The Morozov Inheritance

Geoffrey Lambert

This 2nd edition 2013 published in partnership by

Glenview Imprints & DoctorZed Publishing

A CIP number for this book can be found at the National Library of Australia

ISBN: 978-0-9873244-1-2

Book and eBook distributed by DoctorZed Publishing
10 Vista Ave, Skye, South Australia 5072

www.doctorzed.com

Printed in Australia, UK and the United States of America

To Zusje for tireless checking of each rewrite,

and for unstinting support.

Contents

The Present

It was the perfect night for a killing.

Jagged breaks in the thick cloud cover cut light from a new moon. The road glistened faintly from recent rain. In the distance, a dog barked once. It was mid-week and no one was about.

He stood well hidden in the shrubbery halfway along the driveway. He shifted weight onto his left foot and flexed his fingers around the hilt of the knife. Tonight the atmosphere felt right. He crouched, tensed like a tightly wound metal spring. The rest of the world ceased to exist as his victim moved closer.

He remained motionless. The man pulling the recycling bin drew level with him. At that instant, he sprang at the man's back. The noise of the bin's wheels deadened the slight rustle he made breaking out of the bushes.

He grabbed the man's head and jerked it back sharply against his own body. He forced the man's chin up, exposing the neck. A feeling of intense pleasure surged through him as the knife bit into flesh on the man's neck. The knife was razor sharp yet it took an effort to make the blade cut deeply. The man twisted against the weight of the bin as the knife sliced. He tightened his grip. An ecstatic charge shot up his spine as warm blood flowed over the latex gloves. It was even more satisfying than the sensual parting of cut flesh. He felt himself hardening.

Suddenly he tensed. He heard a noise that should not be there. The moment of pleasure passed as he sensed danger, a voice. He dropped the dying man and slid into the shadows and away into the night.

Graham Harding liked the quiet, tree-lined streets and the calm of the leafy gardens in the exclusive suburb. Nothing ever happened.

The brittle crash of shattering glass startled him.

"That you, Angus?"

He heard footsteps moving rapidly away toward the street. Curious, he peered over the fence. That, as he later told police, was when he saw the bin on its side spewing bottles onto the driveway. On the far side of the bin, he saw the legs of Angus FitzWilliam.

Without anyone knowing, the slice of the killer's blade reignited events that had begun over a hundred years before.

Part I
1897–1940

Moscow

It had been quite some time since the need had been so strong. Most times he could manage it, sublimating into work. Strenuous physical activity, he noted on more than one occasion, helped. Acting out a fantasy at the brothels where he was tolerated delayed the compulsion for years at times.

He tightened the silk cord around the girl's neck with another twist. It was not necessary. She had ceased struggling some time ago. All breathing had stopped. Her arms hung limply beside her body. Her face looked untidy. The tongue was sticking out. He would have to fix that. Glazed unseeing eyes stared at him.

His breath came in great sobs. The actual act of killing was intense, so utterly self-absorbing, so sensual, an out-of-body experience for which time stopped.

He had satisfied himself with the girl. He then told her of one final game. She submitted willingly enough, as they all did. How weak they were. He had straddled her with his legs, pinning her arms, and put the cord around her neck. It had been so satisfying he was hard again.

He eased his tall frame off the prone body and stood facing her, unclothed. As he stood looking at the body, the image of his mother lying naked on her chaise lounge, looking mockingly up at him as she so often did, came unbidden into his mind. He dismissed it angrily. After all these years, the memory of her perfidy upset him. He still loved her intensely even though she had betrayed him so casually, so callously, that he could never forgive her. He knew that eventually none of them could be trusted.

He released the cord, unwinding it from the girl's throat, and placed it in his coat pocket. He took a step back and surveyed the body. The raw bruising around the neck showed how she had died. He looked at the full white breasts with their rose red nipples, the thatch of blonde hair between her legs. No longer will she offer temptation, he nodded to himself, satisfied.

He walked across the room and sat, leaning back in the chair, facing the girl's body. He had always known it should be done in a palace or wealthy house; it was the proper place. He had lived with his mother in a house just like the Ignatiev Palace.

The girl was one of the Ignatiev maids. She had caught his attention on a visit to his friend's house several months ago. With the other ones, he had not been able to safely arrange to meet them in a house. He had to make do with the cheap hotel rooms where he always started his seductions. To leave her body in a place such as this was far more appropriate. She would not have wanted to be left in a cheap hotel. *She* would never have had need of a cheap hotel room.

After some time had passed, when the tension had left him and his heartbeat returned to normal, he gathered the set of earrings he had bought for the girl. He made sure no other evidence lay in the room that could possibly link him to the scene. In this regard, he was meticulous.

An icy calm settled over him. One final matter remained. He could not leave her like that. She had been too willing; she had succumbed too readily. That was wrong. He needed a reminder to take with him.

From an inside pocket of his overcoat, he extracted two slim leather cases that he laid neatly away from his clothes, opening them to reveal three metal implements. Still naked apart from a pair of tight leather gloves, he picked up one of the implements, a razor sharp surgical scalpel, and moved back to the body.

He inserted the scalpel about two millimeters from the edge of the areola and cut what he considered to be a perfectly executed circle, removing the complete nipple. He repeated the procedure with the left nipple. He squeezed each of the excised pieces of flesh to remove any weeping fluid. Then he placed them in the other leather case, careful not to touch any of the ooze from the two open wounds.

Next, he reached down and seized the girl's pubic hair, making sure he had a complete handful. He twisted and lifted it. With his left hand, he used the scalpel to crudely cut the handful free. This was more time consuming.

When he had finished, he checked his watch. About an hour and a half before the Ignatievs would return from the function. Half an hour before the household staff would come into the back area to lay out a cold supper.

He packed the gloves and instruments away, making sure no traces of blood remained on his skin. He dressed quickly, pulled on his overcoat, placed the trophy bag and scalpel case in his pocket and quietly left the house through the back entrance, confident no one had seen him.

Across the lane at the rear, a ten-year-old girl, unable to sleep, gazed out the window. It seemed to her that the tall man in the dark coat moving through the snow away from the Ignatiev house walked like a wolf. She squeezed back, away from the window, in case he should look her way.

§ § § § §

Maksim Nickoliavich Rysakov had been a successful investigator for the Customs Service before joining the Imperial Police Service. Years ago, he declined an offer to join the Okhrana. He told them he preferred to remain an investigator "in the open" rather than the underworld of the secret police. And he enjoyed the work. Most of the time.

Rysakov wore a deep blue serge suit that served as a nondescript uniform. Too much *bliny* and *pelmeny* had left him carrying too much weight, but it didn't bother him. Crimes were solved by intellectual effort, not physical force, he believed. Once during an investigation, a man asked him if he were a Jesuit priest. The description fitted him well, the look of interrogatory intellect, and an air of relentless persistence.

As he arrived at the scene of the murder, he had to push his way through a crowd of Muscovites who, out of morbid curiosity, began to assemble outside the Ignatiev Palace once word of the gruesome nature of the murder spread.

The militiaman at the door glanced at the identity papers declaring M. N. Rysakov to be a senior investigator and ushered him in out of the frost laden air.

Prince Ignatiev, agitated and distressed this horror had occurred in his house, led him to the rear of the mansion where the body lay. Rysakov thanked him and explained he would be able to carry on alone. As Ignatiev left the room, Rysakov carefully lifted the sheet draped over the body. What he saw did not shock him. The initial report to the police had stated there were mutilations. To Rysakov, they were more than that. He had seen similar desecrations before, twice. The other police investigators with whom he worked had shown little interest as the women had been found in cheap hotels known to be frequented by prostitutes and other "low class life." Granted, the deaths were not the usual murders, with drink or infidelity the main causes. In his Moscow, women had few rights and severe beatings by men (generally husbands) were not uncommon, occasionally resulting in death. Killing a woman was against the law. But to get sufficient witnesses to gain a prosecution could be difficult. To Rysakov, however, any crime warranted investigation. Unusual crimes simply presented a greater intellectual challenge.

He walked slowly around the body, the bruising on the neck showed the same cause of death—strangulation. The same mutilation of breasts and genital area. The third murder by the same man. Rather, the third killing that he, Rysakov, could justify linking to the same perpetrator. Yet he had the feeling that if he studied the records there would be others that fit the pattern. He would have to explain this in his report, but he needed to be diplomatic in his choice of words, his superiors did not like alarmist speculation. To his mind, however, there was no doubt. A vicious, deranged killer was loose in Moscow.

That this latest killing had taken place in the house of one of the aristocracy raised the profile of the crimes considerably. The police would not be able to conduct their usual desultory investigation, attribute the deaths to person(s) unknown and file the report. The Moscow newspapers would report this murder in lurid detail, of that he was sure. While he usually had little sympathy for the wealthy and idle rich, he did feel for Prince Ignatiev—he was about to become innocently notorious, pointed at in the street and discussed in whispers at balls and the opera.

His office would not want mention, at this stage, of the other two murders. If the papers got hold of that it could start a panic. That would impede the course of the investigation at this early stage.

"If we don't make progress a bit of panic might not hurt," he muttered to himself.

He studied the body closely, lifting the shoulders to check if anything had been missed by the murderer. Carefully, he searched the room. He opened the back door and walked outside. A number of buildings overlooked the back entrance to the house but he doubted anyone had seen anything unusual.

The best description he had been able to get at one of the hotels where a previous body had been found was "a man in a dark overcoat, perhaps a bit taller than average, did not speak." That covered about half the men in Moscow. However, one reception clerk had said the man was "upper class." As the witness was in the habit of drinking a bottle of vodka a day, he had not attributed much value to the comment. Given the location of this latest crime, perhaps that possibility was worth revisiting. It certainly narrowed the field *and* added considerable complications to the investigation.

"The man's clever," he said to himself, "never leaves anything. But at some stage they all make a mistake. Then I shall be waiting."

One of the earlier murders had been in a hotel in the industrial district not far from a number of textile factories, the nearest owned by the industrialists Morozov & Son. Rysakov knew Ivan Morozov from his years in the Customs Service and had called at the firm. There he spoke to Ivan, telling him about the murder, seeking his assistance should anything unusual come to his attention. Nothing had.

§ § § § §

As winter began to relax her grip on Moscow, the commercial capital of Russia, Ivan Morozov and his son sat eating breakfast. Ivan placed the morning newspaper on the table. No news about the murder. The sensation of the horrific killing at Ignatiev's no longer filled the front pages. With no arrests, the papers had gone on to new stories and scandals. However, Ivan, like the rest of Moscow, remembered this was not the first such brutal slaying. They could only hope it might be the last.

"I've decided we'll go to London this summer. We need more funds to expand," he said, his mind now on other things.

"But, we had an excellent year last season and we've got the loan from the Trade Bank," said his son, Mikhail. "Why do we need more money?" At times he had difficulty understanding his father's relentless drive to expand.

"The Trade Bank loans are short term. They won't be sufficient for the expansion I have in mind. It'd be so much easier if the new tsar released his controls on the economy." Mikhail had heard this complaint many times. Anything that limited his father's capacity to grow the business annoyed Ivan. Mikhail felt it went even further. At times, he thought his father was in fact offended constraints were imposed on his plans. Even though he didn't intend it, irritation showed on his face. Ivan hurried on.

"There are good businesses to be bought. For example, old Baranov is not well and he has no sons. None of his daughters' husbands could run the business. They put far too much energy into spending the profits. I think he'll sell to me. They specialize in woollen fabrics and have good contacts with the Siberian merino herds. It'll expand our range."

"But couldn't we buy Baranov from our own funds?" asked Mikhail.

"Yes, we could," Ivan said, pausing. "But I intend to build a new factory to rival Konovalov's, with the best British spinning and weaving equipment."

Mikhail sat silent, astonished. He knew the size of the Konovalov factory. It was huge, the four-story main building stretched for well over 150 yards with numerous other one to three story buildings, power generation plants, dye works, a men's dormitory, warehouses, and storage. The whole complex covered over one-and-a-half square miles.

The concept was dazzling. With a modern factory of that size, they would rival the largest textile firms in Moscow or Saint Petersburg.

Mikhail was as tall as his father with the same muscular shoulders. He looked across the table with a mixture of admiration and concern. They were already wealthy beyond their needs, so why did they need to embark on so huge an expansion? Ever since he could remember, his father had been driven by the next opportunity, always striving to make the business larger, frequently in big leaps. Risky leaps. He wondered whether, if he had to make the decisions, he could take those risks. He doubted it; the less risky alternative always appealed more. He didn't share his father's relentless drive.

But he wouldn't challenge him directly. His father rarely made a wrong decision.

"Can we do this?"

"Not without the sort of funding that's only available outside Russia. Captain Johannsen has recommended me to his solicitor, who he says is well connected in the City of London. I've arranged to meet with him after our arrival."

For now, the murders were forgotten.

London

When Katy O'Connor left Dublin to make her way in the world, London shimmered like a beacon, the center of the world's greatest empire. She knew she had to leave Ireland. There was no future there. Yet the image of her mother standing on the dock fading into a blue haze as the ship pulled further into the Irish Sea still saddened her.

Within a month of arriving in the capital, she discovered that this was the most exciting year ever to be in London—Queen Victoria's Diamond Jubilee. What a wonderful time to have left Dublin.

Wherever she looked she saw evidence—in shops, on the streets, in conversations, and in the newspapers—of the ordinary Briton's pride and belief in their empire. Even her employer, Mr. Somerston, pointed it out to his family that morning.

"It's colored red," he said surveying a map specially printed for the jubilee. "You can see quite clearly that the sun never sets on the Empire."

"More champagne has been imported than ever before," Katy overhead him say. "Nine-and-a-half million bottles of it." As a solicitor in the city, he seemed to know this sort of information. He must have connections in the government, was the only explanation Katy could think of.

Late in the morning on that third week in June, as all London buzzed with excitement, Katy joined a huge crowd of onlookers watching the jubilee procession led by the naval brigade with guns. Over 50,000 troops from every corner of the empire marched in two columns behind; the largest military force ever assembled in London.

As this grand procession made its way slowly through the city, she strained to see over the sea of heads in front of her. Unable to see more than the horsemen bobbing high above the crowd, she moved closer to the stands, some of which were four levels high, hoping to gain some elevation. She glanced up at the nearest one. Even in the stands, there are foreign-looking people, she thought as her eyes stopped on two, tall, good-looking men above. *How exciting that we have visitors from strange lands as well as the empire.*

Mikhail Morozov sat next to his father in the second level of a stand adjoining the Gresham Life Assurance Society.

The procession, with all its pomp and finery, seemed never to end.

"This is without doubt the greatest empire the world has known, Misha," his father turned to him as he spoke. "Not wanting to do business with the English would be like not opening your eyes to see the sun in the morning. It would still rise high in the sky, but you would miss seeing the brilliant light it spreads across the ground."

The stirring strains of Elgar's "March Imperial" faded slowly into the distance as the last band marched smartly toward St Paul's Cathedral and the jubilee service.

"Come, let's walk among the crowd," said Ivan.

As they strolled through the crowd, women noticed Ivan, glancing sideways as he passed. He had the air of a man who could look after himself. A full head of steel grey hair brushed back from the forehead, and a thick moustache gave him a distinguished appearance. Ivan walked oblivious to the glances he received from women, young and not so young. None, he knew, could measure up to Nataliya, who remained forever young and beautiful in his mind.

Ivan missed little, absorbing the surroundings. Accustomed to making decisions on which his future depended, he was pleased he had decided to come to London. He glanced at Mikhail.

His son had the same self-confidence, but there was a softness about him. Ivan wondered whether he would develop the toughness necessary to build the business.

Ivan felt on edge. Perhaps it was the spectacle they had just witnessed; perhaps it was something else. He felt certain some event of great importance to their future would occur in London.

§ § § § §

Albert (Bertie) Somerston came out of the reception room as the maid closed the front door.

"My dear Morozov, delighted you were able to come," he said shaking Ivan's hand. He caught Mikhail's eye and nodded. "Come and meet our other guests."

When Gustav Johanssen, the shipping captain, had recommended the firm to Ivan, he said, "They're a medium-sized firm in the city specializing in shipping, trade, and investing their client's profits. They also try to limit the damage if the ships do not return. You'll be as safe in their hands as in any lawyer's." Johassen laughed. Then to emphasize the point, he added, "They've handled my business in London for years. They are what the British call an *establishment* firm, solid and reliable"

When Ivan called on Somerston soon after his arrival from Moscow, he found Johassen's description of Freshman, Withers & Somerston to be accurate.

As the two Russians followed Somerston into the reception room, Johanssen strode toward them with a mariner's gait, thrusting a powerful calloused hand around Ivan's wrist. His large fleet of ships, most still under sail, often carried Morozov cargoes.

"Ivan, it is good you are here!" Johanssen said.

The dozen other people in the room turned as the Morozovs entered. Ladies, in long skirts, glanced appraisingly at the two foreigners. More than one of them thought, *the evening is already more interesting.*

This is not so different to Moscow, Mikhail thought as he began to enter the room. For a family as wealthy as the Morozovs, a business expanding rapidly, and a son of marriageable age, social invitations came in a constant stream. So far, he found most of the young women he met on these occasions uninteresting, or plain boring.

Before he could take another step a violent force hit the back of his right leg. He staggered before regaining his balance. As he turned, he saw a young girl on the floor looking up at him.

"He pushed me," she said tearfully, pointing to what he assumed to be her older brother.

"Did not," he retorted with a big grin on his face.

Before the exchange could develop, a young woman with dark hair bent down and scooped up the girl. As she straightened, she looked up at Mikhail with the bluest eyes he had ever seen, a smile dancing around the edge of her mouth.

"I hope you're not hurt, sir," she said. "I'll be taking them to bed now."

For what seemed like minutes the two stared at each other before Katy, curtseying, chased the boy up the stairs.

"Did you see the jubilee parade, Morozov?"

Mikhail started, "Yes, it was most impressive. My father and I had excellent seats arranged by Mr. Somerston."

§ § § § § §

As she chased the children up the stairs, her feet did not seem to touch the ground. When she reached the bedroom doors, she felt breathless. Katy hummed a happy tune as she bundled the children into bed. Unable to stop smiling, she closed their bedroom doors and climbed the stairs to her own room. She sat in a chair in front of the mirror and looked at her reflection. Surely they were the very same two men she had seen high in the stand at the jubilee procession. Her eyes shone bright, her cheeks flushed. "Silly girl," she said to herself without much conviction.

How can I ever explain to Ma and Neave back home how wonderfully exciting London is? And now I have seen the most handsome foreigner. And spoken to him. "They'd never believe me," she said to the smiling face looking back at her.

§ § § § § §

Conversation at the dinner table revolved around the jubilee and the latest gossip surrounding the Prince of Wales, of which there was rarely a shortage.

"Has your wife visited London, Mr. Morozov?"

"No, Mrs. Billingsgate, she died in childbirth. It was a long time ago."

"Oh, I am sorry. Bertie should have told me. My husband, William, died in a hunting accident two years ago. I do apologize, Mr. Morozov."

Ivan looked at the attractive woman seated beside him. Since his wife died he had had a number of liaisons but none had been able to replace the love he still felt for Nataliya. Yet, there was no mistaking the spark of interest in his dinner companion's eyes.

Mary Billingsgate, now well over her mourning, still had a zest for life. She was, she knew, not unattractive. Finding a suitable, discreet man presented the challenge. She found affairs with married men, though enjoyable, were not fulfilling. Although she tried not show it, her interest in Ivan increased. He was a widower, a strong man, attractive and a foreigner, which meant he would leave London in due course. She mentally ticked off the advantages.

When the food courses came to an end the conversation began to drift toward business.

"If you men are going to be boring and talk business I shall take the ladies into the next room," said Emily Somerston, pushing back her chair.

The men stood as the women followed their hostess into the sitting room across the hallway. As Mary Billingsgate moved away from the table, she said to Ivan, "I hope I shall see you again whilst you are in London." She placed her gloved hand on his arm before following the ladies out.

As the dining room door closed, the men relaxed. Chairs pushed back. Waistcoat buttons were undone. It was early and they could now talk freely.

Ivan selected a cigar from a box and passed it on. Somerston had procured a fresh shipment from Cuba, young leaf off the new crop. As they lit up, a light blue haze soon hovered in the air.

Ivan looked around the table. The room held no knights of the realm or lords. Yet, he noted, the air of confidence, the connections to power held by these men was unmistakable. They made decisions and lived by them. They had money and made money, quite a lot, he suspected. He felt comfortable and at ease. He reflected once again that Somerston had been a good choice. If these men trusted the lawyer with their business affairs he would be in good company.

He looked across the table at Mikhail in conversation. Ivan decided they would stay another month to enable them both to improve their language skill. After all, if his plans were successful, they would both need to be fluent in English.

"I say, Morozov, where do you store your goods?" asked a man on his right. "Do you have your own warehouses? If you don't, I'd be pleased to store 'em in mine. We have several large general storage locations. Handle a lot of foreign trade. Always like to help out friends of Bertie, and we've got some spare capacity at present. Some chap in Australia went broke on us."

"I would be pleased to consider using your warehouses, Mr. Smyth," Ivan said.

Why don't we own our warehouses in London? he thought. The idea had never occurred to Ivan. This could be the missing ingredient in his plan. Years ago, Ivan began planning to expand the business internationally. After initially toying with Berlin and Paris, he fixed on London. Apart from its obvious advantages, he enjoyed visiting the great city; it was always stimulating and exciting. The opportunities for an astute businessman in this center of empire were manifold.

Before they left that evening, Ivan arranged to meet Bertie Somerston the following week.

§ § § § §

When his clerk knocked on the office door, Somerston finished reviewing the contract for purchase of a small country estate. He checked that the firm held adequate funds in its trust account. He knew he had full power of attorney to draw down enough to buy the estate.

Bertie Somerston derived deep satisfaction from the knowledge that his clients had sufficient trust in him and the firm to leave substantial funds with them. He knew few legal firms in the city held that degree of client confidence. The firm had built its reputation on its discretion and integrity, principles adhered to over generations— that, and the ability to open doors throughout the establishment and Whitehall. He often found a quiet word in the right ear at the club over lunch sufficed.

"Sorry to barge in like this, old man, but passing by I thought you may have a spare moment. Not inconvenient, I hope," said Philip Armitage as the clerk showed him in.

Somerston thought it unlikely Armitage was just passing by, but let it go.

Even though he liked the man, each time they met Bertie was struck by how ordinary Armitage looked. *An average man, one who would not stand out in a crowd,* he thought, *the perfect man for the job.* Thinning hair and a quiet, unassuming voice; his eyes gave the only clue to the real man behind the façade.

Bertie knew this unremarkable man belonged to a small, dedicated group of men in London who collected information, or intelligence, as it was now called, independently of the civil service and not only from the colonies. Armitage once explained it to Bertie.

"Accurate intelligence from key foreign capitals is valuable input to assess how foreign governments' actions may affect the interests of the empire. Where we can, we seek men and women with an affection for, or sympathy with, Britain. We don't ask them to betray their country. Rather to offer candid assessments to avoid misunderstandings and encourage cooperation between their country and the empire. For our mutual benefit," he added.

Armitage, however, had no illusions. The information gleaned was used solely in furthering the aims of the empire. After fifteen minutes, Armitage left Somerston's office. He stepped onto the pavement busy with the late morning crowd and melted into the bustle.

Somerston sat at his desk for a few minutes after Armitage left, considering what the spymaster had said. Then he stretched, pushed back his chair, and picked up the file for the next matter of the day.

§ § § § §

The Savoy Hotel was the most glamorous hotel in London. Built by Richard D'Oyly Carte from profits promoting Gilbert and Sullivan's operas, it had a sense of style and service usually only found in the top Parisienne hotels. Ivan had stayed there on a previous trip. Now he could not contemplate staying elsewhere. He found the address and the smooth, unquestioning service assets that offset the price. When he told people, "I am at the Savoy," it immediately identified him as a man of substance. It also helped overcome the instinctive British distrust of foreigners. He knew his foreignness made him something of a curiosity and that the British could not help looking down on anyone who was non-British. On the other hand, Ivan knew, money overcame many obstacles. In Moscow, the tables would be reversed.

Dressed for the theater, the two men strolled leisurely through the foyer toward the entrance. The doorman, seeing Ivan, called a hansom cab.

It had been a balmy summer's day, but, as evening drew on, a slight, cool breeze wafted in from the east. As they passed Buckingham Palace, Ivan nudged Mikhail and pointed.

"They may control the largest empire, but we have far grander palaces in Saint Petersburg," said Mikhail. Past the palace, they joined the line of cabs delivering customers outside the Albert Hall.

Tonight, the famous Belgian virtuoso, Eugene Ysaye, was performing Beethoven's "Violin Concerto." Like so many Russians, Ivan loved music. He had taken Nataliya to an early performance of Tchaikovsky's "Slavonic March." The emotion of that music still rekindled his feeling of loss each time he heard it. Within months of the performance, Nataliya was dead.

The concert was magnificent. Ysaye played with the verve and flourish of the true virtuoso. He took four curtain calls, a satisfied smile creasing his face.

Ivan and Mikhail slowly made their way through the crowd to the reception room. Inside there was an air of eager anticipation. By the time each had a glass of champagne, clapping announced Ysaye's arrival. The star made his way around the room, acknowledging congratulations and praise, pausing to speak to those he knew or who caught his interest.

As Ysaye moved past the Morozovs, Ivan said in his deeply accented English, "That was magnificent, monsieur, it touched the soul."

"Ah...," Ysaye said, "do I detect a Polish accent?"

"Russian, maestro."

"Ah. I have not played in Saint Petersburg. Is it as beautiful as I hear?"

"Even more so. You would be welcome in Russia. I haven't heard such music since the great Wieniawski."

"Henri Wieniawski? You knew him?"

"I had the privilege of meeting him on several occasions. He promised to teach my son to play the violin but unfortunately died before my son was old enough."

"I owe much to Wieniawski. He was a valued tutor in my early days."

"Monsieur, the instrument you played upon this evening, it seemed to glow with light. I've never seen such a violin," said Mikhail.

"Ah, you have good taste. My violin is indeed an outstanding instrument. It was made by one of the greatest makers of all time. Some say he was even greater than the incomparable Stradivari. I'm fortunate to own a Guarneri del Gesu, one of the great violin-making families of Cremona in Italy over 150 years ago. You can't get a violin like this anywhere in the world today."

"It must be very valuable," Mikhail said.

"I'm made offers for it every month, and I say 'If I accept your very generous offer on what would I then play?'"

Ysaye turned to Ivan. "If you can purchase a Cremona violin made by Guarneri or any of the great Cremona makers, buy it; it'll be a good investment. I recall hearing that Wieniawski owned a Guarneri when he played in Russia. Do you happen to know what happened to it?"

"I've been told that Wieniawski had large gambling debts when he died and that many of his assets were sold to pay the debts," Ivan replied. "I don't know whether the violin was part of that sale."

"If you're able to trace that violin, please contact me through my home in Brussels. The genuine Guarneris, like all the great Cremona violins, have the maker's label inside the body. It can be read through the 'f' holes."

Ysaye nodded and moved smoothly to the next group of admirers.

Ivan decided to inquire about the value of Cremona violins, in particular Guarneri. It would be rare indeed if he could combine a love of music with a good investment.

Several blocks from the Savoy, they left their cab to stroll through the late evening crowd. Ahead, on a street corner, a small group came and went. As they got closer they slowed their pace, watching people buy newspapers as fast as the boy selling them could pick up the next bundle.

"Body found in Whitechapel," the boy yelled.

A placard stood beside him with words written in bold black letters that even Ivan and Mikhail could understand. It asked:

"Is Jack Back?"

§ § § § §

Next morning at breakfast, they sat at a table with a guest who introduced himself as Peter Carstairs. He seemed well to do and claimed connections, in a somewhat vague way, with Scotland Yard.

"Did you see the morning papers?" he asked, continuing without waiting for an answer. "A body of a woman was found in the Whitechapel area yesterday. The police are treating it as a clear case of murder. The poor woman was savagely attacked with what appears to be a razor sharp blade."

"We heard some reference to this last evening," said Ivan. "The news placards also made reference to a man called 'Jack.' What do they mean?"

"Yes, the lead article also puts the question, 'Is the Ripper Back?'" said Carstairs. He then outlined the bloody history of the Jack the Ripper murders. "I understand that there may be new evidence coming to light in that regard," he said, without any further details.

The similarity of the Ripper killings to the Moscow murders caught Ivan and Mikhail's attention. Back in their suite at the hotel, Mikhail remarked how strange that murders in the two great cities shared such gruesome detail. It was months since either had thought about the Ignatiev house death.

A knock on the door interrupted them. A bellboy delivered a letter addressed in small, neat handwriting. "Mr. Ivan Morozov, Savoy Hotel, The Strand." Not simply "Mr. Morozov." Clearly, the writer intended it should not mistakenly be given to the younger Morozov. He opened the envelope and pulled out a single sheet of fine quality paper.

As he read the letter, Ivan smiled.

"I've been invited to tea with Mary Billingsgate next Thursday," he said. "Apparently, she assumes you have other engagements," he added.

"I'm sure I can find something to amuse me, Father," Mikhail retorted. He smiled as several diversions immediately came to mind. In fact, he found the prospect of being on his own very appealing. His father was so used to control Mikhail at times longed to be able to make his own decisions and live by them. *They may not be what Father would choose, but it's my life,* he often thought.

He had noticed Mary Billingsgate's quiet conversation with his father and the light, almost intimate touch to his arm as the ladies left. He was not unaccustomed to Ivan's occasional liaison, and in fact felt pleased for him. He knew from an early age how much he missed his wife. He sometimes wondered if Ivan would have become so driven in business had she lived. He felt anger at being deprived the warmth of a mother's love. His father at least had the memory to cling to. He had nothing.

The cab drove through a light blue-grey haze covering the city, smoke from the many factories. In the right conditions, it would combine with thick fog rolling in from the ocean. In winter, heavy, sweet-smelling smoke from coal fires added to the potent brew producing the infamous London "pea souper." With no wind, these fogs cloaked the metropolis for days. It could be dangerous walking out alone in such conditions. It was in thick fogs, Mikhail recalled Peter Carstairs explaining, that the Ripper usually struck.

"Good morning," Bertie Somerston said, as they entered his office. "Did you enjoy the concert last night? *The Times* gave it an enthusiastic review this morning."

"I find it difficult to read newspapers. My English is not good enough. However, the concert was wonderful," Ivan said.

"I trust you had an opportunity to consider the alternatives we discussed," Somerston asked.

"Yes, and I have talked over the possibilities with Misha, as it's important he understands."

Ivan discussed the type of properties he wanted to buy. "I'd leave it in your hands to find such property as I don't know London," he said finally to Somerston.

"That may mean you'll have to stay in London some time," the lawyer said.

"We can stay for perhaps another month."

"Good," said Somerston.

"In whose name will the property be purchased," Somerston asked.

"Is there a way of owning it, but not in my name?" Ivan said.

"Yes, it could be owned in trust."

"Is that a legal way to own property?"

"Certainly," Somerston nodded.

"I see," said Ivan. "So in this trust I can buy whatever I wish and it will own them and my name will not appear?"

"That is correct."

"And who makes the decisions for this trust?"

"You or anyone you nominate. For example, now it would be you alone. But if you were to die, then provision can be made that the control would pass to Mikhail," Somerston looked across the desk at Mikhail. "And on his death to his children, should he get married, and so on."

The possibility of marriage had recently begun to germinate in Mikhail's mind. He wanted a woman's love, love that he alone could enjoy. This was one area in which he was determined his father would be a bystander, not part of the decision making. Several young women had been paraded before him in Moscow. "Very good families with substantial wealth," his father had said. *Or titles, in at least one instance,* thought Mikhail. None had impressed him sufficiently. Several were clearly ripe and sensual, but they lacked some other, indefinable dimension. He couldn't put his finger on it. If he had difficulty with hard business decisions, would he really know what he was looking for? He returned his attention to the discussion with Bertie Somerston.

Ivan spent the next half hour asking the lawyer questions and discussing his plans before finally agreeing on a course of action.

With the business settled, Bertie said, "I was chatting recently with a friend of mine, Philip Armitage. He's at the Foreign Office. He thought you might be interested to visit the FO, see how the British system works. He suggested tomorrow, if that's convenient. Perhaps we can meet here and go over together, make sure you don't get lost. I daresay Armitage'll be good enough to stand us a spot of lunch at the club afterwards."

"I'd be pleased to meet Mr. Armitage tomorrow," Ivan said.

"Good. Say half past ten? Mikhail, if you get tired of looking at old buildings I'm sure Emily would be pleased to entertain you over tea. I'll mention it to her tonight."

Ivan was intrigued. As they made their way back to the Savoy, he turned to Mikhail.

"So, I get to meet the Foreign Office. It seems Bertie Somerston has the right connections in London. I've no doubt this Mr. Armitage will want something from me." He was increasingly pleased he had decided to do business with Somerston.

He remained deep in thought until they approached the Savoy. "You should start to think of marriage and a family, Misha—sons who'll grow up with the business as you have."

Mikhail smiled. This time he did not dismiss the concept out of hand. Perhaps his father was right.

When they alighted from the cab, the hotel door was opened by a tall, fierce-looking Sikh with turban, luxuriant beard, and moustache who had taken over as doorman. As the two men walked through the lobby, Mikhail said to his father, "I wonder what Rezanov would make of that."

Rezanov was a hetman of the Ural Cossacks who Ivan had known as a young man. He spent many summers (and some winters) living with them, learning the strict Cossack code. After Nataliya died, Ivan took young Mikhail to stay with Rezanov for several months, and his son returned regularly for many years.

In his stays with the Rezanovs, Mikhail learned to swim and became an expert horseman. In the rough and rollicking lifestyle of the Ural Cossack, Mikhail also learned to fight using the freestyle of the steppes and the deception of the mountaineers.

No Cossack ever left his sleeping quarters without his dagger or saber, and Mikhail had since adopted the habit. When he turned sixteen and was due to return to Moscow after a visit, Rezanov presented him with a double-edged and fluted damascened Cossack dagger. It was not the normal two-foot dagger every Cossack carried, but a smaller, still deadly, replica. Speechless with pride, Mikhail joined the other Cossacks that night, drinking, storytelling, dancing, and singing. It went on all night until, as the early grey dawn began to light the eastern sky, they lay down where they were and slept.

§ § § § § §

Katy woke happy. She could not define why. The day was dull and the air still. Clearly, it was not the weather. Even the blue-grey overcast from factory smoke suspended over London did not affect her mood. Lessons with the children went past the allotted time simply because they were all enjoying themselves.

"Time to go to the park," she called.

When she had arrived at the Somerstons', Katy took over as the children's governess on a provisional basis. The letter Emily Somerston had received from her sister in Dublin introducing Katy explained that she had been educated at one of the better Catholic schools in Dublin "…on a scholarship. She is also well read for someone in her position." When Emily saw how well Katy handled the children and their lessons, the position had been confirmed.

Katy checked once more through the window and decided she would not need a parasol. Not the sort of day she would have ordered, but it would still be fun in the park. She looked forward to seeing people in the latest fashion strolling under trees in full summer leaf. The children loved the park and the freedom to run and chase.

Katy remembered herself on a summer's day at their age. She had not had a leafy park in which to run. She had only the streets of Dublin. Yet it had still seemed fun. *Children could invent games wherever they found themselves,* she thought. You grew up tough in Dublin. You had to know how to fight. Not very ladylike. She shrugged the memories away.

Once they left the Somerston residence, the trio turned right and strolled along the pavement. Katy smiled as both John and Amanda talked excitedly at once.

"Good afternoon, Miss O'Connor," a deep voice said as its owner lifted his trilby in greeting.

Both the children stopped their chatter and Katy, who knew instantly to whom the voice belonged, flushed. She looked up at Mikhail Morozov.

"Oh, Mr. Morozov, we…I'm taking the…"

"I'm coming to visit…"

Katy, blushing, lowered her eyes and made to gather the children who were already standing still beside her.

"I was invited by Mr. Somerston to call and have tea but lost track of time and see I am too late. I'm pleased to see you again," he said, "and the children."

Katy regained her composure and said, "I'm taking the children to the park."

"May I walk with you?" he asked.

Katy blushed again. "We would like that, wouldn't we children?"

"There is going to be band playing and they have just returned from fighting in the colonies," said John.

Mikhail laughed.

"In that case, I think it would be very exciting to come with you," he said looking at Katy, "but first I should tell Mrs. Somerston I won't be calling for tea."

Katy tried not to show her pleasure, but her eyes sparkled.

Mikhail soon rejoined the trio. They reached the park in time to see the band setting up their instruments. The tropical helmets, red coats, and black trousers could only mean one thing, John assured his younger sister, "recent expeditions." Katy said the two could go and look at the soldiers but must come straight back as soon as the band commenced playing.

Katy chatted happily to cover her nervousness. As she talked, Mikhail listened carefully so as not miss any of her words. When he had first seen her at the Somerstons' she had left a lasting image in his mind. To look at her in the daylight, close by, greatly improved that image.

The clear soft cream of her skin contrasted with the deep blue of her eyes. *Her dark hair,* he thought, *would look much better loose around her face rather than pinned in a roll behind her head.* She was as tall as his shoulder, and when she looked up at him, as she did from time to time as she talked, her face seemed to glow. He noticed when she glanced away that she had a full figure, firm shapely breasts and a feminine waist. But it was not a dainty figure; she had an athletic quality about the way she stood and moved.

Katy knew that when she turned her head to check on the children Mikhail was looking at her. Normally she would have dismissed the appraising glances she often received from men without a second thought. But, when Mikhail looked at her, she found it intensely exciting. She turned back to face him. He had strong handsome features and dark, grey-green eyes. She noticed the broad, muscular shoulders. When she looked into his eyes, she could see kindness and, she sensed, not far below the surface a potential for danger that thrilled her Irish soul. This was a man who would protect those he loved.

Mikhail asked her about Ireland and her home. She made no attempt to hide her family's circumstances but described the fun they made, how her mother had passed on her love of poetry and song, and of her own love of books. Mikhail found her answers to his questions on the "troubles" in Ireland direct and well reasoned. He had no knowledge of the rights and wrongs of Irish history but the fact that she could think and hold clear opinions of her own impressed him.

He told her about Russia, the long cold winters, the glorious, but short, hot summers, the fabulous wealth of the rich and of the tsar, how his father's business had been started by *his* father and how he had learned to ride with the Cossacks. He told her that he had never known his mother. She saw how proud he was of his father's achievements and how he expected to take over from his father in turn. *He is a man for whom family is important,* she thought.

Not until the two children came running up and collapsed on the ground in front of their seats did they realize the band was about to begin the concert. The bandmaster, resplendent in a black fur busby, brought his baton down in a commanding sweep.

By the time the band took a break, a large crowd had gathered. Katy noticed that while they had been playing the air had become distinctly cooler. When the band resumed, they launched into well-known selections from Gilbert and Sullivan's operettas "Patience" and "The Mikado," to the appreciative applause of the audience.

When the recital ended, the temperature had dropped another five degrees, and the crowd had thinned considerably. Katy, Mikhail, and the children got up and walked behind the rostrum toward the far side of the park.

"Come on John, Amanda, a brisk walk will warm us up," said Katy. Neither she nor Mikhail were in any hurry to go back to the Somerstons' house if they could snatch more time in each other's company.

When they reached the far side of the park, the light had faded as if dusk had come early. Katy turned and looked back toward the rostrum. She could barely make out the outline. A wispy white film of fog obscured it.

A slight breeze, cold and moist, slid past, causing them to shiver. When she looked again, the rostrum was gone.

"I want to go home," said Amanda, "it's cold."

"Come on then, we'll walk along this edge of the park till we get to a street that'll take us back to our road. I expect that'll be quicker than walking back the way we've come," said Katy.

As they walked down the far side of the park, the fog continued to thicken. By the time they reached a bend in the street visibility was less than twenty feet. Factory smoke, cooled by the drop in temperature, began settling into the murk, making it almost impenetrable.

After some minutes of careful walking, they stopped. Katy saw what appeared to be a street heading at right angles to their current direction.

"That looks like the way to our road," she said, although it was difficult to tell. She could barely see the other side through the gloom.

As they crossed the road the sound of their footsteps on the cobblestones gave no echo. An ominous silence descended with the fog. Their world became a featureless capsule from which there seemed no way out. They moved closer together. The two children held hands between Katy and Mikhail.

They walked on in silence.

The street turned gradually to the right. *If it continues to turn it will go back the way we have just come,* Mikhail thought. *These roads are worse than Moscow's; they can go anywhere.* He didn't say anything; this was not his city. The slight sense of unease he felt when the rostrum vanished became stronger. What had Carstairs said over breakfast about the Ripper? The Ripper selected his victims out of a thick fog.

It was John who first saw the movement.

"What's that over there?" he asked.

Mikhail saw the fuzzy outline of a person ahead on his left.

"Hello," called Katy, "can you please tell us what street this is?"

"Hello, missus," a rough voice with an East London accent replied, "lost, are we? I'll just come over where I can see you better. You stay where you are."

Mikhail sensed another movement in the murk passing back on his left.

A stocky figure dressed in a shabby coat and a cloth cap took shape in front of them.

"Oh, a gent out walking with his family," the figure said. "I think we can set you in the right direction, but it'll cost you a fee, eh lads." He laughed. "Now if you'd just be so kind as to put y'r wallet in here," he said holding out a cap with his left hand to Mikhail, "and you, missus, put your rings in. Make it quick and no one will get hurt. Then you can take your kiddies home." The voice had a hard, menacing edge as he stood waiting, his right hand in his coat pocket.

Katy, affronted by the man's callousness, but used to the rough ways of Dublin, spat back in a broad Irish brogue.

"Ya lazy layabout. Y'r wife and family'd be ashamed of ya. Put ya silly cap on ya thick head and lead us out o' this muck or I'll get me da and brothers to give ya a visit."

The figure was momentarily nonplussed.

"You're not in Ireland now, luv, so do as you're told," he said stepping closer to Katy.

Mikhail had not moved. Now, he reached forward as if to put his wallet into the man's outstretched cap. As his hand came level with the cap, he grabbed the man's wrist and half twisted. Using his weight he yanked the arm toward him. Expecting such a move, the man whipped a lead-weighted cosh out of his right coat pocket. The raw power of Mikhail's pull on his left arm momentarily unbalanced him. The cosh still swung at Mikhail's head, but it had no real power.

Katy gasped, horrified, as Mikhail dropped. He went back on his right foot and fell to his right. *He's going down,* she thought with alarm. The cosh bounced off his left shoulder. Then Mikhail's left leg, fully extended, swung to the right. It hit the man hard behind the knee. His legs buckled and he fell back, desperately trying to regain his balance. Mikhail sprang to his feet and kicked the man's right heel. Despite landing heavily, the man immediately rolled to one side. It took him several seconds to free the cosh in his right hand. That was enough. Mikhail stomped with all his weight on the man's hand. The crisp snap of fractured bones preceded a shriek of pain that cut through the fog. The man fell back on the ground, groaning. Mikhail's left foot kicked him hard in the temple, stunning him. Mikhail lifted his right foot to knee height bringing the heel of his boot down on the bridge of the man's nose. Katy heard a crunch as the bone smashed, driving fragments inward into the man's face. The man lay still, not moving.

"Look out, behind you," Katy yelled.

Out of the fog a tall figure moved rapidly towards him. Mikhail had a fraction of a second to react before the cudgel crushed his skull.

He launched himself hard at the man's right side. His right hand slid under his coat at the same time. The cudgel was already in its down swing as Mikhail's left shoulder hit hard. He felt a numbing crunch as the heavy wood smashed into muscle in the small of his back. Mikhail's right arm now swept back high over his right shoulder. Their faces pressed hard against each other and Mikhail smelt the stale stench of bad ale and rotted teeth. His assailant's eyes, glinting in triumph that he had Mikhail, changed instantly to fear as he saw the flash of silver in its downward arc. Mikhail's right hand plunged the double edged blade into his assailant's neck at the base of his skull, severing the spinal cord. Blood welled along the fluted blade. As the dagger sliced through an artery in the man's neck, the blood spurted.

Mikhail had been vaguely aware of Katy's scream as he hit the man with his shoulder. Now he heard her yelling in rage. He pulled the tall man closer, slicing the cut wider as he withdrew the dagger. The man convulsed and tried to raise the cudgel but had no strength in his arms. Mikhail watched as all expression drained from the man's eyes. The cudgel fell from lifeless fingers and he let the man drop to the cobbles.

"Let go of me you dirty scumbag," she yelled.

Mikhail saw a third member of the gang had grabbed Katy and was frantically trying to restrain her free arm. The man already had deep scratches down one side of his face where Katy's nails had raked him. She fought, belting at him with her free fist, kicking his shins with her feet. The man had just seen his companions felled. He now saw Mikhail running toward Katy with a dagger in one hand and knew he was outnumbered. He released his grip on Katy's arm and turned to run. As he did, he swung his fist. It caught Katy a glancing blow on the cheek. Then he disappeared into the fog.

"You bastard," yelled Katy and, outraged, began to give chase.

Mikhail caught her after a few paces, dropped his dagger, and grabbed her shoulders. She spun around ready to face the next assailant, saw Mikhail's face and collapsed against his chest. He put his arms around her and held her.

At that moment, he felt certain. This was the girl he wanted to marry. Katy had made the same decision about him some time ago.

"The children, where are they?" Katy pushed away from him, alarmed.

Mikhail had completely forgotten about them in the melee.

After a few anxious calls, they found the two of them, huddled in a doorway alcove, John shielding his little sister.

"You are a brave young man, Master John," Mikhail said, putting his hand on John's shoulder.

Over an hour later, the weary foursome turned onto the front stairs of the Somerston residence having retraced their steps to the park, and, foregoing any shortcuts, walked back to the rostrum. With this as a reference point, they slowly made their way home.

§ § § § § §

"Oh, thank heavens. I was beginning to get quite worried about you in this fog," Emily Somerston exclaimed.

The two children ran to their mother.

"We got lost and these men attacked us, Mother, and Katy and Mr. Morozov had to fight them and I protected Amanda and…"

"They were horrible," both of them were talking at once.

"What on earth are they talking about?" Emily asked Katy. Then she saw Katy's bruised face. She looked over at Mikhail and noticed he stood rather stiffly, favoring his left side. Some of the color drained from her face.

With the children upstairs resting, Emily, Katy, and Mikhail sat in the kitchen. Cook bathed Katy's bruised face as she explained what had happened. On the way home, Katy persuaded Mikhail that they should not mention at least one of the thugs had been killed. The bodies would be found the next day, she said, and it would be written off as a feud among the criminal class. It was not likely the one who had escaped would rush to the police to confess. As a foreigner in London, he had seen the merit in her argument. No evidence existed for the police to follow up as he had retrieved his dagger. In any event he had no sympathy for three armed men who would attack a woman and two children. He felt no remorse for having killed at least one of the assailants. He had acted as a Cossack. Nothing less.

Mikhail had been silent since they sat down. Now he told Katy's employer how she had fought one of the thugs on her own rather than allow the children to be placed in jeopardy and how he admired her courage. Emily, in spite of her horror at the potential danger they had all been in, noticed the exchange of looks. The connection was unmistakable. She sighed lightly to herself. They were both of the right age, just so long as it did not cause complications with his father, her husband's client.

Mikhail tensed as he moved on the seat.

"You are hurt, Mr. Morozov." Despite Mikhail's protests Emily soon had his coat off. Faint bloodstains oozed through his shirt from the cudgel hit. Katy pushed the cook's hand away from her cheek and picked up the bathing cloth. The grazing was not serious and the large black bruise would heal over time. For now, it was painful, but Mikhail liked the feel of Katy's hands on his back.

"You must stay for dinner, Mr. Morozov," Emily insisted. "I will send a message to your father at the hotel."

That evening, the story was told again to Bertie and Ivan. Katy had been invited to join them, and Mikhail made sure he mentioned her bravery. Ivan noted no mention was made of the dagger he knew his son carried. He also knew how Mikhail fought as he had learned the same skills many years earlier. While Mikhail spoke, Ivan noted, he looked across at Katy. She was undeniably attractive, but he sensed more, an inner strength, someone who could tackle adversity head-on. Perhaps this girl had more than just a pretty face. Mikhail finished speaking and glanced at Katy, who smiled.

As they left to go back to the hotel, Bertie clasped Mikhail's hand.

"I am in your debt, Mikhail. If I can ever be of service, please do not hesitate to ask."

Back at the Savoy, Ivan asked Mikhail whether he had used the dagger. His son explained. The second attacker was definitely dead, perhaps also the first.

"Katy suggested it would be better if we did not mention this to anyone. From her experience in Ireland, it could only cause trouble."

"I agree," said Ivan. "She is a sensible girl."

"She is an exceptional girl," Mikhail said.

The next day, Ivan received an invitation for them both to join the Somerstons for a weekend in the country, and Katy wrote a long letter home to her mother.

§ § § § § §

In the morning, Ivan related to Mikhail what had occurred at the Foreign Office the previous day.

"I arrived early at Somerston's office, and we discussed the purchase of the property," he said. "Bertie then took me to Burlington House, which he said overlooked Whitehall. Armitage led us down a corridor into an elegant office with neatly dressed men chatting quietly or writing. No doubt drafts of dispatches, or advices to the foreign secretary," Ivan said. "Our passage caused the activity to stop momentarily as they regarded our passing. They seemed as interested in the presence of Armitage as in me, a foreigner. That I found particularly instructive. Their whispers and looks suggested that he appears rarely in the main office of the FO. Eventually, Armitage opened the door to a large office overlooking St. James's Park, or so he said.

"On the other side of a large desk sat a distinguished looking man. This, it transpired, was Sir Algernon Law, head of the Commercial Division of the Foreign Office," Ivan said.

"He asked about the textile factories in Moscow and Saint Petersburg. He obviously had some knowledge of the industry and knew of our involvement. He then asked about the Siberian Railway. He knew Britain sells rails to build it. After some general discussion, he excused himself for another meeting. As he left, he said,

'If we can be of any assistance, let Armitage know and we'll see what we can do.' That was the most important sentence of the entire meeting," said Ivan, pausing.

"Sir Algernon, Armitage later told me, has a particular interest in Russia. No doubt influenced in part by Britain buying nearly a quarter of our wheat last year. Armitage then asked if I had an interest in politics. Not unless it affects business, I told him.

"The discussion continued for some time with Armitage probing my connections with the Russia Government and bureaucracy. Finally, he got to the point. He said, 'If you have the opportunity, from time to time, we would certainly appreciate your views on emerging trends. Nothing confidential, of course, just an informed view of what's going on. I'm sure your comments would be more objective than those of our journalists based in Moscow whose reports we read in *The Times*.' So, this was what he wanted. I said, 'I cannot promise anything, of course, but I would be pleased to give you the doubtful benefit of my observations from time to time, Mr. Armitage.'

"This was what I had hoped for in this meeting, Misha. Now he had to offer me something in return. I said, 'I am hoping to meet with some financiers to raise money for expansion.' He immediately said, 'I'll make some inquiries of the Commercial Division and get them to suggest some names—always happy to help our friends,'" Ivan paused, smiling.

He told his son they then went to one of the more exclusive gentlemen's clubs frequented by senior civil servants and well-connected successful members of the city.

"It exuded an air of privilege," he said. "We climbed a polished timber staircase to the first floor where Armitage led us into the dining room. The head waiter immediately appeared and showed us to a table by the window.

"As we made our way, Armitage stopped at one of the tables. One of the men there appeared to be a banker. As if suddenly struck by an important thought, Armitage said 'You may be able to assist a friend of mine.'

"So, now I am meeting Mr. George Fox, a leading financier in the city," said Ivan, pleased with himself, "with the imprimatur of the Foreign Office. Fox is apparently one of the more ambitious bankers in the city. His firm already has dealings with Russia."

Ivan finished and sat back. So far this visit looked as if it was delivering everything he had hoped.

As he watched his father, Mikhail sensed a crossroad in his own life had been reached. He felt a growing excitement and, at the same time, apprehension. They would raise the additional capital to build a truly great enterprise. He had met a woman like no other. He had left Moscow a privileged son of a powerful industrialist. That had not changed. It was his sense of self that had changed. It seemed a rite of passage, leading him toward a turning point that promised a rich and fulfilling future. *If anything,* Mikhail thought, *this London trip will be more propitious than father could have imagined.* For the first time in his life, he began to believe there was a woman whose love really was worth winning. This time he felt no anger at never having had a mother's love.

Moscow

Prince Vasily Emilovich Koslinski disliked the early spring. Not warm enough for flowers to begin budding, not cold enough for the winter ice and snow to remain frozen. There was snow and mud everywhere. Tall, handsome, and aristocratic, he paid no attention to the mud he trod in through the door of the Moscow Commerce Bank. After all, he was the largest shareholder and related to a grand duke. He showed little interest in the shocking news from the Ignatiev house, other than to inquire as to how the body had been found and what efforts were being made to find the killer.

He walked around the polished mahogany desk and sat carelessly in a leather upholstered chair, oblivious to the paintings hanging on the wood paneled walls, one by the new French artist Matisse. He took these trappings of wealth for granted.

Just over a year ago, when the owners had run short of capital, the bank had invested in a recently finished textile mill equipped with the latest British machinery. He learned last night that the profits from the first year of operation exceeded even the wildest forecast of the founders. The new looms were far more productive than he ever imagined.

The bank had not previously invested directly in textiles, preferring tea importers and fur traders. So imbedded in the Russian economy, these businesses were reliable and steady profit earners. They could not, however, compare with the profits from the new textile factories. Koslinski's attention now focused on how to gain a greater share of this fabulous wealth—for as little outlay as possible.

He knew Russia's industry lagged well behind Great Britain, Germany, and France. For the prince, this meant opportunities to make money. Meanwhile, the prospects for huge profits had not passed unnoticed by the rest of the world. Russian banks could not provide finance at the speed development demanded, and Koslinski watched, along with his contemporaries, as London, Paris, and Berlin poured money in to meet the demand.

A knock on the door interrupted his thoughts. Before answering, he jotted down on a leather clad note pad: "London." The bank's own capital for investment had been exhausted. To pursue the profits he now knew to be in textiles, he must raise new funds.

He listened to his manager and all thoughts of textile expansion left his mind. One of the bank's traditional customers had a problem. He could not afford a large loss if he intended to raise new capital.

Koslinski followed the manager into Ilinka Street, the financial heart of Moscow, and turned left. As they reached Red Square they turned right and entered the Upper Trading Rows, a vast two story retail center with offices on the third story. The bank's customer, Abrovsky, a small, established tea importer and merchant had its premises here.

London

A light breeze slowly drifted thin white clouds across the sky. Late-morning strollers dawdled as they walked through the park. Professional men, reluctant to leave the warmth for the workload waiting in their offices, doffed hats to promenading young women.

Ivan climbed out of the hansom cab, mounted the stairs to Mary Billingsgate's front door and pressed the bell. A maid ushered him through the spacious entrance foyer into the reception room and went to summon her mistress.

Across the street in the park, an impeccably dressed man in a lightweight dark suit watched as a tall man entered the door opened by the maid. As the door closed, he was not sure whether he had recognized the tall man or not; he had not gotten a clear view. He adjusted a white carnation in his buttonhole and, after staring at the door for several minutes, continued on his way.

"Mr. Morozov, how nice to see you again. Please sit down."

"Mrs. Billingsgate, I assure you the pleasure is mine," said Ivan.

Mary smiled and said, "Martha, please bring in the tea, or would you prefer coffee, Mr. Morozov?"

"We Russians drink more tea than even the English. Tea would be fine."

They made conventional small talk, discussing the weather and the jubilee celebrations until the maid returned with tea and small cakes.

When the maid had left the room, Mary asked, "I trust that your business in London is working out the way you expected. London can be a little exasperating at times in the summer."

"Bertie Somerston has been very helpful in making introductions, thank you. I am hopeful I'll be able to achieve all I had planned."

"I trust that will not mean you will be leaving us too soon."

Ivan laughed.

"It has been my experience that when money is involved those who have it do not part with it easily. I do not believe we will be leaving for several weeks at the earliest."

"I am pleased. It is refreshing to meet a charming man with a different outlook on life. You must tell me about Moscow; I know so little about Russia."

As she asked Ivan about his house in Moscow, Mary Billingsgate stood and picked up the teapot. She bent over directly in front of him so that her head was only slightly above Ivan's. He could not miss the soft whiteness of her clearly visible cleavage.

"More tea, Mr. Morozov?"

"Thank you," Ivan replied.

As they talked, Ivan relaxed, his early impression of Mary Billingsgate as an attractive and desirable woman confirmed. But it was more than that. She was a woman confident in her identity, independently wealthy and determined to enjoy life on her own terms. They exchanged stories on society in their respective cities. He discovered she shared his cynicism on the hypocrisy of the generally accepted public mores of the time. One had only to instance the goings-on of the Prince of Wales as a prime example, she said.

By the time he rose to take his leave, he felt a warm empathy with this attractive woman.

"I hope I may call to see you again in the near future," he said.

"Most certainly," she replied, looking at Ivan's strong, masculine features. As she walked to pull the cord to summon the maid she reached into a pocket in her dress and handed Ivan a folded sheet of paper.

"Please show Mr. Morozov out, Martha," she smiled.

In the hansom, Ivan opened the paper.

"*After* one p.m. next Tuesday"

Ivan smiled. He had earned some recreation. His last affair in Moscow had been in the winter, before the Ignatiev house murder. That sensational event had indirectly ended a less than satisfactory liaison with the estranged wife of a distant landowner. In his home city, he needed to be circumspect. She had become too insistent, so he used the prospect of a killer loose in Moscow to end it. With Mary Billingsgate, it would be quite satisfactory. They both knew he would be leaving London. Ideal. He settled back in the cab.

§ § § § § §

Following some discussion, the Somerstons agreed the children should go back to play in the park as soon as possible after their ordeal in the fog. Bertie summed up the logic behind this decision.

"It's the same principle that one should get back on a horse straight after one had been thrown. Conquers what may become a fear of riding," he said.

"It may help the children's confidence, sir, if Mr. Morozov accompanies them," Katy suggested. No doubt existed in anyone's mind as to which Mr. Morozov she referred.

"Quite sensible, sterling chap young Morozov," said Bertie. Emily Somerston noticed the quick flush of pleasure on Katy's face.

Mikhail arrived mid-morning and the foursome set out excitedly for the park. After their shared danger barely a moment's awkwardness arose between them and the conversation flowed effortlessly. While the children romped under the trees, Katy said, "Misha, teach me some Russian words."

They spent the next hour laughing at Katy's pronunciation. Soon the Somerston siblings came clamoring to be taught Russian. Then, to their delight, Katy announced she would teach them Gaelic.

As they walked slowly back to the Somerston house, Mikhail suddenly realized Katy was pointing out objects in Russian with near perfect inflection. It happened so naturally he simply accepted it and began speaking in his native language, much to her laughing protests. He looked at her; this beautiful young woman had a natural ear for languages. However, he doubted he would ever master the strange Irish words she insisted they all try. The more he saw of her the more time he wanted to spend with her. When she looked at him or her hand brushed his, he felt a thrill of excitement.

At the same time Mikhail and Katy set off for the park, Ivan arrived at the offices of the British & Foreign Credit Bank. George Fox met him promptly and showed him into an office with fine English furniture and several large paintings of ships under full sail.

"We were involved in financing some of the clippers that ran tea from China and grain from South Australia. Never had an interest in the *Cutty Sark,* unfortunately, though we did have money in the *Themopylae,* which held the record for the Australia run for some years," Fox said, pointing to the paintings. "I hope you don't mind but I have asked one of my co-directors to join us. Might speed up the process if we feel we can assist."

When Godfrey Langley joined them Ivan explained his plan for expansion in the Moscow textile industry, and that he was prepared to offer as security a charge over a half interest in Morozov & Son.

"That is quite generous security," Fox said. After the meeting at the club he had made inquiries of both the FO and Bertie Somerston. The reports had been more than satisfactory and after discussing the matter with his board of directors Fox had authority, with Langley's concurrence, to conclude a deal. But before that happened he intended to probe some more. "If you're unable to repay the loans, the bank would have effective control over your firm."

"I'm confident the loans will be repaid," said Ivan.

After some further discussion, Fox said, "Will you excuse us for a few moments, Mr. Morozov, I'd like to confer with my colleague," and the two left the room.

Fox returned alone and sat down at his desk.

"We would be pleased to offer you the funding, Mr. Morozov," he said. "We suggest it be by way of letters of credit, which can be drawn at any bank in England or any reputable bank in Moscow. If that's acceptable, I can have the papers ready for you in a few days."

Over dinner that evening, Ivan told Mikhail he had secured the funding. They toasted success with champagne—finding good vodka in London was all but impossible.

The following Monday, Ivan took the early train to Liverpool to meet a cotton broker with whom he had corresponded. The merchant had assured him he could source good quality cotton from Egypt and the United States. Ivan asked Gustav Johanssen to make discreet inquiries among his shipping contacts about the broker. The reports had been generally good: "a bit sharp, always on the lookout for extra profit, but delivers quality merchandise." In fact, all the reports had been unanimous on that point. The broker prided himself on the quality of his merchandise.

When Ivan arrived in Liverpool, he was astonished at the number of masts filling the port. *There must be hundreds of ships here,* he thought. Activity surged and flowed, from ship to wharf, from ship to ship, and from huge delivery wagons manhandled by thousands of stevedores into the holds of the vessels. All manner of goods were being loaded, machinery, wooden crates, textiles, and a bewildering array of other goods. Raw materials and foodstuffs of all kinds were being unloaded. It appeared to rival London for size and activity. No one, he thought, could doubt the English were the pre-eminent maritime nation—and he had only seen two of the great English ports.

After seeking directions several times, Ivan found the broker's office. "Scragg, Jones & Milton, Cotton Importers and Brokers," the sign pronounced on the side of a large warehouse with offices on the ground level.

Mr. Harold Wallace, the sole proprietor, the other gentlemen being long dead, was short and corpulent with a ruddy face and small brown eyes, a little too close together. His office had piles of papers, bills of lading, shipping documents and tide tables in untidy array. Ivan sat on one of the two uncluttered chairs and explained what he wanted.

"I need a reliable supplier of cotton that will make me independent of the major cotton merchants in Moscow and Saint Petersburg," he said. "I may even source the fiber direct from growers unless I can establish arrangements with a reliable broker in England." Ivan explained he needed a certain amount for immediate shipment, then regular shipments thereafter. The quantity would steadily increase to treble the amount over the next three years.

"Quality is of particular concern," Ivan continued. "These are the grades of cotton and the quantity of each I require." He handed Wallace a sheet of specifications. "Just as important, this source must supply exclusively to me. Can your firm handle such an ongoing order?"

Watching Wallace as he spoke, Ivan could see that the size of the order and the prospect that such an order would be ongoing was of singular interest to the broker. Ivan suspected it may be the largest single order he had ever received. He expected the trader was already calculating the profit.

"Mr. Morozov," Wallace said, drawing himself up several inches in his chair, "there is no doubt that we can supply this quantity and quality to you. We would in fact be most honored to receive your order.

"I should, however, point out some of the factors that we in the cotton-trading business must deal with. At this time of the year, most of the large mills in England have secured their raw cotton for this season with forward orders, so I cannot be totally sure of securing this quantity until next season. Secondly, I do not have sufficient storage facilities at my warehouse here to store this quantity at once. Thirdly, I do not know what price I may have to pay to obtain the cotton now. Of course, I would have my staff do their best to buy it at the most competitive price, plus our own modest commission. We pride ourselves in securing the best deal for our customers. Finally, I can only ship against confirmed letters of credit."

"Let me answer the last point first," Ivan said and produced the letter of credit drawn on the British & Foreign Credit Bank.

Wallace picked up the document and, in spite of himself, could not stop his eyebrows rising as he saw the sum for which the letter of credit was drawn. Wallace read it again then placed it on his desk.

"They are a well-regarded bank in the maritime trade," he said. "Perhaps you would be kind enough to allow me to buy you lunch to discuss the details of the transaction."

By mid-afternoon, when the time came for Ivan to catch the train back to London, they had agreed to terms for the order. Ivan signed the order form specifying the full quantity of cotton to be progressively delivered to Saint Petersburg. Finally, Ivan gave him details of the letter of credit and authorization to draw against it for deliveries once loaded on ship. As the express rattled its way to London, Ivan knew he had his source of cotton. Now he could break Wogau & Co's control of the Moscow raw cotton market. Just as he had not told Wallace how he intended to expand his operations, he had not told George Fox he intended to source his own cotton direct, or which mill he proposed to acquire immediately upon his return. It was wise, he had found, not to expose all your plans to any one party.

§ § § § §

At fifteen minutes past the hour of one the next day, Ivan Morozov knocked on the door opposite the park. Mary Billingsgate opened the door herself.

"I hope you don't mind, but it's the staff's afternoon off today so you will have to put up with me," she said.

Across the road, a man in a perfectly cut, dark lightweight suit watched Ivan enter. A look of dark annoyance crossed his face as he saw Mary open the door. He had been about to surprise her this Tuesday although it had been several months since he had seen her. He straightened the carnation in his buttonhole and walked away, staring at the ground, deep in thought. He absentmindedly handed the bunch of summer flowers he had bought from a street vendor to a young girl playing in the park.

Mary Billingsgate showed Ivan into the sitting room, saying, "Please, call me Mary, if I may call you Ivan; it's so much easier," she said.

"Of course, Mary," he smiled.

Ivan told her how he had gone to Liverpool and been astonished at the size of the port. She told him an amusing story about a friend who owned a small dog that developed an appetite for antique furniture legs. Desperate for a cure, the owner smeared the furniture legs with a thin paste of crushed quinine. The bitterness of the application ensured thereafter the furniture was safe.

An expectant silence fell on the room. Mary's mouth was suddenly dry.

"I would like to show you the upstairs rooms. There are some fine paintings," she said breathlessly. *This is silly,* she thought, but she found Ivan's closeness in the empty house very arousing.

Ivan had been puzzled that Mary's curves seemed more fluid under her dress than he remembered. She seemed to move more gracefully. Then, as she stood, he realized. She was wearing no corset or stiff undergarments.

Mary took his hand and led the way up the stairs. They walked past several paintings on the wall and into a room with a large brass bed against one wall.

"This is my room," she said walking on to the side of the bed. There she stopped and put her hands to her shoulders. As she turned the dress fell down about her ankles and with a single step she faced him, naked.

Ivan looked at her; she looked delicious. He took off his coat and began fumbling in his haste with the buttons on his shirt.

"Let me help you," she said brushing her rigid nipples against his hand as she reached up to undo the last buttons. As his trousers dropped to the floor Mary could not resist looking down with anticipation at what she could feel hard against her. Ivan picked her up and carried her to the double bed.

Some hours later, as Ivan left Mary's house, she made him promise to call again next Tuesday.

§ § § § §

The carriage that brought them from the railway station rolled to a stop on the crushed stone driveway. Mikhail stepped down after his father. He stood for a moment taking in the house before him. The grey-stone mansion looked bigger than he expected. There appeared to be wings on either side and to the left a smaller building with a railed yard. *That must be the stable,* he thought. The house had been built on an elevated site in the gently sloping Surrey Hills. To the right, a small wood fell gradually away into the valley.

With their luggage stowed, Bertie took them on a tour of the grounds. He pointed toward the railed yard. "I only keep a couple of horses here and a pony for the children, but I've brought in some extras for the weekend from a neighbor. I hope you ride, Mikhail," Bertie said.

"I look forward to having a ride," Mikhail said, although foremost in his mind was the prospect of seeing Katy several days in a row.

"Then we shall ride tomorrow morning. I've invited some friends to join us. Come, let me show you the wood. At the bottom of the hill is a stream where local anglers often catch trout. Don't have the patience myself, but I'm happy to eat 'em when they're offered to the cook," said Bertie and she led them off across the field to the wood.

Mikhail was aching to talk to Katy. When the children clamored to ride their ponies, Katy had to admit she could not ride. Without hesitation and much to Katy's delight, Mikhail volunteered to oversee the riding after lunch. They talked for several hours while supervising their charges.

Too soon the morning for the return to London came around. That meant no opportunity for private conversation. The carriages arrived and they were off to the station for the mid-morning train.

Mikhail did not know how best to raise the subject with his father so began by asking what plans he had for the future growth of Morozov & Son. Did he see a branch being established in England? Would they expand into mining or railroads? Would they need to expand the capital and take in outside shareholders or could they fund expansion and keep ownership within the family, which may expand one day?

Ivan was pleased to discuss the future, although they often discussed many of the topics together. As the talks progressed, he began to suspect the direction in which the conversation appeared to be heading.

"Father," Mikhail said with as much nonchalance as he could muster, "you have recently suggested that I should begin to consider the possibilities of marriage."

"Yes, Misha, you are certainly of that age," said Ivan. *At last he is getting to the point,* he thought.

"I think I've found the person I want to marry."

"What, only think? Marriage is a serious business and should not be contemplated lightly," Ivan said.

"Then I know. I want to marry Katherine O'Connor."

"Who?" Ivan said, caught off guard.

"Katy."

"Ah," Ivan smiled, "we have all had more than a sneaking suspicion that you might."

"How did you know?" Mikhail asked, surprised.

"It seems that not only in Russia is love blind. Have you asked her?"

"I told her I would like to take her to Russia and show her Moscow and I told her how much she would love it," Mikhail said. "I know she will marry me."

"Yes," Ivan said, "I think she might. Have you thought what a huge change it would be for her, a different language, a much colder climate, a different way of life, her family a long way away."

Once the dam had been breached, the answers poured forth. She was learning Russian, from him. He would arrange a tutor to teach her in his absence. He reminded his father what courage she had and how she would bring a new dimension to their lives.

Ivan looked out of the train window reflectively. He liked Katy; she had qualities that set her apart from other young women he had met. In some ways, she reminded him of Nataliya.

"If you're sure, if you're certain that she is the one, then you have my blessing, Misha," he said, putting his arm around his son, hugging him.

"However, I want you to wait until next year when we return to England. If you both still feel the same way then we'll arrange for you to be married. But I ask that you don't commit the young woman to you formally so that neither of you feel an obligation you may both later regret."

On Tuesday morning, Ivan recalled his promise to Mary Billingsgate.

A few minutes after one in the afternoon, the man wearing a lightweight dark suit sat on a seat under the shade of a plane tree in the park opposite Mary Billingsgate's house. He had not intended coming again; instead, he had resolved to leave his card and arrange to see Mary as he had in the past. That way he felt he could reestablish his casual but rather enjoyable arrangement with her. He had never married. Never felt the need. Recently, however, for the first time, he had begun to consider the advantages. Dining at the club had after all become a little repetitive and tiresome. It had been a rather vague thought, he admitted, but he had begun to think of Mary Billingsgate as a possible candidate. So, try as he might, he had not been able to resist coming to the park once more.

As he settled on the seat, he watched Mary open the front door and admit the same tall strongly built man he had seen the previous week.

"Damn cheek," he muttered under his breath, now certain he recognized the man. It was Ivan Morozov.

"Bloody foreigner. Only been in London a few weeks. Damned hide," he muttered. His indignation rose in outrage at the thought of anyone, particularly a foreigner, upsetting what he had found a most convenient arrangement. The possibility that Mary may have taken the initiative and made all the moves never occurred to him. A foreigner had stepped in and taken his place. It was an insult.

He sat staring at the house for a moment, then stood, adjusted the carnation in his buttonhole and walked away back to his office, fuming at the injustice of life.

Unaware of the angst she had caused, Mary took Ivan's hand and without any pretence at preliminaries led him up the stairs to her bedroom. Once in the room she dropped her light chemise and walked to the bed naked but for a silk garter on her left thigh. She turned, sat back on the bed, resting on her elbows facing him, raised her knees with her legs wide apart and looked straight at him to see his reaction. She was not disappointed. She found it both amusing and exciting to play the wanton in private with a man as virile as this Russian.

Over the succeeding weeks, Ivan visited Mary Billingsgate once a week until the last week in July when, as he explained to Mary, he had to make a trip to Birmingham and Sheffield to meet with suppliers of manufactured goods that were in steady demand by the expanding Russian railways.

Ivan made a number of visits to the FO, taking Mikhail on each occasion. Ivan's objective was to ensure that the contact with the FO went beyond the personal and became a longer lasting relationship. As Armitage had demonstrated, the FO could open many doors in England, and no doubt the empire. He knew this could be of immense benefit to Morozov & Son.

Bertie Somerston located a large, four-story house, with basement servant's quarters, in a fashionable part of London. After several inspections, Ivan agreed to the purchase. Ivan also inspected several potential warehouse sites with Bertie. By the time they had seen half a dozen, they had agreed on the type of property and location that would best suit the needs of Morozov & Son. Ivan now felt content to leave the final selection to Bertie.

One Wednesday, Emily Somerston gave Katy the afternoon off. She told Mikhail excitedly they would be able to spend the whole afternoon together. Mikhail said he had seen what looked like a river in a park. After a brief discussion with the driver of the hansom, they headed for Hyde Park. Once he saw the boats, Mikhail suggested they join the other young couples on the water. Katy now sat in a boat on the Serpentine, her hat tied loosely under her chin. She held onto the sides with both hands as Mikhail fit the oars in the rowlocks and began to row. She looked across the water at the other boats and their cargoes of lovers. Feeling the warm sun on her face, she leaned back against the transom.

"I wish this could go on forever," she said.

An hour later, as he returned the boat, Mikhail turned to Katy. "In a few weeks, we'll be leaving London to go back to Moscow. I wish I could stay longer. I'll miss you so much, but I have fixed in my mind the image of you lying back in the boat with the sun on your face, your eyes closed. That'll see me through the winter." He smiled.

"We'll return next year, as early as I can persuade father. If you still feel the same way then I hope you'll come back with me." He reached across and took her hand in his. It took all his self-control not to declare his love immediately and ask her to marry him.

"I'll wait for you, Misha," she said, grasping his hand. "I'll wait for you."

Katy was bursting to confide in someone that night back at the house, but to whom? She had no friends in London to whom she could talk about such intimate matters. She felt instinctively that, although likely to get a sympathetic ear, Emily Somerston as her employer was not the right person. Instead, she sat down and wrote a long letter to her mother, whom she knew would be both thrilled and apprehensive at the prospect of her daughter marrying a foreigner and going to live in a strange land. Later, as she lay on her bed, she began her nightly practice of Russian, revising in her mind the new words she had learned that day and recalling all the other words she now felt she knew. She said them softly out loud. Halfway through the expanding list she slid into a deep and happy sleep.

Two weeks later, Ivan and Mikhail caught the Calais packet across the channel and then the train to Paris where they stayed a week on business before embarking for Geneva, Berlin, Saint Petersburg, and on to Moscow. Ivan intended a leisurely journey home, arriving in Moscow at the end of August.

Moscow

Vera Nikolaevna Rysakova insisted her husband take holidays in early August.

"You are always working, Maksy," she said. "Do they really appreciate the long hours you put in? I don't think so. If they recognized such dedication you would have had a promotion by now, and we would be able to afford a better apartment." Vera dropped her voice and added, "Don't forget that your son is growing up. Before you know it he will be leaving home and you will not know where the time went."

Maksim could not honestly argue with any of what his wife said, particularly the need to spend more time with Pavel. So he rented a dacha south of Moscow in a lightly wooded area perched on a slight elevation above the prevailing plain.

Together they went on rambles through the forest, watched birds searching for insects and worms or conducting noisy conversations in the canopy overhead. At night they played games. Maksim told Pavel he would teach him to play chess, only to find his son a more than competent opponent. It took some time for him to recall that he had taught him several years ago. Several *years* ago. What had happened? Who had stolen the intervening days? He worked hard, often long hours. He knew he became absorbed in the intellectual challenge of his cases. But, for time to slip past so unnoticed—he resolved, and for Rysakov this was a commitment, to spend more time every week with his son.

Late one evening, with considerable pride, Rysakov conceded defeat to his son after a hard-fought battle. Maybe he had been a little careless at the start and let his mind wander, he thought, trying to justify the loss. Pavel had swiftly, and ruthlessly, taken advantage of every opening. He was a worthy opponent indeed, a son to be proud of.

Rysakov sat outside in the early evening sun, relaxed and, he admitted, feeling refreshed, mentally and physically. He had not thought about work for almost a week and had not felt the slightest guilt about all the unfinished cases and paperwork. In fact, he felt just the smallest amount of pleasure that someone else, not he, must worry about it all. *Of course there will be a pile on my desk when I return,* he thought, *but for the rest of the week, to hell with it.* If only he would play the politics in the department, he had no doubt he would by now have been promoted to a seniority that freed him of all the paperwork. But he refused. Call a spade a spade, an incompetent just that. He would not become a deputy director, but he would catch criminals.

He stretched his legs, resting his feet on a stump, and closed his eyes. As he did, the details of his most puzzling case floated unbidden into his mind.

After the Ignatiev house murder, he reviewed all the details of two similar, earlier deaths and began to wonder if there could be other unsolved murders that might fit the profile of this killer. No one had ever thought to look for patterns in such deaths before. There had been multiple killings in the past but there was nearly always a clear connection—family, lovers, village, and so on. In this series of crimes he had so far been unable to identify any connection between the victims.

What did he know? He ran through the common factors in his mind.

The victims were all young females, in their twenties. All were in service and worked for wealthy households. Robbery was not a motive; nothing had been stolen. He had interviewed those who worked with or knew the victims. None had mentioned the name of any new beau, although in all cases it appeared likely the girls concerned had a new lover. In one case, the victim had told a friend she expected a marriage proposal soon when she would at last be free to reveal her lover. No one had seen the girls' lover, not even in the distance.

Their meetings appeared to take place away from the girls' place of domicile. Although the last murder had, most audaciously, taken place in the girl's employer's house. The only direct evidence of the killer came from his interview with the drunken hotel attendant from one of the earlier crimes. Even then the evidence did not amount to much. He cast his mind back to that time.

"I think the man wore dark clothes and was wealthy," the attendant said.

"Did you see his face?" Rysakov had asked.

"No."

"Did you hear him speak?"

"No."

"Then how do you know he was wealthy?"

"I just did; you can tell; it's the way they move."

"What do you mean? That they move confidently?"

"Yeah."

Rysakov had been unable to get more from the man. Thinking back on that interview, as he lay stretched out in the sun, the value of the attendant's evidence had to have a question mark over it. The man drank. What he described could just as easily be any businessman or official cheating on his wife in a cheap hotel where no questions were asked.

In reality, he had no concrete leads, nothing upon which to pursue the investigation. Had he missed something? He let his mind drift. He found it surprising no one, including the victim's friends, had seen the killer. He had no description. The man was either very lucky or very careful. Or both, Rysakov thought.

Then, he remembered. Perhaps he did at last have one piece of evidence.

A week before embarking on holidays, he went back to the Ignatiev house. He sometimes did this, months after a crime, in the often futile hope of gaining a fresh perspective. He did not go into the house. He didn't want to seek special permission from the prince. Instead, he walked around to the rear entrance. The back of the house was shielded by several large chestnut trees in full leaf. As he stood there, a young girl walked past and stopped.

"What are you doing?" she asked.

"I'm a policeman," he said.

"Are you trying to find who killed the girl?" she said.

"How do you know someone was killed?" he asked.

"My mother told me, and she said it was in all the papers. I saw a man leaving the house that night," she said.

"What do you mean?" he asked.

"I couldn't sleep, and I was looking out the window to see if I could see an owl."

"But there aren't any owls in the city," he said gently.

"My friend says she saw one at night."

"What did you see then?"

"I saw a man walk out of that house," she said, pointing to the Ignatiev house.

"Are you sure, I can't see anything from here."

"I was in my bedroom up there." She indicated a second floor window overlooking where they stood.

"There weren't any leaves on the trees then," she added. *Of course not,* he thought, *there was still snow on the ground.* Sometimes the obvious escapes you.

"What did the man look like?" he asked.

"He made me think of a wolf," the girl said. "I got scared and went back to bed."

And that was all she had been able to give him, a man who made a ten-year-old girl think of a wolf.

What did that mean? he mused, his eyes still closed. *Obviously she did not mean that he walked on all fours. Perhaps the man had walked with a loping motion that reminded the girl of a wolf. Perhaps she was very familiar with wolves. No,* he thought, *she's a city girl. It's unlikely she's seen many wolves. Unless,* he corrected himself, *she spent a lot of time on her family's rural estate, assuming they had one. This is getting nowhere,* he decided. He'd speak with the girl again on his return. *What was her name? Irina. Nice name for a young girl.*

Wolves. I wonder if they deserve to be feared as much as they are? Some even credit them with supernatural powers. He mind drifted. Something else was on the edge of his consciousness. Was it to do with wolves, was it something else the girl had said, or was it something he had seen? He could not quite crystallize it. Like the last rays of the setting sun, it slipped silently out of his grasp.

"Papa! Papa!"

He rose slowly from the soft depths of peace upward toward the distant noise. It sounded vaguely familiar. As he floated upward, he felt himself suddenly shaken rudely from side to side. Then he saw Pavel's face and felt him grasping his shoulder.

"Mama says it's time to come inside or the bears will eat you."

He stretched, laughing, now wide awake.

"I must have slept for over an hour," he said looking at the sun low above the horizon, "and they had to send a chess master to wake me,"

He stood and ruffled his son's hair.

"And I'll beat you again tonight," Pavel said and raced off toward the house with his father in pursuit.

§ § § § §

At the end of August, Prince Vasily Koslinski boarded the train at the Brest Station in Moscow on the start of his journey to London. He dined well in the elegant restaurant car drinking a smooth vintage French burgundy before retiring for the night to his sleeper berth. As his train sped toward Saint Petersburg, another steamed past, heading for Moscow. The Morozovs, ensconced in their sleepers, slept soundly, wholly unaware a train had passed them.

Koslinski had spent the last few months arguing successfully with the Abrovsky family. They had two choices: they could sell personal assets to repay the bank, or, they could transfer ownership of the tea importing firm to the bank in full satisfaction of their liability and keep all their personal assets. Once he had Abrovsky's Koslinski proposed a simple deal to Perlov. Merge with Abrovsky and create the dominant tea firm in the city. The Moscow Commerce Bank would continue to fund the combined business and become a large minority shareholder in the new enterprise. After endless argument and discussion, the commercial attractions were so persuasive Perlov agreed. The bank now effectively controlled the Moscow tea trade.

For Koslinski, he was simply pursuing the bank's traditional business. A Moscovite without his tea would be like a bear without a temper—unheard of. Tea would continue to be a good steady business as long as a samovar remained boiling in Russia. However, the really large profits were in textiles. To pursue those opportunities he had to seek foreign funding. The London trip took on critical importance.

Within two days of their return to Moscow, old man Baranov contacted Ivan. He had decided to sell his textile business as his children had no interest (and, as he put it, even less ability) in the firm. If this was what the good Lord had ordained, then so be it. Once Ivan paid the agreed price, he said, he would settle sufficient funds on each of his children to pursue their chosen vocations. He would then devote himself to glory of the Lord. We must forsake the Antichrist and rediscover God with the Old Believers, he said.

Ivan's father had once followed the Old Believers, although he had not been a man who placed a great deal of faith in religion. Every day, the village had to deal with too many hardships, most of them man made. As a young boy, Ivan had been awed by the fundamentalist fervor of the Old Believer's sermons. By the time he reached adulthood, these impressions had been tempered by his father's scepticism and his own observations of life. Then, any chance God may have had in Ivan's life was shattered when he willfully took Nataliya from him. "How could there be a true God," he said, "if he let my beautiful young wife, with whom I spent so little time, deliver a perfect child and then not allow her to shower her son with love and share in the joy of his growing. No, until that can be explained to me, God is someone else's problem." That bitterness underlay his drive to build his business ever larger and more powerful. If Baranov wanted to waste his money in pursuit of such hollow ideas, so be it.

They met the next day at Morozov & Son offices to agree the deal. Baranov wanted cash and Ivan was now in a position to pay it with the letter of credit drawn on the British & Foreign Credit Bank.

Ivan was delighted.

"The Baranov factory will make us a major force in the textile industry in Moscow," he said that evening. "And I now have my own source of cotton. Direct from overseas." Mikhail remained silent. His father's eyes did not see him. They were focused in the future.

"Nothing can stop me now," he said in almost a whisper.

The third week after their return from London began badly and got worse, much worse. If there was a God, then he was not yet done with Morozov.

In the morning, the warm, fine weather that had greeted them on their return turned wet and oppressive. Then, in keeping with the day, something totally unexpected happened.

The first hint of trouble came in a telegram from their small office in Saint Petersburg.

"Request urgent permission rent second large warehouse store cotton."

"What does this mean?" asked Mikhail.

"I don't know," Ivan said. "Send a reply 'Explain need second warehouse.'"

The response was immediate. "Very large shipment cotton arrived. Bales unloaded on dock. Urgently need warehouse storage protect."

"Permission granted. Will arrive P tomorrow," Ivan replied.

"I'll go to the capital and find out what the hell is going on," Ivan said.

"We're due to pay Baranov the balance of the purchase price in two days," said Mikhail.

"Go ahead and settle with him," said Ivan, "tell him I've been called to Petersburg urgently and I'll celebrate with him on my return. The old bastard will insist on a bottle of vodka to seal the deal, even when he's got my money."

Ivan's local manager waved to attract his attention at the train window as it pulled into the Moscow Station on Nevsky Prospect in Saint Petersburg the next morning. By the time the horses pulling the troika stopped outside the office, Ivan had been briefed on the essential facts.

Harold Wallace, the overweight Liverpool cotton broker with his eyes too close together, had shipped more than half the entire cotton order on a number of large chartered Baltic traders. The cargo filled the entire holds of each vessel.

"The cotton is all American," the manager said. "When I spoke to the ships' captains they said the cargo was transshipped immediately after it arrived in England. First, however, the agent insisted they load a large quantity from the Scragg, Jones & Milton owned warehouse. As soon as the ships from the American south arrived, they had the rest of the load."

This was far more cotton than Ivan had planned for. He had expected the order to be filled gradually, as he called for it. Now it was here sitting on the dock in the weather. The manager had acted swiftly to secure additional storage. As Ivan walked beside him along the dock, the first wagons were already on their way with others lined up to load. If the rain in Moscow did not spread north for a couple of days they would have the cotton safely in storage.

A second wagon rolled past them. Ivan remained silent. Thinking he should make conversation, the manager said, "The captains reported wild weather in the North Atlantic. Somewhat unseasonable for this time of the year." Ivan did not respond, and the manager was not even sure he had heard him.

"I took samples from a number of the bales as soon as they arrived," the manager said, "the quality is good."

Now Ivan nodded. *Thank God,* he thought, *at least all the news is not bad.*

"Can I inquire what the plans are for the cotton, sir? How long will we need the extra warehousing?"

Damn, Ivan thought. It would not take long for the whole market to hear that Morozov & Son had bought a huge quantity of cotton. Even when the news of the Baranov purchase got around (which was after all best known as a woolen fabric factory) it would be clear they had far more cotton than they could use this year. Damn Wallace. Damn that venal bastard. *First, I must solve this problem,* Ivan fumed. *Then I will deal with Mr. Harold Bloody Wallace.*

"I am a little surprised," said Ivan, determined not to show any alarm, "the shipment arrived far sooner than I expected. How long did you rent the warehouse for?"

"I wasn't sure what your plans were so I thought it safer to take a short lease, for a month."

"Extend that to a year," Ivan said. We Russians love to gossip and Saint Petersburg is the capital of that pastime. The only way to counter the inevitable rumors is to show confidence. Keep them all guessing. That will at least give me time to plan what to do, he decided. For some weeks, the industry will find the puzzle of my plans intriguing. Then, if it doesn't look as though there is a clever strategy behind the purchase, more serious rumors will begin to circulate.

He imagined what they would say: *"Morozov is heavily overstocked; what possessed the man? He won't be able to sell it, what with the fleet of ships due in soon bringing new cotton for Wogau. There will be some very cheap cotton around before long!"* This perfidy by his agent would cause a temporary slowdown in his plans, but with funding in place it was not too serious.

When Ivan arrived back in Moscow several days later, he was confronted with news of a far more serious kind. News that could destroy the whole business.

London

The trip to London went without incident for Vasily Koslinski. In Germany, he stopped for several days to meet with banking associates before proceeding to Paris and onto the cross-Channel steamer. The Moscow Commerce Bank had correspondent relationships with several London banks, including the British & Foreign Credit Bank.

"My dear Prince, how delightful to see you again," said George Fox. "The last time we met must have been over a year ago in Moscow."

"Indeed, it was Mr. Fox. You were kind enough to accompany me to the opening night of the Bolshoi season," said Koslinski as a gentle reminder that Fox was well dined and feted on his visit. "Our bank has expanded considerably since that time."

The two bankers discussed matters relating to the correspondent relationship between their organizations and how the sharing of business intelligence would assist both in assessing credit risks of potential customers. But Koslinski knew he could be of more use to Fox in providing information on the Russian market and its participants than the reverse. What he needed to do was establish in Fox's mind just how valuable this relationship would be for the British banker.

As Koslinski explained the reach of his contacts in Russian business circles and within the Imperial Government, Fox began doing his own calculations. He had no doubt a deepening of the relationship would be of significant benefit to the bank. And if it increased the bank's profit, it helped his career. He now needed to determine the price the prince had in mind for this cooperation.

"Profits from the new textile factories are huge," Koslinski said, having decided this was the time to broach the real purpose of his visit. "We made several times our outlay in the first year." He explained to Fox in detail just how successful this investment had been. He now had Fox's full attention.

"We intend to expand our interests in textiles and would be more than pleased to recommend opportunities to our English associates."

"We'd certainly find such returns of interest," said Fox, "but investing directly into the business would be difficult when we are so far away." Fox thought he could see where the prince was leading.

"Our bank would be happy to act as your agent."

I'll bet, thought Fox, *and would we really know whether we were getting the best or only the second or third best deals.*

"I suspect my board would still feel a little uncomfortable," unless we only invested where you put your money, prince.

"On the other hand, if we were to invest in the Moscow Commerce Bank we may be able to provide you with the capital to take such investments," said Fox, watching carefully to judge Koslinski's reaction.

Koslinksi showed slight surprise, acting as though he had never thought of such a possibility. He paused, considering the idea. Then he said, "That may be possible, but it would depend on the terms."

By the end of the morning, a deal had been brokered. The British & Foreign Credit Bank would take a significant shareholding in the Moscow Commerce Bank. They would raise funds in the London market to finance Koslinski's plans. Koslinski would remain the largest single shareholder, and Fox would join the Moscow board.

They discussed the future possibilities over lunch, each convinced he had obtained the better deal. Koslinski had taken advantage of the strong interest in Russia by the London market. He had secured the funding he required. Fox had a valuable foothold in Moscow with connections he could use to expand his bank's business. The only money Fox would risk would be for the shareholding in Koslinski's bank. The rest he was confident he could find from other investors and earn a large fee for the bank in the process.

"Prince Koslinski," said Fox as they sipped a fine vintage port after the meal, "with your knowledge of the textile industry in Moscow you may be able to give me some advice on one of the more entrepreneurial members."

"Certainly. It's very likely I know them."

"As we are now partners, so to speak, I imagine I can talk to you in confidence. About a customer, you understand."

"Of course," said Koslinski, now deeply intrigued and already wondering how he could use the information to his advantage, as no doubt Fox intended. *Why else would he tell me?* thought the prince.

"Ivan Morozov, the principal of Morozov & Son—do you know him?"

"Yes. I've met him a number of times. His firm is an aggressive competitor and keeps expanding. There are some who don't like him as a result," Koslinski said and waited for Fox to elaborate.

"Several months ago, we agreed to lend Morozov a large sum of money to fund an expansion he proposed and which I must say looked very promising. So you can imagine our consternation when we find that a Liverpool cotton merchant has drawn down on these funds. No mention was made of purchasing raw cotton. How large are his operations in Moscow? Would we be in any danger if he were to default," asked Fox, a little too disingenuously.

"He has several, medium-sized but efficient factories and is rumored to be seeking ways to expand dramatically," Koslinski replied. "In the spirit of our new partnership arrangements, we would be delighted to enforce the debt for you and to take over his factories if he were to default," he added.

"Excellent," said Fox. "There is an unrelated matter which has arisen that gives me personal cause for concern over Mr. Morozov. He'll be given no period of grace if he's late with any repayments."

He looked straight at Koslinski, silent for a moment.

"I understand." Koslinski smiled.

Fox smiled back. "I look forward to a mutually profitable relationship," he said.

"Salut." Fox raised his glass.

"Salut."

As they rose to leave the table, Fox straightened the carnation in the buttonhole of his dark, well-cut suit.

§ § § § § §

Since Mikhail's departure, Katy had kept busy with the commencement of the school term for the children.

She wrote several long letters to her mother in Dublin and her mother sent a short, one-page reply warning her not to rush into marriage but giving her blessing and inquiring whether she would have an opportunity to see her daughter again before she left for "foreign parts." The letter brought home to Katy the reality of how complete the separation from her family would be. For a brief moment, she wondered whether she was doing the right thing, leaving the familiar for the unknown. Then the image of Misha rowing the boat on the Serpentine, his arms strong, his eyes smiling down on her, dispelled any doubt. "My heart belongs to him," she said to herself. "I will follow him wherever he goes."

Her mood soared once she opened the second letter the post brought, her first letter from Moscow signed, "Your ever love, Misha."

Katy's Russian progressed well with the help of a Russian-born tutor. She still quietly spoke Russian to herself out loud each night before falling asleep. Pleased with her progress so far the tutor told her that to speak the language properly she must go to Russia, to which she demurely replied that she was hoping to arrange a trip next year.

It'll be months before I see him again, she thought. *What an interminable time. What if he's changed his mind when he returns, or, worse, what if he doesn't return?* In her heart, she knew that could not be so. She felt so much love for this man she knew he must feel the same way.

Misha had written her a lover's letter, from home. Her worst fear— that his return would rekindle some old love affair in Moscow— receded into nothing.

"I hope he's missing me as much," she said to her mirror.

That night she started a long letter, "My darling Misha."

By the time the letter reached Mikhail there would be serious doubts about the survival of the firm of Morozov & Son. If the business did not survive, he could never return for Katy.

Moscow

The Department of Police was located in an unimposing building not far from the Kremlin. People who had to walk past its doors did so with purpose. No one loitered. It was not a place in which to spend any unnecessary time. The dull grey of the walls did not encourage sightseeing.

At the rear of the building, on the first floor, Maksim Rysakov shared an office with two other investigators. The only window overlooked an internal courtyard and admitted limited light on a bright day. The three shared two desks, as one of them, generally Rysakov, was usually out on the job. Today, however, they were all in residence. Rysakov arrived late and had to take the chair on the far side of one of the desks, against the wall.

"Damn paper work. Do you think anyone actually reads all these reports?" complained one.

"Only if you don't submit your report, Gregori," said his colleague. "Then an alarm goes off and everyone thinks you have something to hide." Gregori Yukovsky laughed.

"Well, if they read this report they won't be much enlightened. We have no leads at all." Smoke from dark Russian tobacco formed a thick blue haze in the room.

"Hey, open the window, Gregori," Rysakov called out as he sat down, "there's no air on my side of the desk."

"I hear the government is proposing to reduce maximum working hours, Maksim," said Yukovsky as he turned back from the window. "Maybe that'll stop the strikes."

"Yes, I heard. A half hour a day for the same pay," Rysakov said. He had been back at work for several weeks and already the holiday seemed no more than a distant and beautiful dream.

"It's one thing to have strikes at individual factories, but that last one…hell. Bad enough that the Moscow and Petersburg textile works shut down. Can you imagine if the strike had spread to other industries, like the trains for example," said Yukovsky. "We'd've been powerless to stop it."

"That won't happen, Gregori," said Rysakov. "You're being too dramatic."

"I know, but it's not impossible. There are already complaints that allowing the strikers concessions will only encourage them. That, they say, will lead to revolution or reduced profits." He laughed. "Which will we choose?"

How soon they forget, Rysakov thought. *Only two generations ago most of the factory owners were serfs. Now, building on their parents' success, they are multi-millionaires.*

Walking home last evening, Rysakov took a short detour to avoid a noisy group of strikers. This took him past a scientific instrument shop. He stopped to glance idly at the window display. One of the items he saw galvanized his attention—a doctor's medical kit. He pushed on the door before he realized the shop was closed for business. Taking note of the address, he resolved to return the next morning. When he did, what he learned from the shopkeeper was very significant. The man took the kit he had seen in the window and opened it. Inside were a number of instruments including two small scalpels.

"These kits are used by students in their studies or for dissection work," the man said.

"What would a surgeon use?" asked Rysakov.

"A surgeon would use more expensive, better quality instruments with larger blades, Investigator," the man explained. He went on, "There are a limited number of establishments supplying the medical profession in Moscow and Saint Petersburg. It's a specialized market, you understand. We've been supplying the profession for twenty years and pride ourselves in always having replacements on hand, for when the old instruments become worn."

"That must be difficult to keep track of," said Rysakov, hoping the shopkeeper would volunteer what he now felt sure would be the case.

"On the contrary, we keep records of our regular customer's purchases," he said. Rysakov nodded, containing his rising sense of excitement.

"Are these instruments available only to the medical profession," Rysakov asked.

"No," the owner replied, "anyone with a scientific interest could purchase a set. But why would anyone want to? They're expensive and not much use for anything else."

This could be the break we need, he thought excitedly. *At last, a positive lead. If we send a request to all scientific supply shops for details of every person who bought surgeon's scalpels over the last three years, it'll give me a list of suspects. It's likely prominent doctors and professors at the universities can be eliminated. Who that leaves poses an intriguing thought. The "Monster of Moscow" has a bloodhound on his trail.*

These shops need a permit to operate so government records will provide the names. I'll also check with the universities, with the medical associations, and with doctors that the department uses. The last may know whether there were any less reputable suppliers where money spoke loudest. An official request from the tsar's police always concentrates the attention. If we add the suggestion of possible terrorist links, implying Okhrana interest, that'll get results.

Finally, he would speak to his own contacts in the Okhrana; their networks turned up surprising information at times. This he would handle informally over a vodka, or two.

The fug in the room finally got too thick for Rysakov and he rose, announced he was going out, and ventured into an overcast, cool day. The new lead dominated his thinking. As he walked along the street toward a small park, he began to review the murders again.

All of the deceased were young, attractive women with full bosoms. They had all been in domestic service and in Moscow less than a year. They came from a diversity of villages, so there was no common link there. None of their friends (the few they had) or their workmates had any idea about the identity of their lovers. Although several had said with certainty they knew the victim was involved with someone. Each appeared to have been lonely, away from the familiarity of village and family.

There were two other similarities. Each was dead, and each had had a part of her body removed.

§ § § § §

"There is no doubt the old adage 'the more successful you are the bigger the target' is right," said Ivan after a week of strikes.

Mikhail nodded. "We're lucky they didn't do much damage. Some of the others didn't fare so well."

"They seem to think violence will get them what they want. Well it won't work," said Ivan. "The police should arrest the leaders and deport them to Siberia."

Even though he deplored the damage done by the strikers, Mikhail thought privately that the action had proved to the workers they did have power. Where that might lead concerned him far more than the small amount of damage to their factories. In fact, the strikes only offered a temporary distraction from far more serious internal problems.

Ivan told his managers they had purchased a large quantity of cotton that had been placed in storage in Petersburg. "With Baranov's factories," he said, "and the new facilities being constructed, I will source all our cotton direct from overseas, straight into our warehouses." He could see from the muted response they had heard from the Petersburg manager. With so much cotton in storage they had decided it could only be wild speculation. Such action might endanger all their jobs.

That evening, in need of distraction from cotton and strikes, Ivan allowed himself to be persuaded to join Mikhail and several business acquaintances to dine at a new restaurant. It was not far off the Tverskaia, past the Brest Station and near the famous night spot of Yar. A gypsy musician, new to Moscow, was playing. His music was reputed to bring tears even to the eyes of politicians, so sad and melancholy the tone.

The place was full of noise and laughter, men with their wives or mistresses, tables of overweight businessmen relaxing after a busy day and groups of students by far the rowdiest.

When they had eaten their first course and consumed several bottles of vodka, the haunting notes of a gypsy violin gradually quieted the room. The violinist, a tall thin man with a wispy beard, well past his prime, walked slowly among the diners, his violin tucked easily between his chin and left shoulder. Following, and also dressed in traditional costume, was a shorter, overweight woman with a sensual contralto voice perfectly suited to the songs of mountain and forest. But it was the pure rounded sound of the violin that really captured the heart and mind.

As the player came to their table, Ivan could smell brandy on the man's breath and see the threadbare state of his costume. On an impulse, he stuffed ten rubles into the man's pocket and said, "When you have finished playing, come to my table with your violin."

Roman Romanski nodded and moved on.

Well over an hour later, the gypsy returned.

"What would you like me to play, sir?"

"Play me your favorite song," said Ivan pouring another glass of vodka. It was months since he had relaxed so easily, among friends.

The violin rolled the rich, bitter-sweet beauty of the theme from Tchaikovsky's *Piano Concerto* across the table and into the room. For Ivan, the sounds revived memories of twenty-one years ago, of Nataliya sitting beside him in Saint Petersburg clutching his hand, thrilling to the boldness and pathos of the music.

When he had finished, tears rolled down many of the cheeks of those applauding.

Ivan sat with his gaze fixed on the violin.

"Roman Romanskovich, sit down," he said pulling a chair from an adjoining table and filling a spare glass with vodka.

"Friends," Ivan called as he turned to answer the cries of "more, more" from the room, "that music was the last I heard with my wife before she died so many years ago. This gypsy's magic has brought her face back to me. Please, your indulgence, I must speak with this conjurer."

"May I hold this wondrous instrument," Ivan said taking it gently from the player and turning it slowly in his hands.

"You played like a man inspired, Roman Romanski; that fiddle sang so sweetly, it saw deep into my heart. Will you sell it to me so that I can keep the sound with me forever?"

"Sell it? But on what would I then play?"

"Buy two new fiddles."

"Fiddles! This is a work of art. Look at the luster of the varnish. This violin is my baby. My father owned it and his father before him. I could not possibly sell it."

Ivan had the advantage in this interchange. One of his friends who knew of Romanski from Saint Petersburg had told him the gypsy had won the violin years ago from a drunken musician in a card game. Before that he had used gypsy violins.

"Your sainted father must've been proud of a son who could produce such sounds. Why I've heard that you could charm an empress with only a gypsy violin so skilled are your fingers," said Ivan refilling the glasses.

"It is true. I have played for royalty," Romanski said vainly but untruthfully.

"If you don't sell it to me I'll never be able to keep that sound."

Romanski looked at Ivan with an expression of profound apology.

"Sir, even if you were to offer me a thousand rubles I couldn't sell; it's too much a part of me."

"I'll pay you 500 rubles," said Ivan. They had now established the violin was for sale. Only the price needed to be agreed.

"No, no. I have a wife to support and I must buy another fine violin so that I do not disappoint the patrons. I don't know where I can buy one good enough to replace this beauty, and I refuse to play on anything less. I'd need at least double what you are offering to even contemplate a sale. Even then I don't think I could sell. I'm sorry," he said and rose slowly to leave the table.

"Thank you for the drinks, gentlemen," he said lingering.

Ivan said nothing, then, as Romanski turned to recommence playing, Ivan reached out his hand. He pressed a ten ruble tip into Romanski's hand together with his calling card.

"Speak to your wife about it."

The other occupants of the table had listened with fascination to this interchange. *Ivan Victorovich has had too much to drink,* they thought. *Either that or his mind has become unhinged. Maybe the rumors about the cotton were true.* They smiled indulgently. *God, he could buy the man as his lifelong servant for that price.*

At mid-morning the following day, Ivan and Mikhail sat discussing the action required to resolve their heavy overstocking in cotton when the manager entered to announce that a gypsy musician had presented Ivan's card and requested a meeting.

"Show him in," Ivan smiled.

Mikhail looked at him quizzically. He knew his father was not given to maudlin spending and was intrigued about why he was seeing the man.

"I see you've bought the violin," he said as Romanski entered the room.

"May I look at it one last time?"

Ivan laid the case on his desk and picked up the violin, inspecting it in detail from the saddle where the player's chin rested, the bridge which supported the strings, the "f" holes, the furling, the neck where the player's left thumb cradled the finger board and, lastly, the scroll.

"It's truly a lovely instrument. I'm sorry you can't sell it," he said handing the violin in its case back to Romanski.

"My wife said that I shouldn't become emotionally attached to a violin. She's convinced me that perhaps I was not understanding enough last night. The sounds and memories that it gave to you are too important to ignore. I once lost a child, and I can understand how valuable it can be to capture the images of a loved one to lessen the hurt. If it'll help you remember your wife, I'll sell it for 1,000 rubles," Romanski said.

"I'll give you 800. No more," Ivan shot straight back.

"Ah, sir, this is a valuable piece of art. It's been in my family…"

"Romanski, you won it in a card game in Petersburg. Do we have a deal or do you take your violin back to your wife with no gold? I have a very busy schedule and don't have time for any more bargaining." Ivan's tone was harsh.

"Sir, this violin is of great value…"

"Thank you for showing it to me again. I must resume my meeting," Ivan said, turning his back on the musician. As he did so, he saw Romanski shake his head with resignation. Ivan suspected 800 was far more than he had really expected and was more than he would earn in a year's playing.

Once Romanski had been paid and signed a receipt transferring ownership, Ivan picked the violin up and passed it to Mikhail.

"Look through the 'f' holes and tell me if I really saw what I thought I saw or if I've made a fool of myself."

"It has a label on the inside base," said Mikhail peering in through the "f" hole. "It says something…I can't make out, then Guarneri and the letters I…H…S.' Under that is 'Cremona.'" Mikhail looked up. "This is one of the famous violins M. Ysaye told us about, isn't it?"

"Thank God, I thought I may've been too drunk last night. My eyes are not as sharp as they used to be. When I looked at it a few minutes ago I wasn't sure I could trust what I saw. So, I now own a Guarneri that is worth far more than that drunken old gypsy could ever imagine," Ivan said with pleasure. "I'll get a display case made for the house."

The thrill of a successful trade had never left him, and he preened with satisfaction as he held the violin at arm's length. It was not the value of the win. It was the winning that was important. It put a man at the head of the pack.

The interlude over, both immediately refocused on the real problems confronting the business.

At half past two in the afternoon, they returned from lunch to their offices in Varkarka Street in the financial district. As they entered, the chief manager, who had clearly been waiting for them, pulled them to one side.

"Sir, the manager of the All Russian Trade Bank is waiting to see you. He seems very worried."

"Why would my banker come unannounced at this time of day," said Ivan, instantly alert. Unscheduled visits by bankers were rarely good news. The day that had begun so successfully was about to become the worst day in the history of Morozov & Son.

Mikhail closed the door to their office as Ivan motioned the banker to sit in one of the soft, leather-covered chairs.

"You don't seem yourself, Vladimir Pavelovich," Ivan said. "How can I help?"

"Ivan Victorovich, I don't know how best to tell you. There is a serious problem."

"Tell me bluntly, Vladimir, it'll save time," Ivan said.

The bank manager began slowly as if trying to marshal his thoughts.

"Mikhail came to me last week, on your instructions, and authorized me to pay Baranov the balance for the purchase of his business."

"Yes, that's correct," said Ivan.

"You'd instructed the bank to draw against the letter of credit from the British & Foreign Credit Bank to fund the purchase."

"Yes," said Ivan impatiently.

"The British bank is well known in Moscow banking and the documents looked to be in order so we had no reason to doubt that they would pay. You had a large sum of rubles on deposit earlier this year but you took half that with you to London. For what purpose, I do not know."

"That's correct. And there is no reason why you should know, Vladimir," Ivan said. This was going to be a slow process as the banker was clearly distressed.

"We've had to use all of the remaining funds to meet part of the cost of Baranov's, but it was not enough."

"What do you mean? I had more than sufficient funds in the letter of credit to cover the cost of Baranov's. The balance of funds I intended to use for other purposes." Ivan was now both annoyed and concerned.

"Get to the point man," he demanded.

"The British & Foreign Credit Bank has refused to pay out on the letter of credit," said the manager, sucking in several deep breaths, his brow creased with concern.

Ivan said nothing, staring intently at the man, waiting for him to continue.

"We presented the documents to the Moscow correspondents of the British bank, the Moscow Commerce Bank. That is Prince Koslinski's bank. He has very good connections with the government."

"I know who he is," snapped Ivan.

"They accepted the documents and said that they did not see a problem but as is normal they would telegram London to confirm the payment. The reply came back the next day. The Moscow Commerce Bank sent me the original. It came as a complete surprise to them, they assured me."

He reached into his coat pocket and pulled out a creased sheet of paper headed Imperial Telegram Service and handed it to Ivan.

It read, "Regret to advise this LC fully drawn. Do not pay." It was signed, "G Fox, Director."

Ivan read it again. Slowly the enormity of this small piece of yellow official paper began to sink in.

His bank, relying on the documents drawn on a London bank well known in Moscow financial circles, had paid out in advance of clearing the funds from the British bank. They were now out of pocket a large sum, far more than they would have contemplated lending Ivan without the LC. Without the loan from the British & Foreign Credit Bank allowing him five years to repay, Ivan was in serious trouble. Unless he found an alternative source of funds, his own bank would be forced to foreclose. If that happened, it would trigger default with the British bank. He had no illusions as to what this meant; he had seen it before. *Hell,* he thought, *I have bought valuable assets at knockdown prices myself in similar circumstances.* He would be ruined. He had to play for time.

"Vladimir Pavelovich, I don't know what has happened. We've not drawn those funds down. They were for paying old Baranov. It must be a misunderstanding of some sort. Please let me get to the bottom of the problem. I understand that you need an answer as soon as possible, and I'll find out what the problem is and get the funds cleared for you."

"Understand, Ivan, we cannot carry a debt of this size to one customer. If it cannot be resolved quickly, you will have to sell assets," the banker said with more firmness than he had used since he came into the office, "there is no alternative."

When he had gone, Ivan sat at his desk with his head in his hands.

"What is happening, Misha, have I offended God again?"

Three days later, a letter marked "Very Private" arrived from Saint Petersburg.

Rather than risk a telegram and the potential for other eyes to get the information before his employer, Ivan's manager had written. A second large shipment of cotton had arrived, this time from Egypt. It would also have to be stored.

The manager noted that the quality was good. However, with the stock of cotton already in storage the rumors would now be uncontrollable, "Please advise urgently what to say," his letter concluded.

Now, it became clear what had happened.

"Wallace, our cotton broker, has misused the authority I left him. He must have decided to sell all his stock, no doubt including some canceled orders," Ivan fumed. "It seems he's drawn down every pound from British & Foreign Credit Bank."

Mikhail knew this placed them in a perilous position. They now owned more raw cotton than they could use for years. The cash reserves were gone. If they couldn't repay their bank, the business would be finished.

Ivan went for a walk across Red Square in the cool bite of an early autumn day. When he returned, he called Mikhail into his office and closed the door. He then analyzed their situation with clarity and icy calm.

"We have only one course of action to take—we must sell the cotton as soon as possible. If that can't be done, I'll have to sell an interest in the business to an outsider. But I won't go easily. I've not built this enterprise on what my father bequeathed to see it pulled down on the verge of my greatest success by faint-hearted financiers. I've worked long and hard, without the love of Nataliya. I'll not allow my legacy to you, Misha, to be diminished. Not without one hell of a fight. And Wallace. Mr. Harold 'bloody' Wallace will face a reckoning before I die, whatever the outcome here. Curse that venal swine."

Mikhail stared at his father. Ivan spoke quietly, with a vehemence Mikhail had not encountered before. When his father looked up, Mikhail was taken aback by the cold fury in the eyes. He knew Ivan fought hard in the fiercely competitive business world of Russia and that he had a reputation for ruthlessness—just how ruthless he had not realized until that moment. It was the cold and pitiless look of an assassin. The almost boyish pleasure of the morning might never have been.

§ § § § §

Some weeks after Ivan's banker had delivered the devastating news, the weather turned colder. Unseasonable wild storms from the northwest made life uncomfortable. Any day, the first snows would fall. Ivan spent considerable time and ingenuity trying to sell all or part of the cotton stocks. He spoke to several of his competitors. He would supply cotton of known quality—they could go to the warehouse and check it themselves—when they needed it. They showed initial interest. The prospect of cheap quality cotton was an enticing possibility. However, they had their own commitments. *Anyway,* they thought, *Morozov may not be around for long, so why help a competitor?* Ivan made little progress, disposing of an insignificant amount of the cotton.

The importers were even less interested. They were expecting their own large deliveries from Egypt and America any day before the winter storms made the journey too hazardous. Then, Wogau, sensing Ivan's increasing desperation, offered to buy all the cotton at a heavy discount, a fraction of the price Ivan had paid; to compensate them for holding the cotton until next season, the Wogaus said. Ivan knew accepting such an offer would put paid to any hope he had of becoming a major force in the industry. But he would survive.

The All Russia Trade Bank gave Ivan one more week to repay the money, then they would take control of the factories and sell all the assets

Today, he decided, he would do the best deal he could with Wogau & Co, get the bank settled and begin the long and arduous process of rebuilding the business. He had run out of options.

Mikhail wanted to accompany him to the importer's offices, but Ivan did not want anyone with him. This he had to do on his own. The humiliation should be his alone. He did not want Misha to see him capitulate.

"Nataliya, I've failed you," he whispered so quietly no one heard him. "Everything I did built the business. I took no risk that was not reasonable. I made no investment that was not the right one." He turned left out of his building and walked to the corner where he stopped. "I swear on your memory, my darling, I will rebuild the business for our son." *To think that such a calamitous result could flow from the greed of one man,* he thought. "And then I'll deal with a particular English cotton broker. His life will never be the same. If he lives."

When Ivan left for Wogau & Co, Mikhail sat quietly in the office on his own. His father was tough-minded, of that there was no doubt. He would not concede defeat until the very last minute. He would fight to the end. Although what could possibly save them now, Mikhail could not imagine.

For a moment, his thoughts strayed to himself. If Morozov & Son became little more than a hollow shell, he could not ask Katy to marry him. He may not have a home to live in. He could not ask her until the business was reestablished. All his energy would have to be devoted to helping his father rebuild. He could not expect her to wait, the rebuilding would take years. A feeling of great sadness enveloped him. His father had experienced far greater grief with his mother's death. He knew that. He also knew he could never let his father down. Together they would work to rebuild the business. The price would be high, very high. It meant giving up Katy. He would never see her again. The thought of not seeing her smile and of never holding her in his arms made the future bleaker than he could have imagined. Every time he received one of her letters, his heart leapt. Now he would have to write the most difficult letter of his life, telling her he could not marry, freeing her to seek another mate. He felt his heart would break.

He walked out of the office to speak to the manager. The day-to-day business had to continue until events overtook them. It was now common knowledge that the firm was experiencing difficulties. In fact, several employees had started showing signs of nervousness on the tenure of their future employment.

"A messenger has delivered a package sealed with embossed wax, sir," the manager said as Mikhail emerged. "I placed it in Mr. Ivan's office, but thought you should know."

"Thank you, Sergie. How long ago did it come?"

"About an hour. The messenger said he had come straight from the rail station as the train had been delayed."

"Which station?" Mikhail asked.

"Petersburg."

His interest piqued, Mikhail went into Ivan's office and picked up the package. The envelope had a red wax seal on the front and was addressed to "Ivan Morozov, Private and Confidential." He looked closely at the seal "Victoria Regina." It was from the British ambassador in Saint Petersburg. Why would the British ambassador send an envelope with clearly little more than a letter in it to Ivan? And send it by personal messenger? It did not make sense. Without any further thought, he picked up the filigree letter knife on his father's desk and broke the seal.

He pulled out a single sheet of paper.

It was headed, "Telegram from Philip Armitage, Foreign Office."

"Received news today that severe storms off Scotland sank large tonnage ships. Including SS Nile and four master Sagacious with all hands carrying large cargoes cotton bound Petersburg. Lifeboat rescued several crew Nile who reported other ships feared lost. Thought this may be of use. Good luck Armitage."

Mikhail read the telegram again. Why would the FO tell Ivan about the loss of ships at sea. Unless of course he had heard of their problems and was trying to help. The full implications of the message began to sink in.

"My God! I hope I'm not too late."

He looked at the clock. Ivan had been gone nearly two hours. He may already have sold their cotton. Mikhail grabbed his coat and hat and bolted out the door, clutching the telegram. He hailed the first troika he saw and promised the driver an outrageous tip to get him to Wogau offices on the other side of the city inside ten minutes.

The driver's face lit up at the challenge and the prospects of the tip. On top of that, this rich boy had not even bothered to negotiate price. Without hesitation, he cracked the whip cruelly over the three horses and they took off at breakneck speed to the total disregard of other drivers and pedestrians.

Mikhail failed to notice how close he came to death as the troika's wheels at times left the ground. The driver, panting as much as the horses, deposited Mikhail outside the Wogau office in eight minutes.

Mikhail pressed a wad of rubles into his hand and raced inside.

He burst so suddenly through the door that a secretary facing the entrance cried out in alarm. A large uniformed doorman lounging against the wall whirled at the cry. He immediately started for Mikhail, unsure what to expect.

Mikhail stopped and apologized to the woman.

"Please excuse me. I am Mikhail Morozov, and I wish to see my father, Ivan Morozov who is presently meeting with Mr. Wogau. It's a matter of the greatest urgency. Could you please direct me to him?"

Quickly satisfying the doorman he was not an anarchist bent on destruction, Mikhail followed the man to the door of an office. The doorman knocked politely. Mikhail could now barely restrain his impatience. He began to push past the man terrified the sale may have been made when after a moment's conversation, Ivan emerged.

"Is there a room where we can speak privately?" Mikhail asked the doorman.

"Certainly, sir. Over here."

Once inside, Ivan looked at Mikhail.

"Have you sold the cotton?" Mikhail asked anxiously.

"Not yet. We've agreed price and are haggling about payment terms. What's this all about?" Ivan said.

"Thank God. This arrived about an hour ago. As soon as I read it I came over immediately," said Mikhail and he handed over the telegram.

Ivan read it, twice, so as to be absolutely clear as to the meaning. He stared at the wall, his mind working at fever pitch.

"Thank you, Misha. If you'd arrived fifteen minutes later, you would've been too late."

He put his hand on Mikhail's shoulder and said with a grim smile, "They don't know. They still think their cotton will arrive within the week. These are their ships. Instead, they're at the bottom of the Atlantic.

"I want you to go back to our office and wait until I return," Ivan said. He seemed to stand taller. No longer did he have the hunted look that had dogged his countenance for the last week. Once more, he was in charge of his own destiny. He had no reason to doubt the veracity of the information in the telegram. If what it said was correct...

He had one final throw of the dice.

Ivan walked back into the room where he had been negotiating with P.I. Wogau and his brother.

"Gentlemen, my son just brought me information of a better offer, and I therefore feel obliged to withdraw my cotton from sale. I very much appreciate your time and the trouble you have gone to in making your offer. I trust that we'll be able to do business in the near future."

With that, he nodded to each of the brothers and strode out of the room.

He walked back to the office. He needed to clear from his head the feeling of defeat that had filled it over the last week. And, he needed to think how best to exploit these new circumstances. He felt certain Armitage and the FO would only have sent the telegram if they were sure of the information. All he had to do now was wait.

I wonder how long it will be before the news of the losses reach the Petersburg market. Shipping ports are generally first to know bad news. "A couple of days, three at the most," he said to himself.

The trip to London was paying handsome dividends in totally unforeseen ways.

§ § § § §

Once he had rejected the Wogau offer, Ivan had little alternative but to tell his bank manager of the telegram. Skeptical at first, Vladimir insisted on seeing it. Once the import of the information sank in he agreed to an extension on the debt until the cotton ships arrived in Petersburg. In this event, Morozov & Son would be required to immediately repay the funds or he would take possession of the factory. Alternatively, once he received confirmation that the vessels had indeed been lost, they would negotiate a new arrangement. Of course, a higher interest rate would apply, he explained to Ivan. Vladimir then decided to use this information to indulge in some personal speculation and bought a small amount of cotton from a merchant in Moscow.

Two days later, rumors circulated in Moscow that some cotton importers were deferring deliveries. Another rumor said at least one cotton ship had sunk.

Morozov & Son went busily about its business. Ivan commenced planning the new mill, engaging architects, and placing preliminary orders for new English machines.

The next day, the Moscow daily papers reported:

"The SS *Nile* and the four-master *Sagacious* have been listed by their agents as officially lost at sea. Serious concerns are held for a number of other vessels, also feared lost. Sources close to the shipping companies say these storms are the fiercest in living memory."

Ivan immediately wrote to Wogaus expressing his regrets at the losses. "As you offered to buy when I was overstocked, I feel obliged to reciprocate." He added, "I am pleased to offer you first opportunity to buy. However, do not feel under any obligation, there are no doubt several other importers who may have an interest."

The next day, Mr. Peter Igorovich Wogau presented his calling card at Morozov & Son's office, requesting an urgent meeting. Ivan decided to make him wait and, sending his sincere apologies that he was unable to meet that day, suggested the afternoon of the following day.

In the morning paper of that day, it was officially confirmed—at least two more ships were now listed "lost at sea."

This created a shortage of raw cotton for the mills. Cotton importers and merchants were unable to fulfill their commitments to the factories. With winter fast approaching, the demand for warm cloth began to rise rapidly.

Ivan could not help but be impressed with Peter Wogau. He had thought out his position clearly. Ivan was prepared for long and arduous negotiations. Instead, they reached agreement within an hour. Wogau agreed to pay Morozov & Son double Ivan's cost, provided they purchased all his cotton. This, Wogau explained, would place the firm in a commanding position to supply raw cotton for the winter season. Other importers, whose cotton also lay at the bottom of the Atlantic, would have no choice but to deal with him, at his price. Ivan had doubled his money, and his own mills had sufficient raw cotton of their own to continue producing. That evening, around the dinner table, they celebrated with friends.

"My friends," Ivan said, standing with a glass in hand, "this is a stunning turnaround for Morozov & Son. Not only do we keep all of our business, we can repay the bank in full. And we have funds to build our new factory. That we will be the leading textile manufacturer in Moscow is beyond doubt."

He raised his glass.

"Na Zdaroviye"

The others all rose to their feet. "Na Zdaroviye!" they shouted. As one, they hurled their glasses into the fireplace, shattering the crystal into tiny shards.

§ § § § §

He tipped the delivery man as the maid showed him out. Muir & Mirrielees, the largest department store in Moscow, had had a small display case available with beechwood inlay. A simple stand now held the Guarneri inside and completed the display. Ivan walked into the drawing room and looked at the instrument. It had been freshly polished. The deep luster of the varnish proclaimed the art and skill of the maker.

"Everyone in Moscow knows I'm a generous supporter of the arts, music in particular. I'll loan the Guarneri to the lead soloist of the Russian Musical Society for special performances. I may even allow its use by visiting virtuosos," he announced to the empty room, "provided they play Russian composers."

§ § § § §

Vasily Koslinski returned to Moscow pleased with the outcome of his London visit. On the first night back, he ate alone in his palatial home. His staff knew their master well enough not to intrude upon his thoughts. Copies of recent Moscow newspapers had been kept for him to read at his leisure. In the top issue, he read that three large cotton ships were confirmed lost and grave fears held for several others. "This could lead to a shortage of raw cotton for the mills," the reporter speculated. He wondered whether Morozov had disposed of his cotton before the shortage and at what price. He would find out tomorrow.

Koslinski felt lonely. He had never married, although had come close several times. Since he had left home all those years ago, he had had difficulty making a full commitment to any one woman. Perhaps that was the problem, he mused cynically. He remembered the occasions. Each of the women had been aristocratic and wealthy, quite suitable matches. When the time approached for a public announcement of a betrothal, they had withdrawn. It was as if, at that late stage, as they became more intimate with the prince, something disturbed them sufficiently to end the association. None of the women had ever been specific, at least in public. They simply moved into different circles and married elsewhere. The prince could never explain why he was emotionally unable to make the commitment each of these women quite reasonably expected. Vasily Koslinski had buried deep within his mind strings that tied his heart elsewhere. Strings he rarely acknowledged, even to himself. So deep seated were the emotions, he was incapable of confronting them.

He had few friends, but many acquaintances. Tonight, he did not feel in the mood to call on any. Tonight, he felt the need of female company. After dinner, he left his palace to visit his favorite brothel.

At the many registered brothels in Saint Petersburg and Moscow, where the women in turn registered as prostitutes, most were peasant girls out of work in the city. Some were of a better class, who became prostitutes due to a drinking problem or had been widowed with a child to support. Koslinski generally preferred the peasant girls. They were more pliable—or the occasional true wanton among the others. In addition to the registered brothels, large numbers of women worked unregistered. They used cheap lodgings or the streets, at times ending as deaths for the Imperial Police to investigate.

Many a socially ambitious wife of a wealthy merchant looked upon Prince Vasily with his wealth and title as a catch worth sending a daughter to snare. Often seen at the ballet, theater, concerts, and balls with attractive women, he also attended alone or with a male acquaintance. Occasionally, whispers that the prince preferred young boys came and went. No evidence to support these rumors ever surfaced, much to the disappointment of the aristocrat gossip circles. Koslinski remained an enigma.

The day after his return, he heard of Morozov's astonishing coup with the cotton. He immediately sought details. Once he realized the extent of the windfall, he arranged to meet with Ivan. *Maybe this Morozov is a bigger risk taker than I imagined,* he thought. *This time, it paid off. If he is a true gambler the temptation to repeat this will be too great. Eventually they all come undone.*

Koslinski now put other matters aside for the rest of the morning. If Morozov repaid the loans from the British bank he, Koslinski, would lose any leverage he might have to pick up textile assets cheaply when the next speculation did not pay off. He considered a range of possibilities before deciding his original idea remained the best. It was simple and gave him leverage on several levels. With the funds raised from George Fox in London, his own bank could extend Ivan a loan equal to nearly half the amount he had originally borrowed. He felt confident Fox, for personal reasons, would support keeping a sword dangling over Morozov. Then, if the man got into trouble again, he, Koslinski, would be in a position to grab the assets he wanted to settle the debt.

Ivan was surprised to hear Koslinski's proposition. He had repaid his own bank and was considering whether to repay the balance outstanding to the British bank even though he no need for several years. In addition, he now had sufficient funds of his own to build the new factory.

What Koslinksi offered, however, would give him the freedom to take advantage of new opportunities. The only condition that, until required, the funds remain on deposit at the Moscow Commerce Bank, Ivan could see no objection to. The funds could earn interest there as well as anywhere. So it was agreed, half the funds advanced by the British bank would be repaid. Koslinski's bank would take over the remainder of the debt, securing it with a mortgage over the Baranov factory. Ivan would use the profit on the cotton sale to build his new factory.

§ § § § §

Russia still used the Gregorian calendar and the Orthodox Christmas was celebrated on January 7, thirteen days later than Katy O'Connor celebrated it in the Somerston household. Ivan and Mikhail decided to stay in Moscow that year and not make the journey to Saint Petersburg for the winter season. The design for the new factory was nearing completion and there were still approvals to obtain from the Imperial Government.

Outside, thick snow blanketed the city but not the festive air. Sparkling lights lit shop windows, small booths sold brightly colored toys, sleds and carriages whisked their charges along the streets. People in heavy fur coats and hats walked purposefully along the roadside, many laden with gifts. Gaily decorated Christmas trees glowed in the windows of some of the larger stores. Everywhere, the coming of Grandfather Frost and the Snow Maiden were eagerly anticipated. Kibitkas, hooded carriages placed on runners and harnessed to a troika, hissed across the snow and ice, bells jingling.

Maksim Rysakov liked Christmas. He liked the warm companionship of family and friends. He did not even mind the cold so long as the temperature did not go below minus twenty. Then it could get unpleasant if one was called out because a thoughtless criminal forgot that even policemen like holidays. Vera loved the pageantry of this time of year and she and Pavel set up a small tree in their modest living room. Maksim smiled broadly as he opened the door with the other two pushing behind him excitedly in this, an annual ritual.

"What a wonderful surprise!" he exclaimed. "This is better than any tree I've ever seen, Mamushka, but we can't afford professional tree decorators, only our tsar can afford such luxury," he said in a mock scold.

"We did it, Papa. Mamushka and me."

Pavel could not resist the bait.

"No, it's not possible."

"Yes, yes, Papa," Pavel said. "And I lit all the candles." He bubbled with excitement.

The three of them stood hand in hand looking at the tree, all talking at once. It was one of those moments he would recall with great affection in years to come. It was also a Christmas Maksim Rysakov would remember in detail, but for quite the wrong reason.

The main celebrations took place the following day, Christmas Eve. On this day, in all of Russia, families sat down to a special dinner. This year, the Rysakov family's dinner would be for only two.

A police constable knocked on the door very early on the morning of Christmas Eve. Another body had been found, and this one was different.

The girl had been found about four hours ago and treated initially as the murder of a whore and not of exceptional interest. The hotel where the body had been discovered lay in a rougher part of town where many unregistered prostitutes sought custom in the taverns, the cheap eating places and outside some restaurants. Many of the women used their own lodgings to earn a living, others, like the dead girl, worked out of dingy, and often dirty, hotels, sometimes hiring the room in rotation with several others. Who came and went into the rooms was of no interest to anyone, so long as the girls paid the rent. One of the other women sharing the room had discovered the body. She had taken a customer to the first floor room. It was after midnight.

"When they drew back the blanket, they were both shocked at the sight that greeted them," he said.

When the constable called to the scene saw the injuries, he immediately referred the murder to the office of the investigators. The one man on duty there had no wish to see his own Christmas interrupted.

"The sergeant knew of your interest in the Ignatiev house murder, sir," the constable said. "He recommended the matter be referred to Senior Investigator Rysakov forthwith."

As the droshky hissed over the snow, Rysakov puzzled in his mind that certain times of the year seemed to bring out more violent behavior than normal. These times should be spent in the company of family or friends. The results were often horrific. *It was easy,* he thought, stepping onto the snow and following the constable into the hotel, *to see how God-fearing men saw in it the work of the devil.*

The body had been left as it was discovered. Almost. The police doctor had been summoned. "Don't let him touch anything until I get there," Rysakov had instructed.

The dead white flesh of the girl looked a sad and pathetic contrast to the dirty grey bed linen on which she lay. He looked first at the breasts. They were intact, to his surprise. He had expected this to be a repeat of the Ignatiev house murder. The nipples lay where they should. Something must have disturbed him before he could gather his trophies.

His gaze moved to the throat. There were clear signs of bruising over the windpipe. He bent down to examine the extent of bruising. It went as far as he could see without moving the girl's head. Two thin lines of discoloration close together, overlapping at the front. The rope had been pulled very tight and had broken the skin in several places.

Rysakov walked around to the other side. The same marks on the throat. He looked at the face. It did not show signs of a struggle. It was almost as if she had slid willingly into death. Then he noticed what appeared to be a shadow on the left temple. He bent over again. It was a purple bruise. The girl had been hit with considerable force. It had stunned or knocked her unconscious. The killer had then wound a cord around her neck and pulled it tight, strangling the life out of the young peasant girl.

He straightened and looked at the doctor, who stood silently watching him. Rysakov followed the doctor's eyes as he glanced toward the pubic area. The dark, coagulated tangle confused him. The pubic hair seemed to be intact, but it was matted with some other substance. It looked like dried blood. He looked at the doctor and raised his eyebrows.

"I found this," said the doctor, holding up a twenty centimeter length of rounded wood.

"It had been inserted between her legs and thrust in with violent force. It would have ruptured the uterus and may have gone into the gut. It looks like this madman made love to her with the wood. Or, maybe he was making some other point."

"What other point?" asked Rysakov.

"That prostitutes are bad, that selling sex for money is wrong, and they should be stopped. I don't know." The doctor sighed.

Rysakov stared at the piece of wood. He had never seen anything like it. It had clearly been premeditated. The murderer brought the wooden phallus with him. Could it have been intended as a toy for some bizarre sex game? Perhaps he had not meant to be so violent with the implement. Or perhaps the doctor was right. Perhaps after having had sex with the girl, revulsion at his own weakness overpowered him. He had had to expunge it. It had certainly been senseless from what the doctor said. The girl would have been dead or dying anyway.

The doctor wrapped the wood in a piece of rag and placed it on the bed next to the body.

"If you do not need me, I'll be on my way. I have to buy some toys for my son," the doctor said.

"Of course. Thank you for waiting," Rysakov said, barely noticing the doctor's departure.

Rysakov stood back from the bed and stared at the body. He tried to reconstruct the movements of the girl and her customer. She would have led the man into the room and sat on the bed. The price would have been agreed before she took him upstairs. Perhaps he told her to undress in front of him. She would have stood and taken off her clothes. She then stood naked, waiting for him to undress. Did he take his clothes off? Where would he have placed them? He felt convinced this murderer had struck before. On the little evidence Rysakov had, and a feeling based on experience, he now worked on the probable assumption that his quarry was wealthy. Perhaps even an aristocrat. He looked around the shabby little room. In one corner stood an unpadded wooden chair and a cheap chest of three drawers. He walked over to the chair and carefully inspected it and the floor around to see if there was even the smallest of items overlooked by the killer. There was nothing.

Rysakov walked slowly toward the bed as the killer may have done having hung his coat over the chair. At the edge of the bed, he stopped. Something caught his eye. He looked back at the chair and retraced his steps with his eyes. There on the floor near the side of the bed was a small white shape. He bent down and picked up a white pearl shell button. He held it by the edges. For a brief moment, he considered the possibility of trying to raise fingerprints off the button. He looked closer at it. The irregularity of the surface and the real likelihood that the fingers slid over the button decided. Reliable prints would not be obtainable.

Did it belong to the murderer? Let's assume it did, he thought. That would confirm his assumption that the killer was wealthy. No ordinary worker could afford that sort of button. *How then did it come to be lying on the floor?*

The girl was naked. The man told her to lie down on the bed as he approached her. Is he naked also? Rysakov, for no reason he could explain, felt certain the man was still fully clothed, except for his coat.

So, he gets to the bed and starts to climb on top of her. She probably asked if he was going to take his pants off. He more than likely replied, I'm paying, so shut up and do as you are told.

Once he is sitting on top of her, he kneels on her arms. He talks to distract her. When he is ready he swings his right fist down with all his force onto her left temple. He may have hit her more than once. But he may have undressed, Rysakov conceded, *and he may have had sex with the girl first. The button could have come off if he dressed hurriedly after killing her because he feared discovery.*

Rysakov stood alongside the girl, pulled his fist back to shoulder level and lightly swung it to within a few centimeters of the girl's head, seeing where the impact would strike. *Maybe he hit the girl during sex,* he thought. He looked closely at the marks again. He could see the outline of the knuckles, a darker bruising, and there was a single bruise even darker than the others a couple of centimeters from the knuckle marks. It must be a ring! He looked intently at the mark. There could be no doubt. It was a ring with a raised center judging by the shape of the bruise. It was, he deduced, worn on the middle finger. Try as he might he could not make out any impression that may give him a clue as to the ring's nature.

The murderer has made his first mistake. However small, it suggested he was getting overconfident. Rysakov now felt certain this was the same killer as the Ignatiev house murder and the other deaths. Now he had a button, and the promising lead of the medical kits. From such small beginnings…a surge of excitement coursed through him.

How like a chess game, he thought, *move and counter move, a slow buildup of tension where one attempts to out guess one's opponent.* This looked like it would be a long game.

He walked slowly, searching carefully on the floor, on the chest of drawers, the windowsill, under the bed, until he was satisfied nothing had been overlooked. He stood at the foot of the bed and looked at the heavy peasant hips and the distended shape of the pubic area where the wooden shaft had been driven in.

Rysakov shook his head. *Moscow is a modern, prosperous city with the end of the nineteenth century rapidly approaching, yet primitive brutal crimes like this still occur. What will the new century hold? Surely it cannot be worse?* He picked up the rag-wrapped phallus and left the room, telling the constable to have the body removed to the mortuary for more detailed examination.

When he arrived back at his office, he slowly unwrapped the wood. Careful not to touch it directly with his fingers, he laid it on the desk. The dark discoloration of dried body fluid covered the wood to within a hand's width of the end. As he turned it over, some of the stain was pressed flat into the wood as if the initial rupture had forced some blood out onto the assailant's hand. In his frenzy to ram the phallus home, he had ignored the fluid and gripped it hard, pressing the blood into the hand-held end. He could even see the indistinct imprint where it had been gripped. That meant he had bloodstains on his hand—perhaps even on his clothes.

Rysakov thoughtfully placed the cylinder of wood, rewrapped in the rag, in a paper evidence bag and locked it in the cupboard.

He sat in the chair behind his desk and picked up the button. He turned it over. Nothing particularly distinctive, it was of a type available to anyone in Moscow with the money to buy it. If it came from the killer, how did it end up on the floor? The man was usually so careful. When he returned to his abode, would he have realized a button was missing, and, if he did, would he care? Arrogance, and an unshakable belief in their own infallibility. That eventually undid even the cleverest criminal. His confidence level rose. He would catch the "Monster of Moscow."

Eventually, he began to write a report on the incident. He pulled his watch out of his pocket and checked the time. If he worked fast he might still make dinner with Vera and Pavel and have time to attend the traditional church service.

§ § § § §

At Christmas, every person in Russia went to church to celebrate the birth of Jesus. Services were held on Christmas Eve and throughout the following day. Church bells rang in joyous peeling, summoning the faithful. Every icon had candles lit in front of it. At the entrance to each church, rows of poor gathered, dressed in miserable rags, begging in the name of the newborn savior. By custom, members of the congregation handed out kopecks or rubles, a worthy act of charity on this holy day.

Light snow fell as the kibitka slid to a halt outside the church of St. Nicholas "The Big Cross," so named for the large cross and relics that originally lay protected there. The church stood on Ilinka Street and the Morozovs drove down from Red Square to the far end of the street. Ivan had decided, once he opened the Moscow office, that he would go to church on important holy days in keeping with his friends and colleagues. The five, onion-shaped domes on the roof of the church were visible from Red Square and from many of the banks with offices on Ilinka Street.

Inside the church, people packed into the pews, not a seat was vacant. Ivan and Mikhail stood near the rear. A golden glow from the masses of candles burning brightly beneath icons suffused the interior. The smell of candle beeswax and incense from the burners mingled with the warm, bittersweet odor of humanity. Resonating off every pillar, the choir's rich harmony filled the vaulted space. The music drew each person inward to the amity of the church. Even Ivan could feel the emotion of the occasion.

As the service ended, people slowly exited the church. Ivan saw Prince Koslinski and paused to exchange cordial Christmas greetings.

As they talked, Ivan glanced at the face of a man walking slowly toward the door. He knew that face.

The Rysakovs had been coming to St. Nicholas for several years following a colleague's recommendation of the quality of the singing and the friendly atmosphere. Vera loved it, and they always ensured an arrival early enough to get a seat at the rear. Maksim saw Ivan staring at him and nodded. As they came abreast, Ivan called him over.

"Maksim Nickoliavich, Christmas greetings!"

"Prince Koslinski, may I present Senior Investigator Rysakov," Ivan said.

"May I introduce my wife, Vera Nikolaevna, and my son, Pavel," said Rysakov.

"Are you still in charge of the investigations of the Ignatiev house murder?" Ivan asked.

"Yes," Rysakov replied. "And there was another last night. I fear we have a deranged mind on the loose in our city."

"Are you investigating both of those deaths? How can you be sure they were by the same person?" asked the prince.

"There are now a total of four and I am quite certain they were carried out by the same person."

"Do you have any clues about the identity of the killer?" asked Koslinski.

"We're starting to get a picture of the person," Rysakov replied. Both Ivan and Koslinski wore shirts with pearl buttons, he noted. Then he put any further thought of murder out of his mind. *It's Christmas,* he reminded himself. He joined Vera and Pavel and climbed into the sleigh. As it hissed away into the snow, the sound of carol singing faded into the distance.

1898

The vibrancy of Moscow cultural life this winter rivaled that of any previous year. Ivan loaned the Guarneri violin to a young Russian violinist for performances of Tchaikovsky's "Violin Concerto." The two Morozovs went to concerts, to performances by the ballet, and the opera. However, for Mikhail, this season's social events lacked the excitement and sparkle of previous years. He knew no one would think any less of him if he indulged in several last flings. London was so far away, and there was no shortage of women who clearly signaled they were available. One night, when he had not received a letter for a week, he came close. After several passionate embraces with a girl he had known for years, and with whom he had had a brief involvement, he struggled to politely extricate himself. His excuse sounded clumsy, but his thoughts lay elsewhere.

For Maksim Rysakov, the New Year brought no special satisfaction. Admittedly, there had been no more murders, so far. The details of purchasers of surgical equipment in the Moscow and Saint Petersburg regions had slowly begun to dribble in. He hoped it was complete but suspected that was not the case. He felt sure names of prominent members of the aristocracy or wealthy merchants might have been omitted by the shopkeeper for fear of offending an important and influential customer. Then, the distinct probability existed that the murderer had not used his real name. Or had someone else buy the instruments for him—a servant, for example, whose master expressed an interest in matters scientific, explaining how he required the scalpels for dissecting frogs and insects. The whims of the wealthy caused no surprise to those who served them. Analyzing the information would be time consuming and frustrating. However, at the moment, these lists provided his best lead.

§ § § § § §

Affairs at the Somerston house in London settled into their routine.

For Katy, the days after Mikhail left at first seemed to drag, then, as his letters began to arrive regularly, full of lover's happiness and intimacy, the days flew. There was never too much time to dream and plan their future together. She had confided in her mother and written her long letters about Mikhail and what she knew of his circumstances. Soon it would be spring. In Mikhail's last letter, he said he and his father must come to London to check on the new factory machinery. He expected to arrive in about a month's time. Katy was so excited, she immediately told Emily Somerston.

"That is good news," Emily said. "From the number of letters he has written, there seems little doubt about his feelings. Make the most of it while you are young. It doesn't always last."

Midway through the first week in April, Ivan and Mikhail were once again ensconced in the Savoy Hotel. The next morning, they met with Bertie Somerston. Ivan was keen to see the properties that had been purchased in the last year. Mikhail had only one thought in mind. He sent a message to the Somerston house that he would be calling in the afternoon and at half past two knocked on the door holding a bunch of early roses.

After the initial awkwardness when both were too shy to start a conversation beyond asking about their health and the trip to London, Emily came to the rescue.

"Katy, why don't you take Mikhail for a walk to the park. It will help refresh him after his arduous trip from Moscow. Please be back by four."

Once they were away from the house, it took all Katy's control not to fling her arms around his neck and hug him. Instead, she tucked her arm through his and squeezed as close as she could. Probably more than decorum allowed, but, for a while, they were oblivious to their surroundings. Mikhail put his arm around her waist and hugged her to his side before releasing the delicious feel of her. They walked on with Katy's arm threaded through his.

"I've missed you, Katya. It's so good to see you again. I'll not leave without you this time," he said. Then, realizing that this may be perhaps presumptuous added, "That is, if you would still like to go to Moscow. I mean, if you'll still have me."

"Oh, Misha, of course I'll go with you. I was so scared that you may return and not want to marry me. I do love you so. We'll be so happy, I know it."

The words just tumbled out. They both spoke at once and laughed, each exhorting the other to go first. Katy bubbled.

It took some time before Mikhail realized that Katy was not the slightly bumbling girl she sounded, getting words mixed up and her grammar confused. She was speaking Russian! And he understood her!

"Katya, you do me a great honor. You're speaking in Russian," he said with great solemnity in broken English. "When we're back in Moscow you'll speak as well as me."

Katy blushed, thrilled at the praise and pleased she had persisted with the lessons and practice every night. She was determined to make Mikhail proud of her.

"How else can I tell you how much I love you," she said. They both laughed.

Reaching the park, they sat on a cast iron seat under an oak.

"Katy, I need to ask you again," Mikhail said, facing her and holding her hands in his, "will you marry me and come to Moscow as my wife?"

"Yes, my darling, yes I will."

At that moment, they were the only two people in the world, and their lips came together in a sublime and lingering kiss, a kiss Katy would remember the rest of her life.

For the next two hours they talked. Mikhail told her about their house in Moscow and that they would be in London for about two months, attending to business matters. Would that be enough time to get married?

"We'll have the wedding in six weeks," Mikhail said. Katy nodded, too excited to talk. "Your mother must come across from Dublin. I'll send her the tickets.

"I'll speak to Bertie Somerston and make sure you have enough time off to have fittings for your wedding dress and to buy clothes for Moscow."

When they arrived back at the house, Katy told Emily.

"Mikhail has asked me to marry him and I have accepted," she said. "We're to be married in six weeks. I'd like to give my notice, though I'll miss the children very much," she added. Tears rolled down her cheeks

Emily secretly admired the young Irish girl. Abandoning the country of her birth, and a city such as London, where she must still feel at home with a common language and heritage. Leaving with a new husband (that could be adventure enough) to a foreign land, there to speak a foreign language—she had to admit the girl had pluck. She could never do that.

§ § § § §

A week later, three men walked up from the Liverpool docks. These men had a sufficient air of menace to give even the tough dockside reason to pause. They all wore the same clothing; knee-high, black leather boots, loose-fitting, white cotton shirts over loose dark trousers, the shirt secured at the waist by a leather belt on which hung a curved Cossack knife, and on their head a fur *papakh*. They were Cossack horsemen straight from a raiding party on the steppes. They marched along the cobbled streets, their grim expressions made all the more frightening by the heavy moustache each wore.

As they passed, warehousemen, stevedores, hauliers, clerks, and businessmen stopped, turned their heads and stared.

"Who are those three?" a burly stevedore asked his mate, his hand unconsciously sliding down to the work knife in his belt.

"Frontiersmen from America," his mate retorted, "and I'd keep me hand off me knife if you don't want your head skinned," he added. "Must be a new ship in the port. Look at the fella in the middle; he's a giant! It'd take ten men to stop him."

"They're from Australia. There's a lot of wild men out there, I hear, and they are all huge," said a haulier overhearing the stevedores.

"Well, wherever they hail from, they are not men to be trifled with, I'd hazard," offered a passing businessman. On this observation, all agreed.

A clerk, dawdling on the journey back to his employer, stood gape-mouthed staring at the threatening trio.

"Where d'ya think they're going?" whispered another clerk beside him as the Cossacks strode past. Several unemployed laborers decided to find out. They began following at a respectable distance. The clerks joined them.

The Cossacks marched on through the warehouses, ignoring the minor sensation left in their wake. At the offices of Scragg, Jones & Milton, they turned left. Straight through the entrance they strode. The clerk at the counter looked up at the unexpected clatter, then seeing, shrank back. Before he could ask their business, the leader said in accented English, his voice deep and threatening, "We're here to see Harold Wallace. Get him."

"I'll see if Mr. Wallace is in, sir," the clerk said, glad to have an excuse to retreat.

As he reached the office at the rear, the three Cossacks saw Wallace's piggy eyes peer above the partition. As the clerk walked back toward the counter, Wallace's head disappeared. Without waiting, the Cossacks strode through the open office area, pushing the clerk aside.

"Sir, you can't go in there. Mr. Wallace is not available."

The leader kicked open the office door. Wallace sat heavily on the far side of the desk, his eyes narrowed to just slits. The largest of the trio snarled in a deep roar at the clerk, who quickly withdrew. *This is not my fight,* thought the clerk, concerned only to get away from the violence about to engulf his employer.

Wallace now showed the first signs of real fear. He had no way out. The only exit stood filled by three enormous and violent ruffians. He began to sweat. They towered over him, glaring. Then the older one spoke.

"Last year, you took an order from a Moscow firm to deliver cotton. They left you access to a letter of credit to draw against. Contrary to your instructions, you drew the full amount of the funds at once. We're here to take retribution."

"I was only following instructions. The cotton was good quality as ordered," whined Wallace, now seriously concerned about his safety. Then he recognized the older man. It was the Russian who had given him the order. He'd thought himself very clever offloading his surplus stock in one instant, and to Russia, it was so far away.

"No, you fat venal slug, you only looked after your own interests. You grabbed all the money and to hell with your customer. We want the money returned."

"I can't. I paid it to the cotton suppliers. You've got the cotton."

Sweat dripped down Wallace's red face, his breathing shallow.

"Then we'll take it off your body; you've plenty to spare," said the leader, glaring as he looked at Wallace's corpulent frame.

The metal sang sweetly as the curved blade left its scabbard in a single fluid movement. At the sight of the raw steel, Wallace jumped from his chair. He pressed against the rear wall, his eyes wide with fear. The glistening blade, poised in the air above him, turned him to stone. He couldn't move. In a daze, he heard the singing slice of steel on steel as two other blades were drawn.

A look of utter horror flashed across his florid, sweat-streaked face as the blade descended. It thudded into the desk, inches from his huge belly. As it hit, his bladder gave way completely, a dark stain spreading rapidly down his legs. The sharp stink of urine rose steamily in the stale air of the room. Wallace pressed hard against the rear wall, trying to sink into it as the Cossacks turned and left.

They were fifty meters from the warehouse when the giant Cossack began to laugh. His companions soon joined him and before they had covered much more distance, all three were roaring with laughter.

"That'll teach the bastard a lesson he'll not forget," said Ivan, tears streaming down his cheek. Mikhail and the giant Sergie, a friend from a Cossack regiment in Moscow, could only nod as they tried to catch their breaths.

As soon as the Cossacks disappeared around a bend in the road, several of the more adventurous laborers who had followed them ran inside to see the gore. What they saw was just as good. That night the story grew in the re-telling around the pubs. At least three giant Cossacks or frontiersmen had attacked Wallace for unpaid cargoes. And so it developed. One thing all the versions agreed—they had scared the piss out of him. The Liverpool docks christened Wallace, "Wet Willy," a name that would stick.

Ivan had been intent on revenge against Wallace; after all, the man had very nearly cost him his business. Had it not been for the fortuitous intervention of nature in the Atlantic storm, he would almost certainly have killed Wallace. As it was, he had been half of a mind to wound the man. A knife cut to the face, slice a tendon in his writing arm, a memento that would remind him every day it was bad business to cross a Morozov. As it happened, the humiliation of pissing his pants, with his staff watching and the layabouts who had followed them all as witnesses, provided more painful and lasting punishment. He would never live it down. The man had lost his dignity. Retribution had been secured. The three conspirators caught the next train back to London, satisfied.

Following their return, both Ivan and Mikhail kept busy inspecting properties and meeting suppliers. Ivan met several times with Philip Armitage at the Foreign Office to thank him for the telegram about the Atlantic storm shipping losses and to brief him on the current situation in Moscow. Mikhail took every opportunity he could to spend time with Katy.

Katy was at times barely able to contain her excitement. Would the dress be ready on time? Would it fit perfectly? The dressmaker was very expensive and clearly had a number of wealthy clients. At times, Katy felt out of her depth. She was being told, rather than asked, what she should have when she came for fittings, as though she were a servant. One day, in for a fitting, she had to wait while a matronly woman who dropped in without an appointment gave instructions to the dressmaker and her staff for a ball gown. It provided a very useful lesson. It illustrated the master-servant relationship. The master had to act like a master or the roles would quickly be reversed. It was a lesson Katy vowed not to forget. She intended to be an effective mistress of Mikhail's house.

During this period, Katy dined with Mikhail and Ivan several times.

"Misha, I believe you have made a good choice," Ivan said after the second such time. "She has her own mind, and it's quite acute. She is not one of those pampered rich girls. Her upbringing has toughened her. She'll be a good companion. She even seems to like you," he added with a twinkle in his eye.

"I know that I love her," Mikhail said earnestly, "and I'm sure she loves me."

"Have you told her about our new London house?"

"No. As you asked, I've not told her of any of the London properties," Mikhail replied.

"Good. Then you can take comfort that she's not swayed into marriage by the thought of becoming mistress of a large London residence. She can find out in due course."

"I'm sure that would not have any influence," said Mikhail.

"I suspect you're right, however, a little caution can't do any harm."

In the week before the wedding, Mary O'Connor arrived from Dublin, her first trip away from Ireland.

She had been more than a little apprehensive about meeting this rich Russian. Katy's description of Ivan's business had left Mary in little doubt as to their wealth. Katy was thrilled to see her mother and even more so when she saw how her mother rapidly became enthralled with Misha. Over the days leading up to the wedding, Mary O'Connor spent many hours talking with Mikhail. On the wedding day. she said to her daughter, "I'll go back to Ireland happy my daughter is marrying such a good man. I'll tell all my friends how proud I am to have a Russian son-in-law. He's a good man, so you make sure you're a good wife to him, Katherine Mary O'Connor. Look after him, be lovin' to him and bear his children. Bear him sons. All men need an heir," she said.

"And you will write to me when you are in Russia, won't you Katy? I daresay I shall not get over there. Your pa and the others couldn't do without me for more than a week anyway. I've kept all your letters, my darlin.' I read them sometimes. It gives me great comfort to know that you're doin' so well in the world, and that you're happy," she said.

"Of course I'll write, Ma," Katy said.

The wedding was held in the small Catholic church not far from the Somerstons.' Katy looked radiant. She glowed from inside. She seemed to glide above the ground as Mikhail watched her walk down the aisle. Her wedding dress fit perfectly. It complemented her smooth, fair skin and flattered her figure. Mikhail felt he could not be more in love.

All too soon it was time to leave. Ivan was keen to return to Moscow. As they embarked on the Channel steamer, the reality of another leave-taking confronted Katy. This time it would be for good. This time, however, she faced the challenge with a husband and friend. Katy stood briefly on the deck as the ship steamed out of the harbor. Then, smiling, she turned inside and joined Mikhail, a new, exciting future ahead of her.

Moscow

Maksim Rysakov neither knew nor had any reason to care that Mikhail Morozov married Katy O'Connor in London. In fact, he had never heard of Katy O'Connor, now Morozov. That would change in the future in ways neither could possibly have imagined. For now, Rysakov's mind was wholly directed toward tracking down the "Monster of Moscow."

He obtained permission from her parents to interview Irina Bourlin, the young girl who had witnessed the murderer walking away from the Ignatiev house. She was now eleven years old and quite self-possessed and confident for her age. Irina's father, Victor Bourlin, was a wealthy merchant with connections through marriage to minor nobility.

Rysakov arranged to conduct the interview at her house and now sat opposite the girl in their reception room. The girl's mother sat on a chaise lounge to one side.

"Irina, when I spoke to you last you told me you saw a man leaving the Ignatiev house on the night the maid was killed. Do you still remember what you saw?" he asked.

"Yes, I do," she said.

"How did you know it was a man?"

"He was tall, and he was not wearing a dress."

"How could you tell that? The person would have been wearing a long coat as it was cold. Maybe the coat covered a dress?"

"When Mama puts a coat over her dress it can't fall straight down because her petticoats make it balloon out at the bottom."

She was right, of course; one could see the ballooning effect of petticoats under women's coats every day in Moscow in the winter.

"This man, then, was tall and wore a long dark coat. What else do you remember about him?"

"He walked like a wolf," she said.

"What do you mean by that? Can you explain that to me so that I can get a picture in my mind, please?" he asked.

"You must have seen wolves," said Irina, a little exasperated.

"Only in the distance, once," Rysakov said.

"Well, they have two sorts of walks," she said as if explaining to a child. "When they are just going somewhere, they trot along in a line. When they are hungry and looking for prey they stick their heads out in front and they walk—they don't trot."

"So which way did the man walk?"

"He walked with his head out in front, of course. He wouldn't have been trotting, would he?"

"No, I suppose not," Rysakov said. "Madam, excuse me, but does your husband have a country estate?"

"Yes, north of Vologda. We catch the Archangel train. It is nearly a day's journey from the rail station and we often see wolves in the area, but for the most part they don't bother us," she said.

"Thank you," he said. He turned back to Irina and asked politely, "Is there anything else you can remember, young lady?"

"I saw the man again, just before Christmas," she said. "At least, I think it was him." His excitement soared. At last he felt he was snapping at the heels of his quarry.

"Where?" he asked, as calmly as possible.

"Walking along Red Square. We were in our kibitka and going to get gifts. When I looked again, he had gone."

"Would you recognize him if you saw him again?"

"Yes, I am sure I would, particularly if he walked like a wolf."

"Thank you, Irina, you have been very helpful. I will leave details of how I can be contacted with your mama. If you see this man again, tell her, and she can contact me."

"Will you arrest him?" she asked.

"If we can catch him we most certainly will," Rysakov said.

Rysakov tried to keep this astonishing new development in perspective. After all, she was only an eleven-year-old girl, albeit a very observant one. Sometimes, he had to admit, children had a greater awareness of their surroundings than the parents. Pavel, for instance, could often see a bird in the forest well before he could. She was quite confident and reported what she had seen in a calm and matter of fact way. On balance, Rysakov inclined to believe her—and to believe that she *had* seen his quarry just before Christmas.

He decided not to include details of this interview in his reports. *Let's keep this to ourselves,* he thought, *a little edge. Probably an illusory edge. No,* he thought, *this is progress, real progress. In fact, there has to be a real chance the girl will see the murderer again if he frequents Red Square.*

The Bourlin's maid closed the front door behind him.

Since seeing Morozov and Koslinski at the Christmas service he had observed many of Moscow's merchant class wore shirts with mother of pearl buttons. Some of the wealthy merchants were Old Believers and some of these old religionists were excessively puritanical, even fanatical so. Was it possible an Old Believer had taken on a self-appointed task to rid the city of loose women? Not a thought to be dismissed too lightly. But how did the trophies fit this theory?

By the time he had walked back into his office, he had resolved nothing. His quarry was resourceful, of that he was certain. He was also cruel and deeply disturbed.

He sat down and stared at the pile of papers on his desk. They contained details of the sales of surgical instruments in the greater Moscow area. Slowly, he had been working through them. So far, he had eliminated all the well-known and respected surgeons. Some hospitals purchased surgical instruments for training purposes. That would warrant a closer look to determine who had access to those instruments. Many general practitioners also purchased scalpels, as did amateur anatomists, entomologists, and botanists.

The laborious work exhausted him. He really needed a staff of three. Instead, he, Rysakov, had to do the work himself. And this on top of the normal police work pursuing petty crime, the bashings, and "normal" murders, as well as providing manpower for Okhrana operations from time to time. Most of his colleagues adopted the "squeaky gate" rule—if enough noise was made by a superior you gave the crime enough attention to solve it, or at least convince them that all possible effort was being applied to solving it. Otherwise, the matter would be shelved as "under ongoing investigation."

Rysakov, on the other hand, continued to be fascinated by the intellectual challenge. He believed every crime capable of solution with the right effort applied.

These murders worried him. More than the "normal" killings, which could be bad enough, these murders had added, sinister dimensions. The brutality of their execution and the clear madness of the perpetrator meant no young woman was safe in Moscow while the killer remained at large. Rysakov intended to bring this maniac to justice. He would not give up easily.

With a sigh, he leaned over and picked up a pile of paperwork. As he turned back to work, something again tweaked at the edge of his mind. Something was there. He had seen something that did not quite fit. What was it? Was it important?

He lost the connection. It happened from time to time. His subconscious registered an oddity without being aware of what he saw. The right prompt would send it bursting into his mind, often at the most unexpected moment. No use trying to force it.

§ § § § §

Katy gazed out the window, absentmindedly curling a strand of hair around her finger. Thick snow fell straight down in large, heavy flakes. Only soft-rounded shapes filled the landscape. This was her second winter in Moscow, and she felt happy and secure, yet the severity of the Russian winter still surprised her. The intensity of the cold sometimes made her wish for the soft rain of Dublin. At those times, she missed her mother, more so now she was pregnant.

She had only been in Moscow for a matter of weeks before the entire household began calling her Katya. As Misha explained, "Katya sounds more Russian, my darling."

"Then Katya I shall be," she laughed.

The house, located on a tree-lined lane just off bustling Prechistenka Street, one of Moscow's radial arteries, was comfortably warm. When Ivan built it as his Moscow residence in the early 1890s, he had installed central heating, and the large furnace in the basement warmed the house throughout the long, cruel winter months.

She felt a deep sense of fulfillment. She stroked the roundness of her belly. She was nearly four months pregnant and felt more wholly a woman than she could explain. At times, she was sure she could feel a faint movement inside her. Her maid, Pinna, assured her that she would not feel any movements until after Christmas. She delayed telling Misha until she was quite sure, as there had been several false alarms over the past year. He was so excited he danced her around the house for half an hour, chattering about what he—no doubt it would be a he—would be named, how he would carry on the family business, behaving like any other prospective, first-time father.

A year ago, Russia had secured control of the town of Harbin in northern China. With Peking weak and demoralized, Ivan decided this was an opportune time to visit the region and make new business contacts as Imperial Russia tightened its grip on Siberia. After over three months away, he embarked on the arduous journey home. This took nearly five weeks, with the train, operating only from Irkutsk on the western shore of Lake Baikal, taking sixteen days alone. When he finally arrived home he looked tired and drawn.

Mikhail and Katya greeted him as he took off his coat.

"Welcome home, Grandfather," Katya said hugging her father-in-law, kissing him on the cheek.

He gave Katya a perfunctory kiss in return and turned to embrace his son.

"It's good to be back; it'll be wonderful to sleep in a bed that doesn't move." Finally, Katya's greeting sank in. "What did you call me?" he said. He looked at Mikhail, who nodded, trying to remain solemn. He looked at Katya.

"Is this true?"

She nodded with a broad smile.

The weariness fell away as a huge grin creased Ivan's face. He grabbed Katya, lifting her off her feet in a huge hug. As he gently released her, he kissed her on the forehead.

"I could not have asked for a better homecoming present," he said, hugging Mikhail.

"We must celebrate. Get a bottle of the best vodka," he yelled to the servants.

Over the next week, she became impatient. She refused to be treated like an invalid.

"Look at the ordinary women of Moscow—they go about their day carrying child," she told them. "So will I. I'm one of them."

More often, these days her thoughts turned to her mother in Ireland. *How nice it would be if she were here,* she reflected. When she first arrived in Moscow, Katy wrote most weeks. As she became more settled as wife and mistress of the house her letters home became less frequent.

Tonight, they were going to the Krasnetsky's ball, one of the most popular gala occasions early in the season. Katya tried to curb her excitement. It was not her first Moscow ball, however, never before had she been pregnant.

In her first winter in Russia, she and Misha had been invited to dozens, most held in the private ballrooms of members of the merchant elite. Ivan often accompanied them, alone, except for one memorable occasion. That night he partnered a well-known ballerina whose husband had run off with a younger dancer. Although she had not danced for several seasons, she retained all the beauty, poise, and presence of a great performer. Ivan was the envy of every older man at the ball.

That first season Katya was swept off her feet. She had had to make an effort to ensure she actually danced with Misha, so much attention did she attract. The beautiful young woman who spoke Russian with a strange but fascinating accent, married to young Morozov, caught the interest of the men, the young friends of Misha and the older merchants. The women also watched her, critically. After that first ball, Katya quickly realized that to become part of Misha's circle in Moscow she must curb her natural effervescence, at least until she knew some of the women better.

Katya began to descend the staircase from the first floor. The rustle of her gown caused the two well-dressed men at the bottom of the stairs to break their conversation and look up.

Both were immediately struck by the radiance of the woman coming down toward them. Her hair was pinned up off her neck and held in place by a diamond clip. The new silk gown fell away from her neck just sufficiently for a glimpse of soft, pure white skin. The long sleeves draped elegantly down her arm from the ballooned shoulder. From the waist, the dress fell in a perfect fit. Pinna followed, carrying a long, thick fur coat.

"My darling, you look magnificent," said Mikhail as Katya stepped off the stairs, smiling at the two men in her life.

"You'll need two men to protect you tonight," said Ivan, thinking once again how well she had fit into their lives. Her uncertainty in the first few months had been overcome by a determination to master the management of the house. She insisted on speaking only Russian and quickly became fluent. Now it was impossible to imagine the house without her.

As they slid to a halt outside the brightly lit façade, a steady stream of guests flowed into the ballroom. The snow had stopped falling, and they followed the line through the cleared entrance. The huge ballroom was ornately furnished with a dozen crystal chandeliers hanging from the ceiling. They moved slowly around the room, nodding to acquaintances, chatting briefly with others. Katya still attracted attention, and Misha delighted in introducing her as his wife.

Near the center of the room, Katya became aware of someone looking at her. A tall, darkly handsome man, clearly a prince or duke from the way he carried himself, was staring at her intently. As she caught his eye, he smiled lightly without any hint of embarrassment.

"Prince Koslinski, I think you know my son, Misha. May I present my son's wife, Katya Marieovna," Ivan said.

"Madam Morozovna. We met over a year ago soon after you arrived in Moscow I believe," said Koslinski, inclining his head slightly toward her.

"Forgive me, sir, but those first few months in my husband's city remain a blur."

"You are forgiven, madam. As I've been away for over a year at my family's estate in the Ukraine, we wouldn't have had the opportunity to meet again. I, however, have not forgotten so beautiful a woman. May I have the pleasure of a dance with you tonight?"

"Certainly, sir, so long as it's not the polka; that's my husband's favorite," she said, threading her arm through Mikhail's.

Nearly 300 guests talked, nodded acknowledgements, gossiped, and observed in the ballroom. The grandeur of the colonnade of Corinthian columns framing each side provided a perfect backdrop to the finery on parade. To see and be seen, to hear and to pass on the latest gossip, was as important to the men and women of the Moscow elite as the entertainment itself. The undulating cascade of conversation muted as the orchestra began to play the first gavotte of the night. The throng parted, and the dancers formed up in the center of the room.

Early the next morning, Katya and Mikhail wearily entered their bedroom.

"Is Prince Koslinski important to the business, Misha?" asked Katya.

"He's one of our financiers, so I suppose he's of some importance. Why?"

"When I was dancing with him, I got the feeling he was suggesting he was available. It wasn't direct. It was more subtle than that. Perhaps I imagined it, but I got the impression that if I was pleasant to him it could influence him in his business dealings with you and father."

"I'm sure that was just his aristo's arrogance, my darling," Mikhail said, yawning.

"There is a dark current running beneath those charming manners, Misha. He makes me feel uneasy," Katya said snuggling closer to her husband in the warmth of their bed.

1900

A spectacular display of fireworks in Red Square welcomed the start of the modern age. Celebrations carried on throughout the night and into New Year's Day. "This is a night to savor, an experience to remember," more than one of the revelers said to the other.

The snow, although deep on the ground, stopped falling that evening. In the cold still air, Mikhail and Katya stood together on the edge of the square with the crowds, marveling at the kaleidoscope of color and sound that exploded above them.

Later that night, back in the warm sitting room of their home, they toasted each other and the new century just begun.

Next day, they rose late. By the time they came to the breakfast room, Ivan had the day's papers spread out in front of him.

"The first edition of the twentieth century," he said, flourishing the paper. "Listen to what they say, 'The Russian economy now ranks fourth in the world, after U.S.A., Britain and Germany. Our scientists lead the world in soil science, in petro-chemicals and in hydrodynamics. In the arts, Saint Petersburg is the most dynamic city in the world,'" he took off his glasses. "Do they think we don't know that?" Holding his glasses in front of his face he went on, "'Rachmaninov is composing rich, emotive piano music; Rimsky-Korsakov has written 'Scheherazade,'" he paused to look up from the paper. "But why does Petersburg get all the mention? In Moscow, we have opera companies with a nine-month season. At the Art Theatre, we've all seen Stanislavski's production of Chekov's *Seagull*."

Mikhail and Katya could not help it; they both burst out laughing. Ivan's enthusiasm was infectious.

"Look at how we lead the world in art." Ivan pointed proudly to the article as he handed Mikhail the newspaper.

"'Moscow merchants and industrialists outdo each other in building great collections of Russian and French art,'" Mikhail read out loud under the heading "Art in Russia." "'Now some of the best collections in the world reside in Moscow. They include Gauguin, Matisse, and Monet as well as other new wave artists. In fact, our art connoisseurs seem to have a better liking for the new Impressionists than their native Paris.' Well," said Mikhail, laughing, "why weren't we mentioned; we have some Monets."

It was a time when all things seemed possible. Thousands of French and British investors held high yielding Russian bonds. In the West, all things Russian were fashionable—its ballet, the exquisite Faberge jewelry, its caviar, and its vodka.

In one area, however, Russia lagged the industrial world. The tsar remained an absolute monarch. His word was law. There was no elected parliament, no safety valve for discontent. When unrest and tension rose to dangerous levels, it lead to violence, assassinations, riots, and strikes. For most of the workers two groups seemed to be responsible for stopping the benefits of the new prosperity flowing down to them—the factory owners and the police.

The huge new factory of Morozov & Son had facilities for many of the workers to live in new quarters within the factory grounds with a hospital and school for their children. All this had not made them immune from labor unrest. At many factories in Moscow and Saint Petersburg, agitators fomented trouble. There had even been attacks where owners and government officials had been badly beaten by strikers. Everyone become more alert, more careful.

The temperature is definitely not as cold, Mikhail thought, as the horses drawing his carriage trotted away from the factory at the end of the day. He leaned back in the seat. *The horses can find their own way if Vanya nods off.* On the protected southern side of the factory, he saw the first tentative snowdrop blooms promising the imminent arrival of spring. But, he reminded himself, spring will not officially begin until the flocks of rooks reappear in the city, and the violets and snowdrops are in full flower.

A sharp cry interrupted his reverie as the carriage turned into Pradetski Street. Was it a cry of outrage or a call for help? He leaned out the carriage and saw three large assailants swinging clubs at a single victim yelling abuse as they did so. He called on his driver to stop. The man under attack looked familiar.

Mikhail jumped out of the carriage and ran back. He could not ignore such an unequal contest. It offended his sense of honor. As he ran, one of the men swung a length of wood at his victim. The man saw it coming and thrust his arm up to protect his head.

They did not hear Mikhail's shouts until he was close. The man with the wood spun around. When he was ten paces away Mikhail's hand slid behind his back. The metal sang as the dagger appeared in his hand. His speed carried him into the man before he could gain momentum to hit Mikhail with the club. The man was as tall as Mikhail and heavier. As they collided, the man grabbed at his throat and shoved the wood into his face. Mikhail raked the knife up and under the man's rib cage, leaning in for added leverage. He used the man's own weight to embed the whole blade in flesh. For a few moments, the man didn't react. He hit Mikhail's face repeatedly with the wood. Using his left hand to fend off the blows, Mikhail twisted the blade violently. The man screamed as the metal scraped bone. He punched the wood at Mikhail to push him away. Forced back, Mikhail withdrew the knife in a slicing motion.

One of the other men now turned to confront Mikhail, while the third thug continued kicking their victim. As he prepared to defend himself, a vicious crack sounded above their heads. A big man with a fur *papakh* on his head ran toward them. In one hand, he cracked a horsewhip. The other waved a curved Cossack saber.

It only took seconds for the thug to realize what was about happen. He yelled a warning to the third man. With one arm each supporting the wounded man, the three rapidly retreated. To face a saber-wielding Cossack was every Russian's nightmare.

By the time, the Cossack reached Mikhail's side, the assailants had disappeared. The man stopped, puffing heavily.

"Couldn't you have kept them here for just a few more minutes," he wheezed, "it would've been good to feel my saber slice into one of those bastard's necks."

"Thank you, Vanya," Mikhail said to his driver. "I may've had my hands full without you. You're a terrifying sight in full flight." Mikhail's breathing gradually returned to normal.

The old man grinned. Then, as Mikhail turned around, his grin turned to concern.

"Misha, you are wounded—your head."

Vanya dropped his saber and grabbed Mikhail by the shoulders. Blood was streaming down the left side of his head and face.

Mikhail put his hand to his head. He felt a trickle of warm wetness work its way done his neck and onto his chest. He stumbled, momentarily off balance. His head spun from the repeated bashing with the wood.

"That motherless swine has given me a headache, Vanya," he said as he regained his equilibrium.

The old Cossack, who had seen much action in the Caucuses, finished his examination.

"It is only flesh wounds; they bleed a lot and, yes, you will have a headache for a couple of days, but you'll live. Come on, let's see if that man they beat is still alive."

The victim of the attack lay on the ground groaning, fresh red staining the snow in which he lay. As the two men bent down to help him, he instinctively threw up his arms in defense, expecting more blows to rain down on his head.

"Take it easy, friend," said Vanya, "we're here to help you."

The two gently turned him over and helped him sit up. The man cried with pain as Mikhail grasped his right arm. It looked broken, probably from using it to shield his face from the wooden club.

"Investigator Rysakov!" exclaimed Mikhail.

By the time they reached the Morozov house, Maksim Rysakov had told them what happened, his teeth clenched in pain as the carriage clattered over the cobblestone pavement.

"They knew I'm a member of the Imperial Police. Maybe they'd been waiting for me knowing my route home," he said. "They belonged to one of the revolutionary groups. I don't know which one. They accused me of being an Imperial agent of repression who had to be destroyed as the first step toward workers receiving just reward for their labor." He shrugged his shoulders before crying with pain from his broken arm.

By the time Mikhail and Vanya carried Rysakov through the entrance, the household had been alerted and servants hurried to assist.

"Send for the doctor," Mikhail instructed, "He'll need his arm set."

"Misha! Oh, my God," Katya exclaimed as she saw Mikhail's blood-covered face, her own face draining of color. Pinna pushed her mistress aside, grasped Mikhail's arm firmly with her strong hands and steered him toward the kitchen.

Having made Rysakov as comfortable as he could on a couch in the reception room, Vanya came into the kitchen.

"It's only flesh wounds," he said, looking at Mikhail.

"I can see that," said Pinna irritably without looking up. "How did you let him get so hurt?"

"Ah, you should see the other fellow," he said winking at Mikhail. "I taught this youngster how to fight when he was still at school. Hey, Misha, you remember the free-for-alls we had in the Urals?"

Mikhail grinned in spite of the sting from the mild carbolic solution Pinna used to clean the wounds.

"You lived with the worthless Cossacks?" Pinna asked, her eyes widening.

"I spent many wonderful summers with Vanya and his family, Pinna," Mikhail said.

When Katya came in, the worst of the blood had been cleaned. What remained were multiple abrasions down the left side of his face, which would heal easily. What caught the eye, however, was a long wound running from the hairline in the middle of his forehead to the eyebrow on his left temple. It would leave a scar.

Vanya nodded with approval.

"An honorable scar," he said. "It'll fade in time. Make you look more distinguished!"

Once the doctor arrived, he recommended Rysakov be taken to hospital to have his arm properly set and his other wounds dressed. The investigator had severe bruising on his ribs and other arm and would be very sore for some time.

"But," the doctor assured everyone, "he'll live."

Mikhail insisted that the Morozov's doctor accompany Rysakov to hospital and ensure he received the best possible attention. He then dispatched another with Vanya to pick up Vera and Pavel. Vanya had strict instructions to assure Vera that her husband would make a full recovery and take them on to the hospital.

Katya slept fitfully that night. The image of Mikhail's face covered in blood kept flashing in front of her eyes. The growing life in her stomach seemed to sense her unease and moved constantly. Finally, she fell into a deep sleep, exhausted.

Suddenly, they materialized. Who were they? Where had they come from? A group of men came up the stairs yelling abuse at her, wielding sabers and wooden clubs. My baby, help me, my baby, she cried. Mikhail appeared in front of her confronting the men. They stopped only momentarily. He had his dagger out and swiped at one of the men. The dagger went right through the man, who kept coming up the stairs, leering at her. Mikhail thrust his dagger at another. Then, one of them hit him with a club. His face was covered in blood as he turned to look back at her with his arm outstretched. She tried desperately to touch his hand, to save him, but she could not reach. Behind him, a man raised a saber.

Katya sat bolt upright in bed and grabbed Mikhail's arm. He groaned as his wounds pulled at the raw edges. He was alive. The dream had been so real her heart continued racing. Gradually, the pounding in her ears slowed. She looked carefully around the room. Everything was as it should be; there were no intruders, no leering ruffians. After what seemed hours, she released Mikhail's arm and lay down, drifting in and out of light snatches of sleep until dawn.

Although she accepted both Mikhail's and Ivan's assurances as to their safety from marauding gangs, deep in her Celtic heart, she harbored doubts. Could this be a premonition of something still to come?

§ § § § §

Rysakov had been in the hospital two days. He felt sore and his arm ached. He had a vague recollection of Pavel talking to him and the voice of someone in authority, *probably the doctor,* he thought. At least his head felt clear, clear enough to feel pain now he was off morphine.

"So, the baby awakes. I never thought of you as a brawler, Maksim Nicholiavich," said a confident voice from the doorway.

Rysakov turned slowly. The face and the voice were familiar in a far-off kind of way. He stared at the smiling, handsome face of the well-dressed man. He looked like a doctor.

"Sergei Alexandrovich! You look more prosperous than ever. How long is it? It must be ten years. Are you in charge of my recovery? Do I need to worry?" Rysakov laughed, wincing as the movement tugged his bruised ribs.

Dr. Sokoloff sat on the edge of the bed, his face serious.

"You're lucky your friends came to your aid. If those thugs had continued beating you you may have become just another body on the streets."

"Which friends?"

"Young Morozov and his driver, the old Cossack, Vanya. They saw you being attacked and drove them off. There were three of them, they said. Young Morozov has a nice scar developing on his forehead as a result. Vera and Pavel have been in to see you several times. He is a fine young lad, Maksim, although what the lovely Vera sees in you is beyond me," Sergei grinned.

"That's right, there were three, yelling I was an agent of repression. 'When the revolution comes your kind will be executed,' they said. They were clearly too impatient to wait for that happy day," Rysakov said.

"I take it you are still a policeman?"

"Yes, but I rarely get involved with labor unrest or revolutionaries."

"What are you involved in then?"

"Well, and this might interest you as a surgeon, I'm heading the investigation into the mutilation murders of those young women. There are now four deaths that we know of. And still we have no firm suspects."

Rysakov remembered the fun they had had at university, the hours the two of them spent arguing in taverns. Philosophy and literature failed to convince the scientist, Sokoloff, who was studying to become a great surgeon. The soul was an invention of romantics, he argued. Rysakov recalled arguing that emotions from deep within the Russian soul influenced their history. Sokoloff had scoffed. He took his "mystic" friend to anatomy classes to see if he could find the "soul" he kept going on about. Rysakov recalled how fascinating he found the classes. While he had not found the "soul"—not that he had expected to; it was the essence of the individual and could, to his mind at least, exist only in the living—he had gained an understanding of the human body, an understanding that helped him significantly in his work in later years.

Over the next few days, they discussed the murders. Rysakov had been right. His friend was interested. He quizzed him on the details as if conducting a postmortem.

On the morning of the fifth day, they sat reminiscing about their university days.

"You were always so confident that you would become a successful surgeon—why did you think that?"

"The body intrigued me. I had to know how it worked and why. As a surgeon, I could look inside. I was confident that once I understood the body I could fix it and fix it better than anyone else. The vanity of youth! Unfortunately, the body is a little more complex," he added.

At the back of Rysakov's mind, something stirred again, the thought that had eluded him. Something he had seen triggered an old memory.

"Sergei, didn't you used to claim that all good surgeons were right handed, as you are, of course, and that you could detect a left-handed cut."

"Yes, and I still believe that. The whole protocol of the operating table is set around a right-handed surgeon. Not only is it, in my opinion, more awkward to use a scalpel in the left hand, not being the natural hand, but it can in some cases disrupt the smooth functioning of an operation. Why do you ask?"

"I don't know; talking about our student days reminded me how arrogant and certain you were—about everything. Then I recalled I had a feeling, particularly in the last two murders, that I was missing something. I felt there was a clue on the bodies; something about the cuts he made for his trophy taking. There seemed to be a pattern. But it's so long since those anatomy classes. I'm not certain, but perhaps this monster is left handed. I don't know. I need an expert to tell me," Rysakov said.

"Next time you have a body, call me immediately. It would be a pleasure, old friend. Besides, without my genius and scientific approach, you will never solve this crime," said Sokoloff. The prospect of detective work excited and intrigued him.

§ § § § §

Katya leaned back in the chair. *How strange,* she reflected as Pinna brushed her hair. *Two people, Rysakov and Pinna, appearing out of nowhere into my life. It was fate, of that there could be no doubt. The Celts and the Russians are not so different,* she mused. *Fate determines your life.*

Both times the senior investigator had a central role.

I wonder whether he will appear again, in the future, when something important happens that affects my family? she thought. Somehow, she felt he would.

Pinna began brushing the other side.

Soon after Katya arrived in Moscow, her maid gave notice and Katya had to find a new one. One day not long after, as part of an effort on her part to get her bearings in this great city and build confidence in her new surroundings, Katya went on her own to visit the markets.

Browsing through the market stalls, she found a colorful embroidered scarf. As she went to hand over payment for the scarf, a hand grabbed it and disappeared into the crowd. Katya, without a moment's thought, picked up her purse and ran after the thief. As she raced past the stalls, she became aware of another figure running from behind the stalls in front of her. Suddenly, there was a melee up ahead. When Katya arrived, a tall, strongly built peasant woman of about thirty had her arms around a small, weasel-faced girl who held the scarf. By this time, the scarf stall keeper had also caught up. She immediately berated Katya, demanding payment.

At this juncture, two policemen arrived on the scene, Senior Investigator Rysakov and a colleague on a patrol through the markets in search of troublemakers and petty thieves. At the sight of the police, the weasel-faced woman broke free and disappeared into the crowd, leaving her apprehender holding the scarf.

The stall keeper now mistakenly accused the tall, peasant woman of stealing and the foreign woman of not paying. Rysakov calmed everyone down by asking to see their papers. Katya listened as the peasant woman's papers were examined. She was in Moscow illegally. She did not have permission to leave her village and now stood accused of theft. At this point, Katya intervened and explained what had happened. She paid the stall keeper, who quickly left, mollified, muttering about foreigners. Rysakov then gave his attention to Katya's papers.

"I see you are married to Mikhail Ivanovich Morozov, madam," he said. "I know the family. I apologize for the inconvenience. You may go. Do you know this woman, Agripinna Ivanovna Tishina?" he asked.

Katya looked at the woman with the traditional scarf tied beneath her chin. There was no sign of fear or weakness, only a faint look of resignation. She felt instinctively she would be able to trust her.

Without further thought, Katya said impulsively, "I'm going to employ her as my maid. She is coming back with me. I am sure my husband can sort out any difficulties with her papers."

Intrigued by the brash confidence of the foreign woman, Rysakov decided to accompany them to the Morozov home.

"If this is the maid my wife has employed, it's fine with me," Mikhail said. He then invited Rysakov to a join him in a glass of tea from the ever bubbling samovar.

"Thank you, madam," the new maid said to Katya when they were alone. "I am called Pinna by friends and family. I'd be pleased if you would call me Pinna. I won't let you down."

Since that time the two women had become friends and Katya had learned her story. It came out over several months, with the details filled in as Pinna came to trust her mistress.

"My village is south of Moscow. As is the custom, I had to marry a man my father chose. I knew he had a bad reputation; what I didn't know was how bad a man he really was.

"I worked in the fields, hard physical work, long hours. But I'm young and strong. I didn't mind. The money I earned greatly improved my husband's income.

"I even accepted the beatings and sex that was more like rape," she said stoically. "Many of the other women in the village suffered like me and survived. It wasn't a happy or satisfying life, but that was normal. In the villages, life is given to be endured. Perhaps if our Lord had blessed us with children," she shrugged, "but he didn't."

"One day I heard my husband had been visiting a widow. If he got his sex elsewhere, that was fine by me. What drove me mad with fury was that he was using some of the few kopecks I saved working from dawn to dusk in the fields to buy this woman small gifts. That was too much."

Katya nodded. "That I can understand." *In Dublin,* she thought, *that would be grounds for murder.*

"The next week, when the widow was unavailable, he came home drunk. As soon as he came in the door, he started to abuse me. He said I was lazy, that I should work harder and save more money. 'You're not even a good fuck,' he said. 'The widow is much more fun.' When he said that, he took off his leather belt and began to beat me. The more he hit me, the more aroused he became. He tried to force me face down on the table to mount me," Pinna said. "That was it. I snapped."

"I grabbed a wooden bowl from the table and hit him hard on the side of the head. The blow stunned him. I pushed him back and hit him again splitting the bowl. The drink slowed him down. Before he could recover his balance I pulled the belt out of his hands and laid into him. I'm strong and I hurt him.

"But the belt is disgusting, a coward's way. So I threw it on the floor and used my fists to hit him on the side of the head until he was unconscious. Then I gathered the few things that belonged to me and walked out of the village." Pinna stopped, reliving that traumatic time.

"The humiliation of being beaten senseless by his wife stopped any attempt by him to find me and bring me back. Now I must stay in Moscow. If I return to the village my husband, who still lives there, would use the law to force me to return to his home. I would rather die," she said.

Pinna appointed herself Katya's protector, and, with Katya now approaching her last month, she became very protective. In this role, she could be quite formidable.

§ § § § §

Now that the Morozov household had a mistress again, Ivan entertained more frequently. The ballroom in their house, small by Moscow standards, could still accommodate over one hundred. Since Katya's arrival two years ago it had received more use than in the previous decade.

§ § § § §

Katya was pleased when her time finally came. She was tired of carrying the weight in her belly. When her daughter was placed in her arms, all thought of the pain of the birth evaporated. She knew without fear of contradiction that this was the most beautiful baby ever as she stared with wonder at the wrinkled face. The midwife smiled politely and took her leave. She had other charges to attend.

Father and grandfather were full of plans for the future. Pinna pushed them out of the room, clucking that men should get out of the way and leave the new mother alone. Both kissed Katya gently on the forehead and left closing the door, leaving Anna Mikhailovna Morozovna, the first of the new generation of Morozovs, cradled in her mother's arms.

These children will inherit the business, Ivan thought happily. *Mikhail will have a large family. The next will be a son.* He smiled confidently. *They will grow up in a Russia bursting with opportunity and promise.* The future could not be more exciting.

Harbin

The Russian press called the construction of the Trans-Siberian Railway "the most ambitious engineering project ever undertaken...one of the great wonders of the world." It stretched 6,250 miles from Saint Petersburg to Vladivostok on the Sea of Japan. It led to large-scale migration and the development of heavy industries. Siberia could now supply food, timber, furs, and grain for Russian consumption and export. And it fostered a growing trade with China. The rail also provided a base for Russian power in the Pacific, centered on the Pacific fleet at the ice-free port of Vladivostok.

These were the years when Germany, Britain, and France were dividing China into spheres of influence. Russia, determined not to be sidelined in this contest for territory, grabbed Manchuria, a rich economic and strategic prize. When construction of the last section of the railway began with thousands of Russian workers and armed guards based in Harbin, Ivan met in Moscow with a Kazakh trader, Yusuf Yudin.

He explained to Ivan, "There are huge profits to be made in Manchuria. I have the contacts with the Chinese and understand how business is done in the East. My family has traded on the old Silk Road for hundreds of years."

"Then why do you come to Moscow seeking partners?" Ivan asked.

"What I need is capital and a strong, well-connected sponsor in Moscow. I believe the future is with Russia. Your railway will bring large numbers of new settlers to the East. They'll need supplies. This I can do in a modest way on my own. But, the big opportunity is to send furs and Chinese silks and other goods back to Moscow, to France and Germany and all the other countries west of Russia. To do that, I need a partner."

"Very well, Yusuf Yudin," said Ivan, and they spent the next week negotiating. Once the terms had been agreed, Yusuf left Moscow and returned east with a sum of capital and letters confirming his partnership with Morozov & Son. Orders for goods to sell in the burgeoning new town of Harbin followed swiftly. Within six months, the first shipment of furs and Chinese furniture arrived in Moscow. Ivan disposed of both at a very satisfactory profit.

His first glimpse of the new Harbin, as the coach crested a hill before crossing the Sungari River, caught Ivan unawares. He expected a rude, frontier town. Instead, he saw a Russian town rising in the midst of the orient. Everywhere, he could see the distinctive wooden architecture of Russia, including dozens of churches with their unmistakable onion-shaped cupolas.

Several days after his arrival, during which Yusuf showed Ivan the scale of potential in Harbin, they set out to meet the Chinese partner Yusuf had written about.

Before he left Moscow, Ivan explained to Mikhail, "Even though our business with Yusuf Yudin has been very profitable, he is now proposing we partner with a Chinese firm."

"If we trust him, shouldn't we follow his advice?" asked Mikhail.

"The Chinese are different. They look at life in a different way. Before I agree, I'll go to Harbin and meet them," Ivan said.

Later that day, Mikhail confided to Katya.

"I'm convinced Father is more excited at the prospect of seeing the full expanse of Mother Russia than any real concerns about the Chinese." He smiled.

As the Russian-style carriage pulled up outside a large but nondescript building in the Chinese sector of Harbin, Yusuf said to Ivan, "Don't be fooled by the outside. It is the way of most Chinese merchants. They try to look poor from the outside so as not to attract the attention of the emperor's tax collectors."

Once inside, Ivan saw what he meant. The furnishings were lavish. Exquisitely carved chairs surrounded intricately inlaid tables and screens with scenes of graceful cranes and bamboo thickets edging serene lakes. Liu Ping-nan greeted them with a formal bow.

A demure young woman sat at his side. This, Yusuf explained, was his daughter, Ching-Po, who would translate, having learned Russian in Vladivostok.

By the end of his stay, Ivan was satisfied he would be treated reasonably and honorably and a new business, Morozov & Liu, Merchants, was established. Liu gained credibility with the Russians in Harbin. For Ivan, the connection into Chinese business would open doors not usually available to a Russian. None of the other major Moscow business houses had gone into partnership with a Chinese. That amused him. He didn't share the widely held view that Orientals were inferior to Russians—different certainly, but they had to be astute businessmen; they'd been trading successfully for thousands of years. It was simply good business.

§ § § § §

Yusuf Yudin checked the manifest one last time. He insisted Liu agree the items and values before the cargo left Harbin. It was the largest shipment sent to Moscow by the new firm in the past year. He had a shrewd idea what it would fetch. They would make a handsome profit on this load.

"Do you think our Russian partner will be pleased with the furniture?" Liu asked Yusuf.

"I'm sure he will be delighted," Yusuf replied in Mandarin.

They soon had ready for dispatch a quantity of sable, fox, and marmot fur. It was by no means easy to accumulate significant numbers of good quality pelts. Many of the more accessible area of taiga and forest had been over-trapped. However, both Yusuf and Liu agreed one acquisition alone made the work worth the effort. Only after considerable discussion and argument could they bear to part with it. The profit on that one item alone was worth more than half the sables if Ivan could find the right buyer.

A Chukchi hunter from the far north, disliking the dealers in Vladivostok, journeyed directly south to Harbin. On his arrival, as chance would have it, he ran into another hunter, a Kazakh, who directed him to Yusuf.

What he showed Yusuf left the trader speechless. The huge white and grey striped Siberian tiger would have been nearly nine-feet long from head to tail and over four feet high. It was rare to find a tiger, even rarer to secure a perfect skin. Both Liu and Yusuf agreed, good fortune had indeed blessed the new venture.

Yusuf's buoyant mood continued all day. When the last of the packing had been completed, he said to Lui, "With the new line south from Harbin to Port Arthur nearly complete we'll need more capital to expand the business. I'll send word to Moscow."

§ § § § §

"That's not the work of the *hunghutzes*," the railway engineer said. "Those Manchurian bandits only want to extort protection money, not destroy bridges and cut down the telegraph."

Engineer Kamenev turned his back on the smoldering ruins of the burnt bridge and faced Lieutenant Valevsky, the officer in charge of the detachment of guards protecting the work group.

"If it's not the bandits, who is it? We're so close to Mukden, whoever they are, they must be very confident," said the lieutenant.

"If it's the new group we've been hearing about then we can expect more trouble," said Kamenev. "What're they called?"

"The 'Boxers,' because of the martial arts they practice," the lieutenant replied. "Don't worry, Boris Alexevich, my men will be more than a match for any Chinese rabble. No matter how they 'box.'"

"Damn them; this'll put us behind schedule. Well, better get the work teams starting the cleanup so we can repair the bridge," muttered the engineer.

An hour later, the work gangs had spread out along the track. They began removing burnt and scarred timber. Each strut had to be tested. If the fire had done too much damage, they replaced it.

Suddenly, a single rifle shot shattered the morning quiet—the alarm signal, from the middle of the work gang.

Before the guards could react, line after line of screaming Boxers surged over the crest of a small rise behind the bridge. Hundreds of fighters, dressed in padded fighting helmets, brandishing swords and fighting sticks attacked the work party. It took the soldiers completely by surprise.

The rail workers dropped their tools and ran. Coolies scattered in every direction. Russian gangers ran toward where the lieutenant stood. Some carried their hammers and crowbars, using them as weapons to fight as they ran. The armed railway guards, spread out over the length of the gang line, began firing as they too fell back on the lieutenant. But they were spread too thinly. The rifle fire was not concentrated enough, and many were slashed by swords as they ran. They dropped to the ground, deep gashes bleeding into the sand. At the far end, the sheer number of Boxers overran the guard's line. Valevsky saw uniform after uniform disappear.

Only a third of the total gang and their guards managed to regroup into a loose formation. The Boxers, ecstatic at the extent of their success, pressed the attack harder. Finally, the last of the guards reached the other survivors. Together, they formed around the lieutenant. He quickly realized they had no choice but to fight a retreat up the line toward Harbin.

Valevsky knew they must maintain speed in the retreat or run the risk of being surrounded and overrun. In the scramble, the line broke, reformed, and broke again. As they reached the top of a rise, he yelled to Kamenev.

"Keep the left-hand line formed. Don't become separated."

He received no reply. It was only then he realized that the main body of Boxers had stopped and formed a cheering crowd in the rear. At the same time, the intensity of the attack dropped.

As the crowd parted, he could see why they were cheering. Kamenev had been captured. As they watched, two Boxers forced him to his knees. Another two stood behind him each holding an arm, twisting it back from the shoulder. A third man grabbed his hair and pulled his head forward.

"Oh my God," gasped the lieutenant, crossing himself as a burly Boxer raised a two-handed, three-foot sword high above his head.

For several seconds, there was total silence. The sword hung suspended in the air. Then, it sliced down. The men surrounding the lieutenant watched in horror as the engineer's head rolled onto the dust.

A victory cheer erupted from the Boxers.

"Shoot that bastard," yelled the lieutenant.

As the shots rang out, the Boxer swordsman dropped dead. For several moments, the Boxers looked around, confused. Then, they saw the lieutenant and his men. Rage replaced euphoria. With fanatical screams, the attack on the dwindling survivors resumed. Now, the Boxers knew they were invincible. They had seen one of the foreigners' heads roll. This time, they attacked through a haze of blood lust.

The retreating Russians fought desperately for hours, putting one exhausted foot back after the other. Suddenly, the Boxers faltered and began to fall back. At first, the lieutenant did not notice. They were all close to the limit of their endurance.

Then, it happened. Without warning, the thunder of horse's hooves at the gallop and the wild yelling of the steppes filled the air. A squadron of Cossack cavalry swept past the defenders and down onto the scattering Boxers. Sabers slashed savagely down on the heads of the Boxers. Horses trampled the foe at full gallop. The Cossack assault was disciplined and relentless. Within minutes, the Boxers turned, routed, running in terrified confusion. The horsemen chased them out of sight over the hill, sabers flashing in the sunlight as they rose and fell, specks of blood spattering their horses' flanks.

An hour later, the Cossack captain swung off his horse and walked to where Lieutenant Valevsky sat under a tree. Of the 200 gangers and fifty guards, only thirty were still alive, and most of them were wounded.

"Sorry we were a bit late," he said, "We were told you'd left Mukden and have been looking for you ever since. Looks like you took a lot of casualties. Good thing you didn't go back into Mukden. Last we heard before the telegraph went down, the town was in the hands of the Boxers. They're massacring all the missionaries and Chinese Christians, and of course any foreigners or Chinks that work with foreigners. You know these silly bastards believe they have magical powers that make them invisible to bullets and sabers." He shook his head at such stupidity.

By the time Lieutenant Valevsky and his Cossack escort reached Harbin, it too reeled under attack. The Boxers had besieged the city, and the Cossacks fought their way back into the town. Once inside the defensive lines, they heard the news that the Imperial Army had mobilized nearly 200,000 troops.

"Then we'll really kick these Chinks in the arse," said the Cossack captain with a wide grin. "Though I hear they destroyed part of the railway out of Harbin."

The Boxer siege lasted eight days before the new troops reached Harbin. With overwhelming numbers and weapons, the Russian Army rapidly put the disorganized attackers to flight.

Lieutenant Valevsky, now a local hero, took command of one of the city sectors. As they helped secure the city, they passed the blackened shells of three wooden Russian churches destroyed in the fighting. Hundreds of bodies lay in the street, beheaded by the fanatics if they were even suspected of being Christian. Many Chinese businesses, and some Russian houses, had been looted or burned. Any business suspected of dealing with the "foreign devils" had been targeted.

Valevesky's sector of the city included the area where Yusuf lived. He and his troops helped protect Yusuf's home during the last days of fighting. The two got on well as a result, and Yusuf accompanied the soldiers as a guide through the district.

As they rounded the corner, Yusuf Yudin feared the worst. He looked down the street and saw only ruins. Fire had totally destroyed most of the buildings.

"Which one was yours?" asked Valevsky.

"That one." Yusuf pointed to a partly destroyed building. It was clear there would be little of value recoverable. The roof had collapsed, smashing what the fire had spared. Some of the steel items, such as the rail ties, could be salvaged, but the rest was lost. The clothing, most of the fashion goods, and all the other inflammable items were gone, including half their stock of pelts. It was a large loss. *Thank God the tiger skin has been dispatched,* Yusuf thought. *If it got through.*

"Can you take me to the Chinese quarter?" he asked Valevsky. By the time they reached Liu's home, he was already there, sifting through the ashes. The Boxers had known which Chinese merchants to attack and had been ruthless in their punishment.

"Our business is no more, my friend," Liu said.

Yusuf said nothing.

"Is your warehouse damaged?" Liu asked.

"Totally destroyed."

"Our Moscow partner will suffer a large loss. That is most unfortunate."

"It was outside our control. Yet, provided the last shipment got through before they cut the line, he'll at least have the opportunity to recover some of his capital," said Yusuf.

Liu looked directly at Yusuf.

"Yusuf, you placed yourself in great danger sheltering me and my family in your home during the fighting. It almost certainly saved our lives. We will not forget your kindness."

§ § § § §

The next day Yusuf visited the bank and discovered, to his relief that, not only was it still intact, it was conducting a busy trade. At first he had difficulty getting the clerk at the front counter to give him any attention, so great was the crush of people wanting to withdraw funds or seek assurance their deposits were safe in the vaults and the bank had not been looted. Once he showed the Morozov & Son letter of credit, the clerk's attitude changed. He was shown immediately into the manager's office. The manager confirmed that his bank would be delighted to advance against the letter of credit, at any time.

Yusuf left the bank and sent a telegram to Ivan.

It took three days for the reply to get through the traffic on the telegraph. Only by calling on the influence of the bank had he been able to get any access to send the message in the first place.

Ivan confirmed his request. He also advised that the last shipment had arrived in Moscow and that he was delighted, particular with the tiger skin. It had been the last train to leave Harbin before the Boxers destroyed the line.

Later that day, Yusuf sat talking with Liu over a pot of green tea.

"Old friend, I had news from Moscow today. The last shipment arrived and Ivan Victorovich is very pleased, particularly with the tiger." Yusuf paused. "In my telegram last week, I told him how the fighting had destroyed all our stock. He was sorry to hear you had also lost your warehouse and home; he remembers how finely furnished it was."

Liu nodded.

"He would like to offer you a loan to rebuild your home and to establish a new warehouse under your own name. Morozov & Son will be a silent partner. No one will know that you are in partnership with a foreign devil so that this cannot happen again. The loan can be repaid when you are reestablished. He has authorized me to draw funds on the Far East branch of the bank so that you can recommence business immediately."

Liu stared at Yusuf, uncomprehending for a few seconds as the offer sank in. He was not ruined. He had a chance, a better chance, to rebuild his family's fortune.

"I see your hand in this my friend," he said. "Please tell Ivan Victorovich I accept his very generous offer. We will not forget his thoughtfulness and consideration. Please convey my deepest gratitude to him."

Yusuf nodded.

"I would like to understand. Why did he do this for me, he is so very far away? What am I to him?" Liu asked.

"He believes you are an honorable man with whom he will do much profitable business," Yusuf replied.

"I see," Liu paused. "He is an interesting person. I hope that I shall live up to his expectations."

Yusuf smiled and poured another cup of tea.

In London, Philip Armitage and Sir Algernon Law at the Foreign Office now feared Russia's emerging strength in East Asia could threaten British interests in the region. So, shortly after Russian troops had secured all of Manchuria, Britain signed a military alliance with Japan to forestall any further expansion by Imperial Russia.

Moscow

On a warm summer's day, the last train out of Harbin before the siege arrived at Moscow station. As the crates were opened in his warehouse, Ivan saw the quality of the pelts and realized his fears of a large loss as a result of the uprising were premature. His capital was intact; it lay in front of him. One smaller crate seemed at odds with the rest. They opened it last, expecting residual pelts. Instead, it created a sensation. Word spread like wildfire throughout the warehouse. It contained a sight so spectacular all other work stopped.

The men spread the huge white and grey striped skin of the Siberian tiger complete with snarling head on a packing table. The power and majesty of the great cat, its huge jaws agape, the yellow incisors ready to seize and crush any foe, was unmistakable. This rare and magnificent find would command a huge price.

All that week, Ivan continued to bask in the magnificence of the tiger. Word spread among the wealthy of Moscow, even reaching the Imperial capital, where a representative of the tsar's court expressed an interest in seeing the animal. Ivan decided to hold a viewing, so many of his friends and acquaintances kept finding excuses to call in to the Morozov household, disbelieving reports on the size of the cat. He received several quite ridiculous offers to buy the tiger. Ivan, however, decided to keep the skin. It was too unique to let anyone else own what he had already come to think of as *his* tiger.

While in this ebullient mood, the telegram from Yusuf Yudin arrived telling of the destruction in Harbin. Ivan reviewed the situation. The sable and marmot pelts would sell at a very satisfactory profit. The Siberian timber would be shipped through Johanssen and the other goods would sell at a good margin. The Russian Army had put down the rebellion of the ill-disciplined rabble in Manchuria with ease. Yes, he could expect the Siberian business to resume its profitable course.

Helping Liu reestablish his business made good sense. It would place Liu in his debt, both morally and financially. At the same time, he did not want to risk a repeat of the destruction wrought by the Boxers. So, Ivan suggested the business name be changed. He would be a silent partner. Out of the ashes of the rebellion a new entity, Tiger Moon Trading Company, came into being.

§ § § § §

After the birth of Anna, Katya had, with the help of Pinna, made every effort to regain her figure. She felt pleased with the result. Certainly, there were no complaints from her husband. Her initial fears, that he may not desire her after the birth, had been clearly misplaced. If anything, he became more amorous.

Each morning as he lay beside her, Mikhail considered his good fortune. Katya was beautiful and intelligent; he couldn't imagine being without her. Yet, she could be very irritating. She had an independence of opinion he found both attractive and annoying. He knew she loved him, but at times he was pleased to be away from her.

As summer drew to a close and the first leaves began to turn, Mikhail and Ivan left for London. Mikhail, his wounds fully healed, was adamant. Anna was too young to make the trip this time. However, in response to Katya's pleas, he agreed that next year they would all journey to London. In the meantime, Katya should stay and look after the household.

On more than one occasion during the last two years, Ivan had noted the interest Katya showed in the workings of the business, particularly matters involving workers at the factories. So, before he left, Ivan told Katya he had asked his key managers to keep her informed of any unrest and that they should take note of her advice. Katya was thrilled to be so trusted and assured Ivan that she would do her best to give the right advice.

To remind Muscovites that winter was not far away, the week after they left produced cold winds and sleet. Then, as if offering a brief reprieve to a condemned man, the north wind died and a bright clear sky shone over the city. A warm breeze drifted in from the southeast. Determined to take advantage of the day, Katya, after countless assurances from Pinna that she could look after Anna perfectly well, took her carriage to visit the shops and promenade with others enjoying the weather.

It seemed as though all of Moscow had decided to follow her example. Everywhere, people strolled along footpaths or across parks soaking up the mild sun. She felt pleased she had decided to go on her own. How indulgent to have no plan, no timetable.

She walked slowly past the Perlov teashop, wondering idly whether she would stop and take tea.

"Madam Morozovna," a deep and cultured voice called.

Katya turned expectantly.

"Please forgive me for calling out so crudely."

"Prince Koslinski," she said, surprised. "I would not have expected to see you in this part of the city. It's a wonderful day to be out of doors, don't you think?"

"I suspect it is the last gasp of summer before the north wind reminds us winter is not far away," he said. "Unfortunately I've been working. My bank has an interest in Perlov. However, my good fortune in meeting you has considerably brightened what promised to be a dull day. Would you do me the honor of taking tea with me," he said, indicating with a sweep of his arm the delights of the Perlov establishment. "I'm sure the staff will be able to find an enticing China blend to match this sunny day."

The prince explained that the interior of the establishment had been designed in pseudo-Chinese style when the Chinese regent, Lu Hung Chung, visited Moscow for the coronation of Tsar Nicholas II. Katya imagined the real China would look just like it. She found it thrillingly exotic. The staff dressed impeccably, Katya noticed—neck ties and waistcoats beneath full dress coats. This was to be expected for a business supplying premium and exotic teas to the Imperial Court and the wealthy of Moscow.

Koslinski ushered Katya to a private area on one side of the main shop where Chinese-style tables and chairs were set out. He then spoke briefly to the manager, who hovered behind the prince immediately after they sat down.

"I've ordered a special blend that I have made for my own use. I'm sure you'll find it to your liking." He paused briefly. "I've heard that you and your husband have a new daughter. May I congratulate you, Katya Mariavna."

"Thank you, sir," Katya said.

"I find it hard to believe that you are a mother. So often, I have observed, new mothers put on weight after the birth of their children. You, however, look as beautiful as the day you arrived in Moscow."

In spite of herself, Katya felt a flush color in her cheeks. It was part pleasure, for such a compliment, and part embarrassment that she sat alone with this unmarried aristocrat. She lowered her eyes, momentarily unsure what to do. She finished her tea and placed the cup back on the lacquered tray. It was time to go.

She looked up to find Koslinski gazing at her intently. He was undeniably handsome, with an arrogance born of complete confidence in his position in society and the unquestioned certainty that his wishes would prevail. This self-confidence would, she felt, be undiminished even in the presence of his peers. Her resolve to leave weakened as he entertained her with gossip from the court. He moved effortlessly through the upper stratum of Russian society as only a wealthy, impeccably connected bachelor could. From his anecdotes and observations, he was clearly an acute onlooker of the frailties of human behavior. "Onlooker"—the description just dropped into Katya's mind, and it seemed to fit. Koslinski spoke as though he were removed from the people about whom he spoke. It was not an academic detachment. It was an emotional detachment. As if he had no feelings about them at all.

Katya heard a clock chime. Suddenly, she realized she must return to Anna. She rose to leave.

"Please give my regards to your husband and to Ivan Victorovich," the prince said, walking with Katya to the Perlov door.

"They are presently in London on business, but I shall be pleased to pass on your good wishes on their return," Katya said.

"I see," said Koslinski. "In their absence, if there is any matter concerning the business, or any other matter, please consider me a friend. As you know, I am banker to Morozov & Son and a business confidant to Ivan Victorovich. I'm pleased to place myself at your service," he said, holding her hand as she stepped into the carriage.

"Thank you for a most entertaining morning," Katya said as the horses pulled away. *One more brief stop,* she told herself.

She stopped the carriage outside the exclusive dress salon of Allschwang Brothers in Petrovska Street. She liked the salon. It had an understated feminine elegance. Finely stenciled designs in soft pastel shades decorated the walls just below the cornices. More intricate patterns decorated the ceiling, framing the electric lighting hanging on a pulley system with multiple beaded shades illuminating the dresses, bonnets, and parasols on display. Delicately proportioned chairs stood in front of glass display cases, showing off gloves and evening bags. Behind these cases sat cabinets full of jackets and blouses. Through a door framed by full-length mirrors was a second, inner room with the most amazing array of underwear, corsetry, stays, long johns, and petticoats.

Katya drifted amiably from one dress to another. The salon always had a calming, soothing effect. She slid her hand idly along the display cabinet, looking at the different colored gloves, ran the fabric of the dresses through her fingers. She did not feel like buying today and after fifteen minutes browsing turned left out of Petrovska Street into Kuznetsky Most. She loved this fashionable shopping precinct.

As she walked down the gentle slope toward the low end of the street, she turned abruptly and strode purposefully back to her carriage. The soft veil of well-being following tea with Koslinski abruptly lifted. She must get back to Anna. But that was not all.

As the carriage threaded its way through the busy streets, Katya sat back deep in thought. Koslinski was charming and attractive, and she felt flattered by his compliments. She felt certain they had been given with sincerity. She smiled. What a delicious feeling to know men still found her attractive. That she had no interest in them was irrelevant.

She searched her memory as the carriage rattled over the cobbles. Neither Misha nor Ivan had ever mentioned a close, "confidant" relationship with Koslinski. Why then would the prince suggest such a relationship? What had Misha told her about Koslinski's bank? Something about the business having money on deposit, she recalled. She should have paid more attention. She recalled the first time she remembered meeting the prince, at the ball. At that time, he had made improper suggestions to her. Certainly, the suggestions had been vague. But in her mind the intent had been clear.

As the driver drew up outside their home, she decided she would be very careful with the prince and not disclose any information about the business. Ivan had placed in her a trust, however limited. Katya had no illusions as to whether she could or should override his managers. Nevertheless, she did not intend discussing anything to do with the business with outsiders. *Surely, it would not be necessary anyway,* she thought. *What could possibly go wrong that would require such action?*

§ § § § §

The number of strikes increased every year. More and more, peasants poured into the major cities. As they did, the cost of living rose at least as fast as wages. In turn, labor unions, banned by the tsar, developed spontaneously. Strikes, not well organized or coordinated, grew in strength and number.

"Is it just the cooler weather, Gregori, or are these strike organizers really building up to some larger action?" Rysakov asked. "We need more men to break up what's happening now, let alone anything bigger."

"If it is, Maksim, we'll need the army to control it," said Gregori Yukovsky, "we don't have the manpower. But I can't see that happening. There are too many would-be leaders claiming to have the answers. If they can't agree amongst themselves then there's no danger of them coordinating any action.

"Hey, there was some trouble at the old Baranov factory the other day. Isn't that owned by Morozov now? A couple of people got injured and my information is that it could flare up again. You know Morozov, don't you? Maybe you should talk to him and warn him. It wouldn't hurt the rich bastard to give the workers a few extra rubles; it'd make our job easier," Yukovsky said.

"I'll try to see him this week. Anything to make your life easier," Rysakov retorted.

Rysakov and his colleague sat in their office, filling out the never-ending paperwork. He shifted a pile of forms to one side and reread a report he had completed yesterday on action taken against the strikers. Satisfied, he signed it and placed it on the pile to be filed. As he lifted the report, he noticed a letter beneath the papers. Curious, he picked it up. It was addressed, "Senior Investigator Rysakov." *A woman's neat hand,* he thought.

He opened the envelope and pulled out a single sheet of paper. It was from Irina Bourlin's mother. Irina had seen the man again walking along Nikolskaya Street toward the Upper Trading Rows facing onto Red Square.

He looked quickly at the date on the letter. Two days ago. *Damn, it must have gotten hidden under the mess on the desk.*

He reread the letter. She had been with her mother in their carriage when she saw the man. As luck would have it, their carriage was stopped by traffic at that moment and Irina pointed the man out to her mother. "He was tall with an aristocratic bearing and dressed in well-cut dark clothes."

This was indeed significant, but it was the last sentence that he read a third time. "I feel sure I have seen this man before, although I cannot be totally certain."

Rysakov jumped up from his seat in excitement.

§ § § § § §

Prince Vasily Koslinski heard about the trouble at the old Baranov factory and decided to use it as an excuse to call on Katya. With her husband and old Ivan away, she may feel in need of support, and he would be more than pleased to provide it. She was different from the Russian women he knew. She looked different, she acted differently, and she had an air of almost defiant independence about her. It reminded him of some of the few Tartar women he had met. But it was more than that. There was no denying she was beautiful. But he knew many beautiful Russian women. Some, he had to acknowledge, were even more beautiful to look at than Katya Morozovna. It intrigued him, this strong, almost irresistible attraction he felt for the wife of Mikhail Morozov. It did not concern him that she was married. To a member of the Court, this represented only a minor inconvenience. In any event, he didn't think much of the young Morozov. A bit soft, not like his father. If Katya had been Ivan's wife, he would have thought long and carefully about the consequences. Ivan was a far more dangerous man. *The son I can handle, if necessary,* he thought.

He waited in the reception room of the Morozov house as the maid went to announce him.

§ § § § §

Rysakov stood, staring at the letter, his mind racing. He had had little time over recent months to do more than give a cursory thought to the mutilation murderer. He, along with the other members of the police force, had been fully occupied with the strikes and unrest in the city. There had not been another murder, and dread of this singular evil had retreated for the time being. One more murder as grisly as the last, however, and hysteria would take hold in the current atmosphere. The letter from Irina's mother galvanized him into action.

He told Yukovsky he had some urgent business to attend to and hurried out of the office. The paperwork could wait. He needed to speak to the Bourlins immediately.

He sat in the sitting room where he had last interviewed Irina. The girl explained how she had once again seen the man "who walked like a wolf." Rysakov was silent for a moment and then asked, "Madam, you said in your letter that you had seen this man before. Can you tell me where?"

"I cannot be sure, and I do not want to cause trouble that might affect my husband's business," she said.

"I can assure you the information will be treated confidentially," Rysakov said with practiced smoothness.

"It may not have been the same person, but he reminded me of someone I have seen at the theater. I think I may also have seen the same person at one of the Imperial balls" she said. "But I really can't be sure. It would be terrible if I was mistaken."

Rysakov could see she regretted volunteering the information. He knew from experience that her initial impression, that she knew the man, was more likely to be right than wrong. It was also his most stunning lead to date.

"Madam, anything you can tell me would be of assistance and may help prevent another young life being so brutally wasted."

"I only saw the man ever so briefly," she said. "He was with friends, but he was tall and good looking, from what little I could see."

"Was he a businessman?"

"No," she said, "at least I don't think so."

She had said no emphatically. The man, whoever he was, did not form part of her husband's world, the world of business. Rysakov felt he had made real progress. His quarry appeared almost certainly to be a member of the nobility.

The woman knew more. Of that he was certain. Now he had to gain her confidence sufficiently to extract the information. He smiled at Irina and relaxed. There was no quick way, and he settled in for a lengthy conversation.

When he took his leave of the Bourlin house quite some time later, he felt both pleased and annoyed. What he had learned could be the most significant advance since the case began. It would not, however, make solving the crime any easier. In fact, it may require a great deal of delicacy with no guarantee of success. It became clear from what Irina's mother said that the man her daughter had identified had connections with the highest levels of society, connections all the way to the Imperial royal family. Even though he felt sure she knew his name, no amount of coaxing could elicit it. The poor woman was terrified of being the one to name the suspect. He could see the thought processes in her mind as she talked. If it got out, and she was proven wrong, she would never be able to show her face in society again.

He decided, since he was out of the office and needed time to think, he would call on Ivan Morozov and pass on Gregori's warning about possible factory unrest.

As he approached their house, a tall, handsome, well-dressed man with aristocratic bearing climbed into a carriage and drove off.

§ § § § § §

The rich notes of the Guarneri violin rolled in resonant waves around the concert hall. Not another sound could be heard. The audience seemed to be holding its breath, enraptured by the magic of the music. The soloist sensed he had the theater in his thrall, and his fingers flew flawlessly over the strings in a virtuoso performance of Paganini's 'Violin Concerto.' As the spirited 'Rondo' came to an end, the audience erupted into applause. After the fourth curtain call with cries of "Encore!" echoing around the hall, the young violinist nodded to the conductor and tucked the instrument under his chin.

The depth of the Guarneri's sound intensified the pathos of the short encore, Tchaikovsky's 'Serenade Melancolique.'

Katya clapped her hands, as enthralled as the rest of the audience. Her excitement made even deeper knowing the violin belonged to her family. She had been thrilled to be invited to the concert by the Countess Anastasia Metchersky, whom she had only met socially several times. However, Ivan was one of the wealthiest businessmen in Moscow and a generous benefactor to the arts. The countess would almost certainly have been aware he owned the Guarneri.

When Katya explained that her husband was away, the countess had not seemed surprised.

"There'll be a number of friends joining me at the theater," she said. Then almost as an afterthought, she added, "I will also not have a husband with me. I would be delighted if you would sit with us."

Prince Koslinski left his box and strolled leisurely toward the bar where he knew the countess would be stationed. The foyer filled rapidly as the audience spilled out of the theater. The entire area buzzed with animated conversation, eyes constantly on the move to see who had attended the first night, and with whom.

"Anastasia, how delightful to see you," he greeted the countess. Katya, talking to a member of the countess's party whom she knew slightly through the Women's Tennis Club, turned unconsciously at the sound of a familiar voice.

"Madam Morozovna, how charming to see you here. But, of course, the Morozovs own that wonderful violin the artist played. It is a great gesture that your husband allows the sound of this violin to be shared with all of Moscow. Ladies, may I offer you a glass of champagne?"

With an imperious wave at the busy waiter behind the bar, Prince Koslinski turned back to the two women. He had held little doubt that the countess would be successful in bringing Katya to the performance, as he had requested. She could be very persuasive. He took the glasses from the waiter's tray and offered one to Katya first. The countess, knowing the game, smiled. What could be more natural than a chance meeting in a place as public as a recital at the Moscow Concert Hall, particularly when the Morozov violin was featured? A representative of the Morozov family would be expected to be there. He felt pleased with himself.

Katya looked at the lush furnishings of the foyer, red carpets, gilt statuettes, shimmering chandeliers, and the French and Italian style antique chairs and settees. What a long way from the drabness of Dublin. Now that same girl stood at ease in a beautiful, fashionable dress, valuable jewelry around her neck, and the diamond and emerald clasp above her left breast. She mixed naturally with the rich and titled, glittering in their finery. She had adjusted quickly to the life of wealth and privilege as a member of the Morozov family and reveled in her place as Mikhail's wife and mother to his children. She could not imagine it was possible to be happier. Yet, deep down Katy O'Connor, who knew the oppressive poverty of Dublin, kept her sense of perspective. Few of those present had ever experienced what it was to be poor.

Katya turned to face Koslinski, half listening to his conversation, making polite responses while surveying the room. As the warning bell sounded for the commencement of the second part of the recital, Katya handed her glass to the prince. She smiled lightly and joined the countess, who, with a slight smirk on her lips, led the way back to their box.

Koslinski made sure that he exited his box promptly at the conclusion of the final encore and positioned himself to be in the path of the countess and her party, as they left to find their carriages.

The audience disgorged at a leisurely pace, talking animatedly, calling to friends, arranging to meet at a club or restaurant. The countess had to admire the natural ease with which Koslinski met up with Katya in the crowd.

"Ah, Madam Morozovna, what a wonderful performance. Unfortunately, all too short."

The prince worked his considerable charm at full power. The countess lingered, fascinated to see the outcome with this foreign girl. She discreetly dropped back slightly in the crowd as Koslinski deftly steered the unsuspecting Katya to one side of the hall. He retrieved her long fur coat. They exited not through the main entrance, but through a minor door that only those patrons whose carriages were to the side used. As they went through the door, the countess saw Koslinski put his hand on the girl's waist, as if to guide her through the exit. Once outside, he slid his arm around her waist, pulling her gently closer. It took Katya a few steps to realize what was happening. She immediately pushed his hand off and stepped to one side.

The countess remained at the top of the steps and watched as they approached the waiting carriages. She recognized the prince's coach. Clearly, he had instructed his driver to place it directly in front of this exit. She saw the Morozov woman search for her own carriage. The countess knew it would be with the general melee in front of the main entrance. She could see Koslinski talking and gesturing to his coach. The footman dismounted and held the door open. The Morozov woman shook her head and pointed in the direction of the other carriages. The prince then placed his arm around her waist and proceeded to usher her into his coach. As he forced her onto the step, the countess saw the girl swivel on her left leg and swing her right fist squarely at the prince's jaw. The impact momentarily stunned the prince. He staggered back, tripping over the leg of the footman. Only a desperate grab for the carriage door prevented him falling flat on his back in the snow. The young woman pulled her coat around her and strode off in search of her carriage.

Countess Metchersky struggled to stifle a laugh as several patrons walked past. *Well done, young lady,* she thought, *that's no less than the blighter deserves. It's a pity more women aren't as confident in who they are.*

Without knowing it, Katya had that night won an ally with powerful connections. No longer would she be looked upon as an outsider.

§ § § § §

On a cold, bleak morning in early November, Maksim Rysakov walked into his office banging his gloved hands together to warm them. He had not taken the fur-skin hat from his head before there was an urgent knock at the door and a constable entered.

"Excuse me, Senior Investigator, there has been another murder, and I was instructed to advise you immediately."

Damn. He'd hoped, irrationally he knew, that the killer was satiated or had left Moscow.

"Thank you. Where is it this time?"

"Another cheap hotel called the Apollo. The local constables are keeping guard until you arrive as instructed," the man said.

"Good. Please have someone go immediately to the Surgical Hospital and ask Dr. Sokoloff to meet me at the scene as soon as possible."

The Apollo was a typical low price Moscow rooming establishment hardly worthy of the name hotel. Rooms for hire by the hour, the day or the week. Some rooms had several families sharing, often with flimsy curtains providing the only privacy between them. Other rooms were used by prostitutes paying by the hour.

By the time Rysakov arrived, Sergei Sokoloff was already there arguing with the constable in front of the door.

"Sergei, thank you for coming," Rysakov said. "The doctor is here at my request," he told the constable who then stood aside as they entered.

"Thank you for calling me so fast, Maksim. If I am to be of any assistance I need to be here as early as possible," Sokoloff said.

The small room had only three pieces of furniture, a cheap chest of drawers, a plain chair, and a single bed. A threadbare cheap rug covered half the bare boards. On the bed lay the body of a young woman about twenty years of age. The mattress and the bedclothes around her were soaked in blood. The fetid, cloying smell made it difficult to breath.

Rysakov stood back, depressed and revolted as always at the causal waste of such a young life. He looked away from the body and searched the room for any clue, however small.

Sokoloff walked up to the body without hesitation, studying it with a practiced, professional air.

"I thought you were exaggerating when you told me about the state of the bodies in the previous murders," he said, shaking his head in disbelief.

The girl lay on her back. Both nipples had been removed and her legs were splayed apart in an awkward and unnatural manner.

Sokoloff bent over and peered closely at the holes where the nipples had once been. He spent some minutes looking at both breasts. Rysakov remained silent, watching his friend, knowing that when he had completed his examination he would report.

Apparently satisfied with the breasts, he next gave his attention to the head. Almost immediately, he found what he was looking for and grunted in confirmation. He straightened and stood at her head, looking down the length of the body with a vaguely puzzled expression. The girl's stomach had a slight rise above the pubic area, like a tightened muscle, which was precisely what Rysakov assumed it to be on following the doctor's gaze.

Sokoloff walked to the end of the bed and bent over peering at the girl's pubic area. With a surgeon's practiced hand, he leaned forward and parted the pubic hair.

"Dear God," he murmured.

Rysakov could now see clearly the end of a piece of rounded wood just protruding from the vulva. Sokoloff put his hand on the muscle on her lower abdomen and pressed down. It was initially unyielding and then as he applied pressure the end of the wood in the vulva moved.

He stood and stared at the body, the way it lay in repose was not quite as he was used to seeing them on the operating table.

"Maksim, come over here and give me a hand to turn her over," he said putting his hands under the left hip.

Rysakov hesitated, not wanting to touch the body.

"Come on, it won't bite you," Sokoloff said impatiently.

Rysakov put his hand under the girl's left shoulder. The flesh was icy cold and clammy and quite unpleasant to touch. The dead weight of the body surprised him and his recently broken arm twinged slightly from the extra strain.

"Mother of God," exclaimed Sokoloff as he saw the blood soaked linen.

They turned the body over.

"What manner of beast would do this to another human being, Maksim? And you say that this is not the first?"

"There've been four others that we know about, but this is the worst I've seen," Rysakov said quietly.

"For God's sake, man, you must catch this maniac before he does it again. I shudder to think what he may do in the future."

"What do you mean?" asked Rysakov.

Sokoloff regained his professional air with some difficulty, visibly pulling himself together.

"Let me give you my verbal report now. With your permission, I would like to take the body to the mortuary and examine it further;

however I don't expect to change the substance of my conclusions," he said.

"Firstly, she was knocked unconscious before any of the mutilations."

"How do you know that?" asked Rysakov.

"See the bruising and swelling on the right temple," he said, pointing to the head. "She must have been alive for the blood to have flowed into the damaged tissue after the impact."

"A weighted object has been wielded with considerable force to do that damage. While the girl was unconscious, the nipples were removed using a sharp surgical instrument." He looked briefly again at the breasts and added, "and your man is left handed. I can tell by the shape of the excision. The initial incision is on the top left with an even curve down to the base of the nipple. The return cut is upward and flatter, not as clearly curved. And the cut has ended slightly above or below the initial incision. See how the final severance is a small straight cut. A skilled surgeon would make a symmetrical cut. So your man is also an amateur.

"The amount of blood loss shows that she was alive when the wooden phallus was rammed into her. It ruptured the uterus, the bladder, and possibly other internal organs causing massive blood loss. The poor girl bled to death. The intense pain of the stake must have partially revived her, and she began to regain consciousness because there was a second blow to the head, above the right ear."

He stopped, clearly shaken, as the import of his evaluation sank in. Someone, something, in Moscow was capable of such a heinous crime.

"Sit down my friend," Rysakov said, guiding the doctor to the chair. "Your analysis has been very valuable."

Rysakov took Sergei to a nearby tavern and after two generous glasses of the best vodka the place had to offer put him in a troika back to the hospital. A return to his normal world would help settle him down.

The manager of the Apollo was of little help when interviewed. All he could confirm was that a tall, wealthy man had come in with a girl the previous night. Whether it was the dead girl or not, he couldn't say.

"There are several girls who use rooms on an hourly basis," he said.

Rysakov would have bet a month's pay the "Monster of Moscow" had claimed another victim.

After this latest outrage, he had to start closing the net around his quarry. The man was clever. He covered his tracks well. He made sure no one saw him well enough to get a description. None of the dead women so far had told their friends anything of use about their new lover.

He decided to make another visit to Madam Bourlin. This time he would arrive without prior warning in the morning, after her husband left for work and her daughter for school.

Next morning at the Bourlin house, he was shown into the reception room. Madam Bourlin came in, immediately looking flustered.

"Madam," Rysakov began as soon as she sat on the chaise, "when I was last here you told me you knew the identity of the man your daughter saw leaving the Ignatiev house. However, you would not disclose his name. I am here today to ask you again to tell me his name."

"Oh, I'm not really sure, Senior Investigator Rysakov," she said stammering. "I wouldn't want to make a mistake about an important person. And I can't be completely certain as I didn't see his face clearly."

"Madam, any information you give me will remain confidential. No one will know of your involvement," he said.

"I don't really want to get involved. My husband would be most upset if he knew."

That is interesting, Rysakov thought, *she still hasn't told him.* He relaxed. He was now very confident his plan would work.

"Madam, Moscow needs civic-minded citizens such as yourself. The information such people provide helps maintain the rule of law to everyone's advantage. Even when the information may not be accurate, as indeed your information may not, it helps eliminate someone who may otherwise be unjustly suspected," he said. He could see the equivocation on the woman's face. At that moment, he thought he had her. Then the maid came into the room to inquire if madam wanted tea, and the spell was broken.

"No, thank you, the investigator will be leaving shortly," she said.

When the maid had gone, Rysakov played his trump hand.

"Madam, if you will not tell me the identity of this man, I may be forced to arrest you for withholding information in a murder inquiry and to hold you until the information is divulged. I regret that this may have unnecessary consequences for your family and your husband's business, but you'll understand that I have no choice in the matter."

Rysakov had no authority to arrest the women and in fact no intention or desire to arrest her. He watched his little speech sink in. There were times when the bad reputation of the tsar's prisons could be used to advantage. As the silence lengthened, he began to worry that his trick had backfired. However, he continued to sit there, showing no intention of leaving. He watched her. After several minutes, the color began to drain out of her face. The initial defiance to his threat gave way to a sober assessment of what might happen if she were arrested.

"You will assure me that no mention of my name will be made in this matter," she asked in a small voice.

"I assure you, madam," he said.

"Very well then," she said and whispered the name.

Although he did not show it, Rysakov was shocked by the name she gave him. This man was wealthy, well known, and very well connected at Court. No wonder she had been reluctant to name him.

As he rode back to his office, he wondered where he could go from here. He would need to tread with great delicacy. He would need proof, proof that would stand rigorous interrogation. And, of course, the two Bourlin women may be wrong. But he didn't think so.

When he walked into the office, his two colleagues were engaged in a lively discussion about the increasing levels of industrial strikes and the action needed to control the problem. Normally, Rysakov would have enjoyed the argument, as he had firm views on the issue. Now, however, he needed to think, quietly. He pulled his fur hat down over his ears, turned left out of the building and walked to the park at the end of the block.

Sokoloff's report would be with him tomorrow. He doubted it would tell him any useful new facts, but it would form an important part of the record for any prosecution. As he walked, he reviewed in his mind the injuries each of the murdered girls had suffered. This last was by far the worst. In the first murders, only two souvenirs had been taken, in the next ones three. However, in the last two deaths, the level of violence had escalated alarmingly. It was frightening to imagine where this might lead.

What was it Sergei had said, "It's as if the murderer's taking revenge on the girl for some vile misdeed." That didn't add up. He felt sure the killer didn't know any of the girls well enough or long enough. It was more likely they were chosen because they were lonely and easily taken in by a wealthy, aristocratic, handsome man. They were available. They were young, pretty, had sensual figures and were village girls. Why then this increase in violence?

Think logically, he told himself, *treat it like a chess game; if there is one thing we Russians are good at it's chess. And madness, and emotional excess,* he thought ruefully. *If it is the person Madam Bourlin named, what drives him? He must have any number of attractive women more than willing to jump into bed with him. So it has to be much more complex than that.*

He's deranged, of that there is no doubt. But what triggers the need to kill, and then to mutilate. There's not even an interval, like a cycle, between the killings. Maybe it's a full moon. I'll have to check, but it seems unlikely. Revenge, Sergei said. If that's the trigger, revenge on whom?

His mind raced. What if for some reason the killer had been rejected in a normal relationship? If the woman he wanted spurned his advances? Peasant girls were easily seduced but beneath his contempt. By killing them, could he be taking revenge for rejection by those he really wanted? Maybe killing reinforced in his mind that he was really in control. Maybe it restored for a brief time his self-esteem? Maybe, maybe.

But that doesn't explain the appalling level of violence. He seems to enjoy it. It must give him a perverted thrill. A person like that would be obsessive and single minded. If he continues to be rejected by the woman he's after, his frustration level might rise to a level that triggers far more violent outbursts. *If I'm correct,* thought Rysakov, *there's a woman somewhere in Moscow who is in very grave danger. I wish I knew who.*

By the time he returned to his office, Rysakov still had not decided how to handle the case or what his next move would be. He sat at his desk and decided to go over all the evidence amassed to date to see if, in light of the Bourlin allegation, a course of action presented itself.

§ § § § § §

The return of Ivan and Mikhail from London was a time of great excitement in the Morozov house. They bought presents for each member of the household; warm, woolen headscarfs with Scottish tartan patterns and scented soaps for the women. Soft English leather belts with finely tooled buckles and a box of Virginian tobacco cigars for the men.

For Katya, the best present from London was the warm body beside her in bed and the greedy abandon with which they grabbed for each other when the celebrations finally ended late that night. Katya knew that her own lusty hunger would take more than one night to sate, and from the intensity of Misha's response, she was certain she would not to be disappointed.

For her, there were dresses of the latest design, fashionable bonnets, and a painting of a river scene with water lilies by a French artist, Claude Monet. Mikhail had seen it in a gallery in Paris where they stopped briefly on their return journey. The gallery owner, pleased to get rid of it, said few people want to buy these modern, impressionist paintings; they all wanted traditional scenes this year. Katya fell in love with the soft colors and the light that seemed to glow from inside the painting. She insisted Mikhail hang it in their bedroom.

With neither of Anna's grandmothers alive or in Russia, Pinna became a de facto babushka, a role that clearly thrilled her. Ivan maintained a gruff demeanor that fooled no one. When Anna waddled unsteadily toward him with her arms out, he melted. The day Anna mouthed her first words, which sounded a little like the beginning of *dedushka,* grandfather Ivan's face shone with pleasure. He couldn't stop smiling for days.

"Misha, Katya, come here," he called, "Annushka just spoke to me. The first word she ever said was to me!"

"Say it again, my darling," he coaxed, but Anna turned her face away.

Business boomed and Morozov & Son expanded its operations. Their social calendar was perpetually full. They also undertook charity work, supporting the Moscow Women's Education Society, which provided free education in typing, bookkeeping, and commercial practice to any woman unable to pay for her own tuition. It was rare to find a factory worker in Moscow or Saint Petersburg who could not read. Most could also write. What most could not afford were the fees for further tuition.

Life for most urban workers remained harsh. They had no security of employment, with more than one in five out of work at any time. Trade unions remained outlawed, forcing men and women to turn to radicals and revolutionaries. Without anyone noticing it, a feeling of alienation and frustration steadily spread ever wider in the cities as well as the country.

Easter

Following Katya's contretemps with Prince Kozlinski in front of the recital hall, Countess Anastasia Metchersky derived considerable enjoyment from discreetly noting Koslinski's black eye to acquaintances, and idly wondering how her "good friend" Madam Morozovna could have bruised her knuckles. Years ago, when she had been Koslinski's lover, she had reasonably thought, given her status, that the liaison would continue and indeed develop even though they were cousins. She never wholly forgave him for dumping her.

After the incident, Katya began to receive invitations to the Court and to join the countess and her friends at luncheons. Initially thrilled she and Mikhail were now mixing in the upper levels of society, Katya tempered her enthusiasm when asked in a conspiratorial whisper on several occasions if she had really hit Koslinski. Instinctively, she neither confirmed nor denied the incident, which added spice to the gossip.

One of the ironies of this turn of events, she noted, was that she saw more of the prince by attending these functions. He remained courteous, while letting her know of his continuing interest. Katya simply ignored him.

Eighteen months after the birth of Anna, Peter Mikhailovich Morozov was born. The son both father and grandfather had hoped for and who would carry on the family name had arrived.

§ § § § § §

Katya discovered in her first year in her new home that Easter was the most important event on the Russian calendar, more important than Christmas or New Year. This year, Katya decided, her expanded family would have the full, traditional Russian Easter, with all the trimmings.

Lent, after the Shrove festival, was the real beginning. Large, sweetly cured hams hung untouched in the pantry for months awaiting the magic day. During Lent, sunflower oil instead of animal fats was used for cooking. Fish dishes dominated the menu, although a side of venison was occasionally slipped in to relieve the monotony.

At the start of Holy Week, preparations for the climax of Easter, the Day of the Resurrection, became frenetic. A few days before Sunday of the Pussy Willows, known as Palm Sunday in London, Ivan arranged for bundles of pussy willows to be brought in from the country and arranged into sprays, tied with beautifully colored ribbons.

The hams were taken from the pantry to be baked in a crust of rye flour and water. On Easter Saturday, the cooks spent the day making *pashka,* the sweet Easter cheeses in the shape of a large dome. Into a large tub in the kitchen, they placed the curds, first drained of every trace of whey, and then pressed through a fine sieve. To this, the cook added beaten butter, whipped cream, sugar and vanilla before the hard work of mixing commenced. Katya insisted on taking her turn at the mixing pole while Pinna watched until it reached the desired consistency. Then came the *koulitch,* raised round cakes made of sweet dough, raisin, peel, and flavored with vanilla and cardamom. It was later iced and decorated with the words "Christ has risen." They baked several *rumbaba,* ten-inch high yeast cakes over which rum icing was poured. The delicious smells of all these preparations permeated the whole house.

The level of excitement rose throughout the household as the last hours of Lent approached.

In the dining room, tables could hold no more food—hams had been decorated, joints of glazed veal, baby sturgeon in aspic jelly, whole fillets of salmon lay on platters dressed with great care with caviar. Nearby sat dishes of pickled mushrooms and salted herring. In the center stood the great dome of *pashka,* the *koulitch,* and the *rumbabas.* Around the table had been placed bowls of brightly painted eggs, crimson, blue, gold, and green with "XB"—Christ is Risen—on them. Bottles of colored liqueurs and many types of vodka, including the fiery Ukraine pepper vodka, completed the vista.

The entire household would attend the midnight mass that night to mark the ascension of Christ on Easter Sunday. Ivan arranged carriages for everyone, including the servants.

As they all left, Katya closed the front door and climbed the stairs to Peter's room. He had caught a cold earlier in the week and had been coughing most of the day. At the Thursday service, Countess Metchersky invited them to her palace after the Redemption Day celebrations. Katya explained that unless Peter was well, she may not even be at the midnight service. She looked down at him in the cot glad she had decided to stay, even though Pinna insisted on remaining in Peter's room. He looked so defenseless, coughing and crying. She cooed softly and gently stroked his brow. Gradually, the coughing eased as he drifted into a light sleep.

"I'll be back soon, my darling," she whispered. "I'm just going to check on the food."

In the dining room, she stood in front of the huge table covered in food. She straightened several of the bowls of eggs. The *pashka* looked delicious. There was more than enough salmon, but only two hams had been laid out. She knew they had at least four. After so much fish over recent weeks, the ham would be descended upon ravenously. *I had better make sure cook has set them out ready to bring up, as there is no doubt they will be needed,* she said to herself. On her way down to the kitchen, she stopped at the base of the stairs that led up to Peter's room. Silence. She smiled. *If he can get a good night's sleep he'll be fine in the morning.* She started down the steps.

Not a sound in the usually noisy kitchen and scullery. The silence felt strange.

A wisp of cold air brushed against her legs. *That's odd,* she thought. *No door should be open.* She shivered slightly under her light house clothes. She stopped at the door to the kitchen. The long wooden food preparation table had several dishes of black and orange caviar and a salmon ready to be carved. The hams would be in the scullery, she knew.

As she stepped into the scullery, she saw a table in the center of the room, empty except for two large crystal jugs ready to be filled with cordial for the children. Food lay set out along the benches lining two sides of the room. She could not see the hams.

She took all of this in a glance and stepped into the room.

Her head exploded in a searing flash of white light. Then there was nothing. She was floating by her arms; her heels were too heavy. She stopped floating. A brittle sound, far away. Pressure on her breasts and then they were free. Cold between her legs. Difficult to breath. Intense pain on her nipples. The pain stirred her toward consciousness. She tried to move an arm. The pain in her head throbbed like a hammer at any attempt to move. Something was wrong. She fought to open her eyes.

Upstairs in Peter's room, Pinna sat half dozing when she heard a loud crash of breaking glass in the kitchen. Then a second crash of glass. She jerked upright. Only Katya was in the house. The kitchen staff were all at the church. Pinna jumped up, suddenly alert. No further sound, just silence in the big house. Katya has slipped and had an accident. Without a moment's hesitation, Pinna ran swiftly down the stairs.

Easter filled the church to capacity. Hundreds of candles flickered in the close atmosphere. The rich sounds of the choir reverberated around the worshippers. Each word of the liturgy rang clear and full of meaning as the choir, unaccompanied by any musical instruments, relayed the word of God to the congregation. And then came the climax with the exhilaration of the Resurrection.

The Easter service had a profound beauty and cadence to which the worshippers moved in harmony. It offered peace between men and hope, even to the poor. For them, the prospect of Christ's resurrection offered one brief moment of a dream for a better future.

"Katya! Come down, the bells will soon be ringing," called Mikhail happily as he opened the front door. He slipped away early from the church to be with his wife as Lent ended and the bells celebrating the Ascension began to toll rapturously across Moscow.

He heard the faint sounds of sobbing and a flash of alarm for his infant son shot through his mind.

"Katya!" he called more urgently, "where are you?"

"Mikhail Ivanovich, down here, down here!"

The urgency in Pinna's voice had him running down the steps two at a time. He raced past the kitchen door—it was empty—and into the scullery. Katya lay on the table cradled in Pinna's arms. On her exposed breasts, he could see angry red marks where the nipples had been twisted. Her skirt was bunched up around her hips. Pinna used her free arm to throw it over the exposed legs.

"What happened? Is she all right?" he asked, his voice urgent with concern.

"Oh, my poor darling," he exclaimed as he saw a trickle of blood running down Katya's right temple. His sudden relief at seeing her alive was soon tempered as he took in the state of her injuries. Clearly, she had been attacked. God, let it not be that brutal murderous monster. Rage surged into every muscle that anyone could hurt his beautiful Katya. It disappeared immediately when he heard her weak, scared voice.

"Misha, what happened? Peter…is Peter…" Katya tried to speak. She lifted her head but winced at the pain and lay back against Pinna. Tears rolled down her cheeks.

"He is sleeping peacefully," Pinna answered. "The coughing has stopped."

"Thank God," she said, turning her head into her maid, her breathing coming in deep sobs. She groaned; a low moan, a mixture of pain and terror. An involuntary shudder shook her as Mikhail touched her hand. Her eyes snapped wide open with fear until she saw him. As she slipped into unconsciousness, her hand dropped limp by her side.

Outside the Kremlin walls the bells in Red Square commenced their peal, signaling midnight and the end of Lent. Immediately, other churches throughout Moscow began their tolling in a rolling cacophony of sound, rising to the celebration's crescendo.

In the Morozov household, the din of the bells had an ominous edge.

"Khristos Voskryese—Christ has risen," Pinna said, repeating it three times.

Mikhail picked Katya up to carry her upstairs to bed. As Pinna eased herself off the table, he noticed that the knuckles of her right hand were raw. By the time he had settled Katya under the warmth of the doona, calls of "Khristos Voskryese" were echoing through the house as the worshippers returned eager to begin the feast after the fasting of Lent. The staff hurried to ensure the samovar was full and the food ready.

When they entered the scullery, they found Pinna seated on the table extracting shards of glass from her lacerated feet.

Within minutes, the whole household knew of the attack on the mistress. As soon as Ivan heard, he raced upstairs, ignoring the stream of friends invited to join the family in the celebration feast.

Pinna, unable to walk easily with her lacerated feet, was helped to a chair in the dining hall where, once her feet had been bandaged, they barraged her with questions. All she could say, she responded, was that she had heard a crash as the jugs were knocked onto the stone floor. No doubt by the mistress to alert me, she added.

"When I came down into the scullery I saw a man attacking the mistress," she said, not going into any of the detail.

"Because I had my soft felt shoes on he couldn't hear me as I ran to help her. When I got there, I hit him with my fist and tried to pull him away. I think I surprised him, because he jumped up and lashed out with his arm."

Her captive audience could see the red beginning of a bruise developing on her left cheek.

"Then he grabbed his coat and ran out the back entrance. He was dressed in black, and tall."

"Did you see his face?" asked one of the guests.

"No," Pinna replied.

"There is no sign of him," said one of the men who had just returned from securing the back door. "He will be long gone by now."

Having determined that Katya was not seriously injured, Ivan returned to the dining room.

"She is concussed," he said, "and will benefit from a night's rest. Her assailant has fled, so please join me in celebrating the end of Lent."

Early the following morning, as soon as the sun was up, Ivan sent a note to Maksim Rysakov.

Within the hour, Rysakov returned in the Morozov carriage.

"I'm sorry to break into your celebration of the Resurrection Day," Ivan said, "but I couldn't think of anyone else to call."

"I am in your debt, Ivan Victorovich. Never hesitate to call me," Rysakov said. "Now, please tell me what happened last night."

When Ivan relayed the essentials of the incident, the investigator asked, "Is Madam Morozov awake and well enough for me to talk to?"

Mikhail came down to report that Katya had just woken and while she still had a headache, she would be pleased to speak to the investigator once she had dressed. So Rysakov decided to interview Pinna first.

Katya had two overarching concerns when she woke that morning. First, that Peter was safe and well. She walked slowly into the nursery and saw the cold had left him. The smile that lit his face as he saw his mother pushed her worries aside. She kissed him gently and went quietly into the ablution room. Several minutes later, Pinna came in and spoke to her softly. She sighed, relieved. She had not been violated by the assailant.

Maksim Rysakov listened patiently, asking questions to clarify the sequence of events. He inspected the scullery while waiting for Katya to join them.

When they had finished, he sat silently for some time.

"Thank you, Madam Morozov, for being so patient with my questions," he said, "Are you well enough to help me a little longer?"

"Yes, I think so," Katya said.

"You said the assailant tore your clothing."

"Yes," Katya said, "he tore my blouse and undergarment."

"Do you remember anything from the time you walked into the scullery?" he asked.

"Only the feeling of floating, but my feet were very heavy. Then pain, intense pain. I think I would have slipped into unconsciousness but the bolt of pain stopped me."

"That may well have saved you from far worse injuries. I'm sure your assailant intended to do you serious harm," he said.

"Somehow, he must have known you would be in the house and expected you to be alone," he went on. "Do you normally wait at home for the guests to arrive for the end of Lent feast?"

"No, never. It's a tradition in my husband's house that the whole household attend the Resurrection service. I only stayed behind as my young son was ill and I couldn't bear to leave him even though Pinna said she would stay."

"Would anyone have known you had remained in the house?" he asked.

"Only our own household," Katya said.

Rysakov looked at Mikhail and Ivan. "With your permission I would like to try to reconstruct what happened."

They both nodded assent.

"Somehow the attacker finds out that there will be no one at home, except Madam Morozov. He times his arrival to coincide with the departure of the household to church and forces entry through the kitchen area.

"I suspect he intended to venture further into the house, possibly upstairs, but hears someone coming down to the kitchen. He hides inside the door of the scullery so he can retain the element of surprise. Instead, the person comes into the very room where he is hiding. He believes there is only one person in the house so does not need to find out who is entering. He grabs the opportunity and hits Madam Morozov on the head with a heavy, weighted object as soon as she enters.

"The man is tall and strong; he is dressed in black, in fine quality clothes," Rysakov added, filling in extra detail gleaned from earlier attacks. "As she falls, he catches her by the shoulders and drags her to the table where he lays her upon it."

"That would account for Katya's feeling of floating," said Mikhail.

Rysakov nodded.

"In the process, her arm rolls over and knocks one of the jugs onto the stone floor, smashing it loudly. As he straightens his victim, he knocks the other jug onto the stone. He is not worried by the noise, as he is sure there is no one else in the house.

"When Pinna hears the crash, she starts downstairs. Meanwhile, oblivious to Pinna's presence, he begins ripping Madam Morozov's clothes. Pinna's soft felt shoes made no sound as she ran across the stone floor, although as she trod on the broken glass from the jugs that should have alerted him. However, so intent is he on attacking his victim he's totally unaware of Pinna until she hits him."

"If I'd had a weapon he would be here today, on the floor," said Pinna.

No one in the room doubted the force with which Pinna could wield a rolling pin.

"Even though the force of her attack takes him by surprise, he retains sufficient presence of mind to immediately lash out at his assailant. He turns his head away from her face making it all but impossible in the heat of the moment to recognize him. Realizing there are now others in the house, how many he doesn't know, he abandons his victim, grabs the only piece of evidence that might identify him, his coat, and runs out the way he came in."

"He may have still been at the rear of the house when I came home," Mikhail said, an expression of cold fury on his face. "My God, if only I had been a little earlier."

The question on everyone's mind, why the attack on Katya, why her in particular, remained unanswered.

"How would this person know Peter was ill and that I was with him? He has only had the coughing for a few days, otherwise I would have been at the church. Then, today we were to have visited Countess Metchersky if Peter had recovered," Katya said to Rysakov as he took his leave.

It was only as he sat in the troika trotting leisurely through the crowded Holy Day streets that the pieces started to fall into place. That the man who had attacked Katya was his murderer, Rysakov had no doubt. Had her maid not intervened Katya, he felt sure, would have been murdered, and mutilated. The maid had hit him and judging from the look of her, hit hard. For the next week, his man would have heavy bruising. A disturbing idea took shape in his mind. Why did he pick on Katya Morozov? Could it be that she was the target of his unsatisfied lust? Had she rejected him publicly, humiliating him? A public humiliation could tip his obsession into outright hatred. Was he now intent on revenge? He would have to warn Ivan and Mikhail. He would also arrange for a police guard to be stationed at the house. This murderer won't stop. He punched his fist into the palm of his hand in angry frustration.

The troika came to a halt for a group of well-dressed men, women, and children, heavily rugged up against the bite in the air and talking animatedly. A young girl looked up at the troika with a solemn expression. A knowing smile ghosted across her lips. It seemed she had deduced his dilemma. For some reason, she reminded him of Irina Bourlin. What was it her mother had said? I have seen him with a grand duchess. It would be easy enough for a merchant's wife to confuse a duchess with a countess. If he could confirm his quarry moved in the same circles as Countess Metchersky, he would have his missing link. It was not proof, but it would be enough. A plan began to take shape in his mind. On the other hand, if he could find a connection between his man and the purchase of surgical instruments then he could approach the courts for a warrant to arrest.

In the week following, Rysakov could find no documented connection with the purchase of surgical knives even though the list of buyers had been significantly shortened by eliminations.

It was time to call in some favors from colleagues in the Okhrana, the largest, most successful and diligent secret police force in the world. He knew that not only did they have success infiltrating anarchist and terrorist groups, they also maintained detailed files on a huge number of citizens, including, unbeknown to most of them, all the members of the Court. It was the files on certain members of the Court that Maksim Rysakov wanted to access.

It cost him a bottle of good vodka but there was enough information in the files to provide him with several useful pressure points.

It took several days before his request for an interview with Prince Koslinski received a response. He agreed to meet the investigator briefly at eleven the following morning at the bank.

Rysakov arrived a few minutes early. This was the first time he had been into one of the famous merchant banks. He had to admit it was impressive. It exuded wealth and success, from the polished wood panels around the wall to what he imagined were fine works of art on the walls to the beautifully finished furniture.

At five minutes past eleven, a clerk ushered him into the prince's office. Vasily Koslinski remained seated as Rysakov came into the room. He silently motioned the investigator to sit in one of the leather upholstered chairs. He then leaned back behind his desk and waited.

"Thank you for agreeing to see me, sir, we do appreciate it," the plural noun established Rysakov was there on official police business and had the weight of the law enforcement service behind him.

"What is it you want, Senior Investigator Rysakov? Haven't we met before?"

"Yes, sir. Ivan Morozov introduced us at a Christmas service several years ago."

"Ah, yes. The Morozovs."

Rysakov needed to be careful. This man had many and powerful connections that he would not hesitate to use. Maksim had no wish to lose his career and let a suspect walk free.

"You may recall I am in charge of the investigation into the series of vicious mutilation murders of young women in Moscow."

"And what has that to do with me?" Koslinski asked.

"It would appear from our investigations that the person who committed these crimes has a set of surgical instruments. We are speaking to all people who may have such items."

"What makes you think I would own such implements?"

"Do you own a set of surgical knives, sir," Rysakov asked.

"Not that I recall."

"Are you a member of the Moscow Medical Anatomy Society, sir?"

"You seem to know that I am, along with a number of distinguished doctors and scientists."

"As part of your involvement with this society would you require a set of surgical knives?" Rysakov asked.

"From time to time, the society arranges for its members to participate in dissections of animals, but such participation is purely for scientific study and is of strictly limited access. Each member is expected to provide his own instruments."

"Have you participated in any of these events, sir?"

"Yes, so I must have a set of implements, Senior Investigator; it had slipped my mind," Koslinski replied.

"Do you know Madam Morozov, Prince Koslinski?" Rysakov knew he was getting into dangerous territory now.

"Of course, I know the family well."

"She was savagely attacked in her home on the eve of Resurrection Day."

Koslinski leaned forward and glared intently at Rysakov.

"What are you implying, Maksim Rysakov?"

A fleeting impression of a cobra about to strike flashed through Rysakov's mind. A knock on the door broke the spell, and Koslinski sat back in his chair.

"Enter," he said in a neutral tone and one of his managers came into the room. Rysakov wondered whether the man could smell the tension in the air.

"I am sorry to intrude, sir, but these bills of exchange must be signed this morning."

This had probably been arranged in advance, Rysakov thought, *in case I stayed too long.*

"Please show the investigator out when you leave, Dimitri," Koslinski said.

Rysakov stared at the banker as he signed the bills.

Rysakov now knew he had his man. Koslinski held the pen in his left hand, which had a dress ring on the middle finger.

However, it was only circumstantial evidence. Without hard proof linking Koslinski to any of the murders or the attack on Katya Morozov, the risk of precipitate accusations against such a person were too high. Instead, Rysakov decided on another course of action.

Two days later, he called at the home of Countess Metchersky. What he proposed doing needed to be handled with just the right amount of delicacy balanced by just sufficient threat. Unless he judged it correctly, it could backfire.

"So, you are a senior investigator with the police?" she said. "I have never spoken to a real policeman before. You must have some wonderful stories you can tell."

"I am afraid not, Countess. The work of criminal investigation is largely hard and boring work," he said.

"Ah, I am sure that is not always the case, Investigator. However, be that as it may, why have you come to see me? I do not recall being involved in any crimes unless listening to that horrible modern music by some young new composer last week qualifies, in which case I plead guilty."

"I understand you are an acquaintance of Katya Morozov," he said.

"Yes. That poor woman. To be attacked so violently and in her own home. The police service should make Moscow safer."

"I am in charge of the investigation into that attack. Do you remember reports of violent murders of a number of young women over the last several years? They were brutalized in the most horrible way."

"Yes, I do recall them. They were working-class women, weren't they?"

"Yes, Countess. We are satisfied that those murders and the attack on Madam Morozov are linked, that, in fact, they were committed by the same person." He paused.

"I cannot deny that I find this all totally fascinating, but why are you telling me?

"Why don't you simply arrest the brute?" she said looking shrewdly at him.

"Katya Morozov thinks highly of you, Countess, and I understand she confides in you. Incidentally, you will be pleased to know that her baby son has fully recovered from his coughing fits. I understand she told you she would be unable to meet you at the church service to celebrate Resurrection Day due to her son's illness and that she would remain home with him."

The countess nodded. "That is so."

Rysakov nodded, now certain he knew how Koslinski found out Katya Morozov would be alone.

"The other matter I wish to tell you is a matter of some delicacy," he saw he now had her full attention.

"We know who the mutilation killer is. We also believe that he is the same person who attacked Madam Morozov. However, he is well born and a person of some influence and connection. As you will appreciate this requires us to proceed with tact and caution. We are in the final stages of assembling our proof. We have a witness who saw him leaving one of the killings. We have an item from his clothing and there is some other evidence that I am not at liberty to disclose at this stage. We believe it is only a matter of time before we make an arrest. Oh, and he would recently have had abrasions on his right cheek. Madam Morozov's maid hit him to save her mistress." He paused to let all he had just said sink in.

"You are a person who is well connected and who can reassure other women that they need not fear to be alone in their homes for much longer. Consequently, I do not believe I need to relay this information to any other parties at this stage."

After a pause, he added, "Of course, there is always unintended damage when a member of a prominent family is arrested for such crimes, particularly if he is a male prominent at Court and in the commercial community. Innocent parties such as siblings and even cousins are unfortunately and, in my opinion, often unjustly tainted by the evil. I thought I would seek your opinion on the best way to handle such a situation."

When he finished, he looked her straight in the eye.

The countess was silent for several long minutes.

"Thank you for telling me this information, Investigator Rysakov. I shall give the matter some consideration," she said.

As he was leaving, she asked, "It was on the evening before Resurrection Day that Katya was attacked, was it not?"

"Yes, Countess, while she was at home with her ill son. The rest of the household was at church. It appears that the attacker knew she would be at home on her own."

§ § § § §

The door slammed behind him as Mikhail walked into the room. Anna jumped up from her toys and ran to meet her father, arms outstretched.

"Ah, my little rabbit," he said, whisking her up off the floor and giving her a hug.

"The amount of strike action and unrest is really getting out of hand," he said to Katy as he gave Anna a hug. "It won't be long before we'll need guards to get to the factory. I passed a couple of factories on the way home with hundreds of workers demonstrating outside, shouting demands. They were throwing rocks to smash the windows."

Katya's bruises had healed and the lump on her head almost disappeared. Outside the front door, a uniformed policeman stood guard as Rysakov had promised.

"I heard rumors today that one of the banks had collapsed. No one seemed to have much detail but the timing couldn't be worse, if it's true. Right now, a bank failure would really affect confidence," Mikhail said as Katya took Anna.

The front door slammed again and Ivan's voice called out.

"Have you heard, the Moscow Commerce Bank has failed. As soon as I heard the rumor I went straight around to check if it were true. I thought *I* had good intelligence, but by the time I arrived a crowd had already formed. It seems they discovered a shortfall in funds last week. The manager expected the chairman to come in and sort the matter out. In the meantime, he continued paying withdrawals hoping desperately for a solution. As soon as the funds dried up the bank had no choice but to close its doors.

"I'd forgotten we had money on deposit with them until I heard the rumors," Ivan said. "It's been there since the time of the cotton shipments. Damn, we should have remembered and withdrawn it the minute we heard the chairman hadn't turned up," he said, shaking his head in annoyance.

"Who is the chairman?" Katya asked.

"Vasily Koslinski," Mikhail answered.

§ § § § §

Some days before the bank closure, Rysakov sat in his office wondering if he had made the right move. The hand had been played. All he could do was wait.

A constable came in as he sat staring into space.

"Vasily Koslinski has disappeared, sir. No one knows where he's gone."

The surveillance team reported no sighting of the target for twenty-four hours. Rysakov immediately went to Koslinski's home and demanded to know the Prince's whereabouts. The startled butler told him, "His highness has gone to visit his estates. He won't be back for several weeks."

Rysakov was certain Koslinski would not appear at any of his family estates. *If it were me,* he thought, *I would get as far away from Moscow as possible. Probably overseas.*

When he spoke to the countess, he had hoped, somewhat unrealistically, he now had to admit, that the ranks of the aristocrats would decide a man so depraved and dangerous should be sacrificed for the common good. *There's the fallacy in that argument,* he thought, *none of them really care about the common good. So disappearance is the next best solution. At least the young women of Moscow will no longer be prey to the beast.* Not an ideal outcome, but a practical result.

Once he heard about the bank failure, Rysakov immediately surmised Koslinski must have stolen money from the bank some time before his disappearance, secreting the funds where they could not be found. As a banker, he would know how.

With a sigh, Rysakov closed the file and started to sign the case closed when an idea occurred to him. If Koslinski's funds ran low in years to come, he may feel the furor had subsided sufficiently to reappear, particularly if he found out the evidence linking him to the murders was largely circumstantial. Rysakov wrote a new note and placed it on the top of the file. He resolved to make a copy and send it to his colleague in the Okhrana. The heading read, "Wanted in connection with fraud and the misappropriation of substantial funds from the Moscow Commerce Bank." If the evidence on the killings was slim, the evidence on the theft was not.

The failure of the Moscow Commerce Bank sent reverberations throughout the Moscow business community. To Ivan, and many other businessmen in Moscow, it provided yet another example of the corruption at the core of the ruling class. While he had never really liked Koslinski, Ivan still found it hard to accept that the prince had absconded with the bulk of the bank's liquid assets. It now seemed he had planned his escape carefully.

"Vladimir told me today it seems Koslinski transferred funds over a period of several weeks to banks in Moscow and Petersburg who had foreign counterparts. The Russian banks were then instructed to get confirmed letters of credit issued overseas, which Koslinski arranged to draw against by telegraph," he said to Mikhail as they sat in the chairman's office of the new factory. "Once the letter of credit had been drawn and the funds taken by Koslinski's agent, they disappeared."

"Maybe the agent did also," Mikhail said with a smile.

"If some of the money wasn't ours, one could even laugh about it," said Ivan.

Once it became clear that Koslinski had indeed left Moscow, Rysakov relieved the police guard from outside the Morozov home. He felt some guilt that his stratagem had worked. He had made his city safe but the "Monster of Moscow" would now visit his venom on other, unsuspecting, people. Rysakov had no illusions. Sex offenders were serial recidivists. Coming so close to being caught and unmasked would not change the beast's behavior. It would simply make him more careful.

Harbin

It was ten o'clock in the morning when Yusuf Yudin knocked on the door of the commissariat in Port Arthur. The trip down on the newly opened South China Railway had been a far more agreeable way to travel than by carriage, particularly in the bitter cold of the winter months. He wondered how long the business provisioning the large military garrison defending Port Arthur would last. The most profitable items were two lines of vodka, Double Eagle, a cheap product distilled in Harbin for the enlisted men and the premium Smirnoff, imported all the way from Moscow for the officers. The talk in the market about the Japanese worried him. *It would be a pity to lose such easy money,* he thought.

Yusuf knocked on the door again, harder and longer.

He stepped back from the veranda of the building and looked out over the battlements of the fort to the bay where the Russian Pacific Fleet lay at anchor. It looked impressive. Seven battleships, including the flagship *Petropavlovsk,* as well as destroyers and support vessels lay quietly at anchor. All had their lights on, brightly illuminating their outline. Small plumes of smoke wafted out of the funnels from turbines deep in the hulls, turning over to generate electricity. Apart from the smoke, he could see no signs of activity. It was too cold to be on deck.

The door opened and Yusuf entered quickly.

When he left some hours later, the warm glow of more than a few glasses of good vodka formed an effective barrier against the damp penetrating cold. A few soldiers wandered quickly across the parade

167

ground. On the impressively thick defenses, he could see a small number patrolling, hunched over to keep warm. An array of huge naval guns sat on rails pointing out to sea. A light dusting of snow, undisturbed by human hand, softened the hard angles of steel and gunmetal. Not one gun was manned. But then, with the Fleet at anchor protecting this Russian possession deep in China, what danger could there possibly be?

As the clock struck midnight, Yusuf lay sound asleep in his hotel. One minute later, a series of tremendous explosions echoed through the town. By the time he woke and got to the window, more explosions rocked the night. From the second story of the hotel, he overlooked the whole harbor. What he saw was spectacular. Flames leapt from the warships. The whole bay was bathed in orange. Then, in the fire-lit gloom seaward of the remains of the fleet, he saw the disappearing wake of two destroyers speeding out to sea.

Yusuf assumed at once that the attack had been by the Japanese. The markets had speculated for some time war was imminent. Now it had begun. He dressed immediately and roused the manager. With his assistance, they got the telegraph office to open and he sent an urgent message to Ivan with instructions it be delivered regardless of the time of day or night, telling him the Russian Pacific Fleet had been destroyed at anchor.

For Yusuf, war was an opportunity. Whatever the goods, in war greater quantities are needed, and fast; price is a secondary consideration. War also carried great danger and risk, both physical and business. He sent a second telegram, this time to Liu Ping-nan.

The initial success of the Japanese did not surprise Yusuf. The Russians had not taken even the most basic precautions against attack. Not a single gun in the fleet had been manned or loaded. The shore batteries remained immobile, coated in heavy grease against the winter storms. He had heard that not only did Japan have a large, modern navy, it also had an army of nearly a million men armed with the latest repeating rifles and mobile artillery. And both were battle hardened from the recent successful war against China. None of this boded well for the Russians, or Tiger Moon.

Within months, the Japanese Army had cut the rail line and captured Port Arthur. It was the first war to be reported, as it occurred, by the world's press. It created enormous interest throughout the

West. In London, Bertie Somerston, reading daily accounts of the war, made a note to ask Ivan about the conflict when he next returned to London.

In Harbin, huge numbers of soldiers had to be fed, clothed, and entertained. Tiger Moon took advantage of every opportunity, completely unaware of and unaffected by the failure of the Moscow Commerce Bank.

During this period, Yusuf heard stories of a Russian with large sums of money who was rumored to have purchased one of the largest and more lavish brothels in Harbin. Among the European journalists covering the war, Harbin was known as the "brothel of the world," a place where everything and anything was procurable. This mysterious Russian had a reputation for being particularly obliging in catering to all tastes, for a price. Curious, Yusuf made discreet inquiries. However, when he heard rumors through the Chinese network that the man also had dealings with the Japanese, his enthusiasm waned. If true, the Russian walked a narrow and dangerous path, one Yusuf did not wish to follow.

In his last article before sailing for Hong Kong, the war correspondent for *The Times* wrote: "The war is now officially at an end, though the fighting stopped some time ago. A peace agreement is now settled between the two sides. While they are to be commended for ending this brutal conflict it is sobering to note that by the time both sides agreed to cease hostilities casualties totaled nearly half a million lives.

"This war should give pause to those politicians who clamor for more aggressive policies in the Orient. Beware! For the first time, a major European power has suffered an ignominious defeat by a modern Oriental force."

Moscow

The level of unrest throughout Russia increased significantly that winter. By the time the Japanese attacked Port Arthur, over 500,000 workers had taken an active part in a strike. The urban workforce was no longer a disparate mass of recently arrived villagers. No longer were they novices in direct action or helplessly disorganized. For the first time in Russia's history, a very real and present threat confronted the established order. Meanwhile, at the center of power, belief in the absolute power of the tsar remained as unshaken as ever.

In the months following her attack, Katya's bruises healed, leaving no physical evidence of the assault. Even her anxiety subsided a little once Rysakov assured them the assailant had left Moscow for good. He reinforced this news by adding he had strong evidence identifying the man and if he ever showed his face in Moscow again, he would immediately be arrested.

"If you know who this monster is why will you not tell us his name?" Mikhail asked Rysakov when he delivered this news.

"We do not want publication of his name to cause him to go to ground. I want to be able to know if he surfaces again so we can grab him immediately," Rysakov replied. None of the Morozovs suspected Koslinski. To them, he was simply an embezzler. When his colleague, Gregori Yukovsky, asked why he had not told the family the name of the killer he said, "I don't have enough hard evidence to get a prince with his connections convicted, so what's the point? If it became publicly known, I'd have been in trouble with the inspector general without adequate proof. Anyway, so long as Koslinski is no longer a threat to the people of Moscow, I've done the best I can. If we'd charged him relying on circumstantial evidence, there's a good chance he'd have got off. At least now he's uncertain as to the strength of our case. Russia is no longer safe for him."

Yukovsky looked at him, eyebrows raised. Both knew the killer was out there somewhere and very likely to strike again.

In daylight hours with the normal activity of the house, Katya soon became her usual cheerful self. When night fell and all lay dark and quiet, the demons from that Easter sometimes intruded into her dreams. The details varied but each time she had the same feeling of helplessness. She knew what was about to happen but was powerless to stop it. She often woke screaming. On some nights, in a semi-conscious state, she beat at Mikhail with her fists as he tried to calm her and wake her properly.

While the dreams became less frequent as weeks passed, something niggled at her. Somewhere, deep in her mind, she felt she should know her attacker. She tried hard to conjure up a face, without success. *Perhaps,* she thought, *my mind won't let me see him.* The ephemeral wisp eluded her grasp, hovering just out of reach.

On the streets, strikes and skirmishes with the police turned increasingly ugly. As Rysakov and his fellow officers were only too well aware, the radicals had action cells dedicated to the overthrow of the government by violence. The most dangerous used bombs to assassinate their targets. Killing innocent bystanders was just collateral damage. Pressure in the cooker now reached boiling point.

"If we keep getting more bad news from the Far East I think there's a real chance the worker groups'll come out on the street," Yukovsky said as they sat in their small office at police headquarters. "If the army and navy can't beat the 'yellow monkeys' of Asia then what hope have they of controlling the Moscow mob?"

"The intelligence is not encouraging," agreed Rysakov.

§ § § § §

By early January in the fifth year of the new century, 25,000 workers went on strike in Saint Petersburg. Persistent rumors of assassination lists kept the police on edge. That night, workers planning a peaceful march to present a petition to the tsar slept fitfully, uncertain what the next day would bring. Word had spread among them that large numbers of soldiers had been brought into the capital.

Unrest on this scale had never happened before and the governor of the city, deeply worried, assembled 12,000 cavalry and infantry. Soldiers' bivouacs could be seen laid out in the streets and squares. Campfires burned brightly in the clear night. The snorting of cavalry horses carried on the freezing air. Overhead, a huge, blood-red moon rose over the horizon, beaming a cold unnatural light into the brittle night.

The next morning, a brilliant clear day dawned in the capital with a temperature of five degrees below freezing. It was one of those rare winter days when no wind blew.

Workers began marching along the great avenues that converge on the Winter Palace. Men and women, some with children, all dressed in their best clothes, gathered together. No weapons were carried. No revolutionary symbols were displayed. Instead, they carried icons and portraits of Nicholas and the tsarina. It was Sunday, so they sang hymns and marched in peaceful, orderly columns.

As they approached the palace, they found themselves confronted by a company of guards. Pressed by numbers behind, they moved slowly forward, unable to obey the guards' commands to stop. Unnerved, the commander gave the order to fire. The soldiers could not miss. The densely packed marchers had no protection or place to hide. An old man and child fell first, dead.

By the end of the day, 200 lay dead with 800 wounded. That day destroyed forever the people's belief in the tsar, their "Little Father."

Within weeks, the wildfire of revolution set Moscow ablaze. Grand Duke Aleksandrovich, governor general of Moscow, was murdered, a nitroglycerin bomb tearing him into bloodied pieces. In a series of coordinated actions, the tsar's troops and cavalry violently suppressed the uprising and the momentum of revolution stalled.

Rysakov noticed no slowing down in the level of activity. Informants, no longer as bountiful a source, still sent in some information. However, with such fluid levels of unrest, he found it difficult to follow up all leads effectively. He also sensed a distinct difference to previous strikes. This time it was more spontaneous and more widely supported than ever before. The other difference, and this had importance for him as a policeman—informants reported a number of factory owners and wealthy businessmen as assassination targets.

Ivan Morozov looked out the carriage window as his driver steered the horses through the streets at an easy trot. Small knots of men and women on corners and in front of taverns looked up as the carriage passed. The looks of idlers had rarely been friendly, now they had undisguised hostility on their faces. *Perhaps it's my imagination,* he thought, *but there seem to be more people than ever standing around, waiting.* By the time he arrived at his office, the feeling of unease had intensified. These workers look like informal brigades, as if they're awaiting the arrival of a general to announce the start of war. *Don't be ridiculous,* he told himself.

"Did you see the number of people standing around?" Ivan asked Mikhail as he strode into his son's office. "I think we're in for some serious trouble."

"We're still repairing the damage at the Baranov plant," Mikhail said. "I hope we get at least that amount of time."

"If there's any more strife at that plant, close it down and install the new British wool-knitting machines. Baranov's old equipment breaks down too often anyway," Ivan said. "Any word on the Harbin shipment?"

"No. It's still chaotic on the railway. Last I heard, the minister had ordered commercial freight left on sidings while food supplies were rushed through to the main cities. They assured me soldiers would guard the sidings until things return to normal. They weren't very convincing, so I think we should be prepared for losses."

"Damned aristos, why didn't the tsar at least receive the petition, then none of this would have happened," said Ivan.

Outside the air felt charged with electricity. All around the city, people waited, anticipating something momentous about to happen.

Gregori Yukovsky burst noisily into the office at police HQ.

"I just heard," he said breathlessly to Rysakov who signed a report and added it to the pile on the desk. "Men on one of the rail lines out of Moscow have gone on strike. It's as though this is the signal everyone's been waiting for. Printers in the city immediately joined them."

Rysakov looked up. "This might be the beginning," he said. "If so, we're in for some serious trouble, Gregori."

Like a vast line of falling dominoes, the strike spread across the nation in the time it took a train to reach the next town. No general led them, but within a week two million workers were on strike across the breadth and width of the empire from Saint Petersburg to Harbin. The momentum was now unstoppable. And this time, the workers armed themselves with guns and sabers.

"This could be the most effective general strike in history," Rysakov said to Yukovsky as reports filtered in showing the astonishing extent of the action. Factory workers, servants, postal workers, janitors, droshky drivers, doctors, lawyers, school teachers, and even the entire corps de ballet of the great Mariinsky Theatre joined the strike. Streetlights went out as the electricity generating plants went down, no newspapers hit the streets, no tramcars operated, and soon food and fuel began to grow scarce.

Katya made certain the children remained inside the house. All the doors were locked and the windows shuttered. Some of the servants disappeared. Others reported a dangerous, expectant air about the city. At times, they said, it was unnaturally quiet with few people on the street. Then, around a corner, a large crowd would be arguing what action they should next take.

When the momentous announcement was made by the tsar's government, Mikhail and Ivan were at home with the family. Their factories sat idle, closed by the strike.

"This is wonderful. For the first time we have an assembly with real power, and freedom of speech and association," said Mikhail when news spread. "We'll have an elected duma, a parliament, that'll approve all laws."

"Those fools in Petersburg must be really scared," Ivan said. "It's about time."

Within a week, workers came back to the factories. As Ivan observed, "They still have to earn money to live on."

The missing servants miraculously reappeared in Katya's household. By common consent, no mention was made of their absence. Almost without missing a beat, the business of running the household resumed. Outside, however, real danger still lurked.

At police HQ, Rysakov and Yukovsky sat at their desks. Both had dark circles under their eyes; they felt exhausted.

"Most of the factories have reopened, I hear," said Yukovsky. "The city looked almost back to normal when I came in today."

Rysakov nodded agreement. "But I fear the trouble is not yet over. The Black Hundreds are out in force." He shook his head in disgust.

"Damn!" said Yukovsky. "Those bigoted bastards are more brutal than all the strikers. Why does the government allow them to operate with impunity?"

"There've already been reports of four deaths and dozens of beatings. Jews in particular are being targeted. Convenient scapegoats. But no one seems to be immune. My theory is that the tsar lets them go about their business to distract workers from thinking about government's policies. And it'll work. They'll worry less about strikes and more about staying in one piece," said Rysakov.

"Hell, we'll get blamed for all the mayhem, but if we arrest any of the Hundreds we're lucky to get a conviction. No evidence ever seems to stand up. Witnesses are too scared to appear in court," said Yukovsky. "It's going to be dangerous to be on the street."

Not long after the proclamation, on a cold and windy day, a large, untidy man dressed in a military-style greatcoat marched into the Morozov factory administrative area and shook the sleet from his shoulders.

"Where are the Jews?" he demanded coarsely. "We know you have Jews here. We're going to rid this factory of the scourge. Once they are gone there will be no more strikes. Get Morozov down here," he called out rudely.

By the time he finished his tirade he had been joined by half a dozen men all armed with clubs. They stood in a belligerent semicircle behind their leader, glaring defiantly. At the back of the office, one of the clerks scurried out to get the chairman.

Ivan entered the office through the back door. The clerk followed closely. Without pausing, Ivan walked unhurriedly through the desks toward the intruder, his eyes fixed unwaveringly on the man's face. The level of noise dropped to a whisper as his staff watched, fascinated. No one who knew him would have countenanced such a direct confrontation with Ivan Morozov.

Ivan stopped inches away from the Black Hundreds squad leader and stared unflinchingly into his eyes.

"Who are you?" he asked quietly. "You march into my factory uninvited and *demand* to see me!"—his voice now booming—"Who do you think you are?"

The squad leader hesitated, momentarily taken aback. "You have Jews here and other trouble makers. We're going to rid you of them."

"I only employ good Russians and only *I* make the decision to dispense with my employees," Ivan said with steely authority. "I do not need help from you or anyone else."

The squad leader looked at Ivan, standing quite alone in front of him. He had no doubt that he and his men could control the room of clerks, but this tall man radiated power and authority. He was used to being obeyed. The squad leader, who had been a sergeant in the army before disorderly conduct got him discharged, stared back at Ivan, deciding his next move.

A door closed and the squad leader spun around. *Now we are seven against two,* he thought, *but neither of them shows any fear. Have we walked into a trap?* He began to feel uneasy.

Mikhail walked into the room, unconcerned. He stopped a meter behind the armed men.

"These gentlemen are leaving," Ivan said, retaining the initiative.

Without another word, the Black Hundreds squad turned and followed their leader out of the factory.

"I had twenty men armed with cudgels outside, just in case," Mikhail said.

"Those types are all cowards," Ivan said. "They rely on intimidation and superior numbers. But you better warn our people and make sure our own guards are very visible as people leave at the end of the shift."

The next morning, reports came in to Ivan that the Black Hundreds had been seen in the vicinity of the factory, but the workers, many of whom had participated in the strike, stayed in large groups until well away from the location. Only a few were physically attacked and none seriously. The main perpetrator in the beatings was the thuggish leader whom they reported took great delight in the attacks. This Igor Donstoy, Ivan discovered, was well known as a bigot with a pathological hatred of Jews and anyone else who did not share his extreme views.

The most direct route from their home to the new Morozov & Son factory went through the edge of the city skirting Red Square. Each day they made the journey by carriage. Now, after the trouble with the Hundreds, a second carriage followed each way. It contained armed guards.

Rysakov took no solace in being right as attacks by the Black Hundreds increased. Worker groups, however, were now better prepared, armed with weapons smuggled in from Europe and the United States and the clashes became increasingly bloody. Rysakov, Yukovsky, and their colleagues could do little to prevent the development of urban warfare. Before long, even newspapers called on the tsar to take action to protect ordinary citizens. The government immediately used this as an excuse to move against the dissidents. In December, they arrested 300 workers in the Imperial capital. This action galvanized leaders of the Moscow Soviet.

They called a meeting immediately. Even on such short notice nearly half the delegates turned up. Anton Pushkin could barely control his excitement. Ever since his rejection by the University in Saint Petersburg, he had become increasingly involved in the revolutionary movement. He had easily beaten most of the other candidates in the entry exam, but money and position gave his place to a young man from a prominent family for whom university was a pleasant diversion. Pass or fail, it would have no impact on his future. Pushkin, on the other hand, knew he would make his mother and godfather, Uncle Vanya, proud. He had the ability. The injustice still rankled. Socialists and Marxists, who made the core of the Moscow Soviet's leadership, encouraged his bitterness, and he soon became a trusted organizer.

At the meeting, everyone was talking. The noise did not abate until a small wiry man with intense eyes stood and asked for quiet.

"It is time to take a vote," he said. By common consent, they all recognized him as chairman of most meetings through sheer power of personality.

"Comrades, I think you all agree, we cannot stand still when the government has taken such repressive action against our friends in the capital," he said. There was a rumble of assent.

"What we must do is make it very plain that we insist on the right to meet freely without fear of reprisals. Our committee recommends a general strike be called."

Heads nodded as calls of agreement rang out.

"What if they send troops against us?" said a voice from the floor.

"This time," the small intense man said, "we have guns. Fire will be met with fire, violence with violence."

Pushkin's adrenalin soared.

Once word of the strike spread, Mikhail and Ivan both agreed they must still go into the factory each day, notwithstanding that it may entail some risk. Even during a strike, there should be enough staff they could rely upon to limit vandalism at the plant.

With the problems caused by the first general strike still fresh in her mind, Katya immediately arranged for double the normal purchases of food for the household in the hope that this might encourage most of the staff to remain in the relative safety of the house. She was not alone. Everyone rushed to stock up. Millions of gold rubles were withdrawn from the banks, so much so that if the run on the banks continued the first closures would take place within days.

Maksim Rysakov was a realist. Both he and Yukovsky agreed they would make a token appearance at the office, but if any serious disturbance took place they would be powerless to stop it. In fact, they would not even try. Rysakov just hoped the strike would be just that, a show of worker power to wrest more concessions from the government and the mill owners. He hoped it would not be used as a cover by extremists to carry out assassinations.

On the first day of the strike, the Morozovs left home early and now stood in Ivan's office looking out over the factory grounds. They had done all they could; the rest was up to fate.

As the noonday whistle screeched its piercing signal all over Moscow, nearly 400,000 workers downed tools and poured out of the factories onto the streets. Large groups of men and women congregated on corners, in parks, and in the taverns. The leaders of the Moscow Soviet were stunned by the success. Now they had to move quickly to control it unless through inaction it again lost momentum.

As fast as it could be organized, they called a mass meeting to pass resolutions supporting the demands. Expecting a large turnout, the meeting was held at the popular Aquarium Theatre, a place known to most of those on strike.

Pushkin arrived early and made sure he had a seat close to the stage. Before long, several thousand had crammed into the venue. The deputies and key leaders sat or stood on the stage. The air was charged with expectation. As the theater filled, a small group moved down the aisles passing out fistfuls of handbills. They had been printed by the Bolshevik combat detachment, but many thought the single sheet was the official statement from the council. They read it avidly:

"Act in small groups. Put one or two marksmen against a hundred Cossacks. Let our fortresses be the courtyards. Make sure it is easy to fire and withdraw."

The instructions struck a chord with the strikers.

As soon as it seemed no more could squeeze into the hall, the small wiry man with intense eyes took command of the meeting. Demands for participation in the political process and the right to freedom of association were noisily agreed to. But it was the handbills and the recent experience of many in the theater of the harsh suppression of strikers meted out by the tsar's soldiers that really occupied people's minds.

Without consciously intending to, Pushkin jumped to his feet and yelled above the din to the leaders elevated in front of him.

"If they send troops against us, we must put up barricades. We cannot just stand in the street and be shot like Bloody Sunday."

He turned to the crowd behind him. The noise abated slightly as people asked, "What did he say?"

"Put up barricades. Protect yourselves from the troops," he yelled.

At that moment the doors burst open and armed troops rushed into the theater. The commander called out, "The building is surrounded. You cannot escape."

Scuffles broke out immediately as outraged strikers grappled with the soldiers. The leaders rapidly dispersed, one of them grabbing Pushkin by the arm.

"Come on or you'll be arrested."

As he followed his rescuer through a side door, a shot rang out and he heard the bullet *thwang* into the wood above his head.

The armed uprising had begun.

§ § § § §

The next day, Mikhail left well before dawn with Vanya driving the carriage as always. There was little more he could do at the factory. He just hoped the presence of a Morozov in the building might help inhibit the more senseless damage.

Dr. Sergei Sokoloff heard shots had been exchanged at the Aquarium and came to the hospital prepared for a long day, most likely to sleep in his office until the strike ended. He shook his head sadly. There would be more widows before the strike ended and more wounds than his staff could adequately treat. *Perhaps the worst of the action would be in another sector,* he thought. If it was concentrated around Presnia district, he would be very busy. As he walked through the wards to the surgical areas, he reflected that, inadequate though the facilities were for any large emergency, they would have negligible capacity without the generous support the hospital received from the wealthy merchant families, particularly the Morozovs.

As the weak light of dawn filtered through leaden clouds, large groups of angry men and women began throwing up barricades. They made them wherever a group assembled, cutting many of the city's main arteries in multiple locations. There was no plan, no organization, no directives. Carts, desks from nearby offices, tables, chairs, boxes from stores, whatever was moveable, got added to the pile. The defenders of each barricade called out to each other whenever they could see another barricade at the next bend in the street or on a corner.

"Victory or death!"

"Down with the tsarist regime!"

"Defend our rights!"

By noon all of the major arterial roads to the center of Moscow were cut. The Kremlin and the center of government were isolated. Government troops in barracks near the Kremlin soon realized they were heavily outnumbered and stayed where they were. Even though barricades had been erected on roads leading into Red Square, no attempt was made to assault the troop positions there. Even the most fanatical revolutionary knew that would be suicidal. A stalemate developed.

The sergeant snapped to attention in front of the desk.

"Well, sergeant?" prompted General Dubasov, the new governor of Moscow.

"When the snow stopped falling, sir, people who had been watching the building of the barricades, slowly, and with some trepidation, came out from behind their curtains, offering cups of hot tea and food to the strikers. None stayed long though. I suspect they were fearful troops may appear at any moment to break down the barricades."

"And did this happen only in one or two locations?" the general asked.

"No, sir, from all the reports that are in, it appeared to be widespread. The strikers took it as a gesture of support, and the reports say it seemed to bolster their spirit."

After a pause, as he digested this information, General Dubasov said, "Thank you sergeant. Please keep me informed of any new activity at the barricades."

"Sir."

This report was the one thing that genuinely scared the governor of Moscow. Dubasov knew that if the strikers won over the people of the city all prospect of reestablishing order would be lost.

"We must take action immediately. The rabble must not be allowed to gain the upper hand. Call the adjutant," he said to his aide de camp. He knew what he must do. He *would* regain the initiative. Radical action was required.

Once the adjutant sat in front of him, he gave his orders. When he had finished the adjutant's face lost its color. He remained seated, thinking he had misheard the orders.

"Well," said Dubasov, "you heard my orders. Don't sit there—get on with it."

"Yes, sir," said the adjutant. This had never happened in Moscow before.

Now that the orders had been given, General Dubasov felt relieved. *This will show Petersburg the true gravity of the situation. Then I'll get my reinforcements.* He smiled.

Anton Pushkin glanced once again at the back of the girl. Although she was dressed in peasant clothes, he knew she lived in the city. He had seen her before at meetings. *She is very pretty,* he thought, *even with the red and blue scarf over her head. How wonderful to be defending the same barricade together.* Even her name, which he had only discovered that morning, added an exotic touch to the day.

Margarita Ologov sensed someone watching her and turned around. As she straightened her back, she stretched, pulling her shoulders back knowing this would push her breasts tight against the bodice. Ah, it was Anton. She looked directly into his eyes and smiled. His face lit up with a look of pure pleasure. She watched as his gaze slid down over her bosom, then dropped her eyes demurely. She had noticed him at that first meeting over a month ago. She knew he was strongly attracted to her. He was good looking, she had to admit. But his aura of excitement made him stand out from the other young men. When he stood up at the Aquarium Theatre and called for the building of barricades, she had felt a thrill surge through her body and her face flush with excitement. She made sure she was at the same barricade as Anton that morning.

Mikhail Morozov finished his rounds with the factory manager. All the doors into the buildings were secure. The gates from the street had their chains secured. Although some of their workers wanted to continue working he had concluded they were insufficient to run the factory safely. The entire establishment would be shut down until the strike was over. Once it had been agreed, Ivan, the manager, and a team of guards decided to remain at the factory overnight. As there was nothing further he could do, Mikhail decided to leave for home. It would be easier to go around the barricades in daylight.

He called Vanya to harness the horses. As the carriage left the factory, the gates clanged shut behind them.

Earlier in the day, Rysakov had received reports that barricades were being erected all over the city. In that case, there was nothing they could do. Now it was a matter for troops, unless the government granted the strikers' demands, which he cynically thought most unlikely. Yukovsky declared he was off for home, and they left together.

Rysakov walked quickly, hoping to keep well clear of the strikers and any trouble. As he rounded the corner, half way down the street, he saw a large group of men and women. They seemed to be busy carrying items of furniture into the middle of the road where a large pile had already taken shape. He stopped to watch, fascinated, until he realized what they were doing.

"God, if they are building them here, there must be dozens of them," he said to himself.

There are going to be some cracked heads over this. He had no doubt that the strikers would not have built barricades on this scale unless they were armed.

"So, Moscow is in for a bloody battle," he said to the empty space in front of him. "I had better let Sergei know he is going to be busy."

Having made that decision, he turned to go. As he did he saw a tall young man who seemed to be in charge stand on the top of the barricade and stare after him. He had the devil-may-care stance of a young Cossack even from that distance. Rysakov turned in the opposite direction and walked fast toward Sergei Sokoloff's hospital.

Pushkin saw the slightly overweight man turn the corner and stop dead, looking with amazement at their work. He watched with satisfaction as the man hesitated then turned on his heel and headed off across the intersection.

By late morning they had finished. To add more would serve no purpose and Anton called a halt. Now that the activity had stopped an eerie silence settled over them. The defenders looked uneasily at one another.

"By heaven, I'm hungry," one of the strikers said. "Why didn't we bring the horses with that cart? I could eat one."

Laughter rippled along the barricade and the tension eased. They began to break into small groups sharing what food they had. Anton walked across to where Margarita sat. Even though he could see she had brought some bread and pickles, he said, "I hope you won't be hungry because I have plenty to share."

They chatted amiably until Margarita asked, "What will we do if the soldiers come?"

"We have rifles and pistols," Anton replied. "If they shoot, we'll defend ourselves."

He pulled out the pistol he had been given and showed her. He had six bullets. There were two other pistols and five rifles. Some had more ammunition but no one had more than eight rounds. Enthusiasm and confidence, on the other hand, they had in abundance. So far, they had not been confronted by well-armed professional soldiers. At that moment, the barricade stood unchallenged. They remained in total control of the street. They had prevailed.

The day dragged slowly into afternoon. The steady snowfalls stopped, to be replaced by occasional light flurries. Messengers came and went, bringing news and occasional instructions that often contradicted the earlier information. Mostly, the defenders stomped their feet against the cold, talked quietly, and waited.

"I can hear horses," the lookout called down from on top of an overturned cart.

All conversation stopped as they looked toward Anton.

"How many?" someone asked.

"Only two or three."

"Maybe they are scouts."

"Are they coming this way?" Anton asked.

"Sounds like it. They are at the end of the street, around the bend," the lookout answered.

"Everyone take cover and get a good firing position," Anton said because it was the only order he could think of. His heart started to pound faster now that it had begun. The first niggling of fear formed deep in the pit of his stomach. The air around the barricade prickled with tension.

Mikhail joined Vanya on the driver's seat. The eerie silence of the city made the inside of the carriage intolerable. Each took comfort from the other's presence. Both knew if action became necessary they could rely on each other.

The streets were almost deserted the closer they got to the center.

Vanya kept the horses at a slow trot. He began to wonder if it had been such a good idea to leave the factory. Maybe they should have stayed.

"I don't like this quiet, Misha. There are no people, and that's not a good sign," he said. "If there are barricades, we won't be able to get the carriage through. Maybe we should unbuckle the horses just in case."

"Not yet," Mikhail said, "let's see what's at the end of this street."

Before the horses had gone two steps further, an explosion of rapid fire shattered the silence. A heavy machine gun had opened up.

Without a thought as to where the firing was coming from, Vanya reigned in the horses and began to unbuckle the harness. No discussion was necessary; Mikhail immediately followed suit. The continued bursts of gunfire made the horses skittish, and it took some effort to take the animals out of the traces.

Mikhail threw his leg over the horse's back and mounted. He grabbed the halter of the other and held it as Vanya, no longer young, struggled to haul himself up. Vanya pulled the horse close to the carriage to use as a step. He grasped the mane in his left hand and was about to kick his right leg over when a tremendous *whuuump* echoed down the street, drowning out the deadly clatter of the machine gun. Vanya knew instantly what it was, and his grip froze at the enormity of what was happening.

He yelled at the top of his voice to Mikhail, but the sound got lost in a deafening blast as a second artillery shell exploded where they had been only minutes before. The solid body of the carriage sheltered them from the worst force of the blast. Pieces of masonry shattered from the building next to the explosion, together with fractured cobblestone, and showered down on them. Vanya felt a piece of shrapnel whistle past his head and then he was on the horse's back.

"Ride," he yelled and both horses raced away from the terror.

When the machinegun opened fire, the lookout on the barricade bravely climbed to the highest point on the structure to seek out the location.

"They're in the belfry tower of the convent," he called. "The bastards can see half the city from there."

Vanya could see the barricade now. The horses did not need any encouragement after the explosion of the artillery shell. They had already covered half the distance and Vanya began to wave his arm at the barricade, yelling at them to open it up and let them through.

"There are two horsemen racing down the street from where the shell hit," the lookout called.

Anton, shocked into immobility by the artillery fire, jumped into action and clambered up the overturned cart. The lead rider was waving his arms and yelling at them. Anton could not yet hear the words but as he came closer he noticed something familiar about the way the rider rode.

"He rides like a Cossack," Anton said out loud.

"Well, someone doesn't like him. They nearly got hit with that shell," the lookout said.

"Open the barricade and let them in," Anton yelled. "Quickly!"

He had a second look to make sure that no cavalry followed and jumped down to help move the cart and allow the horses through.

The Cossack pulled his horse up. He was older than the defenders had expected, with a full head of grey hair. Trickles of blood ran down his temple and left cheek where shards of stone had nicked the skin.

"Thanks, friend," he said.

"Uncle Vanya!" exclaimed Anton. "What on earth are you doing here?"

Before Vanya could answer, there was a second *whuuump*.

"Take cover!" Vanya yelled.

The shell exploded much closer to the barricade.

"The bastards were using us as sighting targets," Vanya swore.

"They have a machine gun in the convent's belfry," Anton said.

"Then they'll also have an artillery ranging officer up there as well," said Vanya. "They'll be able to see the whole city! No wonder they used us."

The realization suddenly dawned that he was talking to his godson.

"Anton, thank God it was you in charge otherwise this lot may have shot at us," he said, then, "What the devil are you doing with the revolutionaries?"

"I think your friend has been hit," said Margarita, standing a short distance away.

Mikhail slumped over the horse's neck, his left arm hung limply down as small spots of blood dripped slowly into a red pool in the snow.

General Dubasov watched the third shell hit the roadway close to the barricade. It had been an inspired choice to put an artillery range officer in the convent bell tower. He congratulated himself. One could see most of the city occupied by the revolutionary scum from this vantage point. He climbed the stairway to the top once the machine gunner was in place and gave instructions to use the carriage as a sighting target. As he watched the two riders disappear around the barricade he smiled with grim satisfaction. His instinct had been correct—they were clearly sympathetic to the rebellion or they would have been fired upon by the defenders. Even though he could only see the far end of the barricade, the guns now had the range and could blast it at their convenience. He barked an order at the range officer.

"Soldier, you are to remain at this post, relaying target information until relieved," he said before taking one more look at the panorama below and heading for the stairs.

Dubasov knew it would be a slow process clearing the barricades by use of artillery. However, he also knew that a constant bombardment of high explosive ordinance would weaken the resolve of even professional soldiers. Ordinary people would very quickly cease supporting the insurgents once they realized the bombardments stopped when an area had been vacated.

The time will come before long, he thought as he slowly made his way down the stairs, *when infantry and Cossacks will storm the remaining pockets of resistance.* But first he was going to soften them up.

Within a week, Dubasov had destroyed most of the barricades. The only area still held by the rebels was the textile district of Presnia. On the ninth day after the general strike had been called, the general marshaled his forces and surrounded Presnia. With his Moscow garrison strengthened by an elite guards regiment from the capital, he had a well-armed force ready to join the artillery batteries positioned on all four sides of Presnia. It took most of the night to deploy the troops and armaments, but before dawn they were ready.

Anton Pushkin and Margarita Ologov fell back on barricade after barricade as the high explosive artillery shells destroyed them. So far, they had survived. Now they sat in Presnia, waiting. He looked across the room at her, her face streaked with dirt and sweat, hair held in check by the red and blue scarf. She glanced up at him, exhaustion clearly visible in the dark blue smudges under her eyes. She tried to smile. He wondered whether his eyes had the same wild, hunted look.

The people in the room stirred as a tall man in a tattered overcoat limped across to the table on the far side. He had been wounded yesterday.

"I have just received the last action brigade report. We have 200 rifles and nearly 600 pistols. No one has more than six rounds; some have only one bullet left. In addition, our fighters have over a hundred sabers and fifty grenades." He had recited the extent of their armaments in a matter-of-fact way, as if reading a shopping list.

"If anyone is interested, Dubasov has been kind enough to set up all his artillery pointing at us. Did someone do something to offend him?"

His attempt at a joke brought forth several subdued chuckles, though most of the people gathered in the room were too battle tired and hungry to see the humor.

"Well, it's better to die fighting than be bound hand and foot. The honor of the revolution is at stake," said a man at the back.

"Bugger the revolution; all I want is a fair wage for a day's work," a woman stretched out on the floor said wearily.

"Try to get some sleep; I think we are going to have a busy day tomorrow," said the tall man.

At precisely seven o'clock the next morning, Dubasov gave the order for the bombardment of Presnia to begin. Firing five shells a minute, the guns kept up an unabating crescendo of sound and terror. High explosives and incendiary rained down indiscriminately on revolutionaries and residents.

As the first shells burst, Anton and Margarita ran from the headquarters room and headed toward where the first assaults were likely to be launched. As they reached the corner, a tremendous explosion hit them in the back. When they picked themselves off the roadway and looked back, the building they had just left was a pile of rubble. They stopped only momentarily before moving rapidly away from the direct hit. As they did, shells began to fall all around them. There seemed nowhere to hide. When an incendiary shell burst in front of him, spreading its hungry flames over a workman's house, Anton swerved to the right to avoid the heat. When he looked back for Margarita, she was gone. Only a blue and red scarf lay near the corner. Rubble and burning wood littered the spot where once had been the intersection of two narrow streets. The sickly sour stench of cordite and spent explosives sat heavily in the air.

The barrage continued unabating throughout the day and into the night. By this time, all of Presnia was ablaze. Anton stumbled into a small group of fighters including, incredibly, the tall man from the morning briefing. Anton assumed he had been killed by the direct hit.

"Have you got any water?" they asked him.

He shook his head. They were all desperately thirsty. Most of the homes in the area had now been destroyed, and no one had had a drink since morning.

"We can't hold out any longer. Most of the ammunition is gone, and it's only a matter of time before they stop the bombs and send in the troops. We must live to fight again. Get out the best way you can and hide. The bastards are bound to try and track down anyone who was part of the revolution," said the tall man.

"Good luck," he called as he and several others disappeared into the flickering gloom.

Anton stared at the two men who remained. They looked back blankly, defeat etched in the dirt-embossed creases of their faces. For the first time, he admitted to himself, "Margarita did not survive. She is buried somewhere back there." He gazed despondently past his new companions.

With a conscious effort, he turned away, the glare of the flames not so bright here.

"Come on, let's get out of here."

The uprising had been crushed.

§ § § § §

Sergei Sokoloff packed his medical bag.

"Your arm is healing well. There may be some residual stiffness where the shrapnel tore the muscle, but with time and exercise you shouldn't notice any restriction of movement," he said to Mikhail. "The headaches will also pass with time. I can't predict when. The brain's a delicate but robust mechanism; however, please avoid any more violent entertainment," he added with a smile.

"Thank you, Sergei," Mikhail said.

"Any news of the young man who brought you into the hospital?"

Just over two weeks had passed since the general strike was so violently put down and Vanya had not heard from his nephew. Mikhail wanted to thank him for getting them both through the barricades and safely in sight of Sokoloff's hospital before disappearing back into the fortified area. Vanya made inquiries of the family and at his lodgings, but to no avail. He seemed to have disappeared. Privately, Vanya thought Anton had died in the fighting. Otherwise, why not at least let his mother know he was alive. *He was a brave young man,* Mikhail thought. He knew Vanya's sister had been a widow since her husband died in a typhoid epidemic, years ago. Anton's disappearance, as the only man in his family of three sisters, left the family exposed. So Mikhail quietly arranged delivery each Monday of enough food for the family for the week. He knew this would relieve Vanya the burden of worry.

Sokoloff called in to check on Mikhail's progress every few days, not that his patient really needed it, but he enjoyed the company, and being in such a huge and luxurious mansion.

"I heard today that over 1,000 men, women, and children were killed in Presnia," Sokoloff said.

"What a tragic waste," said Katya, who insisted on nursing her husband and sat in on every visit by the doctor. Both had come to regard him as a friend, and he joined them for dinner that evening. As was the custom, several non-family members joined the table as guests most nights

"I hear unrest is widespread throughout the countryside," Mikhail said. "Apparently, the *narod,* the peasants, are burning homes and stealing food from the barns. The damage they are causing in the country is far worse than that caused here."

"The government," he said, "has sent troops along the railway all the way to Harbin with orders to clear it of rebels immediately. They're confident this will be achieved within a couple of weeks. Judging by the methods used in Presnia, I daresay he'll be proven right."

"I fear the government's violent response may not work this time," said a university professor. "The resentment that promised reforms have not been brought in is widespread. I hear it from students and radical groups daily. People are better educated than they were a decade ago. Most of them can read, and they do. They read newspapers. They read revolutionary pamphlets. Many of them have a lot of sympathy for radical ideas when they see how the tsar looks after his people," he said. A regular visitor to the Morozov's, the professor provided a perspective they found both stimulating and refreshing.

When the guests finally left, Ivan sat quietly with his son in the library.

"Misha, I forgot to tell you, I attended a meeting of the committee of creditors of Koslinski's bank yesterday. They are proposing to sell the assets to raise funds to repay some of the depositors' money. They asked if we wanted to buy the bank's shares in the Perlov tea business. I told them I drank the stuff but that was the extent of my knowledge of tea. I did say, though, that we could have an interest in the shares in some of the factories Koslinski held, but only if there was no other bidding to force the price up. They suggested these assets could be sold in an orderly way so we may yet get some of our money back," Ivan sat back in his chair.

"I wonder where that snake in the grass is now. There have been no rumors of any sightings. Usually these aristo's are not that bright and make contact with their family, and something eventually leaks out. The bastard has been damned clever," Ivan mused.

"Vladimir, who represents our bank on the committee, told me after the meeting he had heard the British Foreign & Credit Bank sustained large losses on the collapse of Koslinski's bank. Apparently, George Fox hadn't laid off any of his bank's exposure, and they lost the lot," Ivan said.

§ § § § §

New Year celebrations in Moscow that year were subdued, the sounds and violence of the bombardment still too fresh in people's minds. As 1906 began, it was as if the winter Gods shrank from the sight of the devastation in Presnia. Snow fell heavily, layer upon layer, casting a forgiving mantle of soft white over the scars of the uprising. A funereal quiet settled on the area so the people of Moscow could avoid facing the reality that the spring thaw would show so starkly.

But it was an illusion.

"Not since the Napoleonic wars has Moscow been shelled by artillery. And this time the tsar's artillery killed his own people. Never before has this happened in Russian history," a radical handbill bluntly stated.

Gradually, as the weeks passed, winter showed signs of easing its freezing grip on the commercial capital. As the snow on the ground began to melt faster than new snow fell, Ivan received a letter from the British Foreign Office sent through their embassy in Saint Petersburg.

London

Sir Algernon Law, baronet, head of the Commercial Department of the Foreign Office and a shrewd opportunist, stared briefly out the window at the verdant foliage in the park. It was an unseasonably warm spring day, and soft light dappled through the trees. For those strolling leisurely along the shaded paths, the cares of the world did not exist. For a brief moment, Sir Algernon's mind wandered back to a day just like it many years ago. The mere thought of the young woman on his arm then brought a smile to his lips.

"Sweet memories?" asked Phillip Armitage from the other side of the desk.

"Youth is wasted on the young," Law said, turning around once more to face his colleague. "The opportunities one had then are, unfortunately, never really appreciated and rarely repeated as one gets older."

"Some of our exporters are uneasy over the ongoing unrest in Russia I hear," he said, returning to the matter they had been discussing.

"There has been some disruption to the flow of orders," Armitage admitted. "But I don't think it was the level of force used in putting down the January revolt in Moscow. After all HM's army has put down many a riot in India, though it must be well over a century since the king's own have turned the guns on their own citizens. And there's talk about the possibility of more unrest."

"The Japanese victory changed the balance in the Far East," Armitage continued. "It may mean the Russians become a little less adventurous, particularly in Central Asia. If the situation in Petersburg and Moscow were to deteriorate, would the tsar and his advisors withdraw west?"

"And, if so, can Britain fill the gap?" Law posed into the air.

"The chaps down the corridor are pretty keen on oil, seem to think it will become ever more important and overtake coal as a fuel for the navy. In fact, it looks like its heading that way already, I hear," said Armitage.

"And one of those Central Asian khanates has what looks like a bit of it, you say?" said Law.

"Yes, Kazakhstan. In the past, the Russians have been applying pressure to our interests in Afghanistan, which borders Kazhak. They seem to think the area is their own sphere of interest. The Jap victory might encourage them to withdraw west out of Central Asia. If this happened, it would relieve pressure on Kabul. We could promise eventual support for independence to the local warlords. We could also offer payment for future delivery of oil, in gold of course and at a price of our choosing, after allowing for the difficulties of transport, etc. I have yet to see one of those eastern potentates refuse a lucrative offer of gold coin. Once the first delivery of gold has been made we will offer to temporarily locate a regiment of Ghurkhas and a seasoned regiment from India in the capital, on the pretext of protecting our interests in the oil."

"The great game is afoot once more," Law said.

"It's a well-trodden path." Armitage smiled.

"Indeed," said Law, "but I think we should get the Political Department on side with this scheme, just in case. Don't want to be left holding the baby, what. It would be jolly helpful if we could get some local information on what the Russians were thinking. Do we have anyone that might be useful?"

"I've been giving some thought to that problem," said Armitage. "We have had a rather loose arrangement with a Moscow merchant called Morozov for some time. He's been very successful and now has interests across the geographic spread of the Russian Empire. He also has interests here in London. He might be induced to help, particularly if it were presented as a means of improving trade between our two countries."

"Good," said Law.

"That reminds me," he went on. "I had lunch with Appleby the other day at the club. Said he has it on impeccable authority that Fox's bank is in trouble. Apparently, they lost a packet on the Moscow Commerce Bank failure. Do you think it could be useful if we had our own bank in Moscow? It could make sure that British businesses trading with the Ruskies had favorable funding. It could even raise money from the damned Frogs and Germans and use it to build British business in Russia."

Armitage stared out the window for a long moment. Then he turned to Sir Algernon.

"That could give us a real edge. In effect, an 'extra seat at the table' with the information we could glean from the inside in Moscow. The only problem is that the Russians prohibit any foreigners from owning banks."

"Do you think we could get our Mr. Morozov to own the Moscow Bank if we arranged the funds?" Law asked. "Didn't you tell me this chap was a lover of music? Perhaps I can persuade the D'Oyley Carte Company to take Gilbert and Sullivan's operettas to Russia or perhaps get Elgar to visit," Law added as an aside.

Moscow

Katya bubbled with enthusiasm. "Misha, my darling, we should sponsor the concert. It would be good to hear music that people really love. It will lift everyone's spirits."

After the destruction of Presnia, the plight of families now homeless and without food and clothing for the winter began to worry many in Moscow. Collections of clothes were distributed through the factories where many worked. Food kitchens opened in several of the more substantial structures still standing in Presnia.

The Morozovs contributed generously, while making it clear, as did other merchants, that their assistance to the families was humanitarian, not support for the rebels.

"People are depressed," she told Mikhail. "Their spirits need lifting. All of Moscow needs lifting. What we need is music."

"What do you mean?" asked Mikhail.

"In Ireland, if there was a fight in the pub, when they were all exhausted with each other, the band would start to play again. Before long a happy mood would return and everyone would go home with a bloody nose and a smile on their face."

"A concert that played Moscow's favorite music would be irresistible," she said, warming to the theme. "It could be a benefit concert. The money raised would go to the women and children. And if everyone's spirits are lifted they will give more generously to help the women and children suffering so much in Presnia in this bitter weather."

"Perhaps his majesty and General Dubasov may not be particularly happy with such an event," Mikhail said.

Katya was not to be easily dissuaded.

"But, Misha, it would show that his majesty cared and that the innocents, the children are not forgotten. No good Russian would abandon the children." She knew this last argument would win the day. And it did.

"Very well," he said, feeling he had lost the argument before he began. "I'll take it up with Dubasov in the morning."

"Can I come, please?" said Anna. "I love concerts."

"And you have such experience with concerts, my little rabbit," Mikhail said, whisking her into his arms.

"We'll have to see how well behaved you are," said Katya.

"Oh, good, good. I'll wear my dress with all the little flowers on it," Anna chortled.

Katya's arguments proved persuasive, and Dubasov obtained permission from Saint Petersburg for the concert to go ahead. A brilliant young violinist, Niccoli Mariinski, newly discovered by Moscow, agreed to play when told the Guarneri violin would be loaned for the performance. The Moscow Arts Theatre agreed to provide the venue. Other wealthy families then added support for the one and only performance, a special gala occasion.

The mood in Moscow seemed to lift. It was widely publicized that all proceeds would go to a fund established to help the children of Presnia. There was even a rumor the tsar himself may attend. Ivan dismissed the rumor, saying: "The tsar is not interested in his people and would hardly leave his family for one concert." Nevertheless, interest in the concert intensified.

Yet, beneath all the excitement ran an ominous undercurrent. Anarchists handed out pamphlets condemning the "murder of innocents." "Blood money" they called the donations, "the guilty trying to buy the forgiveness of the people of Presnia."

The day of the concert arrived. A thick mantle of snow covered the ground. Overhead, the pale blue sky had the infinite clarity of a motionless sub-zero winter's day. Objects far in the distance appeared defined in sharp detail. Sounds arrived crisp and brittle to the ear.

The level of anticipation ran high that evening in the Morozov house. Six-year-old Anna's first real concert and her excitement infected Pinna and the other servants. Katya felt glow of satisfaction from the culmination of weeks of organizing. Not only would this be a memorable event, it would help families who had lost everything. Guests began arriving for pre-concert drinks. Throughout the house rang a commotion of greetings, laughter, and eager anticipation.

At last, they were ready to leave.

Overhead, thousands of stars sparkled like festive lights in the clear night sky.

Inside the theater, hundreds of patrons steadily made their way to their seats, resplendent in regimental dress uniforms, aristocratic insignia, and formal evening dress. A buzz of light conversation and laughter filled the space.

The Morozovs decided to sit in one of the boxes instead of the front-row stalls below so that Anna could see the stage. Once most of the audience was seated, General Dubasov, representing the tsar, his wife, and aides, entered from a side door. To a round of polite applause, they sat in the center of the front row. An expectant hush descended over the theater before the applause erupted as the conductor walked out and mounted his podium. He was followed by the soloist, Niccoli Mariinski, bow in one hand, the Guarneri nonchalantly tucked under his other arm.

As the last emotional notes of Tchaikovsky's 'Violin Concerto' faded into memory, a loud, harsh voice ripped discordantly into the silence from somewhere above the boxes.

"Death to the ruling classes—remember Presnia!"

As the audience turned to look in the direction of the outburst, a tall young man in a long coat leapt to his feet, his arm fully extended behind him like a javelin thrower. As his arm reached the end of its trajectory his coat caught on his seat and a large round object, its fuse sputtering ominously, flew out of his hand too early. It fell on the edge of the stage and rolled into one of the lighting holes as it exploded.

Niccoli Mariinski was blown forward off his feet, the Guarneri hitting the ground with a flat thud. Two members of the first violins were killed instantly as wooden shards severed their throats; an elderly colonel in full dress uniform with decorations had the top of his skull separated from his head as a piece of the metal lighting embedded itself; the woman next to him had her lung pierced by an arrow of wood shot as if from a bow at close range.

The screams of the injured shattered the instant of silence after the blast. Many in the audience had blood pouring from wounds. People at the back began pushing for the exits, clambering over seats to get out. Near panic took hold. Closer to the explosion, those not seriously injured began to help the badly wounded. On the upper level, as the bomber tried to run from the theater, four young officers overpowered him, punching him viciously to the ground.

Katya recovered quickly and grabbed Anna, who was sitting, sobbing quietly. Katya looked quickly at Mikhail and Ivan to confirm they were unharmed and turned to comfort her daughter.

"Mama, I'm hurting," said a faint little voice.

Katya put her hand on Anna's face to sooth her, but it felt wet and warm.

"Oh my God, oh my darling, what has happened?"

Blood was running from her head all down the right side of Anna's face.

Ivan and Mikhail spun around at the alarm in Katya's voice. Both their stomachs turned inside out when they saw the little girl's head.

It took all of Mikhail's self-control to gently push Katya away and carefully examine Anna's face.

"It's a flesh wound," he said. "It's not serious. It looks like a splinter of wood shot up here by the explosion grazed her scalp. You are a very brave girl, my little rabbit," he said, putting his arm gently around her shoulder.

Mikhail wiped away the blood, which had now stopped running. He felt an icicle pierce his heart; if the splinter had been a fraction lower and an inch to the right it would have speared her eye, and she would be dead.

He hugged Katya fiercely as he gently handed Anna to her grandfather. For Ivan, the empty horror at the thought of losing his son all those years ago in Petersburg flooded back.

Outside the theater, a young man heavily rugged against the cold, the collar of his coat pulled up high at the back, stood opposite the entrance. He heard the bomb explode and watched as the first of the fleeing audience spilled out onto the street. He was sorely tempted to stay and confirm Dubasov had been killed, but he knew that could be dangerous. He wondered if the young anarchist student managed to escape. He doubted it. No matter. There was no way he could be identified as the organizer. He had made sure of that. As he turned to leave, Anton Pushkin said softly, "That's one for Margarita."

Maksim Rysakov hurried down the street. He had promised his wife he would be there before the concert began, but had been caught at the ministry office in an unscheduled meeting. He knew he would miss part of the 'Violin Concerto.' As he rounded the corner, he heard the *whump* of the explosion in the theater and immediately broke into a run.

"My God, Vera," he said to himself.

In front of him, the heavily clad figure with the collar up turned suddenly, and they collided. He barely registered the grim face of the young man who, without a word, strode off, away from the theater.

Rysakov muttered an apology and raced on toward the scene of the bombing.

§ § § § § §

The bomb killed six people and badly injured dozens more. The target of the bomb, General Dubasov, survived unscathed. The next morning, he told the people of Moscow he had the perpetrator in a cell in the Kremlin and would seek the death penalty for the madman.

Under intensive police interrogation the bomber kept repeating, "Death to Dubasov. I was given the bomb. It was easy to get it into the theater. I should have killed the murderer." He could not give the police a name or address that checked out as real. He thought the man who had given him the bomb was a social revolutionary. The police had very little to go on. It seemed to be a dead end.

In the Morozov household, the bombing had a profound effect. Anna's wound healed quickly as Mikhail had predicted, although it would leave a scar just below the hairline. But for Katya, the nightmares began to reappear. This time, the dreams were more confused. Sometimes, a man dressed in black would enter her room and pick up Anna. When she cried out to her mother to save her, Katya was unable to move. The man then took her daughter away, and Katya knew she would never see her again. Other times, in her dream, she would be awakened by a disturbance outside the bedroom. Once she reached the top of the stairs, she could see Mikhail at the bottom arguing with a group of men. He had Anna in his arms. As he turned to mount the stairs, she could see one of the men raise a sword to strike him in the back. She tried to shout a warning but no sound came out. As Mikhail fell, the man grabbed Anna. He turned a horrible leering face toward Katya before carrying Anna out the front door. Each time Katya awoke, sweating, her heart pounding. She sat bolt upright, listening for sounds, but the house remained quiet and secure.

Anna's wounding affected Mikhail in ways he could not have predicted. His own wounds from the revolution caused him mild inconvenience, but he never doubted he would recover. For his daughter to be exposed so innocently to danger horrified him. To think how close he had come to losing her. He had to force himself to stop dwelling on what might have happened.

One night, about a month after the bomb blast, Ivan announced at dinner, "I have some business that is overdue my attention in London. I thought perhaps I might take Anna to help me."

"Ooh yes, Dedushka, I would love to come with you," she said.

Ivan smiled. "Well, that's settled then."

There was a moment's silence before Katya, knowing Ivan was waiting for her to bite, could not restrain herself.

"She cannot go on her own; it's out of the question," she said.

"But she would be with me," Ivan said with mock seriousness.

"She is not leaving this house without me," Katya said with finality.

"Well, my little rabbit, it looks like we will have to take your mother," Ivan said, laughing. "In fact, I think we should make it a holiday. Misha, the factories are now well managed and will survive our absence for a few months, the streets have returned to normal, and we can take Pinna to look after the children. What do you all think? Is it a good idea or too boring?"

Everyone spoke at once—chastisement, laughter, excitement, questions. After much discussion, it was agreed they would leave in three weeks. They would go by train to Paris and then on the Channel steamer to London.

The next day, Ivan received the letter from the British FO.

Ivan was intrigued. It had been years since he had received a letter from the British. Most times, informal conversations with an embassy member or discussions on his trips to London sufficed. While it was widely known that Morozov & Son had extensive business dealings with Britain, regular correspondence with their embassy could draw the attention of the Okhrana and lead to awkward questions being asked by the Russian government.

He sat quietly in his reading room and reread the letter. The envelope in which it had arrived was addressed in Russian with a one-ruble blue and green stamp emblazoned with the double-headed eagle of the Romanov crest in the center. It was postmarked Petersburg. Nothing out of the ordinary there, Ivan received regular letters from his office in the port. The letter was short and, if it fell into suspicious hands, quite innocent. In fact, it was exactly what one might expect the British government to write to a prominent merchant. It contained three queries after all the usual flowery diplomatic phrases:

Firstly, Sir, it is apparently well known in Moscow of your generous support for the arts, in particular music. Indeed we have been informed that you are the fortunate owner of a rare Cremona violin by Guarneri. We are most interested to foster cultural exchanges between our two great countries. Several of our more distinguished composers and conductors have expressed an interest in visiting Moscow and St Petersburg. Edward Elgar and Sir Arthur Sullivan in particular are both admirers of Tchiakovsky and may appreciate an invitation to visit your great country. We would be greatly indebted to you, Sir, if you would consider sponsoring the possibility of such a tour with your Government. We recognize that this may seem a trifle unusual and that such a request may normally be sent to the appropriate Ministry, but in this instance your own well known love of music may be of some assistance.

Secondly, Sir, our Commercial Department has been approached by Gormack & Whiting a leading British manufacturer of motorized tractors, which are quite successfully used in agriculture in Britain, as to whether there may be a market for their goods in the new areas being opened up in the Russian East. We would value your advice as to possible interest in this market for such products. If we may further impose upon you, we would greatly appreciate suggestions as to possible agents for the importation of these goods.

Finally, Sir, there is as you may know, an abiding interest in this country in Russian art and culture.

A tour of Britain by any of your fine performers
would, we are certain, be well received.

The letter was signed by Sir Algernon Law.

Ivan put the letter on his desk. They were clearly offering him the agency for the importation of the new motorized tractors. He had little doubt there would be a ready market, but would send a telegram to Yusuf Yudin forthwith for confirmation.

Why offer it to him? He felt sure Gormack & Whiting could send a representative to Moscow and interview prospective agents, no doubt including him. But here he was being offered the agency without any competition. The FO wanted something. No doubt they would reveal exactly what in due course. If harmless, he would assist, if not he would have the agency and its profit in any event.

The concerts would be easy to arrange and would be well received. He had heard the music of Elgar when in London and he felt sure its imperial grandeur would strike a chord in Moscow. He may even be able to persuade the increasingly popular young virtuoso, Alexander Petchnikov, to play if offered the Guarneri for the recital. He sat for a further fifteen minutes, then locked the letter in his desk and left the room, a satisfied expression on his face.

§ § § § §

The next day, a letter arrived from Dublin for Katya. It was from her sister Neave.

Dearest Katy,

Ma passed away during the last cold month of win-
ter. She caught cold in the damp walking to the late
shift. We took her into our house but by the time we
knew she was ill she was too far gone.

We knew you would not have had time to get here
for the funeral, which was held in the parish
church. It was a nice service and we bought a couple
of bottles to send her away in proper style.

The money you were able to send helped make her
and Da more comfortable, but she would not stop
working. She just did a little less.

The letters you wrote were a great source of com-
fort to her. Each time she received a new letter she
would show it to all the family and some of the

neighbors. One of us would read it out to her as her
eyes were not good enough anymore. She enjoyed them
so much she has kept them all in an old biscuit tin.
I think it made her feel as if she was closer to
you.

   Please write to us every so often to let us know
how your family is growing up.

   Everyone here sends you their love and best
wishes. I am enclosing a photograph of Ma for you.
It was taken a few years ago on a holiday outing and
we persuaded her to use some of your money to pose.

Your loving sister,

Neave

Katya sat looking at the photo as tears trickled down her cheeks.
She turned it over and written on the back with a pencil in a
copperplate hand was the inscription: "Mary O'Connor, Kingstown,
1904." Katya looked once again at the photograph. Memories flooded
back. She knew the huge harbor piers and the squat Martello tower in
the distance that dated from the Napoleonic wars. The yearning to see
Dublin just one more time, to see her family, was almost a physical
pain, it was so intense.

That evening, it was decided, Mikhail would take Katya and the
children to Dublin while Ivan attended to business in London. Katya
nodded, her eyes red from crying. It would be good to see her da. She
felt the tears well up once more; she would visit her mother's grave to
say good-bye. As she said good night to Anna and Peter, she
explained as best she could that they would come with her to the land
of her birth, to the city in which she grew up.

The next day, Katya wrote a letter to Neave.

§ § § § § §

In the middle of the following week, on a cloudy day with the snow
melt forming puddles on the roads, a messenger arrived at the
Morozov house. He delivered an envelope containing a single sheet of
paper:

"Mr. George Fox of London wishes to inquire whether it would be
convenient to call on Mr. Ivan Morozov the day after tomorrow to
discuss several matters of mutual interest."

§ § § § §

"Hey, Maximus. I've got a job for you. It will almost certainly mean a promotion, and it will present one of those challenges that are so close to your heart. A mystery."

Gregori Yukovsky had long ago dubbed Maksim Rysakov "Maximus." It was a name, he said, that carried a gravitas more suited to a serious investigator. Just like a philosopher/general of ancient Rome, he added, laughing. The name stuck and Rysakov's colleague used it whenever his irrepressible sense of fun surfaced, which was often.

"If I get promoted again, Gregori, I shall have to sack you for showing insufficient respect to your superiors." Rysakov grinned.

"You remember, my friend Lev Belyi. I used to work with him before I moved here. He took up one of those land offers and moved east to Siberia. I just received a letter, from Harbin. It seems that a number of young women have been disappearing and now several have turned up dead. At first, it was only the local Chinese girls. Who knows what they do with their women? I've heard they sell them to brothels to buy opium. Anyway, no one took much notice until a couple of young Russian girls disappeared. One of them was only twelve years old. She hasn't been seen again. The other turned up on the river bank naked but wrapped in an old cloak. 'Vicious things had been done to her,' he says. A jealous lover, I'd say, or a religious fanatic of a father shamed by his daughter taking a lover. I've heard they go a bit crazy out there."

Rysakov laughed. "You have a vivid imagination, Gregori."

He turned back to the piles of neglected paperwork on his desk, determined to clear away as much as he could today.

"How is Vera?" Yukovsky asked more seriously. "Has she recovered from the bombing?"

"Yes. She was lucky, only scratches and bruises from the crush of people trying to get out of the theater after the explosion. There's no doubt the student who threw the bomb was not acting alone, no matter what Dubasov says to calm the populace. It might ease public concern but it certainly doesn't address the real problem. I don't think we have heard the last of the revolutionaries. Not by a long shot," Rysakov said.

§ § § § § §

George Fox arrived precisely on time, neatly dressed in a dark suit of the latest London style. Ivan decided to receive the Englishman in the library rather than one of the reception rooms. It was a more overpowering room. It had several walls of morocco-bound books, two large Monet landscapes, and a vibrant van Gogh, which stood out alongside more traditional Russian paintings. In one corner, a small display cabinet sparkled with exquisite gold and silver ornaments by Faberge. A beautifully crafted wooden desk with leather inlay stood with its back to large glass doors opening onto a south-facing terrace. In front of the desk and to one side were several leather upholstered chairs.

Ivan guided Fox to a comfortable two seater before sitting in a more upright and higher chair opposite him. Between them on the floor lay the skin of the Siberian tiger, its jaws agape in a perpetual snarl, looking directly up at Fox.

After the obligatory small talk, Ivan knew he had made the right choice to use the library. Fox was impressed. Ivan had no doubt his visitor would have been in many such rooms in England. Yet, he felt smugly certain, Fox would not have expected such a display in Moscow.

"My wife has a keen interest in art and I see you have some fine examples of the modern French style," Fox said.

"I didn't know you were married," Ivan said.

"Yes, took the plunge last year. You may have met her I think when you were last in London. Mary Billingsgate was her name, now Mary Fox," he said casually, looking directly at Ivan.

Ivan hesitated only a moment. Fox was clearly making a point.

"Yes, I do remember her. A charming lady. My congratulations to you."

With this revelation behind him, Fox seemed to re-gather some of his equilibrium.

"How long are you in Moscow?" Ivan asked. That Mary Billingsgate had married the banker was really of little consequence to Ivan. He had never intended to compete for the lady's hand and felt sure she would not have expected him to do so. No doubt she decided she had reached an age where she needed a husband for reasons of comfort and propriety. A pity she would no longer be able to receive him privately at her home, but life moves on, he thought to himself.

"As you know, my bank had a significant exposure to the Moscow Commerce Bank which collapsed after Koslinski's defalcation. I'm hopeful I may be able to sponsor a proposal to recover those losses," Fox said.

Over the next hour, Fox outlined his plan to revive the Moscow Commerce Bank and recover his losses. The British and Foreign Credit Bank would advance Morozov & Son the money necessary to recapitalize the bank. Yes, he knew that foreigners could not control Russian banks, which was why he was proposing that Morozov would control it. By recommencing trading with the Morozov name behind it, the bank would soon regain a position of importance in Moscow. It would eventually be in a position to progressively redeem the letters of credit that the British bank had been forced to honor on its collapse. Morozov & Son would repay the loan out of future profits. Of course, Fox's bank would require the normal charge over appropriate assets to secure the advance.

Ivan listened carefully, interrupting only to clarify a point here and there. *Curious,* he thought, *Fox arriving in Moscow so soon after I receive the letter from the Foreign Office.* A coincidence? Perhaps, but Armitage of the FO had introduced him to Fox in the first place. It all seemed a little too convenient. No matter, with Fox offering to finance the whole enterprise, then maybe. Possibilities began to take shape in Ivan's mind.

"Your proposal is interesting. Unfortunately, I am a manufacturer and merchant. I don't understand banking and don't see how I could own and manage a bank successfully. There must be others with more banking background than I who would welcome such an opportunity," Ivan said.

"I have no doubt that's so," said Fox. "There are, however, few more successful businesses in Moscow than Morozov & Son. You already have an association with Koslinski's bank, and it owes you money. Your involvement would ensure its success."

"We would set up a management committee," he said. "My own bank will second several managers, one of whom already speaks passable Russian. You would, of course, have your own nominees on the committee. All of the normal day-to-day banking would be handled under the oversight of the committee. Once all the advances had been repaid, you would control the bank. My bank, in return for providing the funds, would retain a small minority interest and would of course remain the London correspondent bank."

Retaining a share in the Moscow Bank had never been part of the plan; it had only occurred to Fox as he sensed Ivan's interest growing. *Why not?* he thought. *It could give me an asset that may pay large dividends in years to come.*

Ivan was reluctant to commit, it was not a business he understood, he was busy expanding his existing enterprises, particularly in the east, and was not sure if a bank was an enterprise he wanted to own. His mind worked at high speed. There could, however, be some real advantages in controlling a bank.

"You would be chairman, of course," said Fox now anxious not to allow Ivan's interest to wane.

"And my son would be a director?"

"Of course."

"And I will nominate the majority of the directors?" Ivan had decided that if he were to proceed then he would insist on the manager of his own bank providing technical knowledge as a director.

"Of course, the bank must be Russian controlled," Fox conceded.

"The lending policy must be determined by the directors."

"Of course," said Fox, "but subject to normal prudential banking principals."

"Yes, as generally applied in the local market," said Ivan.

"Agreed," said Fox reluctantly, hoping this would not vary significantly from London.

Finally, Ivan pushed back in his chair.

"I am beginning to see some merit in your proposal," he said.

Fox smiled. "I am pleased to hear you say that, sir. Subject to the documentation, I can have the funds available within the month. Will Morozov & Son or one of your other enterprises provide security for our loan?"

Ivan did not answer at first. Then, he looked unblinkingly at the British banker, his grey eyes steely.

"The only security for your loan, Mr. Fox, will be the Moscow Commerce Bank shares," he said calmly but in a tone of unquestionable finality.

Fox made as if to reply, then, thought better of it and nodded, acknowledging that if the deal were to proceed it would be on these terms.

§ § § § §

Some time later, Philip Armitage sat in Sir Algernon Law's office overlooking Green Park in London.

"Well, I think we have our bank in Russia," said Law as the door closed on Fox's departure. "Now we have to fund it and get one of our men into the management."

"A young chap recently joined us after some years in the city. His mother's Russian and he has spent holidays in Saint Petersburg. Apparently keen to go back, so that part shouldn't be a problem," said Armitage.

"Fox will arrange for the funds to be lent to the Moscow bank. However, we will have to arrange to get the money into Fox's bank," he said.

"I've had a chat with the governor of the Bank of England; we were at Eton together, you know. He'll provide a guarantee to the British and Foreign Credit Bank so they can borrow in the money market, provided they reduce the level of the guarantee to zero in half yearly steps over the next three years. I have assured him that the FO will ensure Fox's bank manage the reductions," said Law.

"Fox will arrange to transfer to us a major stake in his bank in exchange for saving his bacon. We will hold the shares in a nominee name so the FO's interest will remain appropriately secret," said Armitage.

"If Fox can't make profits out of this Russian bank, we can transfer funds from the Central Asia appropriation. However, with a bit of luck we shall have our bank in Russia, an invaluable source of intelligence and keep our funding allocation intact to expand our influence in Afghanistan and its neighbors."

Law nodded. "We're rather good at this, don't you think?" he said without a trace of arrogance.

"The nice bit is that if the Russian bank doesn't work out," said Armitage, "we will still control our own British bank. I have no doubt we can find a use for such an animal."

§ § § § § §

The week after Fox left the commercial capital, Ivan and Mikhail met with a craftsman in the smaller of the three reception rooms. This room was nearer the kitchen, and Katya, discussing the day's menu with the cook, heard the voices and came to investigate. As she watched from the doorway, the artisan carefully unwrapped a violin covered in a thin sheet of velvet. The Guarneri. She knew Ivan had recovered the beautiful instrument after the bombing and sent it to Moscow's leading violin restorer. Fortunately, it sustained little damage. When Niccoli Mariinski was blown over by the blast, the violin hit the stage flatly and without any great force. Mariinski absorbed most of that, though she remembered little of that night outside their box. Ivan told them later that the restorer said the only damage was scratches to the lacquer on the underside, and weakening of the glue holding the neck to the body.

She saw Ivan take the violin and inspect it carefully, turning it over and holding it up to the light to check the luster on the underside. He handed it to Mikhail, who placed gentle pressure on the neck to test the glue. Satisfied, he handed the violin back to his father.

The craftsman then began what appeared to be an explanation of the work he had done. Katya could not hear the conversation. With the violin back on the velvet wrapping, the man pointed to the area beneath the bridge near the "f" holes, through which the rich sound resonated.

While the man was still explaining, Ivan once again picked up the violin, but this time peered at the area the man had pointed to. He held it closely under the electric lamp fixed to the wall. After some minutes of scrutiny and apparently satisfied, he spoke to Mikhail and handed him the violin. Katya, no longer interested, turned back to more practical matters. The smooth running of the household demanded her constant attention. Each day brought its series of little crises needing resolution. Firm control ensured matters did not get magnified out of proportion. That would cause friction in the close knit world of the large staff the Morozovs employed and could not be tolerated.

London

They arrived in London on a warm and humid summer's day. Katya had forgotten how crowded and busy the center of the world's greatest empire could be. Anna and Peter stared awestruck out the windows of the train as they steamed amid shrieking whistles, venting boiler valves and the sickly sweet smell of coal smoke into Victoria Station. They could not imagine a city this large. Moscow had a lot of people and sprawled for miles. This city, on the other hand, seemed never to end. Wherever they looked, they saw ladies in the latest fashions, parasols stylishly resting over their shoulders; workmen in cloth caps, sleeves rolled up, kerchiefs knotted around their necks; hundreds of horse-drawn cabs, carts, and wagons; new and noisy motor vehicles; and people—people everywhere, moving in every direction casually, purposefully and in a rush. By the time they reached the Savoy Hotel, the children were bubbling with excitement and questions.

In the morning, Ivan and Mikhail met with Bertie Somerston. Katya took the children to visit Emily Somerston's, where they would all dine that evening.

"That is a substantial sum of money you wish to invest, Ivan," said Bertie as they sat discussing business in his office. "Do you wish to invest any in the stock market or in other business ventures?"

"Not at present," said Ivan. "I want to buy additional property, houses in prestige locations and warehouses near the docks. I would like your firm to handle the purchases and to manage the properties for me."

"We would, of course, be delighted to act for you," said Bertie. "I must say I have a better understanding of your reasons now you've explained what happened in the '05 revolution. It must have been an awful shock."

"My businesses will always remain in Russia, and we will always live in Moscow, but I'll be happier knowing that should anything happen to me or Mikhail then there are assets safely secured in this country," Ivan said. He decided not to tell Somerston he now controlled a bank with George Fox's money, or of the strange letter from the Foreign Office.

Bertie nodded and proceeded to discuss the paperwork required.

Katya was thrilled to see John and Amanda Somerston, both of whom had matured beyond her expectation. John was in his final year of law at Oxford and rowing for the university. Amanda had "come out" and was being courted by several eligible young bachelors. Katya proudly showed off her own children. Peter soon pointed out Anna's "bomb scar" to the Somerstons.

That evening, Mikhail and Ivan told stories of the uprising, of the trip on the railway to Harbin and of the size of the Siberian tiger that now terrified small children from the floor of their Moscow library.

John's eyes shone with the romance and adventure of it all.

"What an exciting place it must be," he said, a young man's thirst for excitement glowing on his face. "I should really like to see Russia."

"Then why don't you come and visit us," said Ivan.

"I have a better idea," said Mikhail, a twinkle in his eye. "John could come and work in our office for a year when he completes his studies. As we have a lot of business with Britain it would be useful for him to have a better understanding of our laws and operations, and we'll gain a better appreciation of how the British system works. When he returns he can represent us in our dealings in London. That is, of course, if his father agrees."

"Rather!" John said.

And so it was settled. Before the end of the year, John Somerston would join the firm of Morozov & Son in Moscow.

Several days later, Mikhail and his family sat on a tram with Katya, happily answering the children's questions about the sights, as best she could remember. As they passed Nelson's column in Trafalgar

Square, Peter and Anna strained to see the top. Mikhail assured them it was the highest statue in the world.

For no particular reason, Katya turned to her right and looked out the opposite window. Before the face disappeared into the crowd, and for only the briefest moment, she locked eyes with a man. It chilled her to the marrow. For what seemed an eternity, she could not move. When she frantically scanned the crowd, the man had gone. She saw only the mass of anonymous faces.

She heard Mikhail's voice and turned.

"What's wrong?" he said. "You look as if you have seen a ghost."

At that, her eyes widened even further, color draining from her cheeks.

"Just a bit of a shock. I thought I saw someone I knew, but I must have been mistaken. They could not possibly be here in London. Where are we now?" she asked completely disoriented.

Later that night, when she and Mikhail were alone in bed, she told him who it was that she thought she had seen. His earlier mild concern immediately turned serious.

"It is possible; what better place to hide than the largest city in the world. We must tell father in the morning."

When Mikhail told Ivan, he wanted details. Where did the sighting happen? Are you sure it was him?

"Are you sure it was the same man; don't forget you were nearly unconscious at the time," he asked Katya. "Do you know who it was?"

"Although it was only for a few seconds, I looked into his eyes. They were cruel and mocking. I can't be completely sure but that look brought back that horrible Easter. Sometimes I think I should know who attacked me but I can't quite grasp who it is."

"Do you think he recognized you?" asked Ivan.

"I don't know," said Katya, shaking her head. "It was so quick and then the face was gone. But the eyes seemed to burn straight through me. It was so unexpected."

"If it was the madman who attacked you then he is deviously clever and utterly ruthless. And, remember, in his mind he has unfinished business with you, Katya. No viciousness is beyond his contemplation," Ivan paused.

"We must be particularly vigilant whilst you and the children remain in London. One of us or Pinna should be with you whenever you go out," he said.

Katya thought she saw the same face in the crowd twice more, once only a block from their hotel. Each time she got only a fleeting glimpse before it turned away. She did not lock eyes with the man again, so she could not be certain. It may have been her imagination now she expected to see it.

The nightmares, of which she had been free for so long, returned. This time, however, they were more terrifying. This time, they involved the children. Only the rough seas of a storm on the Irish Sea distracted her enough for the dreams to subside.

Two days after the ship left Liverpool for Dublin, Ivan had a meeting with Phillip Armitage at the Foreign Office. He had not told Mikhail of the meeting nor did he tell Bertie Somerston. No one else knew.

Dublin

As the ship approached the docks near the mouth of the Liffey, the river that ran through the center of Dublin, a wave of emotion swept over Katya. Tears filled her eyes as she excitedly pointed out landmarks to her children. She had never expected to see Ireland again.

Neave met the ship and traveled with them in the cab to the Grand Hotel in the center of Dublin. She alternated between talking excitedly to Katy and staring with a mixture of curiosity and awe at the tall Russian next to her sister. Although clearly not Celtic, he had the air of a man confident of his place in the world. Whether that came from the physical power she felt sure he possessed, she didn't know. What she had no doubt about was the tenderness he showed toward Katy and his obvious love for the children. She found his lack of formal stuffiness, so common an attitude with the English, refreshing. Anna and Peter obviously adored him.

On the trip over, Katya had tried to explain to Mikhail that the British still controlled her country. When they landed, the clearly visible presence of British troops at the dock and the khaki uniforms along the route into the city graphically confirmed it.

They spent a month in Ireland. Anna and Peter struck up friendships with their cousins, teaching them phrases of Russian in exchange for their improving English. Dublin entranced Mikhail, particularly the pubs and the Irish love of music. He listened with interest to the discussions and arguments about the best path to independence from Britain. He tried to imagine how he would feel if

Russia were under foreign domination. He knew how his country had united against the invasion by Napoleon. He would fight. Of that, he had no doubt. He and all Russians would join with Mother Russia and her vast unending horizons to crush the invader. *The Irish,* he thought with a smile, *are almost Russian.*

The turmoil and unrest, Mikhail noticed, had a depressing effect on business. English investors were trying to sell out and the Irish had little in the way of capital to help them on their way. Property often sold at a discount.

Neave told Katy the new house they had recently moved into they could barely afford even though her husband had a steady job. With three children and an ill father, they needed the space, but it was a struggle.

"At least we aren't the only ones. Everyone I speak to has difficulty making ends meet. We'll get by all right," she said, smiling. "It is so good to see you Katy." She gave her sister a hug.

Katy and Mikhail took Neave and her brother and their families on sumptuous picnics, on happy summer outings, and the children on one special day to shops of their choice to buy presents. The Morozov visit would be long and fondly remembered by the O'Connor clan.

A letter from Ivan reminded Mikhail his real life lay in Moscow. Ivan had completed his business in London and proposed they return to Moscow in two weeks.

Once back in London and safely ensconced in the Savoy, Ivan and Mikhail, after some discussion, had two further meetings with Bertie Somerston, instructing him on one final item of business.

Moscow

Rysakov didn't understand why, but, since the uprising in '05, a new and unrestrained mood blossomed in Moscow. Maybe it was the lifting of censorship on the lewd and the licentious. Always the food and entertainment capital of the empire, his city had rediscovered a fascination with sex. Not only were the poor selling it as they had always done. It seemed a number of bored, high-bred women had begun enjoying the new freedom. Exciting as it may have appeared in the beginning, it did not always end as expected.

When Rysakov received the call, he at first checked the name and address of the hotel to make sure he had not made a mistake. This was a far better class of establishment to the ones he was normally called to.

"I don't understand it, Inspector. We have a reputation amongst the more well to do for our discretion and the consistency of our service. No one has ever been murdered," the manager said as he lead Rysakov to the room where the body had been found.

"When was the body discovered?" asked Rysakov.

"Not until early this morning when the maid went to make up the room for the next guest."

"Then you didn't expect whoever took the room to stay on? They were intending to vacate early?" said Rysakov.

"The lady who took the room often stayed for only one night; she always left early to go about her affairs," the manager said delicately.

"I see," said Rysakov. "I gather she was a regular customer."

"She has been staying with us once a week for over six months. A perfect client—paid her bills in cash with impeccable regularity. A charming person, very popular with the staff."

"I take it you know who she is?" Rysakov asked.

"Of course," said the manager as he stopped outside what appeared to be the door to one of the hotel's premier suites.

"I insisted nothing be disturbed so that you may have the best chance of catching the brute who did this," the manager said as he unlocked the door. "She was one of our most valued clients."

He walked through the entrance vestibule into a sitting room and pointed to the right where a door led into one of the two bedrooms. Rysakov gestured to the manager to stay where he was and turned into the room.

As he entered, he saw on the bed one of the most perfectly formed women he had seen in a long time. She lay naked on her back. She had sumptuously rounded hips, narrow waist, full breasts, and, by the look of her, yet to have children. *Too late for that,* he thought sadly. A normally pretty face with high cheekbones was distorted by bulging eyes and a swollen tongue hanging out of her mouth. He could not see her neck from where he stood. He stood quite still, confident in what he would find. She had been strangled.

He looked down the body. Long, shapely legs. Then he realized what had caught his attention—her pubic hair was not as luxuriant as he would have expected. It looked sparse, as through it had been trimmed for some purpose. *Was it trophy taking or fashion? Thank God it was not as grisly as the "Monster of Moscow."* The most likely explanation was fashion, he decided, so evenly was it done.

Once level with her head, he could see the tell-tale discoloration around the neck from where the garrotte had choked her. On her temple, a deep, blue-black bruising suggested she had been hit by a heavy object.

He left a constable at the door to the suite with strict instructions to let no one enter and went to get Dr. Sergei Sokoloff. He wanted a second opinion.

§ § § § §

Although Pinna had known for some weeks, all the signs were there for someone who grew up in the intimacy of village life. Katya did not tell Mikhail until it was beyond doubt. She was pregnant again. When she finally broke the news, it delighted both father and grandfather.

"We will call him Yuri. Yuri Victorovich, after his great-grandfather," pronounced Mikhail.

"What if he is a girl?" laughed Katya.

"Then we will call her Maria Nataliyanova," he said, "after both our mothers."

Not long after this bit of excitement, John Somerston arrived in the Morozov household. In addition to learning the intricacies of the Morozov business, he would need to master the subtleties of the Russian legal system, a system significantly different to the one in which he had been trained. To do this, he needed a working knowledge of the language or his time would be wasted. John assured them that he had already learned some Russian in London and his vocabulary was indeed good. But, as his tutor told him at their first lesson, "Your pronunciation is atrocious!" The tutor, Oleg Lukan, had learned English when he lived for a time in London with his parents. Only a few years older than John, they soon became friends.

"There is only one way to learn a language," Oleg told young Somerston, "and that is to speak nothing else so that you are forced to learn or die of thirst. And the best place to avoid dying of thirst is at a tavern."

Soon they became regulars at one of the many taverns frequented by students, radicals, and the intelligentsia. At first, John felt he would drown in the sea of strange words, but the regular visits to the taverns continued with John, now a firm member of the group, becoming an eager participant in their discussions.

"Your system of electing a parliament with real power sounds very desirable. We still have an autocrat who sacks the duma elected by the people," said Anton Pushkin, who often visited the taverns seeking potential recruits. "It is only a matter of time before the people take power by force. And then socialist collectives will own all the means of production. Every man and woman will receive a fair wage on which they can live without fear."

Argument erupted on all sides. Pushkin enjoyed prodding the students with radical ideas; it encouraged them to think. Occasionally, he found one sufficiently committed to socialist ideals that he introduced him to the other members of the party. One had to be very cautious, however; agents of the Okhrana lurked everywhere.

The young Englishman interested him.

Some weeks later, the two left the tavern together deep in discussion. They turned the corner onto a narrower street, a short-cut to the main boulevard where they would go their separate ways. Pushkin stopped talking and put his hand on Somerston's arm. A group of five men were walking toward them, all wearing the same distinctive cap. Even at this distance, there was an air of menace about the aggressive "V" formation.

"Black Hundreds," Pushkin said. "Vicious thugs."

As the leader passed under a street light, Pushkin muttered, "Igor Donstoy, as good a murderer as you are likely to meet in Moscow."

Donstoy and his gang looked hard at the two before swaggering arrogantly down the street in search of victims. Pushkin ushered Somerston around the corner and out of sight.

Rysakov and Yukovsky had been watching the tavern for some time after receiving a tip-off Black Hundreds were in the area. Rysakov preferred to nip trouble in the bud before it started. He knew it would be futile to arrest Donstoy and his like after they had beaten a student up. They watched with apprehension as the gang faced off in front of the two young men.

"They seem to know each other," said Yukovsky softly.

"Let's catch up with those two and find out what they're doing. They might be in league with Donstoy and setting up a trap," said Rysakov.

The two policemen crossed the street rapidly.

"Hoi there!" Yukovsky called out.

Pushkin half turned but kept walking.

"Police," Rysakov called.

Pushkin turned again and saw that the two men following them were almost upon them; there would be no point in running.

"Papers, please."

"What's wrong?" Somerston asked Pushkin.

Rysakov immediately picked up the heavily accented Russian.

"You're a foreigner? Where are you from?" he asked.

"London," said Somerston.

"What are you doing in Moscow?"

"I'm working, learning about the legal system in Russia," he replied.

Rysakov turned to Pushkin.

"You appear to know the group who just passed here," he said.

"If you mean that bastard Donstoy and his pack, yes, I know them, and I stay well clear of them. I have no desire to get beaten," Pushkin said.

"And where do you work, Mr. …" Rysakov glanced at the papers, "Somerston?"

"At Morozov & Son. I am staying with the family while I am in Moscow," he said.

"The Morozovs. I know them. They're a respected family. So, why are you frequenting this tavern; it's one used by radicals."

"My language tutor introduced me to it. He meets with fellow students, and he thought it would be good for me to meet and talk with them. I must say it has done wonders for my understanding, and, I'm told, for my pronunciation," Somerston said.

Rysakov allowed himself a wry smile. *I'd hate to think what it was like before you went in there,* he thought.

As the two young men went on their way, the policemen turned to head back to their office. Rysakov stopped. He looked again at the retreating figures. The taller one with the collar of his coat turned up against the cold looked familiar, the way he bent slightly forward. Then they were gone. Had he seen him before? Rysakov shrugged and rejoined Yukovsky.

Somerston and his new friend walked along in silence for some time before Pushkin spoke.

"I didn't know you were staying with Morozov," he said.

"Do you know them? They're a wonderful family. My father acts for them in London."

"Yes, I know them. My uncle, Vanya, has worked for them for many years. They've been very kind to my mother since the revolution," Pushkin said, but would not elaborate further.

§ § § § § §

Rysakov finished reading and put the report down. "There are distinct similarities, however, I would not say the killer is the same man," Sokoloff concluded in the report. He didn't know whether to be pleased that the "Monster of Moscow" had not returned, or terrified they had a second killer on the loose. Sergei had been quite serious and restrained when he delivered the report.

"I thought we'd seen the last of this madness. I don't know how you cope with it," he said to Rysakov.

The manager identified the body, and, surprisingly, Sokoloff confirmed it. He knew the family.

"It's Olga, the youngest daughter of Princess Zelenin," he said. "She's a bit of a social butterfly, seen at all the fashionable parties, often in the company of an older man, I understand. The Zelenins are aristocratic, but have limited means. As the youngest child, I don't know how Olga would have kept up with the fast set. Probably on the lookout for a wealthy husband."

"But this double life she appears to have been leading?" Sokoloff continued. "One hears rumors and gossip about bored wives taking lovers, even earning some extra income on the side. Yet, I hadn't heard such things whispered about Olga. She must have been very discreet."

Rysakov placed the report on top of a small pile of papers.

"Let's hope this is a one-off," he said aloud.

"What?" asked Yukovsky.

"Just thinking out loud about that hotel murder."

"Oh. How long had she been taking paying 'guests'?"

"About six months, or that's how long she had been operating out of this hotel. The manager said she tipped well to keep her secret. He made sure that the same staff always looked after her to limit the risk of it getting out. They all liked her so far as we can tell from the interviews," Rysakov said.

"Did the manager know any of her 'guests'?" asked Yukovsky

"I'm sure he does, but it will take a little time before the implications of not cooperating with the police sink in. For instance, a hotel needs a license to operate and a word to the mayor of Moscow could make it difficult to carry on business," said Rysakov. "I have assured him that any information he provides will be strictly confidential. I sincerely hope this was a crime of passion, a once-off, and not the start of another series of killings," Rysakov added, returning to the pile of reports on his desk. Yukovsky nodded and gazed out the window.

"How well do you know Ivan Morozov?" he asked.

Rysakov looked up. "Reasonably. Why?"

"Do you think he'd engage in large-scale fraud?"

"No," Rysakov retorted immediately. "He's tough, a ruthless competitor who would have little hesitation in forcing his competition into bankruptcy, but then they would do the same to him." He paused thoughtfully before looking up at Yukovsky. "No, he is wealthy beyond most people's dreams. He doesn't need the money, so why would he get involved in fraud?"

"I was over at the Finance Ministry today," Yukovsky said. "As you know, they regulate the banks, issue licenses, and prevent foreigners from coming into the industry. Russians should lend to Russians, they say over there. Have you ever tried to get a loan? God, sometimes I think it would be better to let the British banks start up. Anyway, a friend of mine works there and knowing how much I like the banks thought I might be interested in getting involved in an investigation they're considering."

"It seems a number of Moscow's merchants and manufacturers have been airing their suspicions about how Morozov came to control the Moscow Commerce Bank," he said. "For a while, it was dismissed as just the usual grumbling about a competitor and the ministry didn't take it seriously. Then, a group lodged a formal complaint. They lost all their deposits, running into several million rubles, he said, and they're not happy. Morozov, they say, also had a million on deposit so he stood to lose that in a collapse. But now that he controls the bank, they say he's certain to get all his money back one way or another."

"Didn't Morozov offer to pay out fifty kopeks for every ruble of the depositors' funds by putting his own money in?" asked Rysakov.

"That's what really got these men mad. They're saying Morozov had a deal going with Koslinski, who, as we both know, had other, more pressing reasons for wanting to disappear. Morozov, they say, agreed to Koslinski taking enough of the bank's money to set himself up in a foreign country with a new identity. The rest Morozov secreted overseas so that he could then lend it to himself to take control of the bank by paying it in as new capital. Part of these funds would then be used to pay back half of the depositors' money. In other words, he is using their own money to pay them back!"

"That all sounds a bit circumstantial," said Rysakov. "You know how envious some of those aristos are of the very wealthy merchants. They can't believe they no longer have a monopoly on money and power and they'd relish the prospect of bringing down one of Moscow's wealthiest."

"True, but what really got them thinking there may be something in these complaints was Morozov's burgeoning relationship with Countess Anastasia Metchersky," said Yukovsky.

Rysakov sat bolt upright. "But she's Koslinski's cousin!"

"Exactly," said Yukovsky.

Rysakov's mind raced. "How long has this been going on? How serious is it? Perhaps it's nothing more than a casual friendship as a result of their involvement in several charities?"

"It appears they're lovers. The relationship's been developing over some months. According to the Okhrana's informers," Yukovsky added.

"You didn't end up telling the Morozovs we knew who the "Monster of Moscow" was, did you?" asked Yukovsky.

"No. There seemed little point without proof that would stand up in court, and then when he disappeared…"

"I wonder what would've happened if you had told them?"

They both sat silently, considering the implications of all this new information.

§ § § § §

"You look in the full bloom of health, my dear Katya," said the countess. "If I didn't already know I am sure I would have guessed. There's nothing makes a young woman look more beautiful than the second stage of childbearing. I must say though that Ivan Victorovich is more excited than the father. He is becoming quite a bore." She smiled.

Katya was delighted romance had blossomed between Ivan and her good friend. *She is old enough to be of the right age,* she thought, *and has wealth and position of her own, so she is not chasing his money.* Her husband died many years ago in an accident and she was reputed to have had many lovers since. She had confided in Katya that playing the field had lost much of its allure. It would be so nice, she said one day, to find a man who can keep me happy—and satisfy me at the same time, she added.

Ivan and the countess now saw each other several times a week and clearly enjoyed each other's company. *They're lovers,* Katya thought as Ivan came into the room. *A woman can tell the signs. They really are perfect for each other.*

"Problems at the bank today," he said, explaining his lateness to the countess. "We'll have a drink in the foyer before the concert."

When the front door closed, Katya stood absentmindedly in the entrance vestibule of the house. She put her hand on her gently rounded stomach and caressed the life growing within. She stood in the middle of the foyer for some minutes oblivious to her surroundings, absorbed with the wonder of life.

What to wear, she thought, coming out of the reverie. It was only two weeks to Countess Shuvalov's Rose Ball and she had to decide. The Morozovs had accounts with each of the best dressmakers in Moscow, and she knew she would get preferential treatment once she decided. The blue silk, imported from their office in Harbin, was her favorite. It must have the plunging backline that was now so fashionable and a bust line cut slightly lower than really necessary that she knew she would catch everyone's attention.

The next two weeks vanished in a blur of activity for Katya. They received confirmation a famous British conductor would visit Moscow and conduct a short series of concerts at the Arts Theatre. Morozov & Son would sponsor the series and Katya was closely involved in making the arrangements. One of the hospitals endowed by the merchants opened a new wing and Katya attended as the family representative. The Ladies Tennis Club had its annual meeting to decide office bearers for the next year. Katya supported the reelection of a friend of Countess Metchersky, at her request. And, of course, she kept the household running efficiently. Her ball gown was finally completed. Just in time, since she had not been able to attend all the fittings the dressmaker begged of her.

Now, at last, the night of the ball had arrived. Katya had her hair fashionably short with the waves and rolls currently the rage in society. Her dress, she felt confident, could not be more stunning.

As they entered the ballroom, Katya and Mikhail, Ivan and the countess, a resplendent spectacle rolled out in front of them to the far side of the enormous hall. There must have been nearly a hundred circular tables, each with eight chairs. On every table bloomed a lush display of fresh roses brought in from the Crimea for the occasion. White tablecloths draped elegantly almost to the floor. Two wine glasses and a glass for vodka (or water) sat behind each place setting of exquisitely patterned fine bone china with the Shuvalov crest embossed. Even the dullest of men, Katya mused, looked smart and dashing in white tie and tails. The officers in their tailor-made dress uniforms looked magnificent. Many a heart will be won, or broken, tonight, she smiled happily.

All of the women dazzled. *Even the frumpiest looks almost attractive,* Katya thought, *with makeup, a good hairdresser, a skilful dressmaker and jewelry. What a difference money makes,* her mind momentarily flashing back to life in Dublin.

As they wended their way through the tables, greeting acquaintances, heads turned and men whispered to their wives. Katya looked stunning. The blue silk shimmered as it caught the light whenever she moved, the softness of the fabric falling in sensual folds. Men looked at her with a singularity of interest, women desperately seeking fault. The blemish-free white of her neck was only enhanced by the brilliance of the large blue sapphire pendant encrusted with small diamonds glittering an inch above her cleavage. It had been a gift from Mikhail on the birth of their son. She wore it only on truly gala occasions.

By the time they reached their table, Katya noticed that at some of the tables men held whispered conversations as they passed. It seemed to be directed toward Ivan and the countess. At first, she dismissed it. Ivan was one of the richest men in Moscow now, and she had become accustomed to the attention the family received as a consequence. And there would be no doubting the vicarious interest and gossip surrounding Ivan's involvement with the countess. In some circles it will almost certainly be viewed as an unnecessary mixing with "trade."

Some hours later, after dancing and the first course of dinner, a friend took her aside.

"Katya," the friend said, "I don't know how Anastasia can be enjoying herself after such a horrible thing."

"What do you mean?" Katya asked.

"Oh, I thought you would have heard. My husband heard from one of his colleagues, who knows a magistrate, only professionally, of course. Apparently, Olga Zelinin was murdered, strangled, he said, in a hotel room. They've kept it all very quiet while they investigate, so perhaps she doesn't know. Olga was her niece."

The more Katya thought about this news, the more she felt disturbed. What was the Zelinin girl doing in a hotel room? She lived in Moscow. She put it out of her mind, resolving not to spoil the night.

"Misha," she said once they were home, "does Anastasia know what happened to her niece?"

"The countess has a number of nieces, Katya, which one?" he said drowsily.

"Olga Zelinin. Maria Antonovna told me tonight that she had been murdered."

"Ah, yes, Father told me," he said, shaking off his tiredness. "The Metcherskys are somewhat estranged from the Zelinins, I hear, so Anastasia was never very close to Olga or her mother."

"Why didn't you tell me?" Katya asked.

"We didn't want to alarm you, my darling, and it happened in somewhat unusual circumstances." He then told Katya what he knew of Olga's death, omitting the similarities to the other violent killings and the attack that had come so close to taking Katya from them.

"More importantly for us, we heard that there are rumors circulating that father may be investigated for fraud in connection with the takeover of the Moscow Commerce Bank. It may just be malicious gossip; he seems to think some of his rivals are behind it, but you know how fast that sort of talk spreads," he said.

"But, Misha, that's absurd. Didn't Ivan borrow the money and put it into the bank so the depositors would at least get something back?" she said.

"Of course, it's absurd. I'm sure it'll blow over; nevertheless, it reflects on our good name."

§ § § § §

It took some time, but the manager of the hotel in which Olga Zelinin had been killed, finally remembered the names of the "guests" Olga entertained. However, two he did not know. No amount of threats about the hotel license or the consequences of withholding information from the police could encourage him to remember. Rysakov reluctantly came to the conclusion he really didn't know.

Once he had the list, Rysakov faced the delicate task of interviewing each of them. Checking on their alibis required even more tact and discretion since all were wealthy or well connected at court. And most, it turned out, were married. That left the two unknowns. The manager could add little about these two other than that one had an aristocratic bearing but had kept his coat collar up and hat pulled well down. He had only visited Olga on two occasions so far as the manager knew. The second one did not fit the type of man she normally seemed to prefer. He had a tough look about him, as if used to manual labor. Maybe she liked a bit of "the rough," the manager shrugged, losing interest in the whole matter.

What did intrigue Rysakov was that one of the maids on duty the night Olga had been killed thought she saw a strongly built man leaving the hotel from the floor on which Olga received her guests.

"He scared me a bit," she said when he interviewed her.

"Why?" he asked.

"I don't know," the maid said, "there was just something threatening about him."

"Had you seen him before?"

"I may have; I'm not sure," she said.

"Would you be able to identify him if you saw him again?"

"Perhaps, sir, but it was only a glimpse. The hotel corridors are not all that well lit."

Rysakov thanked her without much hope of a result from that source.

Some days later, the maid, a stolid village girl, a bit slow, but immovable once she had made up her mind, called into the police office in her area and asked for him. The officer in charge referred the inquiry on several days later, and it was nearly a week before Rysakov got the message.

The next day, he called at the hotel. The manager called the maid into his office before leaving Rysakov alone to conduct his interview.

"I understand you called into our local office and asked to see me," Rysakov said. "Unfortunately, it took several days for me to get the message as my own office is elsewhere," he explained.

"Oh, thank you, sir," she said. "I wasn't sure if my information was important enough to take up your time, but you did ask me to contact you if I thought of anything else."

"All information is important," he said, waiting for the girl to tell him in her own time.

"On my last day off, I was walking with my friend—she's from the same village," she said. "We sometimes spend the morning looking in the shop windows, although we can't afford to buy anything. Anyway, this day we decided to look at some of the jewelry shops. Not the ones that the really wealthy go to but the ones that display all their things in the window. We had just started down the street when five or six men pushed passed us. They were all wearing a black cap with a high peak in the front. At first, we thought they were soldiers, but the cap wasn't right really and several of them were carrying axe handles. As they passed, one of them said to us "good Russian girls shouldn't be around Jews—go back to your homes." As he said that their leader turned toward us. I think it was the man who visited the poor Princess Olga."

"What did you do then?"

"We turned around and left. They looked like violent men, and we'd read in the papers that groups of men sometimes beat up Jews because the Jews are the betrayers of Christ." She crossed herself and sat there, silent.

"Did you see where this gang went?" he asked.

"They were heading towards the jewelry shops," she said, "but that's all we saw."

He had heard of some recent trouble in the jewelry and diamond areas of the city when a gang of Black Hundreds had smashed several of the shops, badly beating the owners, and allegedly stealing gems and the day's takings in cash. No one had been apprehended over the assaults and he doubted anyone would be.

"Thank you," he said, "you've been very helpful."

As she stood to leave, he asked, "Do you think you might recognize this man again?"

"Yes, I think so, sir," she said.

So, he thought, *one of the Black Hundreds. Well, they are brutal and vicious enough to be capable of just about anything. Was this man the last to see Princess Olga alive? On the one hand, he may be nothing more than a thug doing what thugs do, and providing some occasional "rough" excitement to a bored aristocrat. Or, he may be our man, if we can identify the right member of the Hundreds, and the maid puts him in the hotel on the night of Olga Zelinin's death. Even then we will still have the devil of a job proving he killed her. These bastards have no conscience, and he'll simple deny all knowledge of Princess Olga.*

He walked back into his office. *First we should find him,* he thought. And then, for no particular reason that he could put his finger on, the name Igor Donstoy popped into his mind.

§ § § § §

Ivan and Mikhail sat in the library talking quietly, the door closed to ensure privacy. The usual dinner guests had all departed. Katya was in the kitchen giving instructions for the following day and planning the forthcoming concerts.

"It's very worrying," said Mikhail.

"Did you speak to Sergei Sokoloff?" Ivan asked.

"Yes, I caught him after dinner. He was a bit reluctant at first, but when I reminded him about the attack on Katya he understood why we're so concerned. He confirmed he had examined Olga Zelinin's body at the scene, at Rysakov's request. In his opinion, there are a number of similarities between this murder and the earlier ones. But he wasn't prepared to say it's the same man," Mikhail said.

Ivan shook his head in dismay.

"Anastasia had a visit recently from Rysakov, who told her her niece had been strangled. He believes her niece must have known the murderer as there were no signs of a struggle. He also said, as delicately as he could, that he understood Olga had a number of male friends, and it would be helpful if Anastasia knew any of them. Of course, she explained she was not close to the Zelinins."

"If it's the same monster, then Katya is in danger," said Mikhail, his face grim. "The bastard may have followed her to London, and now he's back in Moscow."

"We don't know for certain if it was the same man in London," Ivan said. "Katya was still upset from the attack when we left, and she may have seen someone in the crowd who revived that fear. It may simply have been a passing likeness to what she thinks she remembers."

"I know," said Mikhail, "but can we take that risk?"

"No," Ivan said. "We cannot. I'll make sure Vanya is with her whenever she leaves the house."

"Or Pinna," said Mikhail.

"Yes, or Pinna," agreed Ivan.

He got up, went to a glass-fronted cabinet against the wall and poured two glasses of vodka. He handed one to his son.

"I received a letter from Yusuf today. He says that, through family connections in Kazakhstan, Kazak Oil has secured two large prospective areas for oil."

"How does he know they are prospective?" asked Mikhail.

"They have old oil seeps. It's on such areas that the producing wells have been established by the British syndicates. The number of motorized vehicles is increasing in Moscow, but the number in London amazed me, and the demand for motorized tractors for farming will create more demand eventually. Though the real profit, I believe, will come from supplying oil for the navies of the world. The British navy is converting to oil-driven engines, and ours will also. That's where the real growth will come from. And we'll supply them. I can't imagine a more profitable business. We pump the oil out of the ground into storage tanks. It's taken to the refinery, converted into fuel, and sold. The profit margins are huge and no labor to worry about, no strikes, no demands for more money."

"Yusuf has performed well," said Mikhail.

"And he will become rich as a result," Ivan smiled. "The Moscow Commerce Bank today agreed to finance the oil field development if good title to the areas is secured. Yusuf's letter confirms the title."

"With Tiger Moon Trading the majority shareholder in Kazak Oil, our dividends from the east'll be huge," said Mikhail.

"Yes," agreed Ivan. "It is time we both visited Harbin. It's too long since I was last there, and I need to see firsthand the potential for our tractor agency. I'd like to talk to Yusuf about more oil deals. The bank was enthusiastic about funding them. Even Fox's nominee spoke very persuasively. Only conservative old Vladimir wanted to 'think about it.' We'll go in a month."

§ § § § §

Two weeks later, Gregori Yukovsky, in the company of Anatoli Davidovich Repin from the Ministry of Finance, called unannounced at the office of Morozov & Son to see Ivan. Once they had established their credentials, Yukovsky began.

"We apologize for interrupting your day, Ivan Victorovich, as we know you are a very busy man," he opened. "Unfortunately, the ministry has received a number of complaints from a range of different persons, all of whom are depositors with the Moscow Commerce Bank."

"Complaints against successful merchants are not uncommon," he said. "Usually on investigation they amount to nothing so we try to avoid wasting everyone's time. However, in this instance, because of the source of some of the complaints, we're forced to at least ask questions so the matter can be laid to rest."

"Anatoli Davidovich has been given authority from the ministry to head the investigation," he added.

This made it clear to Ivan that, notwithstanding the gentle tone used by the policeman, the investigation was serious. To place a senior man from the ministry in charge meant that the minister himself had approved it.

Ivan nodded. "What do you wish to know?"

"When Vasily Koslinski disappeared, millions of rubles in bank funds also vanished. We've been able to trace these funds to banks in Berlin and Paris, after which…poof, into thin air. No trace of where the money went," said Repin. "The banks have been very cooperative. The problem is that once the deposited funds had been cleared they were immediately withdrawn in bearer bonds and cash. The bonds issued by these major European banks can be used like cash to purchase any asset or deposited in any bank. The bonds are also traded by the banks and by wealthy investors on the Paris Bourse, for instance. There's no way of tracking them. Whoever holds them can convert them into cash equal to the face value. So, the money stolen from the Moscow bank could now be anywhere in the world."

"I see," said Ivan, marveling at the elegant simplicity of Koslinski's theft. "So what has this to do with me?"

"When you took control of the Moscow bank, I understand you funded it with a foreign loan."

"Yes," said Ivan.

"And that loan came from the British & Foreign Credit Bank in London?" asked Repin.

"That is correct." Ivan felt his anger rising as it had countless times in the past that his government, *correction,* he thought, *the tsar's government,* should snoop and spy on everything its citizens did. Outwardly, he remained calm and controlled. He knew it would achieve nothing if he allowed his anger to show. It would only give this bureaucrat satisfaction.

"Was that not the bank that had a correspondent relationship with Vasily Koslinski for some years?"

"I don't know," replied Ivan.

"Did you have some dealings with the British bank some years ago? On cotton shipments, I believe," Repin asked.

"Yes, we did."

"And have you met with a George Fox, a director of the British bank since that time?"

It was now obvious to Ivan that the ministry had been investigating him and his financing for some time, no doubt using the Okhrana's army of informers.

"Where is all this leading? You clearly know that George Fox was in Moscow and that he came to visit me on several occasions. So have other foreigners. We do business with many countries."

"Can you tell us why Fox came all this way to visit you?"

"It was a business matter," Ivan said.

"Can you be a little more explicit?"

"No."

Repin looked across at Yukovsky.

"It may help our inquiries if you could explain the nature of the business you do with George Fox."

Ivan did not answer. He stared at Repin, his face impassive. He thought he could see where the questions were heading. The rumors he and Mikhail had heard must have some influential backers.

"Mr. Morozov, the tsar and his government are concerned that the public has confidence in our banking system. It is particularly important as our industry develops and our trade with foreign markets increases," said Repin.

"I totally agree," said Ivan. "That is why I have invested a substantial sum of my own money into the Moscow Commerce Bank. I wish to ensure that the bank survives and that depositors get back at least some of their money."

"But, it seems, from complaints made to the ministry, that your actions have not improved the level of confidence," said Repin.

Ivan started to say something, then changed his mind and remained silent.

Yukovsky, who so far had said nothing, but quietly observed the exchange, straightened in his chair.

"Mr. Morozov, there have been a number of rumors circulating about your involvement with the Moscow Bank, you've probably heard some of them. Normally we do not take any notice of rumors. If we did, we'd have no time for real police work," he smiled.

"I'm pleased to hear it," said Ivan.

"However, there have been some very specific complaints, and we've had no choice but to investigate them," Yukovsky said in an almost apologetic tone.

"By whom?" asked Ivan.

"You know I can't answer that," the policeman said. "However, the more information you can give us, the easier it'll be to settle the complaints and put the matter to rest."

Ivan was under no illusions the matter would be dealt with so easily.

"We understand you have been accompanying the Countess Anastasia Metchersky to concerts and balls, and that a closer relationship has developed," Yukovsky continued. "How long have you known Anastasia Alexandrovna?"

This question momentarily threw Ivan off guard.

"That's none of your damned business," he retorted. "I'm a widower of many years standing, and I will see what women I want, when I want."

"Quite so," said Yukovsky quietly with a hard edge to his voice, "but Anastasia Metchersky is not just another woman. She is Vasily Koslinski's cousin. In fact, she was once *very* close to him, and we believe she may know where he is hiding."

§ § § § §

"They virtually accused me of conspiring with Koslinski to defraud the bank and use the money to buy control. The fact I've become close friends with Anastasia they took as almost conclusive evidence I was involved." Ivan swore.

Mikhail and Katya sat appalled as Ivan relayed what had transpired.

"Surely, if we show them the funds were genuine borrowings from the British bank they can't still suspect you of stealing with Koslinski?" said Mikhail.

"I thought that was the solution at first, Misha. Then I looked at it dispassionately. Consider how it looks from their perspective—most of the depositors' funds in the bank disappear and cannot be traced; Koslinski disappears; Morozov is approached by the British banker, George Fox, with whom Koslinski had close business ties; Fox's bank lends me the money to take control of the Moscow Commerce Bank; we offer to pay only fifty kopecks for each ruble to depositors over time—in fact, part will be repaid out of future profits. Then, to complete the whole conspiracy I have become close to Countess Metchersky, a cousin of Koslinski, with whom she had been very close. In fact, they were lovers. I asked Anastasia. They believe she knows where he is. With our national penchant for drama and conspiracies, this adds up to incontrovertible proof."

"Fox comes to visit me in Moscow," he went on, "we have extensive dealings in England; having control of our own bank enables us to take advantage of opportunities that may not otherwise have been possible. Take the Kazak Oil deal, for instance. God, if it was someone else, I would take little persuading they were involved with the theft; there are too many coincidences. Damn. I should have thought through Fox's offer more thoroughly before agreeing to it. Curse that man. He's been nothing but trouble."

"What can they do?" asked Mikhail. "They have no proof, just supposition based on rumor."

"I don't know. They won't cancel the bank's license. That would be the end for the depositors. Nevertheless, I'm sure they'll think up some devilment if they can't be convinced I had no part in the theft. In the meantime, I'm sure my enemies will make the most of it," Ivan said.

"You have done no wrong," Katya said. "Without your action, the Moscow bank would have failed completely, and they would have lost everything. There can't be any evidence of wrongdoing because there was none," she said firmly. "We must tell everyone that these rumors are lies and that Morozov & Son is depositing money with the bank.

That will convince them the bank is sound. Then we will make sure that the concert we're sponsoring is a resounding success. That will show everyone we don't give these rumors any credence and that we hold our heads high."

Ivan smiled, "Thank you, Katya. You are right, of course, and we shall do just as you suggest. Women see problems in a very practical way, don't they, Misha?"

When they had gone, Ivan remained in the library, deep in thought. It was not quite as simple as Katya suggested. That the ministry had appointed an investigator showed they did not treat the matter as trivial. He knew that, over the years, in building his empire, he had not endeared himself to some with close connections to the Imperial Court. In addition, some of those in business whom he had bested on more than one occasion would dearly love to help along any move toward his demise.

There was no theft, and there was no fraud. If the ministry decides to confiscate his shares in the bank, then they would have to deal with Fox and his loan. *With no other security for the debt, the rest of our assets are safe,* he told himself. Then, he realized, that in itself presents a problem. If the ministry finds out that the only security for the loan from the British bank are the shares in the bank, they will take it as one more piece of evidence to support their theory. *Why would a British bank make such a loan without much better security, for instance, a charge over one of our factories? With the only security for the loan a charge on the shares in the bank I stand to lose nothing if the bank collapses. If I had some of my own assets at risk, then the rest of the ministry's case would be weak. As it stands I have a problem.*

Even if Fox were here, they would be unlikely to believe him if he said he had no involvement in the theft and that his bank was not a party to it. As a foreigner, his evidence would be suspect.

He stood up, his mind racing, considering his position from every possible angle.

"Even in England, where they claim you are innocent until proven guilty, a strong case could be made against me. In Moscow, you are guilty if sufficient number of those in power say you are. Ivan Victorovich, you had better use the power wealth has given you before those bastards grab it," he said to the empty room.

§ § § § § §

Over the next few weeks, Ivan used all his connections and influence to have the investigation dropped. He met with members of the government in Moscow and even journeyed to Saint Petersburg. His reception was not universally sympathetic. Many in the nobility were secretly pleased one of the nouveau riche, and one with such a high profile, was getting what some felt were his just desserts. The idea that such wealth could be acquired legitimately in such a short space of time was obscene. Particularly by men who a generation ago were peasants. They had no breeding. It stood to reason some impropriety would inevitably be involved in the amassing of such a fortune. A scandal as juicy as this should not be easily pushed aside.

Then there were those who knew Ivan and how he supported charities, training institutes, and hospitals, giving generously and without publicity. They tried to intervene on his behalf.

He had to be careful not to complain too loudly or too widely so as not to raise even more suspicion. In the end, he felt his efforts had blunted the more outrageous suggestions. Nevertheless, there seemed little doubt an official investigation would proceed, albeit quietly. Ivan had his legal representatives make it known they would instigate libel actions to silence the more salacious gossip. Meanwhile, he prepared to fight the likely conclusions. Even with all the support he could muster, Ivan suspected he may never completely clear his name of suspicion. Some doubt would always remain, unless he could produce unchallengeable evidence from an unimpeachable source that would make it clear he was not involved in Koslinski's embezzlement. At the end of the third week, only one possible solution remained. In a course of action fraught with danger, he wrote a letter.

Maksim Rysakov found the conversation with Gregori Yukovsky disturbing. Yukovsky laid out the evidence against Morozov and while Rysakov did not believe the industrialist guilty, as he told his colleague, he had to admit it presented a persuasive case. He had seen too much of the Morozov family to believe them capable of such a crime. His old friend, Sergei Sokoloff, had told him of their unstinting support for his hospital and he had first-hand experience of their generosity.

Key parts of the body of evidence are circumstantial or supposition, he told Yukovsky. These items should be reexamined to determine whether they were fact or not. If this evidence was nothing but hearsay, the case would collapse.

With an effort, he pushed the bank fraud out of his mind. It was only money, after all. Money could be replaced. Life had far greater value, and there had been another murder. Whether it was related to the murders by the "Monster of Moscow" he couldn't be certain. The details he'd received had not been encouraging.

As he climbed the stairs to the room where the body had been found, he wondered yet again when the decay of moral standards had really begun. Last night, when he had discussed the problem with his wife, Vera, she argued the lifting of censorship and calling of the second Duma clearly caused the problem. If the tsar had only retained absolute power, she said, and set the example of the perfect family then the standards of sexual behavior would not have dropped so alarmingly.

He didn't consider himself a prude. He saw evidence of man's weakness too often to be surprised by any new folly. However, even he was taken aback by the explicit sensuality of the new wave of literature and art. There had been a burst of novels, greedily consumed by the reading public, giving accounts of rape, incest, sodomy, sadism, lesbian and homosexual sex, and suicide. If they can read freely of such acts and even be encouraged to try them, would this tip a weak mind over the edge? Would it pull down the barriers society has erected to control such excesses? Where was the line between freedom of expression and licentiousness? *If men and women could indulge themselves for no other reason than self-gratification, surely there would be a breakdown in law and order,* he thought. *Laws I have undertaken to uphold.*

The majority of Moscovites will go about their lives, immensely titillated; a few will experiment. As he knew, more than half the adult males (and more than a few women, though he could never tell his wife that) already visited prostitutes in the city. It was that small number with deeper problems that gave Rysakov his real reason for concern.

A constable opened the door for him.

The woman had been identified as a would-be poet, someone who inhabited the fringes of the bohemian world. He walked around the bed. At first, it looked like nothing more than a random killing. Then, he looked more closely at the body. She'd been strangled. Vicious bruises stood out on both sides of her temple. He straightened up, a sick feeling in his stomach. If he hadn't bent over to check the left temple as well he would have missed it. Her long hair had been cut shorter on the left side near the neck. He could not be sure if it was souvenir taking or perhaps an avant-garde fashion. He assumed the pubic area had been depilated by the woman, not the killer. *No doubt part of this "new wave,"* he mused.

London

"Interesting," said Philip Armitage as he placed the letter on the desk.

"I thought I might send a rather innocuous reply, saying that while we have made no specific inquiries, we have no reason to believe that the British & Foreign Credit Bank has been involved in any improper activities," said Sir Algernon Law.

"It's been quite useful having a man on the ground, so as to speak, at the Moscow Commerce Bank. That young chap we sent over as one of Fox's nominees has sent back some helpful information," he went on. "Don't think that Morozov chap has twigged. Even if he is a bit suspicious, can't really do him much harm; he still has control of his bank. For us, though, jolly useful to know what the Russkies are doing in oil in Kazakhstan."

"Hmm," Armitage stared at the desk. "It's an unusual request. Morozov must be under intense pressure. We had heard through the embassy rumors of his possible involvement with the Koslinski fraud. Someone must be taking it more seriously than idle gossip."

"It's nonsense, of course," said Law.

"Indeed," said Armitage. "Do you think Fox has told us the full story?"

"I'm sure he hasn't," replied Law. "We all keep some secrets, Philip. Nevertheless, he wouldn't be in the spot he's in if he'd contrived to help this Russian fellow rob the bank. No, I'm confident Fox is *our* man and has told us all we need to know to control the British & Foreign, and I must say that it's working out rather well."

"Perhaps we should give further consideration before replying to the letter. I'm going to be away for a bit, and don't you usually go to Scotland about this time of year?" Armitage said.

"I see," said Law. "Yes, the grouse season starts next month, and I always like to get in the first two weeks."

"Perhaps after my return we could discuss it again?"

"Any particular reason we shouldn't reply?" Law asked.

Armitage looked at the bland expression on his colleague's face. They had known each other since Oxford, and he knew that the simple aristocratic air Law affected masked a clear and incisive mind. However, as principal spymaster in the Foreign Office he knew no one should be entrusted with full information, except the prime minister, and even then...

"We don't wholly trust Russia's motives in the Balkans. There's popular support in Russia for the pan-Slav movement that's likely to push Russia to come to the aid of its Slavic brothers. The tsar's government says they won't interfere in another state, but if Turkey should falter, the temptation may be too great. In my opinion, we don't have much protection against Russian expansion in the Balkans or Central Asia," said Armitage.

"If we write the letter, it would almost certainly end up in government hands, otherwise I suspect it would be of little use to Morozov. And even if it were to be written in a bland and anodyne form, a wily politician like the Russian prime minister could choose to interpret it as interference in domestic affairs by a foreign government. They could use that as an excuse to put pressure on India from the north. At this juncture, I suspect it may not be worth taking that risk."

"I see," said Law, "then perhaps we should shelve the matter for the time being."

"After all, Algy," added Armitage, "you seem to be getting all the intelligence you need from your man in the Moscow bank anyway."

Law smiled. "And we still have the British & Foreign."

Moscow

Anatoli Repin walked into Ivan's office alone and right on time for the appointment.

"Will Yukovsky be joining us?" asked Ivan.

"No. This is an unofficial visit from the ministry, nothing to do with the police," Repin said.

"The evidence against you is largely circumstantial," he went on. "There is no hard evidence of your involvement in the Koslinski theft. However, there are those in the ministry who believe there is more than enough upon which to take strong action. I am not one of those who recommend such a course. In fact, it has been my advice to the minister that unless Yukovsky and his department can uncover some hard facts we discontinue the investigation. Unfortunately, that is most unlikely to happen; too many people of influence were affected by the loss of deposits and are more than a little suspicious of your offer of fifty kopeks to the ruble."

Ivan sat silently, his face expressionless.

"Yukovsky and the ministry will continue to seek real evidence. Only you know whether they will uncover any. If there is no evidence to discover then my prediction is that in time the ministry will tire of the effort and the matter will die. If evidence is found then you can expect harsh penalties. In the meantime, you are to be asked to remain in Moscow and to make no transfers of funds out of Russia until the matter is resolved."

"That's ridiculous. I've done no wrong and I have a business that must import cotton and other goods and export timber and furs. How am I expected to continue to operate?" Ivan said.

"Arrangements will be made to approve payments for specific imports and sales," said Repin. "There's no intention to damage your business."

"Of course not," Ivan retorted.

"I can assure you that is the case," said Repin. "The restriction is to be on the sending of funds abroad for investment or other uses. The minister needs to be able to assure people that if you are found guilty then there will be sufficient funds available here for restitution to be made."

Repin spoke in such a dispassionate tone that Ivan found it hard to take offense at the implied accusation.

"The value of my factories and warehouses in Moscow and Petersburg far exceeds the amount that bastard stole," said Ivan, "so what's the point of such restrictions. I can hardly take the factories overseas, and I'll never leave Russia."

"I agree. You have more than enough wealth, including the shares in the bank itself, to cover the loss. But," he said, his tone softening ever so slightly, "it's perceptions that count in politics. If the minister can tell certain persons he has imposed these restrictions pending the outcome of the investigations, then justice is seen to be done, however illusorily. Then the pressure on the minister to act will cease. In a way, it will also ease the pressure on you, if you accept the restriction voluntarily."

Ah, Ivan thought, *at last we get to the point of this visit. They want me to agree voluntarily to the restrictions no doubt because they don't have enough real evidence to enforce them legally.*

"And if I don't agree?" he asked.

"Then I'm sure they will be imposed anyway," said Repin. "However, I would urge you to seriously consider agreeing voluntarily. That would surely be the course of an innocent man and is more likely to be taken to be so by those affected."

Ivan had already reached that conclusion. With no response to his letter from Sir Algernon Law, he really had no alternative. Repin had indicated they could continue importing so the restrictions would have little impact on the operations of Morozov & Son. The Moscow Commerce Bank would be unrestricted in the funding it could provide to all its other customers. And Tiger Moon Trading was a totally free agent. No one knew of his interest in this business on the other side of Russia.

"Very well. You may tell the minister I agree to the restrictions voluntarily, but under protest. An innocent man should not be subjected to such insulting restrictions," Ivan said.

"Thank you, Mr. Morozov," said the ministry man as he rose to leave. "I believe you've made a wise decision."

What a grey and characterless man, Ivan thought as he shut the door on Repin. *A perfect bureaucrat.* He smiled grimly.

§ § § § §

Once Ivan explained to Mikhail and Katya why he could not travel, they agreed the restrictions on movement did not apply to Mikhail. As the planned visit to Yusuf Yudin was long overdue, Mikhail would go on his own to Harbin. They held a farewell dinner to which several regular visitors to the house and some old friends were invited.

"Are there really as many Chinese as the newspapers report?" asked Dr. Sergei Sokoloff.

"It's hard to imagine how so many people can live in a city and work the land," Ivan said.

"What music do they play, Ivan?" said a friend, a gifted amateur violinist who occasionally appeared with the Moscow Symphony Orchestra.

"What little I have heard of the singing is not at all pleasant to the ear. It's a strange, shrill, whining sound. The orchestral music is mostly drums and cymbals, although they do have an instrument with only one string," he said nodding slightly to his friend. "It produces nothing like the sounds you have occasionally been known to grace our halls with Arkady Emilovich."

Ivan knew his friend hoped he would be invited to entertain them and that the Guarneri would be brought from its case. Arkady did not disappoint. The guests left soon after, humming gypsy airs as they dispersed.

The three family members and young Somerston sat quietly in the drawing room as the door closed on the last guest, Ivan reverently cradling the Guarneri.

"What a wonderful gift to be able to play so well and without music," said Katya. "It makes the heart sing."

Ivan was silent for a few moments and then looked at Mikhail and Katya.

"This violin in a way represents our family," he said. "The harmony of the family, in its rich and vibrant sound; our wealth, in its value; and our longevity, in its very old age. I would like you both to promise me that this violin will always be kept by the eldest member of the family and that if for some reason you have to move or leave Moscow you will always take it and keep it with you. So long as you have this violin, I know that the future of the family will be secure."

Katya put her hand on Ivan's arm and squeezed it gently.

"That is a wonderful sentiment, Father; of course we will always keep the violin, and it shall always remain on display resting in its case," she said.

Mikhail looked at his father and simply nodded.

Two days later, Mikhail boarded the Trans-Siberian train in Moscow, destination Harbin. Bubbling with excitement, John Somerston stood beside him on the step as the train picked up speed out of the station. Somerston had jumped at the prospect of visiting Harbin even though it would extend his time in Russia.

The soft golden hues of autumn leaves slid past the windows of their carriage as they left the city. Mikhail had to admit, some of Somerston's anticipation had infected him. This would be a good trip.

As the train wound its way across the endless steppes of Central Asia, Ivan faced a new set of problems in Moscow. A wave of strikes and unrest broke out in several of his larger factories. Strikes were not new. These, however, were well organized and coordinated. Ivan's level of concern rose several notches. It appeared as though the Morozov businesses had been specifically targeted. All the inquiries he made pointed to one key shadowy figure, a member of the Black Hundreds. From the information Ivan gathered, that figure could only be Igor Donstoy. It came as no surprise that he held a grudge against the Morozovs. Ivan had humiliated him. Now it appeared he had decided to cause as much trouble as possible. Ivan had no proof it was Donstoy. Yet he had no doubt.

All of that was disruptive but manageable. Today, one of his foremen reported something far more disturbing. A member of the late shift had been at a meeting where Donstoy addressed the group.

"Your children are short of food and clothing," Donstoy told them. "It is your children who die through lack of money to seek help. Maybe the owners should suffer the same loss."

The woman who told the foreman said that while she supported action to secure more money and better conditions, she did not support action against children and felt the Morozovs should be warned. Ivan decided the police must be involved. He would not risk injury to his grandchildren.

"I see," said Rysakov when Ivan had finished. "Donstoy is a vicious man. We suspect he is guilty of more than one murder though I can't take action unless I get more evidence. From what I know of the man, I doubt your children are in any immediate danger, but take care, Ivan Victorovich. If you get any more information, please tell me immediately. In the meantime, I can confirm to you that Donstoy is a person of interest to us. And he knows it."

"Good," said Ivan.

"How is Katya Mariavna?" asked Rysakov.

Ivan looked at the policeman.

"She is well, thank you, Maksim. I have a new grandson, Yuri, since I last saw you."

"Yes, I'd heard. Congratulations."

Ivan paused. "I still have Vanya or Pinna accompany her and the children whenever she goes out."

"Good, that's wise," said Rysakov, nodding as if he had been awaiting confirmation of the guard on Katya.

Harbin

The train slowed as it approached Harbin on the northern side of the Sungari River. Mikhail pointed out the Pristan area on the other side, which housed the wharfs and warehouses, as well as slums and the highest human dwelling concentration outside Saint Petersburg.

"Over 5,000 vessels berth here each year," said Mikhail. "It's the busiest port in Siberia, bringing timber, grains, and soya bean down the Amur River from the surrounding areas."

Somerston nodded, agog at all the activity as the train slowly rolled across the river. Looking toward their destination, he could not help but notice the low rise of the city skyline, punctuated at random by the towering presence of the familiar, onion-shaped domes of the orthodox churches. Highest of all was a Vologda-style cathedral, perched on a rise. Its roof reached to the heavens in a peak topped by a small onion dome from which rose a cross, a further twenty feet closer to God.

"Harbin's a 'Russian' city," Mikhail explained. "The Chinese leased it to us under the China Eastern Railway Treaty. Our CER have their own police and guards. China recently declared Harbin an open city and Petersburg immediately set up a consulate. Japan, U.S.A., Britain, and other Western powers all soon followed. Each has poured money into businesses here, but most aggressive by far are the Japanese."

The train glided past the lumber yard and freight offices into Harbin Station. As they alighted, a mass of humanity surrounded them. Clearly, the arrival of the Moscow train was still a significant event. People hurried in every direction, and encompassing all the activity was the station. Somerston found the sheer scale of the station building astonishing. He had not seen a grander building than the art nouveau pistachio-green station since leaving Moscow.

Out of the crowd, a man with the dark good looks of Central Asia strode toward them. With his loose-fitting trousers and Cossack-style shirt, he looked neither Russian nor Asian.

A broad smile broke across Mikhail's face as he embraced the man in a Russian bear hug.

"Yusuf, it is indeed good to see you. It's been a long time," he said.

"I was beginning to think that you were scared of the tigers, Misha," smiled Yusuf Yudin.

Yudin shouted several orders in Chinese and a group of porters quickly gathered the travelers' luggage and disappeared out of the station.

"Come," said Yusuf. "Harbin has changed a lot since you were here last. I'll give you a tour on the way to your hotel."

As the horses pulling their carriage kept a steady but unhurried pace, Yusuf briefed Mikhail on the latest developments in the business, in between pointing out new buildings, hotels, baths, roads, and theaters. Anyone listening would have assumed, quite reasonably, that Tiger Moon Trading was the eastern agent for the Morozovs.

Over the next week, while Somerston explored the exotic East. Yusuf and Mikhail discussed business. Yusuf already knew of Morozov & Son controlling holding in the Moscow Credit Bank and had heard rumors of trouble surrounding it. Mikhail told him in detail of the allegations and of the restrictions placed on Ivan and their ability to invest freely outside Russia.

"That's ridiculous," said Yusuf at the end. "I know your father to be an honorable and trustworthy man. He would never be party to a fraud. It's wrong a man is unable to clear his name when so unjustly accused. Is there no evidence that can help you do that?"

"The police have no evidence of misdeeds and the ministry have only circumstantial evidence with no proof. We believe it'll wither on the vine, much to the chagrin of our competitors," said Mikhail.

"You're sure no one knows of your investment in Tiger Moon?" asked Yusuf.

"Only Father and I," Mikhail replied.

"Only myself and Liu Ping-nan know here. Although I suspect Ching-po, his daughter, and Li Yu-Tang, his eldest son, also know. The old man is not getting any younger and to protect the family's interests, I expect he has told them in the strictest confidence. There is no danger of a leak from here," Yusuf said. "So, Tiger Moon can invest in any venture you choose." Yusuf smiled.

Mikhail laughed. "We're more than happy with our investment in Tiger Moon," he said. "In the short term, our share of the profits should remain in the business. Before I leave, I'll give you the details of a solicitor in London to whom we may ask you to send funds from time to time."

They discussed the refrigerated trade in butter to the Moscow and Petersburg market and the rapid growth in soya bean extracts. The developments in Kazakh Oil Mikhail found particularly exciting. In the week before they arrived, there had been approaches from several British firms and one from an American oil company. All were pressing to joint venture the development of the field by drilling wells and then setting up refineries to treat the oil for export. The profits promised to be huge.

At the first meeting with Liu Ping-nan, Mikhail made it clear his father had complete trust in his Chinese partner and that they had no secrets from each other. He explained the problems Ivan faced in Moscow. Liu Ping-nan simply nodded and observed that the injustices of life were to be endured and overcome.

"Your family will suffer no ill effects in Harbin from this unfortunate series of events," he said. "You have firm friends here in the East who will help you should you ever need it. It will be many generations before we forget the honor you bestowed on my family by trusting us to rebuild the business when all we owned had been destroyed."

Only Yudin knew how important to Liu Ping-nan and his family was the trust Ivan Morozov had shown by providing the funds with only the old man's word as to the equity share in the business. Yudin knew for certain that there was not one other instance in Harbin where a Russian (and in fact he was hard pressed to think of any other foreigners) had entered into such a business partnership with a Chinese. Let alone with the trust shown by Morozov.

Toward the end of their first week, they had just sat down for dinner when a powerful-looking man of action burst into the room, threw a Cossack fur hat in the corner, and flopped into a chair.

"Sorry, I'm late. My bloody horse went lame a couple of hours out of the city and I had to cadge a lift on a farmer's cart."

"May I present Tomas Emiliovich Valevsky, late of His Imperial Majesty's Hussars and reputed to be a hero of the Boxer Rebellion," said Yusuf.

"Reputed? Ha!" Valevsky replied, obviously used to the banter. "I defended Harbin single-handedly!"

Mikhail and Somerston both immediately liked the Hussar.

Over dinner, Valevsky allowed himself to be persuaded, against the protests of Yusuf, who had no doubt heard it many times before, to regale his audience with the tale of his retreat to Harbin. Their drinks had to be refilled several times as the story unfolded.

"A wonderful story," said Mikhail. "I remember reading about the fight in the Moscow papers at the time."

"Tomas Emiliovich oversees our security and transport," said Yusuf. Mikhail later found that Valevsky was a very competent manager and Tiger Moon had an enviable reputation among the trading houses for the efficiency of movement of its goods and its ability to avoid most of the theft and banditry in the region.

"After the war with Japan, I persuaded Tomas to resign his commission and join us," said Yudin.

"The money he was offering was barely adequate," said Valevsky, "but he asked so elegantly."

"I suggested that with Tiger Moon he could earn three times his subaltern's pay," said Yudin. "I could not think of a more elegant way of expressing the offer."

Valevsky roared with laughter. "Well put," he said

§ § § § § §

While John Somerston assisted in the more mundane tasks of a new soybean mill project, the swashbuckling ex-Hussar and his easy bachelor's life entranced him. As soon as the opportunity presented itself, Somerston volunteered to accompany Valevsky on one of his trips north up the Sungari to the Amur River. There they would arrange transport for goods down into Harbin. They would be away for about a week.

The pace of activity in Harbin amazed Mikhail. Ivan had told him it was prosperous. In fact, it was booming. It still had the rawness of a frontier town. Even the many new, substantial brick buildings couldn't disguise the frenetic bawdiness.

He soon found that the Harbinese worked hard and played hard. Night life was wild—restaurants and cabaret, gambling clubs, opium dens, and brothels of all description, catering to all tastes. Yusuf explained that the Chinese owned the gambling. Japanese, Korean, and Chinese ran most of the brothels. Russians had little involvement in the flesh trade, except for the mysterious Sergei Brokhoff.

"People whisper any perversion is procurable from Brokhoff, for a price," said Yusuf one night over dinner. Although no proof had ever been presented, he went on, rumors persisted that young girls had been kidnapped and forced into service by Brokhoff for selected customers. Some vanished.

"As I told you coming down on the ship, John Somerston," said Valevsky a few days after they had returned to Harbin, "you are now in wild Siberia, in Manchuria, home of Genghis Khan, not in your home town of London. This is an opportunity not to be missed. Here, in the brothel of the world, you can sample exotic delights unimaginable elsewhere."

They dismissed the *droshky* and strolled through the crowded streets of the Chinese sector. Somerston felt both excited and apprehensive. His new mentor had told him stories of beautiful women eager to service Englishmen in particular. His initial reticence rapidly dissolved in the heady atmosphere of spicy fragrances and the warming glow of several glasses of vodka. Valevsky had very quickly worked out the young student was a neophyte in matters of the fairer sex and resolved to be the agent of his coming of age.

"Only the most attractive women are retained by the House of Heavenly Pleasure," he said. "There are Chinese, Russians, Europeans, and I hear there is even a black from the Caribbean. Long legs, short hair, big tits or small, young virgins or experienced courtesans, they've got it all."

Somerston did not know what to say so he simply nodded.

Valevsky stopped and turned to Somerston.

"Forgive me, John, but I've thoughtlessly assumed that you like women. I can assure you that Brokhoff also has lovely young boys if that would be your preference, and perfectly all right it would be too. Not my sort but…"

"Of course I like women," Somerston snorted. "I'm looking forward to seeing them," he added with bravado.

"Good, good," said Valevsky, pleased he now had his young charge committed.

"Here we are." Valevsky turned in through a solid polished timber door in a well-maintained but nondescript building. They walked through a second door designed to keep out the cold and into a foyer with soft upholstered chairs and dimmed lighting. A women with a hard face and a smile that did not extend beyond her mouth stood up from behind a desk and said, "Good evening, gentlemen, can I help you?"

"Is Brokhoff in tonight?" asked Valevsky.

The woman considered him thoughtfully for a minute and then, apparently satisfied she recognized him said, "Go through into the lounge."

As they passed her desk, Valevsky gently placed a small bundle of rubles near her hand.

They had barely sipped from their first drink when a tall saturninely handsome man with aristocratic bearing and a neatly trimmed grey speckled beard walked over to them. His shoulders stooped slightly and there were dark rings around his eyes, but the eyes themselves were intense and penetrating.

"I am Brokhoff," he said. Years of seeing men (and women) in pursuit of pleasure had given him the ability to immediately assess their likely needs. The two in front of him were easy. The older one he thought he recognized from previous visits; the younger one almost certainly a foreigner and totally inexperienced, no doubt here to be "blooded."

"Sergei Alexandrovich may I present John Somerston from London."

"Welcome, I trust we can be of service," said Brokhoff, inclining his head slightly in Somerston's direction. "Are you to stay long in Harbin?"

"No, I am visiting with a friend from Moscow where I am staying for a year."

"I understand Moscow can be very attractive at this time of year. The season must be about to begin. I trust you and your friend will be able to enjoy the balls and theater on your return," said Brokhoff.

"I'm told the Morozovs *are* the season, so I am sure he will get the best of it," said Valevsky.

Brokhoff's interest seemed to sharpen momentarily. "You are staying with the Morozov family?" he asked.

"Yes, sir," said Somerston.

"I have heard of them. And are they with you in Harbin?"

"I am accompanying Mikhail Morozov on business. His wife and father stayed in Moscow," said Somerston.

"I see." Brokhoff paused. He looked at the young Englishman thoughtfully for a moment, as if framing a question in his mind. "Please convey my regards to the Morozovs in Moscow," he said, then he was back to business, the brief exchange forgotten. "I'll send through a selection of girls."

"Now, if you see one you like point to her. She will lead the way to her room. If you can't decide between several, and I always have that problem, tell them to take off their clothes so you can get a better look," said Valevsky.

§ § § § §

By the time Mikhail concluded his business, early winter snowfalls had become more frequent. He boarded the train for the journey westward content the relationship with their partners had been strengthened and that Tiger Moon would produce large dividends in the years ahead.

And another milestone had been passed. He smiled as he watched Valevsky give Somerston a bear hug. A naïve student had left Moscow and in Siberia made the transition to manhood.

Moscow

After two years in Russia, John Somerston made his final emotional leave-taking in early autumn, the year after he conquered Siberia.

"I'll never forget my time with you," he said, hugging each member of the family manfully. Even Pinna got a cautious hug. Ivan charged the young man with a portfolio of instructions for his firm to execute on his return to London. Mikhail presented him with a damascened Cossack dagger.

"This is the mark of the making of a man," he explained.

"I think we have a firm friend there. He can now even speak passable Russian." Ivan smiled as the train slowly pulled out of the Brest Station in Moscow, sending a deafening shriek from its whistle through a thick cloud of coal smoke and steam.

One Tuesday afternoon, some time after Somerston left Russia, Rysakov walked into Okhrana headquarters. He came to exchange information on a case and hopefully to pick the brains of a friend who had long given up trying to recruit him to the secret police. As he walked through to his friend's office, he saw a young man being escorted down the corridor toward him. The man's hair was unkempt and he had several weeks' growth of beard. As they came abreast, the prisoner lifted his head and stared defiantly straight at Rysakov. An involuntary flicker of recognition passed across his face. In a second, it was gone, and the man lowered his face quickly as the guards ushered him past.

Rysakov turned and watched until the trio disappeared from view down a stairwell he knew lead to the cells, well below street level. The interrogation chambers were also located there.

"Who was that?" he asked his friend.

"Oh, just another revolutionary. They seem to think we're stupid, but we have them all under surveillance one way or another," his friend said. He wearily picked up a file on his desk.

"Anton Pushkin. A student at the university, then after '05 he became increasingly involved with the Socialist Revolutionaries. We finally got sick of him distributing seditious literature. He'll get ten years exile east of the Urals. Do you know him?"

"I've seen him several times around student haunts and felt I'd seen him somewhere else but haven't been able to pin it down. Seeing him just then it suddenly came back to me. I ran into him at the theater bombing several years ago, when they tried to kill General Dubasov," Rysakov said.

"That's very interesting," said his friend, looking up from the file. "We've strong suspicion he's close to the top echelons of the Socialist Action Group. He may even be one of the planners behind the assassination of Prime Minister Stolypin in Kiev, but we can't get proof." After a pause, he closed the file.

"Ah, what the hell, he's going to be out of action for a long time. When we told the judge of our suspicions, he took a much sterner view of Mr. Pushkin than of the normal student ratbag. So, what information have you got for me?" said his friend getting to the business at hand; the other was over and dealt with, not worth wasting more time on.

Rysakov stored Pushkin in his compartmentalized mind. He felt somehow that his friend's suspicions were probably correct and that Pushkin was more than a little dangerous. It was the collective experience of the police and the Okhrana that the really dedicated revolutionaries, those near the top echelons, did not reform after exile. In fact, they became even more dedicated to their cause, using whatever means required. *It may be ten years before you surface but I expect our paths will cross again,* he thought.

Some months later, Rysakov received some good news. Igor Donstoy, Rysakov's favored target as the killer of Olga Zelinin and the poet, had been placed under obvious surveillance from time to time, sufficient to let him know the police had marked him. Whether or not he really was their man, Rysakov didn't know. Perhaps it was coincidence that the murders had stopped, but Rysakov did not think so. Importantly, they had stopped. That mattered.

"Good news, Maksim," said Yukovsky as Rysakov came into their office. "I heard from a friend in the Okhrana that your Mr. Donstoy has left Moscow and is gracing the citizens of Kiev with his temper."

The Moscow Commerce Bank began to repay depositors under the rescue scheme. Officially, the restrictions on Ivan's remitting funds overseas remained in place. Privately, the ministry indicated that with old depositors now receiving money it would be most unlikely the ban would be enforced, should he wish to send funds to London. Ivan, wily to the nuances of the competitive world of Moscow business, declined to take any action. *If I send funds overseas, even with the blessing of the government, competitors will be bound to hear of it and start the rumor campaign all over again. It isn't worth it. In any case, the excellent profits earned by Tiger Moon means regular transfers are made to London; and no one in Russia knows about it.* He smiled.

In the meantime, their business empire expanded at breakneck pace.

The family attended concerts, watched in awe the artistry of Anna Pavlova at the ballet, attended lavish balls, and entertained constantly. They gave generously to charities and supported young musicians of promise.

When all appeared to be so full of promise and excitement for the future, a dark cloud of sorrow blew over the household. Katya's fourth child, Alexander, succumbed to one of the regular epidemics of diphtheria that ravaged Russia and died, aged fourteen months. The blow was keenly felt by the whole household. For Katya, the pain would never really go away. There would always be the hurt of unfulfilled potential, of wondering what sort of person Alexander would have become.

Several years after the death of Alexander, Katya sat one afternoon in the sunroom gazing in a reflective mood through the glass windows at the bright green of new spring leaves, wondering whether John Somerston was now married with a family of his own. The Moscow newspapers had recently been speculating about the prospects of war with Germany. If this eventuates, it may be that England will not be caught in the conflagration and John won't be taken from his family to fight. She thought of the last time she had seen him and smiled. He had been so young and full of excitement at the prospects of life ahead.

Then, something he had said on his return from Harbin snapped unbidden into her mind. She had not thought of it since he left for London all those years ago, yet it still sent a cold shiver down her spine. She knew there was no rational reason why she should feel that way. She simply could not help it. It was involuntary.

He had said, "Mr. Sergei Brokhoff inquired after your health and expressed the hope that he may see you again."

Katya knew no one with the name of Brokhoff. When she mentioned it to Ivan he knew no one of that name. Mikhail then explained with a smile that Sergei Brokhoff was a brothel owner. He was probably doing nothing more than creating a little mischief with John Somerston. He had probably never even heard of Katya or the Morozovs until John mentioned the names. She had accepted the explanation. Yet, deep down she had a sense of misgiving about Sergei Brokhoff, even though she had never met him. Why she had that feeling she could not explain.

She shivered. Her reverie broken, she got up and left the sun-filled room.

§ § § § §

Philip Armitage sat quietly with Sir Algernon Law in the private dining room at the FO. The few other senior servants of the crown entitled to dine there had returned to their desks, leaving the spymaster and the head of the Commercial Division free to talk more openly.

"I don't like the reports coming in from Russia and Austria, let alone what the Germans are doing to inflame the situation. The German Kaiser seems determined to support his Austrian allies against the Serbs. No doubt the Russians will feel obliged to support the Serbs," said Sir Algernon. "What are you getting from your sources?"

"I'm afraid it's worse than you've been told. In Russia, there are street demonstrations and articles in the press demanding immediate war with Germany," said Armitage. "All our intelligence points to only one outcome, war in Europe. It seems as though the main protagonists are only looking for the excuse to justify it."

Law shook his head.

"I attended a cabinet briefing yesterday and the minister was quite graphic. I hoped it was just the politician talking. He said, 'The dogs of war are about to be unleashed, and once off the leash, a darkness will descend on Europe that has not been seen since the days of Bonaparte.' I thought it a bit dramatic but I gather you agree."

"I'm afraid so," said Armitage. "And it'll get worse. Reports from Saint Petersburg and Moscow suggest that unless the tsar and his government bring the unrest under control it may have reached the stage where there will be revolution. And this time it'll be bigger and more widespread than '05. The Russian people are disenchanted with their ruler. We believe the country is at a crossroad. One road'll lead to peaceful evolution, the other to violent revolution."

"How do you think that chap Morozov will fare if there is a revolution?" asked Sir Algernon.

"Well, money always seems to survive, and big money seems to survive better. A lot will depend on just how the Russian government reacts," answered Armitage.

"There's another matter concerning the military fellows," Armitage said as they rose from the table. "They don't think the Russians have anywhere near enough rifles and artillery to equip an army of the size needed to meet the combined Germans and Austrians if there is war."

§ § § § § §

Mikhail and Ivan were as appalled as the rest of Moscow at press reports of German officers taking command of the Turkish Army.

"There'll be no turning back now," Ivan said reading aloud from the morning paper two days later. "Berlin has given orders to upgrade Turkey's railways for war within six months. The newspaper has got it right this time. Listen: 'Serbs have been seeking independence for years, fighting the Ottoman Turks. Now the Germans are helping the Turks. This makes Germany anti-Serb and therefore anti-Russian.'"

"Have you heard?" Rysakov asked Yukovsky. "The German kaiser has sent a message of support to the Austrians and Austria's issued Serbia with an ultimatum."

"It'll be war for certain," said Yukovsky. "There's no possibility of us not going to the aid of the Serbs."

Three days later, Austria declared war on Serbia. The next day Russia issued a mobilization order. Then, on the first of August 1914, Germany declared war on Russia.

§ § § § §

"The conditions have not improved at the front; if anything, they're worse," said Mikhail as he sat down at the table for the evening meal. His eyes had dark smudges beneath them and his face was haggard. He had that afternoon returned from personally overseeing the delivery of heavy clothing, made in the firm's factories, to soldiers fighting to repel the Germans.

"The war has been consuming lives for nearly two years. The official figures grossly underestimate the casualties. More than half our soldiers have no weapon, no boots, not enough clothing for winter and rarely enough to eat. Nothing has improved," he shook his head. No one at the table spoke.

"I could see the explosions of the German artillery shells, throwing up huge fountains of dirt, no doubt mixed with pieces of loyal Russian soldiers," he added. "There must be more we can do to help these poor fellows."

"Misha, you are doing all that you can," said Katya, horrified he had once again gone so close to the front as to see the action. Katya was terrified he would get killed, but she knew better than to try and stop him. Three times he had been to the front. Each time he delivered stores for the troops. He insisted on helping in the war effort. He had even wanted to join one of the regiments before Katya exploded with a fear-induced rage. However, she knew she could not stop him from going. She reasoned that if he only went on trips to deliver stores the chances of injury would be limited. He would survive. Now he had been right to the front. She suppressed her terror. If she protested too much he could always delegate the deliveries and join one of the regiments. As he said many times, "I will not let other Russians fight to protect our land while I am safe at home."

"We have expanded the hospital again," said Katya in an effort to distract him. "Every time we complete a new ward more wounded arrive. We're giving them the best care we possibly can, but so many are so badly damaged it's hard to imagine them ever returning to a normal life when this is all over."

"Misha," said Ivan, "look at your wife; she works long hours at the hospitals as well as running the household."

Mikhail lifted his gaze and looked at Katya. His father was right; she looked as tired as he felt. He smiled weakly, the melancholy that had engulfed him since he left the front lifted a little.

"If the soldiers' conditions do not improve soon, I suspect there'll be mutiny. I'm told there have already been rumblings stirred up by socialists fighting alongside the farm boys. Our men don't have enough to fill their bellies. Many of them have no choice but to take greatcoats off the dead. Rifles they pick up where they have been dropped, sometimes with a hand still gripping the butt. I spoke to some of the wounded as they were carried on carts to the rear. 'Why do we have to fight?' they asked, 'this is not our fight; what do I care about Poland when my crop needs harvesting at home.' On the way back from the front I stopped at one of the field hospitals. We used our vehicles to help carry some of the wounded back."

He stopped as a tear rolled down his cheek. "It was little more than a barn. Men lay groaning on thin layers of straw, wounds roughly bandaged with whatever was to hand. Not enough doctors. Many of them die before they get treatment. No medicines." His voice rose with anger and frustration. "They don't know what they are fighting for but they fight and die with great bravery. And when too many of them have been killed, new innocents are pushed forward to fill the gaps. I'm sorry; I can't get the images out of my head."

He picked desultorily at the food. The others at the table felt helpless. They could not ease the pain he felt because they had not been where he had been nor seen what he had seen. After an awkward silence, Ivan began to tell Mikhail of the unrest in Moscow.

"On the way back I saw one of the radical newspapers circulating among the troops," said Mikhail. "They're already saying that capitalists must be controlled if Russia is to win the war. We're making too much profit out of supplying the troops to want the war to end, they say. They must be mad to think anyone could want this slaughter to continue. If you saw some of the simple men at the front worried about their crops back home, yet fighting with courage to defend the land for all Russians. If they survive and return they will expect better conditions. And they will have earned them." He rubbed his eyes, gritty from tiredness.

§ § § § §

Pavel Rysakov limped as he walked away from the train in Saint Petersburg. It had been packed to overflowing with wounded, troops returning from the front and deserters. He was a deserter, but he had little fear of being caught, there were so many like him. He carried a small duffel bag with his meager possessions and a crust of stale bread. He pulled the greatcoat around him against the freezing air. The February temperature sat at minus twelve. Sleep had only come in fitful snatches on the journey and in his weariness he felt the cold more keenly. He was impatient to deliver the message from the front and get out of the weather. With his injured right leg he could not force his way through the crush on the platform so resigned himself to moving at the pace of the crowd. As he eventually emerged onto the street, thousands of people filled the thoroughfare, some carrying placards, others chanting slogans.

"What's going on?" he asked a man wearing rough, dirty clothes and a cheap cloth cap.

The man looked appraisingly at Pavel and said, "Just returned from the front, have you?"

"Yes. Medical Corps."

"I was there in '14 and '15. I came back here to work in the factories and found my family worse off than when I left. There's no food, because there's no one to grow it or bring it in when it's ripe. I also heard that a lot of villages are hoarding grain, so don't expect your rations to improve here, brother," he said.

"Is that what all this is about?" asked Pavel again.

"Today is International Women's Day so all the girls have downed tools and gone onto the streets to protest the shortage of bread. And it's not surprising when you see the bloody price. The capitalist bakery owners have increased it 400 percent. The bastards!" the man swore again.

Pavel raised his head above the masses in front of him and caught a glimpse of a banner, "Bread for the Workers!"

No one on the streets knew it that morning, but one of the most momentous events of the twentieth century, the Russian Revolution, had just begun.

Pavel resigned himself to a slow journey. He turned painfully away from the mob and made his way slowly toward the factory area to meet one of the leading organizers in Saint Petersburg.

For two years, he had seen the senseless, criminal waste of human life month after month. He thought it would become easier over time, and he worked hard, long hours. But it never got any easier. It seemed that no matter how many men were killed, no matter how often the surgeons repaired the torn and brutalized bodies, the slaughter never stopped. Finally, close to his breaking point, when he could no longer stand the desperate work, trying to repair bodies, knowing they would be sent back to the front as soon as they could walk, he went with the transport companies to gather the wounded. Before long, he carried whatever supplies he could scrounge, food, clothing, boots, and ammunition, to the soldiers dying so pointlessly in the trenches. It made no difference, he knew. The same number of dead and mutilated would still be there on his return. But, at least for the days or hours they had left, what he brought may offer some dignity and the knowledge for that soldier that someone cared. On one of these journeys, a piece of shrapnel from a shell burst scythed into his leg and he became one of them.

Before long, Pavel met agitators among the troops who denounced the war and called for peace. With little encouragement, he secretly joined the Socialists, supplying them with intelligence and carrying messages to group leaders on his trips around the front. The message he carried now for one of their leaders in the capital was explosive. The infantry battalions, close to mutiny, would not take action against workers if they were recalled to quell riots in the capital or Moscow.

Now that he was back, Pavel had every intention of staying and playing a part in the coming revolt to overthrow the tsar.

Finally away from the crush of the massed crowd, he increased his pace. He did not feel at home in Saint Petersburg. As soon as he had delivered the messages he would head for Moscow. In Moscow, he knew people, friends, who would help after he had delivered the same messages. And, of course, his mother and father who he had not seen for two years. He was anxious to see his mother, whom his father had written was not well. The other matter would require delicate handling. He thought for the hundredth time of the conversation he would have with his father. Somehow, he had to warn him. When the uprising came, and he had absolutely no doubt it would, members of the Imperial Police would be in real danger from the mob.

§ § § § §

It took Pavel five days to make the journey home. At times, he didn't think he would make it. In Saint Petersburg when, troops began firing on the protesters, it seemed it would be 1905 all over again. But then the Volynsky Regiment mutinied, refusing to obey orders to fire into the crowd. Instead, they turned and shot their commander dead. The Volynskys were soon joined by other regiments. Together, the soldiers broke into the armories, handing out thousands of revolvers to the crowd. When a quartermaster tried to intervene, they shot him dead.

In Moscow, the Moscow Regiment refused to obey orders. Their officers, seeing the lie of the land, faded quietly into the crowd.

"How do they expect us to retain even a semblance of order," Gregori Yukovsky grumbled. "If the army has mutinied there is nothing we can do."

"Pavel came home two days ago," Rysakov smiled. "It was so good to see him. Thank God he is still alive."

"That is wonderful news," said Yukovsky. "You have only the one son. At least we have two others. Thank heaven they were too young to go to the front."

"I am sorry, Gregori, I had forgotten in my pleasure at seeing Pavel. I should not be celebrating when you have lost a son."

"Don't be silly, Maximus," Yukovsky said. "We will always miss him but nothing will bring him back. How is Pavel?"

"Much changed, he went away a happy young man full of plans for the future. He has come back tortured by what he saw, and he's totally disillusioned with the government." Rysakov stopped. He had been on the verge of telling Yukovsky Pavel had joined the revolutionaries. It was enough that he knew; if the police found out in due course, he would face that problem then.

"He is not the only one who's fed up with the present system," said Yukovsky. "The price of potatoes has quadrupled, if you can get them;

bread has done the same. It's even difficult to get wood for heating. Something has to be done," he said.

The two policemen were quiet for several minutes. Then Yukovsky looked up.

"Maksim, I heard that several police officers were beaten by the mob yesterday. We had better be careful."

"Yes, I heard. Make sure you wear ordinary clothes."

"Word of the revolution is spreading to the front. I hear soldiers are demanding an end to the war," Yukovsky said.

"What really worries me, Gregori, are the anarchists. With the police more or less ineffective and the army either fighting the Germans or arguing with each other, who will impose law and order?" asked Rysakov.

Exactly one week after the protest Pavel walked into in Saint Petersburg had sparked widespread spontaneous revolt, Nicholas II, last of the Romanovs, abdicated his throne. For the first time in its history, Russia had no tsar.

§ § § § § §

Six months later, on a chill damp day in the capital in late October 1917, elegant figures in black ties settled in to listen to Chaliapin singing 'Boris Goudunov' at the Mariinsky Theatre, the Restaurant de Paris was full of wealthy diners, and the many nightclubs had two sittings to accommodate the crowds. Outside, in a well coordinated move, Bolshevik troops took control of the bridges over the River Neva, the main telegraph office, the post offices, the railroad stations, the power stations, and the Central Bank.

Within thirty-six hours, the Bolsheviks had control of the Russian government. To retain momentum, they immediately entered into discussions with the Germans. In December, they concluded a cease fire. By February the next year, a peace treaty had been signed and the slaughter of young Russians in the trenches finally ceased.

As troops began withdrawing from the front line, one of the many problems confronting the fledgling government was repatriation of prisoners of war. And by far the biggest part of this problem was the Czech Legion, a 45,000-strong, fully armed, battle-hardened, well-disciplined force keen to rejoin the fight against the Germans. They expected that fighting with the Allies would ensure independence for the Czech nation at the end of the war. This fighting force presented a serious problem for the Bolsheviks. They wanted them out of Russia. However, the Germans were not about to let such an army pass through its front line to join the Allies, so the only way out was by way of Siberia and boat to Europe. That the Czechs opposed the Bolsheviks complicated the matter even more.

§ § § § §

"Anna, it's not safe to be out alone," said Katya for the tenth time. She looked at her daughter, who had matured into a beautiful young woman.

"Dedushka and your father dare not go to their own factories without an armed escort, although we may not own them for long the way this new government is talking. There are bands of criminals and rapists roaming around. Many are still carrying their weapons from the war," said Katya. "What do you think they would do to a young woman as pretty as you?"

Anna knew her mother was right but was determined to get her own way. She had seen groups of unshaven dirty men carrying rifles coming out of her friend's house last week. The family had moved to their country estate immediately after the Bolsheviks seized power, and the home had been taken over by deserters and anarchists. Stories abounded of wild orgies, drunkenness, and vandalism in many of the grander houses in Moscow abandoned by scared owners. But she was bored and desperately wanted to see her friends, even though there could be no certainty they were still in the city.

Katya sat in the downstairs reception room where the Guarneri stood in its display case. Peter and Yuri stood looking out the window as if guarding the fort. Pinna hovered in the background.

"Are we safe here, Mama?" asked Yuri.

"Of course, my darling," she replied. "No one can hurt us here. I have my two soldiers to protect me."

Pinna, strong and stolid, did not smile. She had spoken with some of the remaining servants, who brought very disquieting stories of an almost total breakdown in law and order. To see for herself, she had quietly gone out to what markets were still open yesterday. For the first time in many years, what she saw really frightened her. She returned convinced they were not safe from marauding mobs.

Immediately, she began preparations for Katya and the children to flee on short notice. She had not yet told Katya and did not know quite how to, Katya loved the house so much. When they did have to flee, and Pinna was convinced they would, they would be no different to any peasant. They would only be able to take what they could carry. So she began an inventory of valuables small enough to be secreted in their clothes.

When Ivan and Mikhail returned that evening with Vanya and their escort, they brought disturbing news.

"At the main factory today, we had a deputation of workers, including several foremen, demanding they be given a say in management. One of them even suggested our offices should be given over to a staff eating facility. Management will be conducted by a council of workers of which we would only be members. Decisions would be by majority vote!" said Ivan. "I asked them who would finance the business and they replied that once the state nationalized the banks, finance would be available on a needs basis to any worker-controlled factory. It can't go on, the city is close to anarchy, and the new government seems powerless to do anything."

After the evening meal, Katya and Pinna took Yuri to bed upstairs. The others remained below in the sitting room discussing what tomorrow might bring.

When Pinna told Katya what she had seen, Katya's unease increased. Midway through a discussion of what items should be taken if they had to flee, a loud banging at the front door startled them. Immediately after came a gunshot and the crash of splintering wood.

A strange, coarse voice started shouting. Other voices, rough from too much vodka, joined in. Pinna moved first with a speed belying her bulk. Katya followed through the door and onto the balcony. She could hear Ivan's voice raised in anger. Then Anna screamed, her voice high-pitched in terror.

Katya reached the balustrade and looked over the rail. What she saw sent an icicle of fear down her spine. She opened her mouth to shout a warning but no sound came out. She stood, unable to move, one hand gripping the rail, the other outstretched toward Mikhail, her face frozen in horror. The nightmare was happening in front of her.

She knew what was about to unfold. Just like her dream, but she couldn't move.

All the actions of the characters seemed to be in slow motion. A tall man with an unkempt beard and filthy clothes had one arm around Anna's waist. He had trouble holding her as she fought to get away. He said something to one of the others, who laughed and took his rifle. The tall man then hit Anna with his free hand, stunning her. He reestablished his grip. With his free hand, he began squeezing her breasts cruelly.

"I told you there were prizes to be had in this house," said a solid man who appeared to be their leader.

"Stay where you are," he snarled as Ivan and Mikhail advanced rapidly to free Anna. He leveled his rifle at them and worked the bolt action to chamber a round. "There are other women in the house, lads, and when we've had enough fucking there is plenty of gold and jewels to be had. This little beauty's mother is to be left for me. I know just how to treat these rich bitches."

One of the gang, staggering from the effects of vodka, dropped his rifle and began to undo his trousers.

Vanya had been last out of the sitting room. He stayed just out of the leader's line of sight, behind the stairwell. Now, as he passed the cloak stand, he quietly picked up his Cossack saber, unsheathing it in one fluid movement. Ivan, suddenly aware of Vanya and knowing instinctively what he was doing, prepared to move. As the drunk dropped his trousers, Vanya lunged. The saber sliced straight into the exposed flesh of the man's stomach. Vanya leaned all his weight forward before shifting his feet. Using his body weight he dragged the razor sharp blade out. One of the dying man's intestines came with it.

As the scream momentarily distracted the leader, Ivan sprang. He grabbed the barrel of the rifle as the man turned back. They glared savagely at each other. Instantly, Ivan knew who the man was, viciousness etched into the face. Ivan jerked the barrel forward to break the man's grip. The man pulled back. At that moment there was a deafening explosion. At first he felt nothing. At the same time he thought it curious his left arm suddenly had no strength in it. He hauled with his right and almost succeeded in pulling the rifle away.

Katya watched as Ivan collapsed with a bullet through the chest. Mikhail smashed his fist into the man's face, forcing him to lose grip of the rifle. It sank, with Ivan still holding the barrel, onto a large Turkish rug.

As the man staggered under Mikhail's assault, one of the other gang members fired his rifle at Mikhail. Katya's legs turned to jelly as her husband fell backward onto the floor.

The leader regained his balance, pulled a revolver from his belt and pointed it at Vanya.

As his finger tightened on the trigger, two men burst in through the smashed front door.

"Police, drop your weapons."

The leader spun his revolver around. The policeman did not hesitate. He fired the Smith and Wesson. The bullet hit the gang leader in the throat and his weapon fell harmlessly to the floor. The second policeman fired a fraction of a second later, killing another of the gang as he turned with rifle at the ready. The Smith and Wesson barked a second time inflicting a fatal chest wound on a third.

The remaining man turned to face the police with Anna as his shield. Neither rescuer could risk a shot. But Anna's captor had made a bad mistake. Pinna had continued down the stairs during the shooting with only one thought on her mind; to rescue her darling Anna. As the man turned, she struck, her fury giving her strength beyond even her size.

Pinna reached up, grabbing the man around the neck. The surprise attack caught him off balance. She then used her bulk to haul him backward. Anna struggled weakly, breaking free as the man fell. Somehow, Pinna landed on her knees, never relinquishing her grip on the man's throat. The man now twisted to turn around. Pinna knew if she allowed this to happen he would overpower her. With a superhuman effort, she lifted the man's head and smashed it onto her upraised knee. Stunned, the man stopped struggling. She raised his head again. This time as his neck hit her knee it snapped, like a chicken being prepared for Sunday dinner.

The crack broke Katya out of her frozen state and she raced down the stairs, tears streaming down her face.

Ivan lay still, dead, in a pool of blood. Mikhail was not moving. Blood streamed from a head wound. Anna knelt trembling, shallow breaths alternating with sobs.

Peter recovered first and ran to his father.

"Papa is alive," he said, and Mikhail groaned and rolled to his knees.

Katya put her arms around Anna and Pinna as her daughter began to cry softly with shock.

Rysakov pushed the Welby into his belt and walked over to the gang leader sprawled dead with his legs buckled under him. Yukovsky kept the Smith and Wesson at the ready in case more anarchists appeared.

I thought I recognized this bastard," said Rysakov, "Igor Donstoy. Thank God we got here in time. He's a murderous bastard." He looked over to Yukovsky. "The women of Moscow thank you, Gregori; they will be safer for his demise."

Later, Rysakov explained to the family that the new commissar of war had issued orders to round up and kill anarchists and any other criminals terrorizing the city and looting. Special squads had been clearing the worst areas. While he and his friend were not part of those squads they had authority to take action where warranted. They decided to call on people they knew to ensure their safety. They had already called at three other houses and found them securely locked. Only the Morozovs had been attacked.

They had no time to mourn Ivan's death.

"You must get your family out of Moscow," Rysakov said to Mikhail. "The Bolsheviks will nationalize all factories; they've already taken the banks. My son, Pavel, has told me that all capitalists will be targeted and imprisoned. There is also the constant danger of other gangs. I wouldn't even be certain of the special squads; they may be just as violent. They know no one cares about protecting the rich."

"I don't even know how long I'll have a job. At the moment they need the police to help restore order, but," he shrugged, "we worked for the Imperial Government."

"You saved my life all those years ago and I would like to return the favor. While I still have some authority, I'll issue you all with passes to leave Moscow. I can't guarantee they'll work, but it's the best I can do. Come around to my office tomorrow. Then slip out of the city as quickly and quietly as you can. Take nothing with you."

§ § § § § §

They felt as though the cold had penetrated to their very bones. When they stopped to rest, their joints ached. It had been days since they had had a halfway decent meal and hunger had become the principal focus of each day. No one seemed to have much food. Not the villagers, the stores or others who, like them, walked unsure what danger lurked around the next bend.

A station lay somewhere ahead. There, they had been assured by a not entirely unfriendly official at the last village that they could expect a train that would take passengers with the right papers. The official had been very vague about when the train might be expected. "Just follow the road," he had said, "it is about a day's walk." And so they had.

Finally, they arrived to be greeted by a large crowd of people, also waiting. So far as Mikhail could determine, no train had been sighted for days.

"One is expected any time," a well dressed man told him. "It will bring food. It must. There is none to be had in the surrounding countryside."

With no alternative, they settled down to wait. Soon after they arrived at the station, a family decided to leave, unwilling to chance the arrival of the train.

"We've been here for a week," the woman said. "There is no train. Everyone is on strike." She walked off into the forest, trudging after her husband and child.

Katya quickly mobilized her family to fill their spots under the roof of the old waiting room. At least they now had a roof over their heads and four walls to break the chill of the wind.

Once Inspector Rysakov had left them on the night of Ivan's murder, the reality of what had happened sank in. As well-known wealthy industrialists, they were certain to be targeted by the new regime. The position that money and social status had brought them was gone. In fact, it now counted against them. They were marked people, liable to be summarily arrested and imprisoned. All their assets, the factories, the art and their house would be taken by the state. They no longer owned anything. The bank had already gone.

A directive would soon be issued, Rysakov told them.

"The palaces of the aristocracy and the houses of the wealthy merchants will be sequestered by the government and used for hospitals, government offices, or even worker accommodation. The inhabitants will have to live with the workers," he said.

They talked for hours. Finally, they all agreed. They must leave Moscow. Anna no longer insisted on seeing her friends. The assault had shaken her badly. Peter and Yuri, serious faced, listened intently to their father.

In the morning, Mikhail generously paid off the remaining staff in the house and bade them visit their relatives. In these uncertain times, all were pleased to do so. Vanya refused to leave. He and Mikhail arranged for Ivan to be buried next to Nataliya immediately. The ceremony was short and simple. It was too dangerous to be anything else. With a heavy heart, the family said good-bye to their patriarch.

Mikhail shook his head sadly. The end of the "new Russia," cut down before it could mature. Now they were to be discarded, prisoners, refugees, fugitives, and émigrés.

"We look like people from a village," said Pinna. Each carried a small bundle over their shoulders. It contained additional clothes and a personal icon. The only extra item, which they took turns to carry, was the violin. Katya insisted they take it.

"Do not forget what Dedushka said," she reminded them, "this violin represents our family. We must keep it with us at all times."

Every day, when she saw the violin case, Katya thought fondly of the man who had embraced her into his family with warmth and trust. His time had been too short and now her children had no grandparents to love and spoil them.

At least all the children have been taught to play the violin, she thought. *I wonder why it is only Yuri who has showed real talent. He's only ten and already he can pick up a fiddle and play a tune from ear. Only last week he saved a difficult situation by playing country airs to the delight of the village women. I wonder if he really knew what he was doing? But it got us a small amount of food and a roof to sleep under that night.* She glanced lovingly at her youngest son.

Finally, a train came. It steamed slowly up the slight incline where the line emerged from the forest. The wheels squealed as it ground to a halt when the engine drew level with the platform. The mood at the station changed dramatically. Everyone began talking, calling out, and jostling for position on the platform.

Mikhail counted only eleven trucks, cattle trucks by the look of them, and two open flat tops on which dozens of Red Army troops sat. As soon as the train stopped moving, the doors of the cattle trucks slid open and more troops spilled onto the ground to stretch their legs. The train appeared full of soldiers. What little space remained would not take many from the station.

It took him until the next morning to get to meet the officer in charge. By that time, he knew the troops were heading for Ekaterinburg, the heavy-industry center at the foothills of the Ural Mountains. There they would join other Red Army detachments in the area.

"We are to reinforce the garrison against units of the anti-Bolsheviks, the Whites, threatening the city," a soldier told him. "Or so the rumors have it," the man added. "I'll believe it when I see it. It sounds just like the Polish front: go here, go there, get killed, but don't ask any questions."

As they talked, it transpired that Mikhail had been in the same area of the German front ferrying wounded to hospital. Without explaining the full nature of his reason for being there, delivering supplies from their own factories, Mikhail soon gained the soldier's confidence. They had shared the terror of the German bombardment, the squalor of the trenches and the indifference of the higher command. This connection, the unexplainable bond between battlefield soldiers, got Mikhail in front of the commanding officer, a young lieutenant with the hard eyes of one who has watched too many men die.

"So, Mishlovski tells me you were on the Polish front," he said, looking carefully at Mikhail.

"Yes, I was working with the field hospital. I was able to commandeer a vehicle and carry some of the wounded from the front. If they had to wait for the carts, they died."

"I know. Too many of my own men died waiting for medical help. Even when they got it some still died for lack of proper attention. What were the conditions like in the field units?"

Mikhail told him of the appalling conditions in the hospitals and how indifferent the command structure seemed to be. The lieutenant nodded in agreement.

"You're right, the field units were often totally lacking in even basic medical supplies. I visited one on my way back to Moscow. Mishlovski says some of the men you transported were from our regiment. Thank you for that." The lieutenant sat down and his shoulders slumped, defeated by the memories of too many comrades dead.

Mikhail got the feeling he had just passed the test.

"We can take you as far as Ekaterinburg. Then you are on your own," he said.

It took the rest of the week to get to their destination with frequent stopping, reversing and long waits. The civil war, now being fought in skirmishes across the eastern part of the country, ebbed and flowed around them.

As they detrained, Mikhail heard for the first time a rumor that surprised and shocked the whole family. Here, in this industrial city, the tsar and his family were being held prisoner under house arrest. The talk among the soldiers on the train speculated that the increased activity of Whites in the area was directed to rescuing the tsar.

Then came the most astonishing news. Mishlovski rushed up, his face lit up in anticipation of being the first to deliver momentous news, news they all found impossible to believe.

"Have you heard?" he asked, rushing on before Mikhail had a chance to reply. "The tsar has been executed, and all of his family. Here in Ekaterinburg."

"Are you sure?" asked Mikhail. He stared at Mishlovski. If true, what would it mean? Would there be popular revulsion against the Bolsheviks? *Unlikely,* Mikhail thought, *the tsar seems to have abandoned his people. But a government that would do such a thing...*

"There is no doubt," his new friend replied. "The rule of the Romanovs is over!"

It was only then Mikhail became aware of the buzz of conversation all around him as the news spread like a grass fire in summer.

§ § § § §

Was this the real nature of this regime now controlling Russia? Mikhail pondered. That it could almost casually murder the tsar *and* his family—if they could carry out such a brutal act against the head of the country, whatever his shortcomings, what did it mean for his own family? Mikhail felt even more certain that if the Bolsheviks discovered he was a prominent industrialist, a member of the bourgeoisie, he and his family would be in danger of suffering the same fate.

They decided to leave Ekaterinburg immediately and make for the village of the Rezanov family, the Ural Cossacks with whom Mikhail had spent much time in his youth. He felt sure they would find sanctuary there and could rest in safety. What they would do thereafter, he did not know.

They made slow progress, trudging heads down, along the dirt road. On the second day out of Ekaterinburg, they came upon a farmer driving a near empty cart. After a brief conversation with monosyllabic responses they found he was headed in their direction. For the price of one ruble a head, Mikhail persuaded him to allow the six of them to travel on the back of the cart. He knew hunger and exhaustion had sapped much of their strength. The cart would allow them to rest as they moved toward Rezanov's village, about three days journey away. They traveled in silence.

They had been on the cart several hours when Katya glanced again at the driver. She did not feel comfortable with the way he kept looking at Anna and smiling. She had no doubt what was going through his mind. Each time he smiled, he exposed two rows of rotted teeth. *He has a decidedly shifty look about the eyes,* she thought. However, they were in no position to be choosy. They had seen no other transport on the road.

The cart had no covering and offered no relief from the heat of the day. The only brief respite came from an occasional dry wind from the south. The farmer's horse, its head hung low in the heat, resolutely hauled its load, steadily eating up the miles. Mikhail wondered when the farmer would stop to give the horse a rest as they had been going without a break for half the day.

"Will you be stopping for a rest soon?" he asked the man.

In response, all he got was a nod. The man did not even turn toward him, just stared straight ahead. Suddenly, Mikhail's senses were at full alert. He detected a slight smirk when the man nodded. What was this fellow up to? He could see no sign of any village. What a fool he had been. They were being led into a trap where they would be robbed, or worse.

Then he saw it, a roadblock, a group of men spread across the road, just visible in the distance. They could be soldiers, or partisans, or bandits in league with this fellow. Mikhail sat on the driver's bench next to the farmer. One glance back to where the two women and his three children dozed decided him. If they jumped off the wagon now, they would almost certainly be seen. With three females, they could not make a speedy escape. He would have to rely on their passes and his wit. That the passes were issued in Moscow must carry some weight. After all, he would say, they have been checked many times since we left the city.

The sun hung low in the sky by the time the wagon crested a small rise and a large village spread out before them. Their escort of the Red Guard patrol surrounded them as they walked slowly along the deeply rutted dirt track that served as the main and only street. Curious villagers stared at them. Women in the full peasant dresses and head scarves pointed at the procession, talking with animated gestures. Finally, they stopped in front of an *izba,* the one room structure in which everyone in the village, other than the miller, lived.

"You will all wait in here," said the leader of the patrol. He had not been completely sure how to handle the Moscow passes. His natural suspicion inclined him to believe them to be bourgeoisie and enemies of the revolution. The farmer, who he knew from the area, told him he thought they were White spies and that he should be entitled to a reward. The patrol leader had been born in the region and after two years of mind numbing terror in the trenches had deserted. He returned to his village and made contact with other Bolsheviki in the area. When the revolution came, he was promoted to command one of the paramilitary units of the Red Guard. Their main targets were *kulaks,* peasants who through hard work raised themselves out of the mire of village poverty. But if the passes were genuine, he didn't want to make a fool of himself.

"When our commissar returns, he'll decide what to do with you."

The walls of the *izba* were made of logs laid horizontally, the gaps between them caulked with oakum to keep out drafts. The roof was thatched and at one end of the room opposite the door sat a large stove and oven made of clay. Several benches lined the other two sides providing the only seating. A table, bare of any implements, stood forlornly in the center of the room.

Katya took all of this in before the door closed behind them. They heard the sound of a bar being dropped in place on the outside. Clearly this *izba* had been prepared in case enemies of the revolution were caught. As the bar clunked into its supports, they realized they stood in almost total darkness. The only windows, set well above the benches, were covered with a barely translucent film that Pinna later told her was stretched and dried bull's bladder. It admitted little light. They stood there silently, shocked, captives at the mercy of the commissar, whomever he might be.

"The stove is cold; this is not being used by a family," said Pinna.

She strode to the windows and pulled the bladder away, letting enough light penetrate the darkness for them all to see once their eyes adjusted to the gloom. Anna went to one of the bench seats and idly rubbed her hand along the wall behind.

"It's all greasy," she exclaimed, looking around with distaste as she searched for somewhere to wipe her fingers clean.

"That is caused by smoke from the stove," Pinna said. "All *izba* are the same. There is no chimney, so the smoke settles inside. This is how all of the ordinary people live," her voice tinged with a mixture of defiant pride and revulsion.

Katya felt too tired and dispirited to worry about the grease and flopped down on one of the benches. Only then did she realize what it was about the floor that had been troubling her. It was dirt, hard packed from the impact of hundreds of feet over many years, but still dirt. If they were to get any sleep, some of them would have to lie on the dirt floor. *No wonder life expectancy in rural areas is not high,* she thought.

Peter had been inspecting the walls and windows for signs of weakness.

"Papa, I think maybe Yuri could squeeze through the window when it's dark and the guards are asleep. He could lift the bar from the door and we could very quietly creep out of the village. We would be well away by dawn," he said to Mikhail.

"If it was just me and you two boys that may be worth a try," said Mikhail in a low voice. "But with the three women we would not get far enough away and they would catch us in the morning. The fact that we tried to escape would make it look as though we were guilty. No, I think we will wait and see this commissar. Rysakov's passes have got us this far, I think we have a good chance of being able to continue our journey."

In his heart, Mikhail remained deeply worried. He knew petty officials this far away from Moscow were virtual laws unto themselves. They could keep them imprisoned for as long as it pleased them. A dedicated Bolshevik could even have us transported back to Moscow for trial.

They spent an unpleasant night; no one got much sleep. The next morning, Pinna yelled at the guard outside that they needed food and water. Eventually, after berating the man on and off for several hours, the door opened and one of the village woman brought in a pot and a jug of water. The pot contained boiled turnips. They became their sole source of nourishment from the time they were incarcerated. After the meager meal, they gradually lapsed into silence, broken only by the occasional rumblings of hunger in empty stomachs.

The gloom of the *izba* was depressing. No one had the energy to make conversation. The sun passed its zenith and, judging by the change in intensity of light, was now headed for the western horizon and darkness. Although it was still summer, a cool breeze picked up from the north and they began to feel a drop in temperature. Without the stove alight, it would be a distinctly cool night.

In late morning of the second day, just after the daily pot of boiled turnips, their guard called through the door.

"The commissar has arrived. He will know what to do with people with Moscow passes," he said.

An hour later, they were roused from their torpor by the sound of the bar being raised. When the door opened, three men came into the room.

"You," one said, pointing at Mikhail, "come with us. The commissar wants to see you. The rest of you stay here."

As Mikhail disappeared and the door closed, they heard the scrape of the bar once more sliding into place. Katya felt a sinking in her stomach, and a premonition she would not see Mikhail again. She hugged Anna closer.

As he walked down the rutted track with his guard, Mikhail saw half a dozen horses grazing off to one side of a larger and better finished *izba*. *That must be where the commissar lives,* he thought. In the miller's home, Pinna had explained that the miller was always the most prosperous person in the village. *Could the miller be the commissar?* he mused, dismissing the thought immediately. The miller would no doubt have been denounced as a kulak and probably imprisoned or killed.

This *izba* had two rooms, its walls more sturdy and better finished, and the roof was a double thatch. Several pieces of crude furniture in both rooms gave the place the feeling of a home. It was lighter inside, he realized. He could see detail, not just the vague gloom of their prison. As he entered the second room, he saw the reason for such good light. Several candles flickered brightly on a table behind which sat the commissar.

As he stood in front of the table and waited, he studied the commissar. He had the gaunt tough look of a man who lived hard. But there was an aura of authority. A man used to command and to being obeyed. He continued writing in a leather-bound book that appeared to be a journal. *Perhaps like a ship's log,* thought Mikhail. Apart from the three who had brought him, only one other man stood in the room, positioned to the left and rear of the commissar, and having given Mikhail a cursory glance, paid him no more attention.

Finally, the commissar laid down his pen and looked up. His dark eyes were piercing. This man had seen others die. Mikhail had seen that look in the trenches. But they had something else—ruthlessness and a touch of cruelty. In that instant, Mikhail had no doubt. His men not only respected him; they feared him.

"Mr. Morozov," he said looking at their passes on the table in front of him. "So you have come from Moscow?"

"Yes," replied Mikhail.

"Leave us," the commissar said to the guards, who slowly left, closing the door, clearly disappointed they would not witness how their charge was to be dealt with.

"And how is the center of industry? It is many years since I was last there. You see, Mr. Morozov, I spent seven years in exile in a remote work settlement. When the revolution rid Russia of the tyranny of the Romanovs and the capitalist class, I returned in triumph," he paused, "to be given the honor of commissar of this region." He said the last with just a touch of irony. "One of our many duties is to search out and capture counter-revolutionaries," he said, looking directly at Mikhail.

Something was familiar about the man seated across the table from him, and Mikhail was momentarily distracted. *Where have I seen him before?*

"I see," he said, unsure what else to say.

"Where are you heading with these police passes?"

"We are traveling to the village of the Rezanovs in the upper foothills of the Urals. I am told it is about three days travel. We intend to live and work there. I have lived there before when I was younger," he said. *Better to say as little as possible, just enough to be feasible,* he thought.

After some further discussion about the conditions in Moscow, the commissar turned to his adjutant.

"Dmitri, please take this order to the village headman," he said, handing him a paper.

"Will you be safe with this prisoner?" Dmitri asked.

"With his wife and children under lock and key, I think so," said the commissar.

When the adjutant left the room, the commissar turned to Mikhail.

"We have limited time, Comrade Morozov, before Dmitri returns," said the commissar. "You have told me much about Moscow in general. Now I would like some information in particular. Firstly, how is Uncle Vanya?"

Mikhail could not stop the surprise registering on his face. Then, in a flash, he knew who the commissar was. Anton Pushkin. He had not seen him since the '05 uprising.

"So, at last you know who I am," Pushkin said, the ghost of a smile playing around his mouth. "How is my uncle?"

"He is well," said Mikhail, recovering his composure. "He insisted on staying in Moscow and is living with his sister, your mother. Before we left, we made sure he had adequate funds for his own use, and he has unrestricted access to our house and its contents. So both he and your mother should want for nothing."

"And my mother, how is she?"

"When we left some months ago, she was ill, but I don't think it was life threatening. Vanya did not seem particularly concerned," Mikhail said. "She is older and no doubt feeling the symptoms of old age. When did you last see her?"

"Seven years ago, and it is unlikely I shall get to Moscow in the foreseeable future. But who knows?" he shrugged. "Life is full of surprises."

"Your family was very kind to my mother over many years when my father died. I would like to repay that debt," Pushkin continued. "However, the revolution has many ears and many ambitious men keen to advance over the bodies of others. Betrayal has become commonplace, loyalty a luxury."

He then proceeded to tell Mikhail what he proposed. When he had finished, Mikhail nodded.

"Beyond that, there is little I can do. If you are brought before me again, I will consider my debt extinguished. Good luck." Pushkin rose and shook hands before calling the guards. As he left, Pushkin thrust the passes back into Mikhail's hand.

Some time after midnight, the adjutant and two of Pushkin's staff soldiers came for them.

"Under no circumstances will any of you speak until we are well clear of the village," the adjutant instructed them. The guards then escorted them several miles to the south before handing over three bags of cold boiled turnips.

"It's all the food we could take without arousing suspicion," the adjutant said.

It puzzled Mikhail that they were taken out of the village by the guards in the dead of night. He asked the adjutant why.

"Wouldn't the villagers think it strange?" he said.

"The commissar is satisfied you are who you say you are," said the adjutant. "If he simply let you go in daylight some of the villagers may have wondered why these strangers are being given the benefit of the doubt. Then they may have begun to question other decisions by the commissar. This way, when they wake up, the prisoners will have vanished; they won't know whether they had been released, taken to another location for interrogation, or taken into the forest and shot. This uncertainty will cause them to fear the commissar a little more and fear is the only certain way to control the *narod*."

Without another word, he and his men disappeared into the darkness.

They walked all night and after a brief rest in the warm sun of the morning, continued for most of the next day. They carefully avoided major roads and any large groups that could be Red Army detachments or peasants seeking kulaks. Nearly a week later, the tired and hungry band reached the outskirts of Cheliabinsk, well south of Ekaterinburg.

Late morning, they walked slowly into the city. With their dirty clothes and tired resignation, they blended easily with other people out about their business. They received a few curious glances, but nothing more. Another family displaced by the trouble affecting us all was the attitude.

"Go to Cheliabinsk, there are Czech Legion units there," Pushkin told Mikhail as he left the *izba*. "Moscow broke up the Legion into small groups and sent them along the rail line. As a result, they now control much of the Trans-Siberian Rail. A directive was also issued to disarm or arrest them. From what I've seen, that's made them even more determined to get out of Russia and back to their homeland. They're well organized and battle hardened. If you can travel under their protection, you may have a chance of getting to wherever it is you are really heading. That is your best chance of survival."

When Mikhail started to remonstrate that they really were traveling to the Rezanov village, Pushkin cut him short. "Don't insult me, Mikhail Ivanovich. Even if you made this village of Rezanov, I know it'll not be more than a temporary stop since you'd soon be found out there and arrested. Now go before I change my mind."

When they reached the center of Cheliabinsk, it looked like a town in a state of turmoil. Large numbers of Czech soldiers strolled confidently among disparate displaced people, desperate to find safety from both Reds and Whites. It quickly became apparent the Czech Legion was a far more cohesive group than local units of the Red Army, and it looked like they exploited this position to get whatever supplies they needed. The Czechs seemed the real power in the city.

Pinna went into the markets to buy food and brought back several rumors. One concerned the Czechs and members of the Romanov family. This, Mikhail dismissed. Don't forget, he said, they're dead. The other rumor, which he also heard whispered, concerned money. It sounded more plausible, and intriguing. Apparently, so the rumor ran, the Czechs had secured a large shipment of gold from the Romanov treasury.

According to the story, when the Bolsheviks took control of the government immediately after the coup d'etat, one of their first acts was to seize the Imperial Bank in Moscow. The funds there would be needed to pay the new civil servants. Instead, the Red Guards found half of the gold had already been moved east to Samara on the Volga River, a precaution against the German invasion.

When the commissar of war attempted to disarm them, the Legion moved on Samara. Terrified they may lose a major part of their gold reserves, the Bolsheviks hastily moved the gold up river to Kazan. The Czechs quickly overran Kazan and captured the gold totaling hundreds of millions of rubles, a truly valuable prize.

This gold, the rumor said, would now be moved east some said to be sent to London, others to America. Which Czech units held the gold was another matter. No one knew for sure. It could be the units now in Cheliabinsk or it might already have been moved further along the line. Everyone had a theory.

As he walked, taking in the surroundings, Mikhail observed the Czechs. They acted with the confidence of an occupying army. *Yet,* he thought, *if I were in charge of that amount of gold in this city, I would not let my men wander around so casually.* If it really was here, it could prove a powerful attraction for any number of opportunists. On balance, he decided the gold did not sit in this city.

The Cheliabinsk market had vendors from all over Central Asia, including not more than a week's travel by horse to the south, the land of the Kazakh, home of Yusuf Yudin.

Anna, like the rest of the family, soon adopted the habit of wandering off in search of bargains. On this day, she bargained unsuccessfully for a parcel of vegetables. Annoyed she had wasted so much time for no result, she turned sharply to walk away. As she did, she collided with a man in military uniform.

He had been watching her for some time. Expecting her to turn the other way, he stood almost at her shoulder when she swiveled around. The impact caught them both off balance, and, without thinking, he put his arms on her shoulders to steady himself. To a casual observer, it looked like nothing more than a friendly embrace. To Anna, however, it reminded her of something altogether different and terrifying. With lightning reflexes, she punched the man with her right fist. Even though they were too close for the punch to have any power, the young man jumped back, startled.

"Mademoiselle, please forgive me, I assure you it was an accident," he said with heavily accented Russian, but in a deep, attractively modulated voice.

With an effort, Anna calmed herself. *There's no danger here,* she realized, *just a silly mistake.*

"My apologies, sir, you gave me a shock," she said, not looking up.

"May I introduce myself? I am Charles Macek, lieutenant in the Czech Legion. How may I make amends for my clumsiness?"

It was the voice that made Anna look up at Lieutenant Macek. Having looked, she noticed his eyes, a clear deep blue, his well-trimmed moustache, his dark brown hair, and his broad shoulders. Somewhere deep inside her, it felt as though a switch had been thrown for the first time. She had never experienced such a feeling before. She found it quite disconcerting. It left her unbalanced and a little breathless. When he spoke again, she realized she had been staring and felt her cheeks burn.

"May I walk with you, mam'selle?"

"If you like," she said, somewhat ungraciously, immediately embarrassed at her rudeness.

At first, their conversation was awkward and stilted. They walked slowly through the markets, passing several stalls twice, each enjoying the other's company. Anna dawdled past the stalls, stopping unconsciously in front of a vendor of sweetly smoked ham.

"That looks like the best ham in the city. I think we should taste it. Two servings please," Macek said to the meat smoker before Anna could protest.

"Mam'selle, please tell me if this meat is good enough to serve to a beautiful woman at a private dinner," he said as he offered one serving to Anna.

She had not realized how hungry she had become. Her mouth watered at the smell of the ham. It was a generous gesture by the lieutenant, and she accepted with an elegant half bow, laughing as she took a mouthful. They both began laughing at the other eating as they continued their aimless and happy perambulation.

This is the most beautiful creature imaginable, thought Macek. *How exquisite she is.* In his travels with the battalion through Europe and Russia, he had seen many sensual and attractive women. None had made his heart skip a beat like this. As the hours passed, the prospect of having to say good-bye and return to his regiment alone seemed almost unbearable.

When Katya saw her daughter's happy face that night, she knew something important had happened. Her intuition told her it must involve a man. However, seeing Anna smile again easily overcame any sense of misgiving she felt.

§ § § § §

As the days became weeks, the two met nearly every day, spending hours talking and laughing together. Mutual attraction slowly blossomed into love. Katya insisted Anna only meet the young man in public places and with a chaperone. To this role, she co-opted the formidable Pinna. The choice pleased Anna as, within reason, she knew Pinna was putty in her hands. Pinna would try very hard to please "my little rabbit." The arrangement worked most satisfactorily. On days when Macek had regimental duties to perform, Anna helped her mother in the cheap lodgings they had found on the outskirts of town. Even when they did meet, it was only for a couple of hours before Anna had to return to the two rooms in which they all lived. Some days she earned a few kopecks or food for a meal doing menial tasks for vendors at the markets. Katya also earned a small regular income teaching English.

Mikhail knew their resources would not last indefinitely. Even the small amounts they were able to earn at present would not make any long-term difference. They all knew that as winter approached this casual work would dry up completely. They had to get east before then.

Anna heard about it first. When she arrived at the markets, expecting to meet Macek later that morning, the place was in turmoil.

"What's the matter?" she asked one of the vendors who she had come to know slightly.

"The Czechs have revolted and taken thousands of Red Guards prisoner," he said.

"What happened?" Anna asked, immediately worried about Macek and whether any harm had come to him.

"Some Austrian prisoners of war were being sent by train back to Europe," said a Kazakh trader who had his stall adjacent. "The two groups started throwing insults at each other, then one of the Austrians threw a piece of iron, hitting one of the Czechs on the head, knocking him to the ground senseless."

"That's right," said a third man with some authority, obviously keen to tell the story. "I spoke to one of the Czechs a few minutes ago. He said that their man may not live, so a group of his comrades boarded the Austrian's train and grabbed the culprit. They then slung a rope over a beam in the station roof and lynched him. When the local Red Guards tried to arrest them, the rest of the Czechs rose up and captured the entire Reds unit, all 2,000 of them. Not surprising, really, most of them are only farm lads who have been given a gun, and there's not much leadership." He shook his head. By now more than a dozen people had gathered to listen. "Only a couple of shots were fired and no one seriously hurt, but the Czechs ended up with thousands of rifles and thirty light artillery pieces."

He paused here for effect, and throughout the crowd there was a collective sucking in of breath. With this one incident, the Czechs had become the controllers of the city. Conditions were hard enough with the shortage of food and other essentials after the Great War, the revolution and now the civil war. Would this mean the Czechs would commandeer what was left and take it on their train? The crowd broke up, new discussions erupting in every direction. None of this penetrated Anna's mind. The man said some had been injured. *Please, God, let it not be my Charles,* she thought.

It was three days before Anna finally saw Macek.

"Oh, thank God you're all right. I was so worried when I heard of the shooting," she said, throwing caution to the wind and putting her arms around him.

"I'm sorry I couldn't get word to you, my dearest Anna, there was too much happening," he said embracing her. "And it's not over yet. Those Austrians were fools to goad us and then to bring down one of our men. What did they imagine we'd do, ignore the assault? Unfortunately, our boys overreacted in the heat of the moment, but I can hardly blame them. I suspect I may have been tempted to do the same thing if I'd been there."

"No, you would never have been so brutal, my love," Anna said.

"It's hard to imagine unless one was there," Macek said. "Now the Bolsheviks have overreacted in turn. We intercepted a telegram from the war commissar ordering the Red Guards to disarm the Legion, take away our trains and break up the units. Anyone found with a weapon is to be shot," he said, the seriousness of the situation reflected on his face. "After a lot of discussion, it's been decided that we'll organize as a fighting force. If necessary, we'll fight our way through to Vladivostok to embark for home. We telegraphed this recommendation to the other trains, who unanimously agreed. Within days, the Legion will have control of the whole Trans-Siberian Line."

Anna looked up at him puzzled. "How many trains does the Legion have?"

"We now have eighty trains spread out along the length of the railway. And we have the best of the rolling stock. If the Reds get too aggressive, we can easily stop all freight along the line and take over more trains."

"Some of the forward units are already in Vladivostok and have telegraphed back that the Allies have landed troops from England, France, America, and Japan," he went on. "All we want is to keep the Legion intact until they send enough ships to take us back to Europe."

"As an engineer, I'm going to be busy working on getting the trains ready, rebuilding some of the rail cars. Some of the flatbeds will be reinforced with concrete to anchor artillery pieces. Others will be reinforced with steel plate armor for machine-gun emplacements or built up with wooden baulks buttressed by sandbags on each side. Each train will then be a complete fighting machine," he said.

"Each train? How many do you have here?" asked Anna as she became increasingly concerned at the turn events were taking.

"Two, and we've heard there is another due in tomorrow. We'll commandeer that as well." He paused and looked at Anna. "Within a week, or as soon as the work is completed, our orders are to embark for Vladivostok."

She stood quite still, knowing her life stood poised at a turning point, not knowing if she could bear to look at him or not. Whatever he said next would affect the rest of her days.

"You know that I love you, Anna Mikhailovna. I would like you to come with me and to be with me forever."

This was the decision she had been both dreaming of and dreading, and she knew that she must make it there and then. With only a moments hesitation, she said, "And I love you Charles Macek. Are you asking me to marry you?"

"Of course," he said, a big smile breaking out all over his face.

"Then I accept," said Anna and leapt into his arms, kissing him with abandon.

But this was only part of the decision that had kept her awake at nights.

"You'll love living in Russia; it's a wonderful country," she said, not game to look at his face.

"But…we must stay with the Legion or run the risk of being captured by the Reds. And we'll all be embarking to return to Europe," he said, somewhat taken aback and not sure how serious she was.

"Charles, I cannot abandon my family."

"I don't think it would be possible to take all of them to Europe," he said cautiously.

"Then we must take them as far as Harbin where they have friends who'll protect them. Then I can leave my country knowing they are safe." She looked up at him with her eyes wide and pleading.

Relieved, he said, "I think I can arrange that. There are other officers who are taking Russian wives. A few extra travelers should not be a problem."

"You are wonderful; I knew you'd find a solution," she said, happily throwing her arms around him again. "Come, I must tell Mama immediately."

He started to protest, but relented, and smiling took her hand and followed her out of the markets.

§ § § § §

Smoke from the engine drifted back down the full length of the train. The large British-built machine needed all of its considerable power to pull the twenty carriages with the extra weight of armaments up the long incline. The Czechs made sure they secured the most modern and powerful steam engines. The bellowing, burping older trains they left for the Red Guard.

Progress east had been slow. Delays caused by fighting ahead and the constant need to replenish fuel dampened the excitement of the first days when they sped along the track. They even had to reverse several times recently to avoid trouble.

Mikhail thought sadly of his father—he should be with them. All the striving and work he had put into building the family's fortune had come to nothing. All they had left was what they carried with them. At least Ivan could have been spared to spend his old age with his grandchildren. With a sigh, he turned once more to look at the endless taiga slipping slowly past the window.

"There seems no end to these soldier's appetites," said Katya as she sat down wearily next to him. Katya, Anna, and Pinna offered to help with the messing arrangements and in tending the wounded and sick. They were immediately welcomed and soon hard at work. None of the three women complained; they were too pleased to feel safe for the first time since leaving Moscow.

"I hope Anna will wait until we reach Harbin. The way she looks at Charles…," Katya said. They had persuaded their headstrong daughter to wait until the trains reached Harbin before she and Macek married. *It is all happening too fast,* Katya thought. *How can they be so sure they love each other enough to spend the rest of their lives together? And Anna will be living in a foreign country, away from her family.* She poured all her worries out on Mikhail. They discussed the alternatives, knowing that they could not forbid Anna to marry the dashing young officer. She would simply go ahead without their blessing. Then Mikhail reminded Katya of a young Irish girl, about Anna's age, who fell in love with a foreigner. She had married him and gone to live in his country. She had been about to say "that was different" but caught herself in time.

"You're right, Misha," she said, "I just hate the thought of losing her."

For the first time in her life, Katya understood the sadness on her own mother's face when she had left Dublin.

When Katya mentioned Harbin, Mikhail's mood lifted. Tiger Moon Trading. Not all was lost. Part of Ivan's legacy remained intact, provided they could get through the fighting safely.

The train reached the end of the long, uphill pull and looking back down the sweeping curve he could see all the carriages and armed flattops of their train. Not far behind were the dual smoke plumes of the two huge engines hauling the thirty carriages and armed platforms of the second train.

Before they had left Cheliabinsk, the third train steamed in late at night when most of the town was sound asleep. Hundreds of armed Czechs immediately surrounded it. They quickly unshackled three boarded up carriages, full of supplies, the officers told them. Working quickly, they located them in the middle of the second train. They then linked the new engine in tandem with the other, leaving the remainder of the carriages behind. Both trains left Cheliabinsk at first light next morning.

Mikhail soon became impressed with the organization of the Legion. They had their own bank, which operated the whole length of the line, a telegraph (which Mikhail used to send word of their impending arrival to Yusuf Yudin in Harbin) and they even printed their own stamps to use on letters. To keep the troops informed, they published a newsletter, operated cigarette, and soap factories (and here Mikhail was able to be of real assistance in improving the smooth running of the operations), laundries, and bakeries.

Many of the boxcar living quarters had been painted with bright, colorful scenes of their homeland. To keep spirits up, musicals were organized and staged when the trains stopped to reprovision. It did not take long for Yuri's skill with the violin to be noticed and for him to be co-opted into the orchestra.

Two days after the trains left, Peter, now of the age when many young Russians had left for the front in Poland, joined in the daily maintenance of the guns and ammunition supplies. When they stopped for provisions, Peter, with the endless energy and enthusiasm of youth, worked alongside the legionnaires. Before long, they began to accept him as one of them, and he spent as much time with his new friends among the Czechs as he did with his family. Most times, Mikhail disembarked with him to help in the reprovisioning, particularly restocking wood for the boiler fires and filling the water tanks to generate steam. "I enjoy the exercise," he told Katya.

The thick forests of spruce, pine, and the ubiquitous birch, Russia's national tree, slid slowly by in monotonous repetition. Occasionally, they saw brown bears and elk staring curiously at the noisy intruder before resuming their feeding. Peter was sure he had seen a wolf, but no one else had.

When they stopped, one of the most pleasurable activities was the search for bilberries and wild strawberries, although with summer coming to an end it became harder to find ripe berries not already eaten by the bears. Some of the Czechs, those who came from farms, often found large pungent fungi, which enlivened the cooking for the next few days. Willow grouse, ruby throats, jays, spotted woodpeckers, and the great grey owls called musically, hooted in disdain, or shouted shrill warnings when disturbed by the sound of the axes.

Katya and Mikhail sat engrossed in discussing their daughter when, without warning, the staccato explosions of multiple gunshots shattered the peace. The noise seemed to come from both sides of the train. Immediately after the initial salvo came another. Then the deafening sound of continuous small arms fire filled the air. Bullets thudded into the wood of their carriage. Mikhail instinctively threw Katya onto the floor. Grabbing a rifle offered by one of the soldiers, he joined in returning fire.

Before he could get his second shot away, the well-oiled fighting machine of the Legion identified the location of the ambush. The heavily sandbagged machine gun nests immediately raked the trees on both sides with a withering wall of lead. Within less than a minute, the boom of the artillery and the deafening crash of high explosive shell bursts overrode all other sounds. The ambushers' rate of fire swiftly dropped as their casualties mounted.

Meanwhile, the train continued on its journey undeterred. By the time the second train reached the ambush site, it was ready, having heard the concussion of the shell bursts. As it came within firing range, the Czechs opened up. The response from the ambushers was desultory and intermittent. The heart had gone out of the attackers.

This was the most serious assault the Legion had experienced, four dead and twenty wounded. Katya and Anna hurried along to the hospital car to help tend those hit by bullets or flying debris.

"From what we can tell, they were partisans and elements of the Red Guards, possibly acting on orders from Moscow, but more likely desperate for supplies and thought taking one of our trains would solve the problem," Macek told them that night. "From intelligence received further along the line, we expect to have to fight our way through to Chita. But with soldiers like young Peter, that will be no problem."

Peter glowed with such praise from so experienced an officer as Lt. Macek. Katya looked at him queryingly.

"Peter was near the machine gun car when the shooting started and ran in to help keep up the ammunition supply. One of the gunners got hit in the head by flying wood splinters. Only a flesh wound but it bled so profusely he couldn't see. Peter jumped in and took over the firing without hesitation. He even cleared a jammed round in the gun. The other gunners were most impressed," Macek said.

Katya could only smile wanly. *Has he grown up that fast?* she wondered. *It seems only yesterday he would jump into my arms.*

Anna leaned back against Macek, her eyes closed, savoring the fresh-scented air as the train moved slowly through the evening. They stood on the flat plate over the coupling between two carriages. It was the only private space on the crowded train. His arms were over hers, meeting around her waist beneath her breasts. She felt a warm tingling at the top of her thighs. *If we don't get married soon,* she thought, *I will not be able to contain myself.* She felt him harden against her and responded to the pressure.

There was nothing said for many minutes, their closeness enough. Then Macek said, as if musing to himself, "I think those fellows today were really after the gold."

"What gold is that, my darling?" Anna said dreamily, only half aware of the conversation.

"Those three trucks we loaded last before we left—that's the tsar's gold."

"Oh," said Anna and pressed herself harder against him, turning her head so she could kiss his lips.

As they approached Irkutsk on the shores of Lake Baikal, Anna noticed the general level of alertness increase. This was an area of heavy partisan and Red Guard activity, not to mention renegade Cossack bands. With such a bounty of gold bars, they were potential targets for any one of those groups. Yet, Charles explained, the Legion had confidence they could negotiate safe passage with the Bolshevik government in exchange for the gold.

"We believe it's about half the country's gold reserves, $330 million. The Reds need it desperately. We have it, and we intend to keep it until we're safe," Macek said. As a fighting force the Legion would be hard to beat, he explained. So, Anna realized, the gold was a potent bargaining counter, provided they could hold onto it.

Autumn began to show its colors in the leaves of the trees, and the air became decidedly crisper. Again, they had been stopped for several days. Even when stationary, keeping steam up used fuel surprisingly fast. Once they got moving again, everyone knew they must stop for fuel very soon. By mid-morning the driver saw what he wanted ahead—a railway refueling depot, a small hamlet where wood was cut to length and stored for the trains. As they came into the depot, a pile of cut fuel could be seen neatly stacked in hoppers near the tracks.

An old man came out of a wooden hut near the fuel dump as the train, with a screech of metal on metal, came to a halt. After a brief discussion, he retreated into the hut and the wood-loading team disembarked to begin their work. On the opposite side to the depot, the ground rose steadily away from the train. It had been logged for the first hundred meters, thereafter it was heavily forested. A group of hopefuls decided to have one last fossick for berries and pine nuts. Mikhail and Peter joined them in a welcome distraction to the enforced inactivity of the train.

Peter was lucky. He found a bush with a small selection of berries. He had just finished picking them when, off to their right, in a sudden beating of wings and hooting a noisy group of great grey owls broke cover. Any birds suddenly disturbed like that deserved attention. For nocturnal owls, it was a danger sign. The Czechs to their right gave the prearranged whistle signal. It was immediately relayed to the left and back to the train, alerting the gunners to possible attack. Without hesitation, the berry party began retreating backward out of the woods, rifles at the ready.

Mikhail and Peter had just left the last line of trees when firing started. The shots came from in front of them, and to their left. From the number and sound of the shots, it was not a large force. Probably a small, partisan group. Then they heard shouting from the train. One group of partisans was targeting the engine and drivers, while another targeted the men loading the fuel. They were trying to disable the train or at least delay it. That could only mean one thing. A larger force was on its way.

The sniper sat well hidden, high in a pine in the second line of trees in from the cleared area. He was an experienced hunter and had chosen his hide well. Two trees in front of him limited his line of fire but the rest of the field was open.

He saw the two men exit the tree line. The down angle was a little steep but easily within his capability. He looked at the artillery flattops. They were his assigned targets. He had been told to keep their heads down to prevent them firing high explosive shell bursts. He sighted and fired at a gunner winding the elevation of the gun up to aim at the hill. The gunner ducked for cover. The two men he had spotted were now moving down the slope. He had to act now to get a clear shot. If he did not, they would be out of his line of sight. He thought of his children back in the village half starved while these bloody foreigners grabbed everything. They looked well fed and healthy, the bastards. With practiced care, he took aim deliberately and slowly squeezed the trigger.

Mikhail felt as if he had been hit with a sledgehammer. As he fell, his feet tangled, twisting his body. He saw the pale blue of the afternoon sky. Then, Peter was looking down at him. *Why can't I hear what Peter is saying?* He tried to breathe, but his chest wouldn't work. *What is wrong?* he asked, but no sound came. There was no pain, but for some reason, he couldn't lift his arms. He found it curious there seemed to be a lot of liquid in his throat. He had a last glimpse of Peter's face. *Why is he crying?* Mikhail thought. Then the sky became white.

Peter was at his father's side in seconds, closely followed by two of the Czechs who had seen Mikhail get hit. They grabbed them both and raced down to the train. As they did, one of the machine-gunners who had been watching for the source of the firing on the artillery saw the unprotected muzzle flash of the shot. The flash had been shielded from the big gun but was clearly visible from the side. In seconds, the gunner traversed the treetops with a concentrated stream of bullets. They shredded the pine and knocked the sniper, with ten holes in him, lifeless out of the tree.

By the time they got him back to the train, Mikhail Ivanovich was dead.

§ § § § §

Katya watched the Czechs walk in an ordered line toward the forest. She could make out Mikhail and Peter walking happily side by side in the middle of the line. Idly, she watched them disappear into the trees laughing together. The scene reminded her how much they all missed Ivan, how much he would have enjoyed joining his son and grandson in the search for berries.

The first gunshot jerked her out of her reverie. She sat bolt upright against the window. The Czechs began to emerge from the trees, backing down toward the train, their rifles facing the sound of the firing. Seconds later, Mikhail and Peter appeared. Mikhail carried a rifle. Peter held the satchels containing the berries.

Her relief at seeing them turned to horror seconds later. About twenty meters from the trees, Mikhail seemed to jump in the air. The rifle dropped from his hands as he fell backward onto the ground. An instant later, Peter dropped down beside him.

"Noooo!" she screamed at the window. "Misha, get up, get Peter, get up, please…"

She saw the two Czechs pick up Mikhail and, half carrying Peter, race back to the train.

"Oh, my God," Katya said as she ran out of the carriage to where the Czechs carried Misha.

"Get the surgeons; they can take the bullet out." She could barely get the words out between sobs. "He must be in the hospital carriage. Quickly, he mustn't lose any more blood," she said. As she looked at Mikhail's face, a froth of blood trickled from his mouth.

The soldiers knew it was too late. They had seen too many chest hits in the trenches not to recognize a fatal injury. The exit hole was too ragged. Nevertheless, they carefully picked him up and carried him to the hospital where the surgeon pronounced him dead.

Only after the brief burial ceremony had concluded did the enormity of what had happened hit Katya. A gut-wrenching emptiness engulfed her. First Ivan had been willfully taken from them. Now, her one true love had so pointlessly been snatched from his family in the prime of his life.

"Just gathering berries," she said incredulously to Anna and Yuri. "What harm was he doing?"

As she spoke, she looked across at Peter, suddenly realizing how selfish she had been in her grief. It struck her then how traumatized her eldest son must be. Peter saw his father shot. He was with him as he died. He could also have been shot. She put her arms around Peter. They held each other, tears streaming down their cheeks, breath coming in great sobs. For the first time since becoming part of the family, Pinna did not know what to do or who to comfort. Unobtrusively, she left Katya and her children to their grief, tears falling down her own cheeks.

§ § § § § §

The train finally left the depot only to stop half a day's journey onward at a small village. Heavy fighting ahead prevented them proceeding for nearly two weeks. Katya found this enforced inactivity almost unbearable. She needed activity to distract her. Without it, she became despondent and depressed, full of sorrow and despair. Only Anna's happiness offered some relief and rekindled memories of the intense joy of her own marriage to Mikhail.

Ah Misha, she thought many times each day, *how happy we were.*

But it was Peter and Yuri who reminded her of Mikhail's legacy. Her sons needed her now more than ever. She must be strong for both of them.

Finally, the train resumed its eastward trek, and Katya concentrated all her energy into work and keeping her remaining family close by. She forced herself to think about the future, unthinkable though it was without Misha. She must still make for Harbin. She had to ensure a safe future for Peter and Yuri, and in Harbin was a business in which the family owned a large interest. Mikhail had told her she could trust Yusuf Yudin (who she vaguely remembered from his visits to Moscow) and their Chinese partner, Liu Ping-nan. What she would find there she could only guess at.

As far as the Czechs could tell her, Harbin was safe. She wondered yet again whether anywhere could be truly safe again without the protection of force of arms. The whole country seemed to be in a state of anarchy. Images of the hundreds of bodies lying alongside the railway as they passed through stations where Whites had fought Reds passed through her mind. Clearly no quarter could be expected from either side. The battle lines clearly moved so fluidly no one had time to stop and bury the dead. It had been horrible to see the bodies, decomposing in the sun. But it had been impersonal, a reality that didn't affect them. And then Mikhail became a casualty, a statistic of civil war. All of a sudden it was very personal.

What did the future hold for them? she wondered. If they encountered a large Red force, even the mighty Czechs may be defeated. Or they may dump noncombatants in their efforts to escape. And what of Anna?

Charles Macek was very solicitous after Mikhail's death. *He seems a decent and thoughtful young man,* Katya thought. *Away from the strictures of war, with the love of a woman, he could develop into a good husband and father. But until they leave Russia, their future is as uncertain as ours,* she thought. *Why should I deny Anna the pleasure of marrying the man she obviously loves; in a month we may all be dead. Anna should marry as soon as possible.*

Within a week, Katya found an Orthodox priest and Anna became Mrs. Macek. The happiness so evident on her daughter's face when the ceremony ended brought tears to Katya's eyes.

"Your father would have been so happy for you," she said, hugging Anna tightly. Memories of a young Irish girl and a handsome young Russian flooded her mind. *Ah, my beautiful Misha, why did you have to leave me?*

After long delays, the train made the spectacular journey around the southern edge of Lake Baikal and onto Chita. Here the Chinese Eastern Railway linked to the Trans-Siberian. This was where Katya, Peter, and Yuri changed trains on their way south to Harbin.

The three stood on the platform watching Anna disappear from their life. Around them swirled a mass of strange people, local Buryats and their Mongol cousins, Russians, Cossacks, members of the Allied Interventionist Force, Buddhist monks in their saffron robes, and Japanese soldiers. Katya looked around expectantly for a familiar or friendly face. Not surprisingly, she found neither. They would buy a ticket and make their own way south. Peter had hidden inside his shirt a money pouch given him by Charles Macek. It contained a large number of rubles significantly replenishing their rapidly dwindling resources. Macek had insisted. "I must know that my new family has the money to get to safety," he said.

Anna, her eyes red rimmed from the tears of parting, leaned further out the window of their train as it slowly steamed out of Chita. She could still just see the three small figures waving on the retreating platform. Then the crowd pressed around them and they were gone. She pulled the window sash down and slumped back against her husband.

"I may never see them again," she sobbed. "Don't ever leave me my darling," she said, grasping Charles arm around her.

Macek hugged her as the train, gathering speed, took them toward their new life together.

In Chita, Katya put her arms around her sons and walked slowly toward what appeared to be an office. They had no luggage, just a roll of spare clothes and the violin clutched under Yuri's left arm. They looked what they were, three more refugees amid the chaos of civil war. As they made their way toward the ticket offices, they passed a seat with two old Buddhist monks sitting talking and looking at them. One of the monks got up and tapped Peter on the shoulder.

"Please forgive me for intruding, but the lady with you looks very distressed. Is she your mother?" he asked.

"Yes," Peter replied.

"There is great sorrow in her face, we couldn't help but notice," the monk said quietly. "Perhaps she would like a seat?" he said, indicating the seat against which his fellow monk was now standing. Katya sat gratefully. Over the next hour, they told the monks their story while Peter bought tea from the ever-present samovar at the back of the station.

"And how do you intend getting to Harbin?" asked the monk.

"By the next train," said Peter.

"It may be safer if you had someone to travel with you."

"We hoped that a friend of my father would meet us here. My father wrote to tell him we would be arriving in Chita, but it has taken so long he's no doubt given up on us," Peter said.

"What does this man look like? Was he by chance a Kazakh?" asked one of the monks.

Katya sat up. "Yes, I think he is," she said.

"There has been a Kazakh coming up here many times, asking about a Russian man and his family of a wife and three children. Perhaps he is your friend," the monk said. "But we didn't think that it could be so as you are only two children. But now you've told us of your daughter, perhaps this is who you seek."

That night they slept at a house run by the monks for travelers, not far from the station. Each day, they returned to look for the Kazakh. A week passed, and they had resigned themselves to risking the travel on their own. Then, one morning one of the monks came toward where they sat with a man of medium height, dark olive skin, and black hair tinged with grey. As he came up to them, he stopped and addressed Peter.

"I am Yusuf Yudin, and I'm looking for the family Morozov," he said.

Katya looked up at him. "Yusuf, I am Katya Mariavna, the wife of Mikhail Ivanovich. We met in Moscow. Ivan and my husband Mikhail are both dead. These are our sons, Peter and Yuri. We would be most grateful if you would take us to Harbin and safety."

Yusuf looked at the woman who addressed him. He was shocked how the wife of his partner's son, the vibrant young woman he recalled meeting, had changed. She seemed shrunken and had grief etched upon her face. However, he had no doubt it was the same person. He looked at Peter. He could see Ivan in the strong intelligent features. The younger one, Yuri, looked more sensitive, perhaps he took after his mother.

"I'm pleased to have found you," said Yusuf. "Thank you my friends," he said to the monks.

Harbin

Katya fell into a routine in the years since they arrived. Early every morning, she joined a group of older Chinese in the little park across the road practicing tai chi exercises. Old Liu recommended the ancient ritual as a means of retaining good health into old age and of recovering equilibrium in life.

"It helps cope with the pain and hurt that inevitably comes into all our lives," he said.

She liked the house in which she now lived. It was modest but very comfortable. Built for a departed American, it had the illusion of space and openness often found in Chinese houses. Yusuf initially suggested she buy a house in the Russian sector. Like most of the European areas, it had wide streets, trees, restaurants, and theaters with a view of the huge, onion-shaped dome of St. Nikolai Cathedral. Katya declined.

"God has deserted me. I don't want to have to look at his house of worship every day," she said.

Where she lived had more Chinese than Westerners, but she felt comfortable there. A twenty-minute walk in one direction brought her to the offices of Tiger Moon Trading. In the opposite direction, another twenty-minute walk brought her to the International School and her part-time work as a teacher of English. She smiled proudly as she recalled how quickly Yuri picked up languages. She often walked with him to the school. He had long become equally comfortable conversing in English, Chinese, or his native Russian. *He has my ear for the spoken word,* she thought.

Both Yusuf and Liu made it clear to Katya that the Morozov equity in the business would provide her with enough income to live comfortably, without the need to work. Nevertheless, Katya needed the distraction and discipline to occupy her time, to prevent her going mad missing Misha. To fill in the rest of her week, she worked as a volunteer at the Hospital of St. Basil, operated by the Orthodox Church, one day each week.

With Liu's blessing, she opened a simple clinic in a building owned by Tiger Moon. Here, any women, Asian or Western, could go without questions asked. There they could sit and talk. Some sought refuge, some, fascinated by Chinese culture, listened to talks by bilingual Chinese women. Others wanted basic medical advice away from the knowledge of their husbands. For these, Katya employed a woman skilled in traditional Chinese medicine and remedies. Most days, Katya spent time at the clinic, drinking green tea, chatting with the women. Of all the activities she undertook in that first year, this was the most cathartic. The sharing of grief speeded the healing.

Her fluency in Chinese improved with the passing months. Gradually she began to master the subtleties and nuances of the language, how the same word could have quite different meanings when used with different emphasis. Chinese characters were an entirely different matter. She could occasionally recognize one or two but for the most part the written language was utterly incomprehensible.

Harbin throbbed with White Russian émigrés plotting endlessly to bring about the demise of the Bolsheviks. For the most part, the same talk and bellicose threats were repeated at meetings and in restaurants month after month. Katya rapidly lost interest in their cause. She thought it preaching to the converted and had more to do with keeping their spirits up. It helped them avoid thinking about what they had lost, she thought. Judging from the Harbin newspapers and what Liu and Yusuf told her, the Red Army had clear control of eastern Siberia, with one exception—the Japanese.

In the last few months, Katya noticed, more Japanese companies had established large offices in the city. As their influence escalated, Yusuf and Liu became increasingly worried. They both had bad memories of the war in '05. The same could not be said for many of the White Russians in the city.

"Your fellow Russians are strange people," Liu said to Katya one morning when she called into the Tiger Moon office to visit Peter, who now worked full time in the business. "The Japanese inflicted a heavy defeat on your countrymen twenty years ago, and yet there are many here who welcome their return."

"Some see an opportunity for profit," said Yusuf. "But I fear many are under the delusion that the Imperial Army will help overthrow the Reds."

"Is that likely?" asked Katya.

"No," said Yusuf. "The Japanese Army has one objective only, to annex Manchuria so that their companies can exploit our resources for the benefit of Japan. If they're successful, they'll be ruthless. Many lives will be lost and we'll be lucky if Tiger Moon survives."

"In China, we have been through many changes of government," Liu said. "We have learned to be like a willow in the wind, to bend in whichever direction the wind blows, but never to break. If the Japanese gain control of Manchuria, it will only be temporary. The Chinese people are very resilient. We will smile and do whatever business we must to avoid attention. We know the Japanese have a thick face and a black heart."

"What do you mean, honored father?" Katya interrupted using the customary title of respect.

Yusuf answered. "I think in the West it is most easily translated as 'they say one thing and do another.' The end justifies the means. Whatever they say, they'll still take whatever action best advances the interest of Japan. If that means killing some of the local people, for instance, then they'll do so without a moment's thought."

"But, we will ultimately prevail," said Liu. "One who is skilled in walking leaves no trail."

Katya thought she knew what he meant this time. Yusuf had explained to her, when she had proposed setting up the women's clinic, that Liu Ping-nan had a close association with the Pure Jade Benevolent Society. The sign of the green triangle. They had connections all over China and while visibly a straightforward self-help organization, Katya suspected there were many layers upon layers within the society, the real purpose of which could only be guessed. If she was right, then Pure Jade had far more serious and secret objectives.

§ § § § § §

Sergei Brokhoff felt distracted. He looked down at the naked body of the young girl lying on the futon. She was on her side crying quietly. One half-developed breast was just visible with red marks where he had squeezed it. She had her legs drawn up, revealing her vulva. He told her to stay in that position after he spanked her buttocks. Each of the cheeks showed stinging red welts. Some of the strokes of the light bamboo cane had hit her sex. He made sure of that. Just enough for tolerable pain; he prided himself in his ability to judge the right level of pain to administer. He was only halfway through his normal ritual with a new girl but he felt his interest waning.

He purchased young girls from impoverished parents. Others, and these he usually preferred, were stolen and delivered to the brothels by organized gangs. Once they had been used a number of times, they were too ashamed to go back to their families and became resigned to their new way of life. The girl on the futon had been stolen in Mukden.

He called out and an old woman came and took the girl away. She would be kept in a locked room and physically inducted into her new duties by the other women. He felt no sorrow for the girl. In fact, he had no feelings at all for her. She was simply an item of merchandise. He wondered if his age could be causing him to lose his drive. No, he concluded firmly, it must be something else.

His mind kept drifting to the woman he had seen yesterday. He was certain it was the same one although many years had passed since he had last seen her. It fascinated and stimulated him that she was here, in his town. He resolved to find out more about her.

Having made that decision, he turned his mind to business. Brokhoff had no misgivings about the increasing presence of the Japanese. He recalled how profitable his past dealings had been. If they had special needs for their brothels, he would supply them, at the right price. He knew they usually filled their own establishments with women purchased in Japan or Korea, but some requirements only he could procure.

Brokhoff also rented them the premises for the brothels. What no more than a handful of Harbinsi knew was that Sergei Alexandrovich

Brokhoff was one of the largest property owners in the city. He cloaked his ownership with a labyrinth of nominees and Chinese companies. More than a few of the larger businesses in the city would be surprised to know that the rent they paid each month ended up in the hands of a secretive brothel owner. He was a very wealthy man.

The other strand of his growing business interests, and by far the most profitable, was opium. Although banned in other parts of China, in the melting pot of Harbin, demand was increasing. Recently, he had received a number of inquiries from Japanese interests. He found this odd. In his experience, they did not use drugs. So what prompted their interest, he could only speculate. *Well,* he thought, *if they pay, I will supply.*

Nothing, however, is totally secret for long in China. There were always a select few, men with the resources and the network to collect information (and who recognized that knowledge is power). In Harbin, two men in such a network knew the full extent and nature of Brokhoff's dealings. Liu Ping-nan was one of them.

§ § § § §

The clear sky and warm sun made it a day when it was a pleasure to be out of doors. Katya felt invigorated after her morning exercising and walked happily toward St. Basil's Hospital. She had heard the hospital, and more particularly the women's ward where she worked as a volunteer, had received a generous donation from a wealthy Russian businessman last week. She was keen to find out more detail. They were always short of supplies and equipment, so donations like this brightened everyone's life by making the provision of care more effective and easier.

"Good morning, Olga," she said as she walked past the nurses' station. "How many new iron beds are we going to buy? And new blankets? Are we all getting new uniforms?"

"You're early, Katya," said the head nurse. "Our new benefactor is here talking with the director. I hear he's asked to meet some of the volunteers, so you'd better straighten your hair and polish your teeth!"

"I shall bow and curtsy." Katya laughed as she moved off to begin her duties, which mainly involved cleaning, assisting the nurses wash the longer term patients, and generally keeping track of the paperwork for stores.

Half an hour later, she heard a slight commotion behind her. She turned to see Olga beckoning her to the nurses' station.

"This is Sergei Alexandrovich Brokhoff, our most generous benefactor," said the director. "He's expressed a wish to meet some of the volunteers. May I present Mrs. Katya Morozov, sir."

"Mrs. Morozov," he said, bowing slightly as he took her hand. *This was old-fashioned courtly behavior,* Katya thought. "Perhaps Mrs. Morozov could show me around a ward? That will prevent me from wasting any more of your time, Director," he said, making it clear the director had been dismissed. Katya and Olga managed to keep a straight face as the director was a fussy, officious little man, always puffing his own ego.

"I'd be delighted, Mr. Brokhoff, if that meets with the approval of the director," she said.

"Of course, of course. Well, look after him," said the director, and he marched off to his office.

Before Katya realized it, Brokhoff had steered her away from the nurses' station and the two of them were walking slowly around the ward chatting. He was a charming and entertaining companion. A tall man with receding, grey-speckled hair and a neatly trimmed beard flecked with grey. He had the air of confidence that only comes with experience and success. By the time she had shown him the small garden on one side of the hospital building, she was relaxed and enjoying herself. The courtly behavior of her guest reminded her of other times, of the society she had once been a part of in Moscow. A feeling of happier times past.

"You have been a delightful guide, Mrs. Morozov," he said. "Thank you. I must return to my business now or I will not be able to earn enough money to make any more donations."

Katya smiled. "I hope we can persuade you to be generous again, Mr. Brokhoff."

"Please, do me the honor of calling me by my Christian names," he said.

He turned to take his leave, then stopped and turned back.

"I am thinking of making a further donation, for the children's ward, but after talking to the director I would like to be sure that I can nominate what the money is to be spent on. I rather got the impression new furnishings for his office might feature high in his consideration." He smiled. "Could I impose on you to give me some advice in this regard? If tomorrow would suit, I could send an automobile to pick you up at say, ten in the morning and bring you to my office. I should only detain you for an hour, although if our discussion were to go on beyond eleven, I should consider it my duty to escort you to lunch."

"I'd be delighted to help, Sergei Alexandrovich," she said.

She watched as he walked toward the corner where his car waited. He was impeccably groomed, wore expertly tailored clothes with an aristocratic bearing, something she had not seen since before the revolution in Moscow. His good looks complemented a slight aloofness that was both attractive and slightly disturbing. She smiled, feeling a light flush come to her face. Tomorrow would be fun. She turned and reentered the hospital. As she did, a memory stirred in the back of her mind. There was something familiar about Sergei Brokhoff. She shrugged. *He probably reminds me of any number of people back in Moscow,* she thought. Then it was back to work.

As Brokhoff climbed into his car, he smiled a cold humorless smile without the slightest trace of warmth.

The next morning, at the appointed time, Katya rode in the automobile to a modern, three-story building on the border of Pristan. She could have walked there in less than twenty minutes. An attractive Chinese girl opened the door and showed her into an exquisitely furnished sitting room on the top floor. Katya looked at the delicate antique Chinese furniture. *Some of the pieces must be over a hundred years old,* she thought.

"Ah, good morning, Katya Mariavna," Brokhoff said as he entered the room from a door to the left. Katya had only the briefest glimpse before the door closed. She had the impression of a much larger room with screens and more beautiful furniture.

"This building is on a slight rise and from this floor you can see the Sungari River," he said, gesturing Katya to come to the window. The view in the distance was impressive. Over the tops of the other buildings she could see the steamers on the river, and the myriad of small Chinese craft sculled expertly between the busy traffic.

"This room looks too good to be an office," Katya said. "It looks more like part of a home."

"It has indeed been used as a residence," said Brokhoff, "but is seldom so used today. I like to be surrounded by beautiful things and as I am often moving around and not always in my office, this suits me well. But enough about these surroundings, you must tell me about the operations of the children's ward."

Katya gave a brief description of the operations of the ward and its needs.

"May I order some tea?" Brokhoff asked.

"Thank you, that would be lovely," Katya said.

Brokhoff rang a small bell on the table beside his chair and a beautiful girl in a cheongsam came in to receive his instructions. As she left the room, Katya had the impression she was naked under the very thin material.

She returned carrying a lacquer tray with two small teapots, one a soft red, the other jade green, and two matching cups. She set the red pot and cup on the table beside Katya. As she poured the tea, Katya could see that beneath the light material of the dress the girl was indeed naked. When she had poured the tea, she smiled demurely. She then poured Brokhoff's tea from the green pot and left the room.

"This is a special blend I have made exclusively for me. I think you will like it, although it may taste a little bitter at first," he said.

Katya took a sip. It was bitter, but not unpleasantly so. As they continued talking, she noticed her cup was empty and reached to pour a refill. Then Sergei was alongside her pouring from the red pot. He handed her the cup and said, "Drink up, it will warm you." As she drank the second cup, she felt a general sense of well-being flowing through her body.

"What an excellent tea," she said, as the girl appeared beside her, refilling the cup.

§ § § § §

It was first light when she stirred. She lay, cozy and warm in her bed, in that half conscious state of early morning. She felt totally relaxed, languorous and sensual. She stretched slowly. Her breasts felt tender. She slid her hand under her nightdress; her breast felt sore. As she touched her nipple, it hardened immediately and as it did she became aware of a tingling between her legs. Her clitoris was sensitive to touch, but not at all unpleasant. Images, as in a dream, flashed through her mind. They were disjointed, and, like a dream, she could not put clear form around them. Ethereal tableaux came and went along with feelings of intense pleasure alternating with sharp pain.

When she awoke again, the sun was high in the sky. She still felt extremely tired, wrung out. She also felt sticky and dirty.

The next day, she was more like her usual self. The blurred images had mostly faded but the emotions of pleasure and pain persisted. She began to feel guilt. If she had been having intense sexual dreams, why had she not dreamed of Misha? She had not forgotten him, of that she was certain.

Pinna told her that a man and a young woman had brought her home in a motor car. They said that you had been working too hard and had collapsed at the office of a businessman you were visiting to raise money for the hospital.

"They helped me get you into the house," she said. "Then I put you to bed."

"What time was that?" Katya asked.

"Late afternoon," Pinna replied.

Katya decided not to tell anyone how she felt. First, she must find out what had happened.

She began to reconstruct the day she had gone to see Brokhoff. Everything was clear, until they had tea. After that, she only had fragmented images, which could be her dreams. Perhaps she had collapsed. She started to go over it again. *The girl in the cheongsam poured me tea. She was in that dress. Then why do I have the image of her naked bending over me? And the memories of pleasure and pain, where do they come from? Are they also in my dreams?*

No matter how much she wrestled with her recollection, she could not remember clearly what happened from the time she was having tea until she awoke the next morning. She had only fragments, unconnected images, but all were sexual.

Slowly, she came to the realization there could be only one possible explanation. She had been drugged and raped. And it could only have happened in Sergei Brokhoff's office. *I must go to the police,* she thought. She went over in her head what she would tell them and changed her mind. Brokhoff could simply deny it. The girl in the cheongsam was obviously in his employ and would corroborate his story. *I have no proof.*

Shame turned to anger and outrage and intense frustration as she realized there was nothing she could do.

Later that week at the clinic, as delicately as she could, she quietly asked Ching-po, Liu's daughter, with whom she had built a friendship, about the effects of opium and other narcotics. Could they make a person lose their memory? Could a person still function under their influence? The answers confirmed her suspicions.

Next, she made inquiries about Brokhoff. Only then did the true nature of the man become apparent. A brothel owner reputed to deal in drugs. An old memory surfaced. John Somerston's visit to Harbin all those years ago. Hadn't he brought salutations from a man called Brokhoff? What had Misha said? He dismissed the message, "He's the owner of the brothel John visited, no doubt just being a little mischievous."

Stupid woman, she berated herself, *how could you let this happen?* He seemed so urbane and gentlemanly. Part of the trap. And that tea. No wonder it tasted bitter. For the first time in many years she swore in Gaelic. *But why do this to me?* That question rolled around and around in her head without answer. *What am I to Brokhof? Could there possibly be a connection to our old life in the capital?*

No one must know, she resolved. *Oh, Misha, forgive me.* Tears streamed down her cheeks. *I'll work harder and in time this will be just a foul memory. I'll put it behind me.*

But it was not over—not yet.

Katya continued her routine of early morning tai chi, her visits to the clinic, her work at the hospital and her visits to Tiger Moon. She made sure she spent more time with Yuri, helping him with his homework and talking together. He excelled at school, he made many friends, and his teachers spoke highly of him. His best friends were Chinese boys his own age. One of these introduced him to the martial arts. Before long he and his friend were regular pupils at classes given by Master Wu in the Chinese sector. Katya had been apprehensive at first until Yusuf assured her that if they had the protection of a man as revered as Master Wu they would be safe and treated with respect. After all, Yusuf pointed out, tai chi is also a form of martial arts.

Immersing herself in activity had the effect she had hoped. She thought less and less about what had happened. She continued to walk from home but became much more vigilant, keeping to crowded streets and thoroughfares.

This particular day started cloudy and mild, a harbinger of waning summer and approaching autumn. She followed her accustomed route, walking from the busy street, through the hospital gardens, to the entrance. Halfway toward the entrance, a tall figure with a cloak around his shoulders stepped from behind a tree. She jumped, startled. It was Sergei Brokhoff.

"Good morning, Katya. I have missed you these last weeks," he said.

Katya looked behind her and to her left preparing to run, but she could not move. The shock of his effrontery robbed her of the will to act.

"Go away; leave me alone," she said at last.

"That's no way to treat a lover," he said quietly.

"You are nothing to me. Don't come near me or I'll call for the police."

"The police? I think not. What would you tell them? I'd say we had a lover's fight and that you are simply angry. They would be polite but they would have no interest. Besides, I have something to show you, something to remind you how much you enjoyed our time together."

Before Katya could protest he said, "Come, sit on this garden seat; it's in full view of the road and the hospital. You'll be quite safe," he added sarcastically as he sat on the seat.

Katya stood irresolute. Deep in her mind, a memory started to form. It was in Moscow. A man had tried to get her to go with him against her better judgment. She looked at Brokhoff, but the image was only half formed. What did he want? How loathsome to be in close proximity to this man.

He opened a thin black leather attaché case on his knee.

"You have a choice Katya Mariavna; you can see what I have here, or you can see it spread all over Harbin," he said.

Reluctantly, she sat down.

He took out a folder and handed it to her. Without looking at him, she opened it. A portfolio of photographs. Pornographic by the look of them. *How sordid,* she thought, about to slam the folder shut. She looked at the face of the naked woman. It was her face. She felt simultaneously shock, and embarrassment. She dared not look at her tormenter, her face flush with shame. She looked back at the photo. She was lying on her back with her legs wide apart and her arms folded above her head. Her eyes were closed. She looked totally relaxed, a languorous smile on her face. She turned to the next photo. She lay in the same position. This time a naked girl bent over her, the same girl that had served her tea. The girl knelt between her legs doing something Katya had only heard about. She could not stop looking at them. The next three photos showed Katya being raped by a man—Brokhoff, she presumed, and in various other poses with the girl. In every photo the camera had been positioned to capture her face. In each of them, she seemed to be enjoying what was happening.

She closed the folder. She felt utterly humiliated, which, of course, must have been what Brokhoff intended.

"You may keep those copies; I have others," he said, breaking the silence. He talked on for a few minutes but Katya did not hear what he was saying until something broke through her subconscious. She was not sure whether it was a phrase or the Muscovite intonation. The memory that had been half formed suddenly became startlingly clear. She was being half forced into a carriage after a concert.

She knew who this man was. She looked at his face. The hair had been cut differently and the hairline had receded. It had grayed with age. The beard changed the appearance of his face, but, she was certain. It was Vasily Koslinski. She almost spat out his name when some instinct warned her to swallow the words. She stared at his face and saw cruelty. A man dedicated to his own pleasures to the total disregard of others. She had no doubt this man was capable of any degradation, any viciousness. Suddenly, she wanted to get away. She stood up abruptly and clutching the folder walked rapidly away to the street. As she did she heard Brokhoff/Koslinski say, "I will be expecting you, Katya Mariavna."

She looked at the photographs many times over the next days until she became so sickened she found a secure hiding place and secreted them out of sight. She had no intention of seeing Brokhoff again, ever. If she did not, he had threatened to publish the photos. *If that happens, I will have to leave Harbin, the shame will be too great, not only on the family, but on those who helped us.*

But where can I go? I have no papers. The Russian papers are no longer valid. I have no British passport, and the local identity card Liu arranged won't let me travel out of China. If I leave, I'll be stateless. She had written to Bertie Somerston advising him of their predicament soon after they arrived in Harbin. With no reply, she had no way of knowing if her letter had actually got through to London. In the turmoil of the time, she had doubts about the reliability of the post.

She felt trapped. She knew she had to make a decision. If she did not, events would overtake her. She would have to explain what had happened to Liu. There seemed no other alternative. It would result in huge loss of face for her and her family. It may even, she thought, result in her ceasing to have contact with Tiger Moon. She felt she would always receive some support from Yusuf Yudin but even that of necessity may have to be limited. Without the connections of Tiger Moon and the income it provided, they would become just another White Russian family struggling to stay alive in the dog-eat-dog world of tens of thousands of displaced people in a city increasingly under the sway of the Japanese.

A week later, she had still not made a decision because she knew that, once made, there was no going back; the die would be cast. To take her mind off the dreadful dilemma, she took to walking through the city streets. On one cold cloudy day, a chill wind from Siberia blew away the sound the first time her name was called.

"Katya Mariavna," he called again.

She stopped and looked around blankly.

"Over here," the voice said. "I was sure it was you. It's good to see a familiar face."

Katya at last identified where the voice was coming from. She stared blankly at the ascetic face of a man smiling at her from the café doorway before recognition dawned. A broad smile creased her face.

"Maksim Nickoliavich, what a wonderful surprise. What are you doing in Harbin?" she asked.

"I was just about to have tea and a cake; won't you join me?" he said.

"With pleasure," said Katy, thrilled to see a familiar and friendly face.

"I'm very pleased to see that you made it. How are Mikhail and your family?" he asked.

"It was your quick thinking and bravery that enabled us to get away from Moscow and for that I'll always be grateful. However, Misha is dead," she said and proceeded to tell Rysakov what had befallen them in their journey begun nearly a decade ago in Moscow.

"I am very sorry to hear about Misha," he said, "I liked him very much."

"And you, Maksim, what about you?" Katya said. As he told his story she could see in his eyes the sorrow of loss so common in this city.

"Vera had been ill for some time as you may recall. About two years ago, my friend, Dr. Sergei Sokoloff, diagnosed a tumor. At first, he was optimistic that he may be able to operate and remove it, but when he did a more thorough examination he found several others and he told me that she had perhaps six months to live. I took what time off work I could to care for her. Initially, she responded and it seemed that she may even recover. Then there was the assassination attempt on Lenin, the Bolshevik leader. My son Pavel had been active in the Social Democrats since he fought on the Polish front. The Bolsheviks used the assassination attempt as a pretext for a terror campaign. The Chekists, the Red's secret police, rounded up anyone opposed to them, regardless of whether they wanted to overthrow the tsar or not. Many were shot, the rest imprisoned. Pavel was sent to the Lubianka prison. The last I heard he was still alive.

"When Vera heard this, she gave up all hope and declined rapidly. Within a month, she was dead. I didn't know what to do, with the Cheka then arresting members of the families of opponents of the Reds. So, I started selling our possessions for what little I could raise, thinking I might be able to use some of the money to get Pavel out of prison. Then Gregori Yukovsky, a friend and fellow officer, warned me I was under investigation and the prospects of my being able to get Pavel freed were negligible. I left some money with Gregori to see what he could do for Pavel and fled Moscow."

They stayed talking for several hours, two lost souls taking succor from each other amid the maelstrom of revolution. A common history and the pain of lost loved ones forged a bond words did not need express.

"I'm now an inspector in the Harbin Police Force, which is largely Russian. Some of the members I used to know in Moscow. They had to leave like me, just because they were members of the Imperial Police Force. We are still loyal Russians," he shook his head. "I fear these new masters will be more repressive than the old."

"The Reds still manage the railway here but the power of the railway police doesn't extend beyond it so they can't take any action in Harbin," Rysakov went on. "However, that's not our real concern. The Japanese military police, the Kempeitai, are becoming increasingly powerful. They treat Manchuria as a Jap colony."

As they talked, a possible solution to her own problem took shape in Katya's mind. Of all the people in Harbin, she felt she could trust Rysakov the most. After all, he had saved their lives in Moscow and gotten them out of the city. Even more importantly, Rysakov had an unsolved crime in Moscow to which they both had a connection.

"Maksim, do you remember Vasily Koslinski, the aristocrat who stole the money from the Moscow Commerce Bank?"

"Of course, we never found out where he skulked away to," he replied.

"I know where he is. What is even more important"—and here she paused, for what she was about to say she had not said aloud to anyone, even herself, but she knew she was right—"I am certain he is the "Monster of Moscow," the murderer who almost killed me."

She felt a great burden had been finally lifted off her shoulders.

"How can you be so certain?" he asked, now excited. This was quite unexpected.

For the next hour, she told him how Brokhoff/Koslinski had drugged, raped, and photographed her and now threatened her. She could not say with certainty that she remembered the face of the man who attacked her all those years ago in Moscow. All she could say was that she had always felt deep down that she should know her attacker, without ever quite grasping why. Now, she said to Rysakov, she was certain.

"Maksim, I don't know how to get out of his trap," she said with a touch of desperation. "Forgive me for burdening you with all of this but there is no one else in Harbin I feel I can trust."

Rysakov looked at her intensely. With his elbows on the table, he leaned toward her. "I have known for many years that Prince Vasily Koslinski was the murderer," he said. "I just did not have sufficient

proof to arrest him in Moscow. That, however, was in different times."
He paused.

"I have unfinished business with this beast," he said. "Let me think
upon this, Katya. I'll contact you in two days."

For the first time in weeks, Katya slept soundly that night.

It was the following week before Rysakov contacted her and she
had begun to fear he could do nothing.

"I apologize for not contacting you earlier, but I had much to do.
From what you told me, Brokhoff is wealthy. It also turns out he has
many connections within the Harbin police. I have had to tread
carefully as I didn't want any word of our suspicions getting back to
him until we are ready to act. Fortunately, it seems not everyone
thinks mister brothel owner is a good citizen. I'm told there have
been many cases over the years of young, prepubescent girls
disappearing. Occasionally, their mutilated bodies have been
discovered months later. Strong suspicion has pointed toward
Brokhoff, but this has only been based on hearsay. There has been
no evidence and so no charges.

"Some of our police have been corrupted by him; some with
money, others with unusual sex where, like you, he took photographs
to keep them compliant. Many in the Harbin force, however, would
like to see the last of him. Now, this is what I propose," he said
leaning forward as he outlined his plan.

When he had finished, Katya was silent for some minutes, then she
asked, "Why do you think he didn't kill me when he had me
drugged?"

"Who knows?" the detective said. "You eluded him in Moscow. He
tried to seduce you. You not only rejected him, you humiliated him in
front of his peers. I suspect he resolved then to make you one of his
victims. At the last minute, you again eluded him. Worse than that,
you may have caught a glimpse of him when he attacked. I've no
doubt he intends to kill you. First, he needs to restore his ego. You
have to be humiliated and debased for rejecting him. When that has
been done, you will be killed. He's a man who enjoys inflicting pain
so I don't think it would be a pleasant death."

Katya shivered.

§ § § § §

When the doorman told Sergei Brokhoff that a colonel of the Japanese police wished to see him, he took immediate notice. He assumed it would be the Kempeitai, who exercised wide ranging power and influence in Harbin. Brokhoff had deduced, quite correctly, that if he wished to retain the high profits from the narcotics trade, he needed to cooperate with them. He was therefore surprised when he came into the sitting room to find a Japanese officer dressed in a smartly pressed uniform and the soft cap of the army.

"I am Colonel Naito Fukashi of the Japan Imperial Police," he said. The other man who had been standing at the window now turned.

"I am disappointed to see you again, Vasily Emilovich. I had hoped you were dead," said Rysakov.

Brokhoff stopped in mid-stride, surprise at seeing his old nemesis clearly evident on his face.

When he regained his composure, Brokhoff said, "You are mistaken, sir, my name is Brokhoff."

"I have explained to Colonel Fukashi that you are a fugitive from justice. That you murdered seven people in Moscow, and that you stole millions of rubles from a large Russian bank. The colonel has generously offered to help in the interests of seeing justice done," said Rysakov.

"And how do you intend to prove this Mr. …what did you say your name was?" Brokhoff said.

"Ah, how remiss of me, I am Inspector Maksim Rysakov of the Harbin Criminal Department," Rysakov said. "As you say, there may be some mistake, but to clear the matter up perhaps you would be good enough to accompany us to Harbin Criminal HQ."

"I do not think that is necessary, Colonel," said Brokhoff, addressing the Japanese and ignoring Rysakov, which didn't worry the inspector one bit. "I have many good friends in the Kempeitai who, on one phone call, will vouch for me."

"No doubt you do, Brokhoff-san, but you will make no calls until you are at the Harbin HQ," said Fukashi in broken Russian. Without any further discussion, he issued a sharp command in Japanese and the door was flung open and a dozen heavily armed Japanese troops burst into the room, filling the limited space. They quickly surrounded the brothel owner and ushered him out into the street. As they did, Colonel Fukashi said to Brokhoff as he passed, "I am not Kempeitai."

When the patrol reached the Harbin HQ, the Japanese troops, having delivered their cargo safely, withdrew. Colonel Fukashi and Rysakov went inside where four of his fellow officers, men uncorrupted by Brokhoff, took the prisoner into a large room with a table at one end. Seated behind the table were three people. Brokhoff was told to sit on the single seat facing the table.

"That is Vasily Emilovich Koslinski. I knew him well in Moscow. My husband had many dealings with his bank before he stole all the money. He tried to kill me; he is a despicable animal," Katya spat at the man across the table.

Brokhoff did not flinch. He stared at her with such malevolence that she shrank back in her seat, appalled.

The second person behind the table stared intently at Brokhoff. This man was well dressed, clearly a prosperous man of considerable means. He was older than any in the room. Brokhoff took his eyes off Katya and turned to this new foe. His heart sank, although his expression remained one of total contempt. For several minutes, there was not a sound in the room. Then the older man spoke. He did not identify himself; it seemed everyone there knew his identity. He turned to Rysakov.

"I am satisfied that this is Vasily Emilovich Koslinski. My wife was his cousin, and we saw each other frequently at court and family functions. We had a large sum of money deposited in his bank. He stole it all. Many of our friends lost money with his theft. The shame of our family's association with this man led to my wife's premature death. Now that he's caught, he must be punished."

"For the record, I also identify the prisoner as Vasily Koslinski. I interviewed him years ago in connection with a series of murders in Moscow," added Rysakov.

Rysakov looked across at Colonel Fukashi, who nodded, satisfied they had apprehended the right man.

The third person behind the table now spoke.

"I am Major Anatoly Davidenko, major in the Red Army temporarily assigned to the CER as head of railway police. I have received a report from Moscow by telegram confirming that V.E. Koslinski is wanted for crimes against the Russian people—fraud, theft, and he is classified as an enemy of the state and a member of the bourgeois class. I'm now satisfied this man is Koslinski. He should be handed over to the Red Army to be tried in accordance with the laws of the Soviet Union. I can assure you, he will be dealt with appropriately as an enemy of the state. I have a squad of men outside who will escort him back to the railway where he will be immediately taken to Chita."

Throughout this exchange, Brokhoff did not utter a word. Now, he said, "I am Sergei Alexandrovich Brokhoff, as the local commander of the Kempeitai will confirm." With that, he rose to his feet and began to stride toward the door. The four police officers moved as one blocking his exit. They twisted his arms behind his back and marched him out of the police HQ. Once outside, they delivered him to the tender care of a Red Army squad. Only then did Brokhoff realize the seriousness of his situation.

"You cannot hand me over to the Bolshevik Army. I am Brokhoff. I am a resident of Harbin. I insist that you call the commandant of the Kempeitai. This farce cannot be allowed to continue," Brokhoff demanded in a loud voice.

Major Davidenko responded by producing a length of rope. He tied Brokhoff's hands behind him and immediately marched him toward the railway surrounded by the Red Army squad. Neither Davidenko nor Colonel Fukashi wished to chance the possibility of the Kempeitai interfering.

Major Davidenko did not slacken the pace. They continued at a quick march. After Brokhoff had complained loudly several times to people in the street that he was being kidnapped, the major warned him he would be gagged if he persisted. That quieted the brothel owner's complaints. It did nothing to reduce his level of alertness. He knew he had limited time to avoid being taken in custody back to Russia.

One block from the rail station, the small group turned the final corner and slowed to a walk. At the far end, blocking their access to the station and safety stood a company of armed Kempeitai police deployed across the width of the road. Brokhoff immediately called out.

"I am Brokhoff, a Harbin resident and friend to Japan. These men have illegally kidnapped me. Help."

Somehow, the military police had been alerted. Davidenko showed little surprise. It had almost certainly been one of the corrupt police in Rysakov's office. His men looked at him. They were clearly outnumbered.

"I suggest you avoid an unpleasant incident, Major, and release me immediately," Brokhoff said smugly.

"Close formation and continue marching," Davidenko commanded.

The troops did as they were told. The small knot of men and their prisoner continued toward the waiting Japanese. None of the Russians had any illusions about the willingness of Kempeitai police to engage in violence, or the viciousness with which they went about it. All of them saw it daily on the streets. Hands tightened around the stocks of their rifles.

At fifty meters from the station, Davidenko pulled a whistle from his pocket. He blew a piercing shriek.

"Quick march," he commanded crisply.

Within seconds of the whistle, a squad of heavily armed combat troops poured out of the station. They took position hard on the rear of the Kempeitai. Following them came six huge Cossacks armed with nothing more than their sabers, left hand holding the scabbard, right hand on the hilt. The Cossacks marched straight through the combat troops. When they reached the Japanese, the keening squeal of metal on metal sent shivers through every man on the street. The sabers sliced into the air. Metal flashed in the sunlight. Each arm stopped at shoulder height in the striking position, above the head of a Kempeitai.

Davidenko timed it perfectly, arriving at the enemy line at the same time. The Japanese officer took one look at the Cossacks and concluded no "round eye" was worth losing half his men. The Kempeitai line parted; they had been out maneuvered. They knew the Cossacks to be samurai, true warriors, men rightly to be feared. With the major and his prisoner through the line, the Cossacks withdrew. Still facing the Kempeitai, they retreated slowly backward as the Russians entered the rail station. Brokhoff knew then that Koslinski had finally been defeated.

Major Davidenko smiled bleakly. He had lived in the East for many years and preferred not to leave outcomes to chance.

A month later, Rysakov met Katya in a café and related what he had been able to piece together of the trial and demise of the "Monster of Moscow."

"What happened to him at Chita?" she asked, concerned he may have escaped again.

"He was taken before a military court as soon as he arrived in Chita. Although I had no evidence I could give Davidenko on the murders, I told him all the details I could recall. He remembered reading about the murders in the newspaper. 'If I get a chance, I will tell the judge of your suspicions,' he promised. 'The charges we can prove, however, are serious enough for the death penalty in any event.' Whether he told the judge or not, I don't know."

"The trial took several days with Koslinski working hard to delay it at every step," Rysakov said, "Finally, the judge found him guilty of the fraud, the theft, and of being an enemy of the people. The next morning, he was taken out and executed by firing squad. Such is the justice being meted out under the Bolshevik regime. In this case, however, I am pleased to say it was totally appropriate."

"Thank God it's over. I don't know how I can thank you, Maksim," she said. "It's as though a nightmare is over, and I've woken to a fresh new day. All these years, the fear I may be attacked again sat in the back of my mind like a trapdoor waiting to be dropped. No more."

When the steaming hot brew had been placed in front of them, Katya turned to her friend and said, "There are some things that I don't understand. Why did Colonel Fukashi help?"

"Colonel Fukashi is head of the railway police for the South Manchuria Railway, which is controlled by the Japanese. They hate the Kempeitai and when I put the proposal to him that he could secure a success at their expense he jumped at the chance. The Kempeitai are gaining control of many businesses in Harbin, amassing considerable wealth, denying a fair share to other units.

"I found that if a member of the Harbin Police tried to arrest Koslinski, he would treat it with contempt and use his connections to avoid detention. On the other hand, he had significant dealings with the Kempeitai. He assumed the announcement of a Japanese police officer was one of his military police friends. Fukashi *is* a police officer, just of a different branch." Rysakov smiled.

"I still don't understand Fukashi's interest," Katya said.

"Well, with Koslinski declared a criminal wanted by the Bolsheviks, it was a simple matter to have his property confiscated. The brothel was assigned to Fukashi for his help. Two warehouses that adjoin the CER have been assigned to the Bolshevik government in compensation for the money Koslinski stole. The remaining properties have been appropriated by the Harbin Council, who I hope use it to pay my salary."

Katya was silent for a few minutes before she asked, "Do you know what happened to the photographs?"

"Oh, yes, I'm sorry, I almost forgot," he said, pulling an envelope out of his attaché case. "Here they are, including the negatives. Fukashi's an old-style warrior and honored his undertaking to return them." He handed her the envelope, which was unsealed.

"They're all there," he said. "Destroy them as soon as you can."

"Thank you, Maksim," she said. She would burn them all as soon as she returned home. She felt no embarrassment that Rysakov had seen the photos; in fact, in a strange way, she felt a little relieved.

§ § § § §

During the early 1930s, Russian influence in the life of the city gradually declined. Many Russian businesses failed and were bought up by Chinese entrepreneurs. Yet, a large Russian émigré community remained in Harbin. For most of these Russians, the bulk of the wealth brought with them gone, life became increasingly difficult, though not all Russians found the going hard. Peter Morozov flourished in the business, soon demonstrating he had his grandfather's steely will and instinctive feel for business.

Katya's friendship with Maksim Rysakov matured, bound as they were by their history, though neither wanted it to develop into anything more permanent. Then, one day, Katya received a letter that was worth more than gold. It was from Anna.

She excitedly called her sons to tell them the news.

"Anna has written," she said. "She says that she has written other letters, but assumes that they did not get through as I haven't replied." She took her spectacles off and said to her sons in an exasperated tone. "How could I reply if I didn't get the letters? I didn't know where to send my letters." She put her spectacles back on. "She and Charles are safe in the new country of Czechoslovakia, and she has one child, a boy named Michael, after Misha, with another due any day. Oh, how I wish she were still here," Katya said. "She says that Charles had a substantial amount of money from his time in Siberia. They have bought a large farm a day's journey from Prague. They are very happy and hope that we may visit them one day. Oh, would that I could," said Katya wistfully. "I must write immediately."

Not long after the letter from Anna, Peter announced his engagement to a Russian girl whose family had also fled Moscow. They were to marry in the spring. Katya immediately put aside plans to visit Anna and became immersed in her son's approaching nuptials.

Yuri had long since finished school and worked with his brother. At the same time, he continued his involvement with his Chinese friends, who, unbeknown to the rest of his family and most of Harbin, were active in the nationalist movement to free China of foreign domination. After some years, he achieved elevation to the one of the highest rankings in Shaolin kung fu, a rare achievement for a westerner. Throughout, Yuri continued playing the violin, joining the Harbin Symphony Orchestra as a permanent member.

Peter's new wife almost immediately announced she was pregnant, much to Katya's excitement, and the possibility of travel was postponed again.

Soon, there were more grandchildren in Harbin, and Katya found her time well occupied. When she reached her mid-fifties she began to realize that the aches, pains, and tiredness she felt could not be cured by a holiday. They were the symptoms of an aging body. The reality of a trip to see Anna steadily receded. Each time she received one of her daughter's increasingly infrequent letters, it was discussed again, more as a wish than a real prospect. She now had six grandchildren, three in the East and three in Europe.

§ § § § § §

In London, by the mid-1930s, Japan's intensifying interest in northern Manchuria did not go unnoticed. A confidential note prepared by the British Foreign Office described the position succinctly.

"Japan's economic fortunes are bound up with the development and exploitation of China. All her eggs are in the China basket. For Japan, access to China's resources is vital," Philip Armitage, the new head of the Commercial Division after the retirement of Sir Algernon Law, finished reading aloud and placed the memo on his desk.

"I think we can concentrate attention elsewhere for the time being, don't you think?" he said to one of his section heads. "I daresay Hong Kong is now more important to HM government than northern China."

"What about Russia?" asked a section head.

"With the Communist regime now firmly in control, the dynamics of our relations with the Soviets have changed," Armitage said. "The old, informal sources of intelligence are of little value. Real spies are the order of the day," he added. He had not given a thought to the Morozovs for years. Life in the FO moved on.

§ § § § § §

At about this time, the Japanese Kwantung Army moved quickly to gain control of most of Manchuria, including Harbin. The Russians soon discovered that they were treated by the new rulers like any other subject peoples, with ruthless indifference.

One of the first acts the new puppet government of Manchuria took was to promulgate the "Opium Law," giving the Kwantung Army a monopoly in the trafficking of narcotics.

Katya noticed the amount of time Yuri spent at rehearsals but thought little of it until she arrived early for a performance one night in the season. It would be the first time Yuri performed as principal soloist with the Guarneri violin. Katya was determined not to miss a minute of it. She entered through the stage door and walked toward the area where the musicians gathered, tuning their instruments. She intended to wish her youngest son good luck, even though he had specifically asked her not to. *Mother's prerogative,* she said to herself, smiling. She felt immensely proud of Yuri's musical abilities.

As she turned a corner in the corridor, she saw Yuri. In front of him stood an attractive young woman she had seen before at concerts. *What was her name? Larissa. Yes, Larissa Andreovna Kamentov. A Harbinsi, born here.* Yuri had introduced her after a performance some months ago.

As she watched, Larissa stopped speaking. Yuri smiled, putting his arms around her. As he did so, she stood on her toes and kissed him on the lips. Clearly, for them no one else existed at that moment.

Katya smiled, her suspicions now confirmed. *And it is about time,* she thought.

At that instant, Katya's shoes trod on a loose floorboard and, startled by the sound, Larissa looked up, saw Katya, flushed a bright red, and ran off in the direction of the orchestra.

"Yuri, darling, I came to wish you luck," said Katya. "I'm told the performance is sold out. Everyone is coming to hear the great Morozov play the famous Guarneri. It will be a triumph," she said, kissing Yuri on the cheek. As she turned away to go to her seat, she stopped. Yuri still stood where Larissa had left him.

"Wasn't that Larissa Andreovna? Perhaps I'll see her afterwards."

Larissa Kamentov quickly became a regular visitor to Katya's house. Katya liked her immediately. She was also a violinist, but not of Yuri's class. Her father held a senior position in the CER and had come to Harbin as an engineer over twenty years ago when the city was little more than a frontier town.

The Kamentovs lived in the Russian sector and seemed to like Yuri, which in Katya's mind meant they were sensible people. Katya soon decided she would be more than happy if the romance developed into the marriage of her remaining son. *Misha could then rest happy,* she thought.

Some months after Yuri's musical triumph, he came home early one evening with a grim expression on his face.

"No rehearsal tonight?" Katya asked, hoping the lovers had not had a falling out.

"No, it was canceled. There's been another kidnapping. This time, they grabbed Simon Kaspé, the young Jewish pianist who's just returned for summer vacation. He was walking home with his girlfriend when they struck. His girl is lucky they didn't rape her as well," Yuri said.

"How horrible," said Katya, "it could have been you and Larissa."

The kidnapping made front page news in the Harbin daily papers the next morning.

"I see Kaspé's father has received a ransom demand for $100,000; how can he find that sort of money?" Katya said to Yuri.

"He owns the Hotel Moderne and is reputed to be wealthy," Yuri replied. "You can count on the Kempeitai being behind it somehow. I heard they have been told by Tokyo to raise enough revenue to pay for their occupation of Manchuria. I'm sure this is just one of their 'fund-raising schemes.'"

"That poor boy's family," said Katya, "how they must be suffering."

The next day, the papers reported that the French consul had advised them not to pay the ransom.

"Dear God," said Katya, "it's only money; pay up and get your son home."

"I expect that they don't want to encourage more kidnappings," said Yuri. "And, of course, with these animals, there is no guarantee that having paid the money Simon would be released unharmed."

"Yuri, you will be careful, won't you?"

Nearly four weeks passed without any sign of the young musician; then, there was a sensational development. Simon Kaspé's father received a package containing a portion of a human ear. Again, the consul advised against paying the ransom.

"It's easy for that official to give such advice," said Katya, "it's not his son. Why doesn't the father ignore the man and pay up?"

"Isn't it strange the Japanese police can't seem to make any progress in finding the criminals," said Yuri. "According to the newspapers, they are making 'strenuous efforts to apprehend the culprits and free the young man.' I'll wager they know exactly where he is."

Nearly two months later, the police found Simon Kaspé's body in an underground pit in near freezing conditions. He had been starved and beaten, his fingers broken with a hammer so he could never play the piano again.

The viciousness of the crime outraged most of Harbin and thousands attended the funeral. Such was the outcry the Kempeitai arrested and jailed the killers. Within weeks, the newspapers reported they had been released on probation. Harbin now had clear evidence of the protection non-Japanese could expect under the new regime.

Pressure mounted on the non-Japanese trading houses.

"Harbin is a city of drug addicts," said Peter, shaking his head in disgust. "There are now more than ninety opium dens all controlled by the Kempeitai. Opium's so cheap even the poor can afford it. Apart from making themselves rich, what do these so-called military police hope to achieve?"

Liu answered. "They have two objectives. Firstly, to pay for the cost of maintaining the army in Manchukuo. The other reason is more unpleasant. They hope to weaken our resolve by making the people dependent on opium. In that objective, I must admit they are having some success.

"In the meantime, Yusuf and I have begun to empty the warehouses as they will not hesitate to steal whatever they can. I have made provision for gold and jade to be hidden safely. Ching-po and my son, Yu-Tang, will know how to access these funds when the Japanese are gone."

"When do you think that might happen?" asked Peter.

"I do not know," said Liu. "I suspect it will not be in my lifetime. However, you may be certain that China will be victorious eventually."

At that moment, Ching-Po entered the room and went straight to her father.

"There is a Captain Yamamoto at the door demanding to see you, Father," she said with an edge of apprehension in her voice.

"Is he alone?" Liu asked.

"No, he has a troop of five soldiers with him," she replied. "They look dangerous."

"Peter, you must leave immediately. You cannot be seen here. Go out the back entrance," said Yusuf.

"Yusuf, my friend, it may be better if you also leave and let me deal with this man. I know him. He is one of the truly venal members of the Kempeitai. I am letting him think that he is bleeding me dry and taking all my assets. I shall let him 'discover' another valuable chest and hope that he leaves satisfied," said Liu.

Yusuf nodded and quickly followed Peter. Liu motioned his daughter to go. He did not want to risk her in the presence of a group of the dreaded military police.

When Katya heard that the Japanese troop had assaulted Liu's maid, cook, and his wife, she immediately went to the house. Yuri was already there. She felt deep empathy for the women and spent the morning offering comfort and support.

"It is becoming dangerous to remain in Harbin," Lui said to her. "There are now reports of Russian women being assaulted and raped by these beasts."

"Yes," Katya said, "I heard that one woman complained of being assaulted to the duty officer at the Kempeitai headquarters. She said that the officers there raped her again, and then arrested her on a charge of prostitution."

"There's no protection for anyone," said Yuri. "On the way here, I walked by the main road to the river near the entrance to the Chinese sector. The Japanese army has erected a large gibbet and hung the heads of three Chinese from it. One was still dripping blood. The message is clear—obey your new masters or suffer the consequences."

A year later, Yuri announced that Larissa had consented to marry him. In the difficult conditions then prevailing in Harbin, Katya agreed with the Kamentovs that the wedding should take place as soon as possible. Who knew when they may all be forced to leave the city? The two married in St. Basil's Orthodox Church and immediately took over half of Katya's house.

"It's far too large for me and Pinna alone," Katya said. Yuri saw through this offer, even though the logic made sense. His mother would have a daughter again.

In the meantime, the orchestra maintained a limited program with greatly reduced numbers of players. It became a small act of defiance to continue to play the music of Russia and Europe. The Japanese tolerated limited performances. All performances had a varying number of imperial citizens and their wives or mistresses in the audience and the orchestra had taken to including one Japanese item in each recital. Great care was taken to first clear such inclusions with the local commandant.

On the evening of a cold wet day, when a north wind drove stinging rain in showers until the sun set, the two newlyweds were last to leave the rehearsal hall. They locked the door and started for the warmth of home. As they rounded the corner, they had the misfortune to walk into an armed, four-man Kempeitai patrol.

Larissa immediately dropped her gaze to the ground and both stepped to the side in deference to the privileged position these soldiers held in the city. It was simply sensible to do so. Most times, the soldiers arrogantly swaggered past without a sideways glance. Sometimes, if they were bored or disgruntled, they would take an unhealthy interest in their inferiors. This was one of those times; they were cold and in need of some distraction.

"Stop!" commanded the corporal. "Papers!" he yelled rudely in poor Chinese.

As they searched for their papers, all four soldiers suddenly noticed Larissa, whose long blonde hair spilled down around her face, almost to her waist. They exchanged glances. Both Yuri and his wife caught the looks. *If I don't do something fast,* thought Yuri, *Larissa is in real danger of being raped by these cowardly bastards.*

"Honored soldiers, please forgive us for our tardiness; we have just finished rehearsing for the concert that your commanding officer has requested. This female is the leading musician, and he has demanded that she play at her best. I am taking her to her quarters so that she may practice for many hours to be perfect for the esteemed officer," he said, hoping fervently they would swallow the story.

He watched as they absorbed what he had just said. A man in charge of a female performer made sense to them. Their commanding officer was a man with a bad temper. If what this Russian said was true, it would not be in their interest to have their pleasure with this woman, and for him to find out they had made her performance below standard. After a few moments, the corporal said, "Take her to her quarters immediately and make her practice an extra hour."

To his squad, he said in execrable Chinese, in a loud voice, "She'll be even more fuckable tomorrow."

Laughing, they pushed past, throwing obscene comments at Larissa in Japanese.

When they had turned the corner, Yuri let out his breath and put his arm around his wife. She shuddered as they hurried down the street and out of sight. After they had walked for some minutes, she calmed down, and they resumed a normal pace. She held his hand, feeling once again the taut muscles and calloused skin of the edge and heel of his palm. It still amazed her that his Shaolin skills had not interfered with the suppleness of his playing.

Two days later, the weather cleared and Harbin sparkled under a brilliant pale blue sky. The remnants of the north wind kept the city cold but it was a day on which it was good to be alive. It was the dress rehearsal, and the orchestra, now down to less than half its full strength, practiced in high spirits. The level of excitement and anticipation always rose before opening night. The rehearsal went off without a hitch. The consensus was that "if we play that well tomorrow all of Harbin will talk about it." Having made sure they had locked all the doors of the hall, Larissa gave Yuri a last kiss. She then joined the rest of the Russians heading back to the Russian sector. She was looking forward to seeing her mother that night. Yuri turned and walked in the opposite direction toward Katya's house carrying his violin. Before her group turned the corner, Larissa turned for one last wave to her husband. Her strangled shout stopped her friends in mid-step.

Yuri stood in front of four Kempeitai soldiers, almost certainly the four that had accosted them two nights ago. Larissa could not hear what they were saying. The corporal screamed at him. As she watched, one of the soldiers hit Yuri with a rifle butt. As he collapsed, they caught him and threw him into the back of a small truck. The other three soldiers climbed aboard and it drove off. Within seconds, it had disappeared.

Only then did Larissa find her voice.

"Noooooo...Yuri! Yuri!" Her face twisted with horror.

When Yuri regained consciousness, he found himself in a small dark room. The only light came from a barred window set high in the wall. He felt his head. A painful lump had formed from the rifle butt impact and his head ached. He stood up and walked carefully around the room. He was not badly hurt. His next sensation was the bitter cold. A chill breeze came in gusts through the window. He looked up. No glass. He put his ear to the single door. Silence. Clearly, he had been kidnapped. He swore quietly. When he found the corner that received the least of the breeze, he settled down to wait.

Katya received the ransom note demanding the equivalent of 50,000 rubles late the following morning. She immediately assured Larissa she would pay without hesitation. She then told Liu Ping-nan and went to see Maksim Rysakov. Liu sat silently for some time after Katya left before quietly giving instructions to his daughter. She looked up at him, seeking confirmation she had heard correctly. Liu simply nodded.

Rysakov returned immediately with Katya. He spoke at length to Larissa, gleaning as much information as he could about their first altercation with the Kempeitai. Finally, once Katya confirmed she was going to pay the ransom, he left to confront the local Kempeitai commander. He did not expect any acknowledgement of their involvement. In fact, there would be a strenuous and offended denial. However, if they knew, after the Kaspé incident, that the Harbin police were investigating, then the best he could hope for was Yuri's safe return once the ransom was paid.

It was late afternoon, judging by the change in light coming through the tiny window, when Yuri finally heard sounds outside his prison. For most of the previous night, he had forced himself to rest, allowing his head to recover. Then, for the last four hours, he had gradually increased his level of exercise to keep warm. Soon after he regained consciousness the previous night, he had searched for the violin, in vain. It was not in the room. He preferred not to think what may have happened to it. That problem would have to be dealt with later. Now, he must concentrate on getting out alive. He felt sure his mother would agree to whatever ransom was demanded. He thanked his luck once again that they had neglected to tie him up. No doubt they thought their superior numbers and loaded weapons were sufficient to keep him under control. There was only one way out of the cellar, the solid single door. *And only one way in,* he nodded to himself.

When he heard the lock being turned, he positioned himself in the middle of the room. He leaned forward, knees bent, head slightly bowed. Two soldiers entered the room. It appeared to them he was still suffering from the previous night's assault. He saw under hooded eyebrows that although both had weapons only one had his rifle at the ready, pointing at him. The other's rifle was shouldered so he could carry a dish. It contained a small pile of cold rice and a beaker of water. He slowly lifted his hands to receive the food. As his hands came level with his shoulders he exploded into action. The flat of his left foot kicked the rifle hard knocking it clattering to the floor. At the same time, as his left foot hit the ground the fingers of his right hand smashed into the man's throat, snapping his windpipe. By this time, the other guard had dropped the food and water and was struggling to unsling his rifle. Yuri swiveled on his left foot, punching the heel of his hand into the bridge of the soldier's nose, shattering the bone. The man stood stunned. Yuri kicked him in the crutch. As the soldier doubled over in pain, he grabbed his head with both hands and twisted violently, breaking his neck. The soldier was dead before he hit the ground.

Yuri spun around to attack the first guard. He lay writhing on the floor, desperately trying to suck air in through his fractured windpipe. He watched the man dispassionately for a moment before realizing that the noise might attract attention if there were others nearby. He kicked the man's head with his heel, knocking him unconscious. Within minutes, he was also dead, suffocated. Quickly, Yuri pulled both bodies out of the doorway and gently closed the door, unlocked. He then placed the two bodies and their weapons against the wall onto which the door opened.

After waiting an hour, Yuri cautiously opened the door and went out. The building was deserted. The only furniture was an old table and three chairs. On the table were the meager rations of the two Japanese soldiers and a flask of water. Once he had disposed of those, he sat down to decide his next move.

The last of the daylight had gone when he heard laughter and the approach of two men clearly speaking Japanese. They seemed very pleased with themselves. *They must have collected the ransom,* Yuri thought. *Good, they will be relaxed.* The main entrance to the cellar opened, and the corporal entered carrying a lighted torch and two bottles of liquor. He shouted a greeting as he walked to the table.

As the second soldier entered, Yuri struck. He knew he had only enough time to disable. He chopped down with all his might on the base of the soldier's neck striking the nerve and knocking him unconscious. The corporal heard the clatter and spun around. He moved fast, unslinging his rifle with the smoothness of a seasoned campaigner. As the barrel began to swing down from the vertical Yuri realized he was not going to be able to make the distance to grab the rifle in time. He had to try to avoid the first shot. He instinctively went into a low forward roll toward the man. That probably saved his life. As he went down, he heard a whisper of wind pass his head. When he came out of the roll, the corporal was standing with his rifle not yet horizontal, a look of total amazement on his face. Out of his neck stuck the hilt of a throwing knife.

Yuri relaxed. He said quietly in Chinese, "Thank you brother," and turned to the entrance. He could see no one.

"We must dispose of these animals so that no one can find them," he said.

Within seconds, two men dressed in rags appeared. They moved with smooth, practiced fluidity. Yuri thought he recognized one but made no comment; anonymity was the best defense. They were almost certainly experienced assassins, probably sent by Liu although he knew he would never know. He bent over the body of the corporal and went through his pockets. He was right; the ransom had been paid. He straightened, making no attempt to hide the wad of notes that he laid on the table. He gestured to one of the men.

"There are two more dead in that room," he said. The man nodded.

Within an hour, all four bodies were gone. All trace of the fight, of blood, had been cleaned away. The weapons were carefully put to one side to be taken separately. The food and drink bottles, emptied, were left on the table. To anyone who came looking, the soldiers had come and gone, releasing their prisoner after receiving the ransom.

As they were about to leave, Yuri called softly to his two conspirators and pointed to the money. They nodded, smiling, and each came and took a portion. Then they vanished as quietly as they had arrived. Yuri picked up the balance of the money. About half was still there. Silently, he melted into the night.

Only three people, and probably Liu, he thought wryly, *would ever know what really happened tonight.*

When he arrived at Katya's house, he immediately had three women crying with happiness and hugging him. Eventually, when they had quieted down sufficiently, they asked him what had happened.

"I had two soldiers guarding me," he said. "Then a couple of hours ago, the others arrived very pleased with themselves. The corporal came and told me the ransom had been paid and I could soon go home. Your family is very sensible, he said. They told me they now had enough money to set up their own business. I got the impression they intended to leave immediately and go home to Japan." He was confident Liu would hear this story and judiciously spread it. *Mama will also tell Maksim Rysakov,* he thought, *who won't believe it but will understand and retell it. For some weeks, the Kempeitai will not know what to think.*

Before he left the cellar, Yuri looked in every corner to see if the Guarneri was there. It was not. They almost certainly sold it to some second-hand dealer, he surmised. The prospect of not having the instrument cast a pall of sadness. It was their last tangible link with his father and grandfather.

Within days, it became increasingly apparent it was too dangerous for Yuri, Larissa, and Katya to remain in Harbin. They held a meeting with Liu and Yusuf Yudin.

"We must leave," Katya said, "but where do we go? We run the risk of imprisonment if we go north to Russia, and, in any event, it's not possible to travel without proper papers. A military pass from the Kempeitai would be of little help, and it would be courting disaster to even ask for one."

"Peter won't leave," said Yuri, anticipating where the discussion would eventually lead.

"But he must; we must stay together, and the children—we can't leave them here," Katya said.

"That's his point, Mama, it's too dangerous to take them. They're too young for such a journey. He told me that he'll trade with the Japanese and put up with their looting until he can find a way to get papers for all his family. He's going to try to get to Britain or America. You know how determined he is."

"Then I'll stay," said Katya. "Besides, we must find the violin. Misha would never forgive me if we left without it."

"There is a way west over the mountains, and then eventually south to Shanghai," said Liu. They all fell silent as he paused. "My daughter wishes to leave Harbin and go to the south. I am happy that she leaves this city, but I do not think it is much safer south. The Japanese Army is like a plague of locusts consuming everything as they move through the land. But she has decided to go. The Green Triangle network will offer what help they can along the way."

As they left the house, Liu placed his hand gently on Katya's arm.

"I am told that Sergei Brokhoff, whom you call Koslinski, had a son soon after he arrived in Harbin. He is now a man and was brought up in his father's house, encouraged to indulge in their mutual interests. I have heard he has sworn revenge for his father's death. That is yet another reason why you must leave," the old man said. "Do not worry about your violin; if it is still in Harbin, I will find it," he added.

Katya nodded. She had heard of this son. He was no better than his father.

Once more, they would be fleeing with only what they could carry. The wealth and status of Moscow was long gone, now even the relative comfort and security of Harbin would soon be in the past. She wondered if it would ever change.

Pinna, after much discussion, decided to stay with Peter and his family. She could not face another flight at her age, she said. It was a sad parting for both Katya and Yuri. Pinna had been an integral part of their lives for so many years, through turbulent and frightening times. They, however, had no choice. They had to leave.

Within two days, they were gone. A week later, they arrived at a small village in a remote valley of the Khingan Mountains. "The head man of this village is a cousin of my father and a Green Triangle member," explained Ching-po. "We will be safe here." With encouragement from the villagers, the three Westerners quickly settled into the steady, predictable routine of rural life.

Not long after their arrival, Larissa announced shyly one evening, "I'm going to have a baby, Katya."

Yuri beamed with pleasure. Katya, after congratulating her daughter-in-law, felt tears rolling down her cheeks. She turned away, not wishing to spoil Larissa's moment. *I have six grandchildren. Three I have never seen, three I have just left and will likely never see again. This child I must never leave,* she told herself, dabbing her wet cheeks with a cloth.

By the time Larissa gave birth to a daughter, Katerin Yuriovna, they had all become part of the life of the small community, working alongside the villagers.

Months later, an itinerant trader arrived in the village leading a heavily laden donkey. He spoke briefly with one of the old men and went on his way. When Katya and Yuri returned at the end of the day, Larissa greeted them with a big smile.

"A strange little man came into the village today. He left a package for you, my darling," she said to Yuri, pointing to the table. On it lay a familiar shape. Hurriedly, he unwrapped the parcel. The case was a little more battered, but inside the Guarneri sat as beautiful as ever.

Katya sat down, relieved at last. Ivan's violin, the family's violin, was back in its rightful place. *Misha would be happy.* She smiled. Liu had been as good as his word.

The years passed and Katerin grew into a strong lively girl. They heard of the increasing violence of the Kwantung Army in the east and to the south, and of the fighting between the Communists and the Nationalists to the southwest.

Occasionally, a Japanese patrol would pass through a neighboring valley, but they were not bothered. Until one day, a survey team appeared at the entrance to their valley. Within a day, they had gone. No one gave it any further thought. Now that Katerin was able to play with the other children, Larissa took Katya's place working with the other women.

On this particular day, Yuri, as he usually did, trekked out with the men to work on the terraces. The women went down to the tree-lined creek at the bottom of the valley to collect wood. Larissa did not return that evening, nor did any of the women in her party. Alarmed, Yuri and a group of the men took torches and began to search. Halfway down, they found two women hiding behind three large rocks, terrified and disheveled. A Japanese patrol, alerted to the village by the survey team, had caught the group, they said. Only they had been lucky enough to escape. The rest had been raped repeatedly, then bayoneted. They had been particularly vicious with the blonde-haired one. Yuri found his wife's bloody and brutalized body and carried her back to the village. There he made a vow with a coldness that chilled Katya.

"I will avenge Larissa's death no matter how long it takes. They are nothing more than animals. They deserve to be treated like vermin and exterminated." Two days later, after fiercely hugging his daughter and being assured by Katya she would take care of Katerin, he joined another man from the village. Together, they walked past the terraces, becoming forever smaller in the distance until they disappeared into the mountains.

That week, Katya took Katerin, and, together with Ching-po, began the slow and perilous journey toward Shanghai. One day, Yuri said, he would meet them there.

PART II
The Present

Sydney

More than sixty years after Katya left the village in northern China, Will Callaghan sat at his usual table with other early risers. Since his divorce two years ago, he had established a routine. After an early morning run or a surf if the waves were up, he would read the papers over a cup of the best espresso in Sydney.

As he took the first sip, he opened the newspaper. "BRIC Economies to Drive Growth," the lead article was headlined. Brazil, Russia, India, and China. *Right countries, wrong order,* Callaghan thought. *China and Russia are the real drivers. In fact,* he thought, *this is China's century.* He read the article and was about to turn the page when a header below grabbed his attention. "Prominent Banker's Throat Cut." Angus FitzWilliam. *God, without his support, my bid's in trouble.*

He had been forced to bid for the brokerage house before he was ready. An overseas insurance group had approached one of the vendors, threatening to derail his plan. To get immediate bridging finance, he mortgaged everything he owned. And the funding was definitely short term—two months, while he finalized the longer term finance from FitzWilliam's bank.

"That'll be no trouble, Will. We'll pay out the short-term funds. Pity we can't act faster, but the matter has to go to the board. I'll prepare a paper recommending the deal, and it should be finalized within a couple of weeks," Angus FitzWilliam said.

There was always a danger in moving too fast, before you had "all your ducks in a row," as he liked to say. Things could go wrong. Then the money outlaid had an interest bill to be paid each month. Soon, you had a hole in the profit. Callaghan put the newspaper down. It looked like this was not going to be an exception. The prospects for expanding the business into China suddenly no longer seemed relevant.

Yesterday, after themselves becoming the target of a hostile takeover bid, the overseas insurance group had withdrawn from the race. It would have been ideal to have generated a quick profit with a sale of the retail business to them. He could imagine the headlines in the financial press, "Callaghan Chooses Cash," "Astute Investment Banker Strikes Again." The lead articles would open with something like "Brilliant investment banker turned asset raider has pulled off another stunning coup, buying the country's largest brokerage house and selling one of its main divisions before the ink is dry. Everything Callaghan touches turns to gold. Intricate planning and attention to detail seems to be the key to his success—that and a willingness to take risks others would blanch at."

If he had been able to sell the retail arm so soon, he knew it would have been pure luck, nothing else. However, he was happy enough to let the journalists spin an aura around him. The press loved him and the buccaneer image they had created.

This was his biggest deal; more than he was worth. Much more. He knew his reputation, as much as the game plan he prepared for the financiers, had got him the short-term funding. And, of course, the promised takeout from Angus FitzWilliam's bank.

"Shit!" he said as he read the report. "In his own driveway…"

FitzWilliam had not completed his report for the bank board. The two of them were scheduled to work on it that day. Without the report, the board would not consider the funding.

As he read further, his spirits lifted a little:

> "Police said that Mr. FitzWilliam was fortunate
> in living next door to the well-known micro sur-
> geon, Dr. Graham Harding, who happened to see
> his neighbor immediately after the attack. Mr. Har-
> ding would not talk to the press; however, police
> sources said that, had he not gone to FitzWilliam's
> aid, he would have bled to death. Dr. Harding was

able to stop the bleeding from the severed blood vessels in the throat and call an ambulance. The surgeon went with him to the hospital where he operated immediately. Mr. FitzWilliam is in intensive care in a stable condition. This reporter has received an unconfirmed report that the assailant may have been disturbed before he could finish the job and this helped save the banker's life."

There was nothing he could do but wait.

Callaghan had no way of knowing that this attempted murder would reignite events begun over a century ago. The result would affect him profoundly.

He called the bank's office and spoke to FitzWilliam's PA.

"He's still in intensive care but we're hopeful he'll be off the critical list by tomorrow," she said

"That's good news. Have the police got any idea as to who did it or why?" he asked.

"They seem to think it might be connected to a number of threatening calls he received. Angus treated them as crank calls but the police are investigating whether it might be connected to a failed loan application."

The next day came the phone call he had been dreading but expecting following the events of the last forty-eight hours.

"It's Harry Belamy here, Will. I'm one of Angus's co-directors. I think we met over lunch with Angus recently. You've no doubt heard of the terrible attack on Angus, who I understand is making good progress. However, the doctors tell us that it'll be some time before he'll be able to return to work. Even then, they're not certain whether there may be brain damage associated with the loss of blood...In the meantime, Will, I regret the bank's board has decided to put a hold on all of Angus's loan portfolio. The police are looking at a number of transactions he was involved in to see whether there may be a connection to the attack. So, unfortunately, we won't be able to proceed with your proposal. No reflection on you or the deal, you understand, just an outcome of the attack. As soon as the police give the all clear, we'd be happy to talk again."

As he put the phone down, Callaghan stared out the window. He would not give up easily. However, there was an increasing probability there would be only one outcome—disaster.

He now owned the largest brokerage house in the country and in a matter of weeks had to repay the short-term funding. He now had no way of making the repayment. He worked feverishly to find an alternative source of funds, to no avail. Finally, he spoke to the manager of the finance company that had provided the short-term funding.

"Sorry, no chance of an extension," the manager said. "In fact, my board is very nervous after the attack on FitzWilliam. The money will have to be repaid on time."

Two days before the deadline, he again met with the funder.

By the end of the week, he was no longer the owner of the largest brokerage in the country. The funder now owned it and had it up for sale. He had no doubt it would be sold, but at a heavy discount. That was what banks did when they became mortgagee in possession. They sold quickly, at any halfway reasonable price. Forget the cost; they had only one concern—what is a buyer prepared to pay right now? Then, he knew, they would come after him for the shortfall. Being a forced sale, he knew there would be a shortfall, a large one. The rest of his assets would go; there would be nothing left.

Callaghan did not complain. He knew the rules. He had gambled and lost. Now he had to pay the piper.

§ § § § §

"What I don't understand is why the bank got the idea there was drug money behind the company," said Nic da Costa. As front man for the property company developing the marina, everyone looked to him first for answers. "It's a good project. What the hell do they care where we get our share of the cost? How do they know we didn't make it on the share market; a lot of people do. This drug story is bullshit. Isn't it, Eddie?"

"Of course," said Eddie Ng, the Vietnamese member of the consortium.

"What about the problems we had getting the rezoning through the local council?" asked Warren Kay.

"But that was a year ago," said da Costa.

"Yeah, but some pretty serious things were said by those anti-development campaigners, and they were reported in the local paper," said Kay.

"As I recall, there were suggestions that the company was associated with drug groups. Eddie was even named by some of them. We had to threaten defamation action to shut them up," said Joe Garand, the company's lawyer. He had been associated with this group for some time. They paid him well and he knew when not to ask inconvenient questions. Several of them had avoided jail more than once through his efforts.

"The bank's lawyer was very thorough, and she certainly made inquiries at the council, they told me," Garand went on. "Maybe that's how they got wind of the allegations. It's just very unfortunate that FitzWilliam told you the bank would fund the deal and you took his word and went ahead."

"It'll cost us. Until we can get a new funder, and that is not going to be easy after the attack on FitzWilliam, we'll have to stop work," said da Costa. "It's going to make the project marginal at best."

"What's the worst then?" asked Garand.

"If we can't get funding, we either sit on a half-finished project or look for a buyer. Neither alternative is very appealing," answered da Costa.

Warren Kay pulled into his apartment block car park in a foul mood. He had not said much at the meeting with da Costa, Ng, and Garand. There wasn't much he could add. What had happened had happened. But it really pissed him off that the project was now marginal at best, instead of the nice little earner he had expected.

He had been one of the early investors on Garand's introduction. Da Costa had a good track record in property deals. As a marina, the project had the added attraction of fast boats and all he associated with them. Now it looked as though he would be lucky to get his money back, and that only after a couple of years. He had sold most of his other property assets, mainly low cost rental investments, to go into the marina. Now that money wouldn't earn anything for a long time.

He slammed the door to his apartment shut and swore again. The banker had told them the funding would be available. They accepted his word. Kay didn't like being lied to, and the banker had lied to them. Sure, he said the deal needed board approval, but he went on to say that "on the information I have, I don't expect any problems." The banker got no less than he deserved. *In a way, it's fitting he survived,* Kay thought, a thin smile breaking his face. He'll have something to remind him for the rest of his life, "Don't promise what you can't deliver."

§ § § § §

Will Callaghan woke thoroughly rested. He had slept the sleep of the just, or so he told himself. He stretched his two-meter, broad-shouldered frame. Maybe wind and sun damaged the skin but he wasn't about to change his habits. The tanned face in the mirror was of a man who spent his spare time outdoors. In Callaghan's case, this meant the beach, in the surf. And on the snow slopes—most years he skied Canada and Italy for as long as he could justify. The demands of business meant it had never been long enough over the years.

Now that had changed. In the week since the last of his assets had been sold, he had, for the first time in years, felt free. No high-powered meetings to attend, no board papers to read, no reports to analyze, in fact, no decisions at all to be made. Getting the morning espresso became a pleasure instead of a necessity. He sat enjoying the rich aroma of fresh ground coffee, not even the daily papers held any interest.

When the news of his spectacular collapse broke, it had been headlines for a couple of days, wise men writing it had all been foreseeable. These "high flying" dealmakers always had a hard landing, and so on. Two months ago, he could do no wrong, everyone waiting on the next deal. He gazed out across the sand to where the waves rolled in, one after the other. The surf looked far more interesting.

He now lived in the old family home on the beach, twenty kilometers north of the city. For reasons long forgotten, his father, William Henry Callaghan, an accountant, had placed the house in a trust for the benefit of his grandchildren once they reached the age of twenty-one. In the meantime, on the death of both parents, their children could live in the house or let it. They could not sell or encumber it. Will had never had cause to think about it before. Now, he blessed his father's foresight, if that's what it was, because the banks could not touch the house. At least he had a place to live in comfort.

His only sibling, a sister two years older than he, died in a car accident years ago, her drunken boyfriend escaping with minor injuries. His mother never really recovered from the shock. Both parents had died within a year of each other. He kept the house vacant, using it as a getaway from time to time. Everything was pretty much as they had left it. He had never had the time, or reason, to really go through their papers and possessions. It just hadn't seemed necessary. Everything was so familiar and comfortable. He liked seeing the reminders of his parents around the rooms.

He picked up the phone and dialed.

"Is Zoe Marranti there, please?" he asked when a secretary answered. As he waited to be transferred, he reflected. It was largely because of Zoe Marranti, the funder's solicitor, that he had a small car and enough money to live on. She had made the point to the finance company board that Callaghan had cooperated fully. He had not tried to challenge any of their actions or hide assets. This had saved them hundreds of thousands if not millions in legal fees. The least they could do was leave him with enough to live on.

"Marranti."

"Hello, Zoe, it's Will Callaghan."

"Oh, hello," the voice slightly on guard.

"I wanted to say thank you for the gracious way in which you handled my meltdown," Callaghan said. "Now that everything is settled, I wondered if you were free for dinner."

He arrived early at the restaurant that evening, relaxed, and at ease with the world. Not only was Zoe Marranti a very smart lawyer, she was also a very attractive woman.

Over the next month, Zoe realized that Callaghan was dating her for herself and not angling to create trouble for her client. She then became all woman, examining him as a man. She liked what she saw, liked it a lot. One night, after a soft and romantic dinner, they both concluded they had gone beyond casual dating. Looking back, the spark of attraction had been there since the first time they met. Now, they both wanted more, much more.

It seemed to work out quite naturally. She had a busy and successful legal career, frequently putting in punishing hours. He lived near the beach, an hour's drive north. So, after dinner on Friday night, they drove north and spent the weekend doing what lovers do. Making love at any hour, swimming, he surfing, she paddling on the shore, cooking meals together, reading quietly, listening to music and talking, getting to know each other. During the week, he stayed one or two nights at her townhouse in Double Bay, depending on her workload.

§ § § § §

Callaghan soon got bored. He started calling business colleagues who had chased him to be part of his next deal. All asked how he was coping. What did it feel like to lose the lot when you were at the top?

When he explained he had several new deals and asked if they would be interested, the response was always the same. You bet; we'd love to have a look. When he explained he had no funds and would be looking for full financial backing, the responses cooled.

"We could structure the funding offshore if this would help," some said. *No doubt,* he thought. *They think I've secretly hidden millions out of sight in a tax haven.*

"I don't have any offshore funds," he explained.

Those he still regarded as friends were more honest. We'll try, Will, but without any funds from you, the best we could do would be to hire you as a consultant with some profit share. Might be best to take some time out, they said.

"To hell with them," he said, putting the phone down on his last conversation.

He put the deal files in a pile on the desk, stood up, and stretched. Out the window he could see a steady line of breakers rolling in from the Pacific. There were already a dozen surfers out there catching the left handers several hundred meters into the shore. He watched as one expert caught a ten-foot monster and effortlessly rode it into the shore break.

This room had been his father's study and library. He walked over to a large leather upholstered chair near the wall mounted bookcase and sat down. Below the bookshelves sat a cupboard with a key in the lock. He opened it and took out the first item that came into his hands, a small shoe box full of photos and papers.

Night had fallen before he realized how long he had been sitting there. After a hastily prepared dinner, he was back in the chair, engrossed in his family's history.

The next day he went exploring through the house. He found cupboards with photo albums, most of which he remembered from his childhood. There were bundles of letters tied together with string, old theater programs, concert programs, school reports, and piles of miscellany. All of these things brought back warm and happy memories. He resolved to collate them into some semblance of order, something he had never had the time to do. *Time, apparently, is one commodity I now have in abundance,* he noted.

He pulled out a large, aged, parchment-quality envelope. Inside he found a document that puzzled him. As he reread it a question of identity immediately came up. More particularly, his mother's real identity. The document was a marriage certificate, for the union of Katerin Yuriovna MacDonald to William Henry Callaghan. His mother had always been known as Katy, never as Katerin. The middle name he could only guess at. As far as he knew, her natural parents had been killed by the Japanese in World War II. She had been found wandering the streets of Shanghai by a gentle childless couple. They adopted the seven-year-old and brought her to Australia on one of the last ships to leave China. She remembered little of Shanghai but had clear memories of China and the rural villages. He remembered sitting entranced as she told them wonderful stories about her early years. The common elements to all of them were how helpful the ordinary Chinese had been, and how terrifying the Japanese soldiers. She had been lucky she said. "I had the most wonderful 'parents,' the MacDonalds."

Callaghan could not really remember them. They had both died when he was very young. He looked at the black and white photograph of an older couple each with a loving arm around a pretty teenage girl, his mother, at the beach. How very British they looked. Long trousers, rolled up, and a decent dress; no shorts and T-shirts for them.

Who, then, was this girl with the foreign-sounding name? He felt an overwhelming desire to discover his mother's roots and through that his own. His father's heritage was easy; he knew it well. William senior's parents emigrated from London in the 1920s. Grandfather

Callaghan came from Ireland, the west coast originally, and then from Dublin. His grandmother was from Glasgow, Scotland. They met on the boat out and married not long after arriving in Sydney.

The discovery of his mother's real name created mystery and romance around the person who had given this house, his childhood home, its warmth and personality. He had to find her.

§ § § § §

He didn't trust Asians, and he didn't like them. It was a family thing he told Garand when the lawyer first proposed the deal. However, the development looked good on paper, and he still liked it when he inspected the site.

"They are only investors, Mix," Garand had said. "And they like the deal."

But Asians spelled trouble in Kay's eyes. His father had always hated them, but never really explained why. His father had so many secrets that young Warren "Mix" Kay knew not to pursue it. Until this deal, he had always avoided them. Now they were stuck together in a project that would be lucky to break even in a couple of years.

When he looked at other projects Nic da Costa had developed, he had been keen to be part of the next one. As for Ng and his Vietnamese friends, he had little doubt they were in the drug trade somehow. The stupid bastards had tried to bribe the local councilor to get planning consents through fast, drawing attention to themselves and the project. At least, that's what the local paper alleged. Ng denied he offered bribes, but Kay wasn't so sure. Even that might have died as nothing more than a rumor if the bitch of a lawyer hadn't started asking questions. But, even allowing for *all* of that, he thought, the banker told them the money would be available. Then, for no good reason he changed his mind, knowing they had spent all their own funds on his say so. That could not be forgiven. Kay knew there was nothing as lacking in appeal as a half-finished project.

He lay back in the chair, letting the complexity of Mahler drift over him. What did the bankers care where their equity funds came from. They helped launder dirty money every day. They didn't go around asking every depositor to prove the source of their funds, did they? How can banks go around reneging on a deal they had agreed to? They had told them they would fund the marina development. That was what incensed him. The lawyer's digging had only unearthed rumor. They should have treated it as just that—unsubstantiated gossip.

The banker got no more than he deserved. It'll be a lesson to others and the scar'll remind the bastard every time he shaves. He let the second movement of the symphony soothe his mind.

He relaxed his muscular frame and closed his eyes. As a youngster, he had been one of the smaller boys in his year with an immigrant father who spoke with a strange foreign accent. The school bullies soon found the gangly, lonely boy a natural target. He tried to fight back but was no match for the bigger and older boys. That did not stop him hating them. Hate filled his face as they taunted and hit him. Soon he was known as "Crazy" Kay. Then, some wag one day yelled out "rabbit warren." Soon it became "crazy as a rabbit" and then "Rabbit" Kay throughout the school. Several years later, a teacher explained how the rabbit plague threatening Australia's wheat and sheep industries could now be controlled by an introduced virus, myxomatosis. Instantly "Rabbit" became "Mix." He did not mind the change as most of the class had nicknames and "Mix" sounded better than "rabbit."

He grew rapidly during high school, spending a lot of time on his own in the gym. He remained a loner, not playing any of the team games. No one bullied him then. In fact, most people stayed well clear; he was not a boy to be crossed. One teacher had been heard to state during his last year that he thought Kay had psychopathic tendencies.

"He holds grudges against his fellow students for unhealthy lengths of time," he told the headmaster.

Some years later, two of the boys who had been the most persistent bullies were beaten with a baseball bat on their way home from university. Both had kneecaps smashed. No charges were ever laid over the assault.

§ § § § § §

To the rest of the crowd at the concert hall of the Sydney Opera House, the four men talking quietly at one of the entrances to the forecourt looked like any other concert goers. "Probably two gay couples," one woman whispered to another.

Detective-Sergeant Mike Smith said, "Any sign of our man?"

"No, but he could go in at the last minute."

"Yeah, I know," he said as the other members of the Serious Assault Squad shook their heads. "You all know what to do. Bill and I'll go in and sit with the ushers on either side; you two cover the exits. If the target takes up his seat, we leave him until intermission— unless he tries to leave earlier—and take him quietly then. We don't want any action." He knew he did not need to state the obvious as they were all experienced officers, but repetition never did any harm.

"Mike, what do you think the chances are of this ticket being owned by our man, and how the hell is he going to get in without a ticket?"

"Well, the ticket office said that they normally don't replace lost tickets. If the holder is a regular concert goer and the seat is still vacant at curtain call, they have discretion to let them in. We've told them that tonight they should be very sympathetic." He smiled. "Anyway, the chances of this being our man are pretty slim. But every lead must be followed, etc., etc.. But, don't worry, you get to hear some classy music for free."

"Pity it's not jazz."

"Amen to that."

"Where was the ticket found?"

"On the roadway outside FitzWilliam's house. It was wet and a bit muddy," Smith said.

"Could belong to anyone."

"Yeah. Well, it beats waiting in a car watching some bastard's house. The scenery is a hell of lot better here. Look at that gorgeous woman."

Callaghan and Zoe Marranti reached the top of the stairs and stopped momentarily in the space that forms at an entrance before people decide just where to join the moving throng. For Callaghan, it was toward the bar to get two glasses of champagne. As they moved through the crowd, Zoe briefly noticed a group of four, slightly overweight men near one of the doors looking at her.

Callaghan had jumped at Zoe's suggestion to join her at the Sydney Symphony Orchestra concert. Years had slipped by since he had been to an SSO performance. The buzz of the foyer added to his anticipation of what lay ahead. Music had been an integral part of his growing up and in his newly acquired leisure he had begun to rediscover the classics he loved. Tonight, a visiting young Russian virtuoso was to play Tchaikovsky's 'Violin Concerto in D Major.' The violin, particularly when played by a master, remained his favorite. The music transported him to another world.

As the warning bell ceased and the doors closed, high up in the Gods, a man leaned briefly over the rail and looked down at the stalls below. Only one vacant seat remained, toward the front. A quick glance at the ushers on either side, and he resumed his seat, a grim smile barely crossed his face. He had been right to buy another ticket, even such an inferior one.

An animated buzz of voices poured out the doors as the first half of the program ended. Eventually, Callaghan secured two glasses of bubbly and stood discussing the music with Zoe. As they talked, laughing, full of anticipation for the *Concerto in D* after interval, a tall, good-looking man made his way through the crowd toward them. As he came abreast of Zoe, he caught her eye. An expression that was neither smile nor smirk momentarily creased his lips as he looked into her eyes. Then he was gone, toward the bar. For an instant, Zoe wondered whether she should know the saturnine face, before Callaghan was introducing her to a friend. The moment slipped from her mind.

When the performance ended, the four police officers waited until most of the patrons had left the hall before agreeing the night had been a waste of time. And yet Detective Sergeant Smith felt they had somehow missed an opportunity. He couldn't quantify it; it was just a feeling.

Warren Kay exited the opera house slowly with the rest of the patrons. He deliberately walked past the four policemen, but was long gone by the time they decided to leave.

§ § § § § §

As Callaghan sat looking out over the beach the next morning humming the theme from the violin concerto, an old memory surfaced. His mother had always loved the violin and often attended concerts in the city. But there was something else, part of a story she had told him and his sister.

The time he had spent going through old papers and photos brought back many happy memories—of fun, and of her stories. Stories full of exotic people of the East, her fear of the Japanese, storms on the high seas, and the excitement of arriving through Sydney Heads. They had never tired of hearing them. He sat there deep in thought, smiling as he relived the fun they had as children. There was something about a violin, he was sure.

He poured a second cup of black Columbian and returned to his seat. The surf had come up overnight and twelve-foot sets were rolling in. He watched as a black wet-suited board rider slipped off the lip of a huge wave, ripping away to his left as the tip of the wave curled in a crushing break. He followed the surfer as he flipped his board back up to the tip of the wave and down again with breath-taking dexterity. Finally, when the wave had shrunken to a size no longer challenging, the surfer flipped the board over onto the back of the wave and was gone, paddling out for the next monster.

The story of the violin—it was really part of the story of how his mother came to be on the boat with the MacDonalds—slipped into his mind as he watched the surfers.

When the MacDonalds found her she was lost in the chaos and confusion of Shanghai as the Japanese Imperial Army prepared to advance into the International Settlement. She told them her mother had been killed by the Japanese.

"Grandmother told me to go to an 'island,'" she said. "But I wanted to go to America. All I had were Chinese identity papers, a small cloth handbag, and a violin in a battered case. Your nanna tried to get me to leave the violin. I said 'No' in a firm voice and told them, 'My Grandma said I must keep the violin whatever happens and must never let it go.' And I was a very determined child," she had added with a smile. "I kept that violin and brought it all the way to Australia."

He smiled, he could still hear his sister asking, "What happened then, Mum?" even though they had both heard the story a dozen times.

I wonder what did happen to the violin, he thought. He had vague recollections of seeing a shabby carrying case, but that was all. Having nothing planned that morning, he decided to look for it.

It was early afternoon when, after drawing a blank in the obvious places, he found it. It lay covered in dust alongside two old cases full of childhood memorabilia in the dry and insulated attic. Believing the roof should keep what the roof produced he dusted the case carefully and took it down into the living room.

He eased the clasps open and lifted the lid. Inside, resting on what appeared to be ancient red velvet lining, lay a sorry-looking violin. The old cat gut strings had snapped over the years and curled up around the scroll. The bridge lay flat on the face of the violin. He gently picked up the instrument and turned it over. The surface still had a lustrous patina.

"I guess the strings can be replaced and the thing made to look like a violin again," he said to himself. "A bit of a polish and it might not look too bad."

He laid it back in the case and considered the bow. That was in an even more lamentable condition. Nearly all the horse hair stringing had sheared and it looked as if it did not belong. He slipped the two slide clips holding the bow in place and lifted it out. As he did the tip of the bow caught in the velvet lining and tore it. The material was so frail the tear lengthened as he disentangled the tip. He laid it on the table and turned to look at the damage. Sticking out from behind the rip was a piece of paper. As he carefully tried to pull the paper out he saw that it was still snug in an ingenious double pocket sewn into the lining. If he had not ripped the velvet he would never have found the secret pocket. As he eased the paper out, it soon became apparent that it was the envelope of a letter.

It was addressed to Mrs. Neave Ryan / Mr. Patrick O'Connor in Ireland, at a Dublin address.

§ § § § §

Zoe Marranti got very irritated as Callaghan explained how he remembered about the violin and how he found it. How in taking the bow out he found the envelope with its letter.

"Will, stop babbling and show me the letter," she demanded.

"Oh, I've read it," he said.

"Oh, give it to me."

She gently smoothed the single sheet of faded copperplate writing and read it quickly to get the sense and then again slowly to absorb the meaning, the habit of an experienced lawyer.

Dear Neave or Patrick, if you are reading this,

The beautiful young girl bearing this letter is my granddaughter, Katerin Yuriovna, Yuri's only surviving child. Yuri has disappeared. I do not know where he is or if he is alive. He hates the Japs so much. Her mother, Larissa Andreovna, has been most brutally murdered by the Japanese. We have traveled across China to get here, but alas too late.

I am very weak (I think cholera or malaria) and do not expect to live much longer (Here the writing became unclear and drifted. On the next line, it appeared the writer had gathered her strength and continued.)

I am sending Katerin into the International Settlement in the hope that a child will be able to slip through the lines and will find a sympathetic soul who will take her to safety.

Please look after her as if she were your own.

My love to you as always

Katya

Zoe looked up.

"Is the young girl your mother, Will?" she asked.

"I'm sure she is," he said.

"How old would she have been when this was written?"

"About seven or eight. And from this letter she had probably been traveling across China with her grandmother trying to avoid capture by the Japs or the Chinese warlords. They must have reached Shanghai because that is where the MacDonalds found her. She was literally wandering the streets on her own."

"How absolutely terrifying for a girl of that age with the turmoil all around her. God, anything could have happened," said Zoe.

"I wonder why she didn't give this letter to the MacDonalds?" mused Callaghan.

"She was probably so traumatized she forgot all about it," said Zoe.

"Yes, more than likely. Or maybe her grandmother was so weak she couldn't explain it clearly. I imagine she would have spent her energy impressing on my mother that she must get through to the International Settlement above all else. And, of course, don't let the violin out of your sight. Hang onto it whatever happens. That part got through to my mother; it was part of the story she told us many times."

Zoe read the letter again. "Thank God, we never had to go through a war."

Callaghan then told her about his mother's marriage certificate, the same name as the letter.

"My mother had Russian names, so did her parents, judging by this letter, so it's very likely I'm half Russian," he said. "Funny, now I know why I like vodka.

"Ever since I found the marriage certificate, I've been curious to find out who she was, and who my ancestors were," Callaghan went on. "This letter made up my mind. I did a Google search, but the records in China for foreigners at that time are almost nonexistent. In fact, I doubt there were many, if any; it was such a tumultuous period. I thought of trying the Red Cross or some of the other international agencies but canned that idea. So I'm going to do the obvious and go to Dublin."

"Couldn't you just write to them, or get a phone number and ring?" asked Zoe.

"I could," agreed Callaghan, "but I'm not excessively busy right now. In fact, I've got bugger all to do, and Dublin is a great city. So why not go and knock on their door? Chances are it'll be a waste of time. The house has probably been demolished. Hell, it's over sixty years ago, but, so what? If I learn any little thing about my mother, or her relations, even ones she didn't know she had, it'll be worth it. Somehow I seem to have Russian and Irish ancestors."

He stopped, looked at Zoe, then said, "Why don't you come with me?"

Zoe stared at him. She hadn't seen him this alive for months.

"What about the adoption papers; they'd show your mother's maiden name and you may be able to trace her that way," said Zoe.

"I've been through all the drawers, boxes, and papers in the house, and haven't seen anything other than the marriage certificate," he said.

"But you can't get married without showing your birth certificate to prove you are who you claim you are," said Zoe.

"Maybe the MacDonalds claimed their original papers had been lost in the escape from China and got new ones issued, including papers for my mother. It must have been something like that because we have the marriage certificate, properly issued."

They spent the afternoon with Callaghan telling Zoe the stories his mother used to tell, and how the violin had simply been mentioned in passing, as if it had always been in the family. He and his sister had grown up with stories far more exciting than the traditional Grimm's fairy tales.

"I thought I had the exotic parents, Will," said Zoe.

"Without doubt, you do, only one of my parents can claim that label," Callaghan said. "Against an Italian father and Polish mother, I retire defeated."

"And both born in Europe, don't forget," said Zoe.

"You haven't really told me about them, Zoe. How did they meet?" Callaghan asked as he twisted the corkscrew into a chilled bottle of aged Semillon. As he eased out the perfect cork with a sweet *plop,* Zoe told her stories.

"My father was born in a small village near Cremona in northern Italy southeast of Milan during WWII and his parents migrated in the early 1950s to Australia. My mother was born in Lublin, a town southeast of Warsaw toward the Belarus border, near the end of WWII. Her parents feared the Russians, and what Poland might become, so left in the chaos at the end of the war. They went from one refugee camp to another until they emigrated to Sydney."

"It was music that brought them together," she went on. "My mother was coming home from a recital by a young Polish violinist and walked past the local hall. My father was being asked to leave the Saturday night dance." She laughed. "A loud Italian male with too much testosterone.

"My mother is descended from a famous musical family. A direct descendent of the Polish violinist and composer Henri Wieniawski. He was soloist at the Saint Petersburg Court in the second half of the 1800s. You never know; one of your ancestors may have met him then." She smiled, passing her glass to Callaghan for a refill.

"I think he died in Moscow, apparently from an excess of alcohol. They say he gambled obsessively, often spending all night at the tables. He apparently lost most of the time. He even had to sell a valuable violin to settle his debts. My mother says that he was tricked out of the violin by a gypsy who wanted it and got him so drunk he didn't know what he was doing. He never got it back despite the efforts of his family. They even appealed to the tsar's court but by that stage the gypsy was long gone.

"She's convinced from the family history that the gypsy sold it on to a waiting client, probably one of the aristocrats or a wealthy Moscow industrialist, and that this had been his plan from the outset. Goodness knows what the real story is. As she's got older she's become a bit obsessive about it and writes letters seeking details of famous violins and their provenance," Zoe confided. "I wish I could get some evidence that the damn thing had been destroyed or donated to a museum."

§ § § § § §

Nearly a week after the concert, Mix Kay remembered where he had seen the gorgeous woman with the glass of champagne. She had been talking to the banker, FitzWilliam, when he had been with da Costa and their lawyer. Garand had pointed them out in the distance. Had he said she was a lawyer, or had he said bank employee? He got the legal firm details from Garand and spent some time in the lobby watching. By midday, and a few innocent inquiries of the receptionist, he had confirmed Zoe Marranti was a lawyer, almost certainly one of the bank's lawyers. By early afternoon, he knew where she lived.

Later that day, Kay parked his vehicle and went for a wander around the streets of Double Bay. He soon discovered Marranti lived in a small townhouse two streets back from the harbor's edge. Box gums lined both sides of the street, but the gardens were tiny, befitting a high-density, high-price suburb. This made observation more difficult. He retreated to an area of restaurants and cafes a street away, sat down to a flat white, and looked around. There were a lot of people, coming and going. He smiled thinly; he could blend in.

After a meeting with Nic da Costa two days ago, Kay decided he had unfinished business. Da Costa told them he had gone over the costing and the project was unlikely to break even. The only thing that saved da Costa, Kay ruminated, was that he had the same amount of money in the deal as the rest of them. He would suffer the same amount of pain. He suggested to Garand that da Costa should buy him out. Garand laughed.

"Nic is so over-committed that this deal could bankrupt him. He can't afford the price of a good night out," Garand said.

If this female lawyer had simply stuck to the mortgage documentation, the bank would have lent the money. Kay could feel his anger rising again. Then he thought of the almost erotic sensation of his knife parting the flesh on the banker's neck. He calmed down. A passer-by, noticing the smile on Kay's face, smiled back but didn't get a response.

§ § § § §

Zoe drove her car into the single garage of the townhouse and got out, pressing the remote button to close the door behind her.

Half an hour later, a taxi pulled up outside and Callaghan got out. He turned with his back to the townhouse to pay the driver, called good night, and walked up the short paved path to the porch. He paid no attention to the pedestrian, one of many that strolled past him, as he walked to the front door. It was a balmy night, and it felt good to be out in the cooler air after the heat of the day. He stood in the porch light for a minute, searching for his key before letting himself in.

The pedestrian walked to the end of the street and crossed to the opposite side, walking back away from the harbor. The germ of an idea began to take shape in Kay's mind. He made a mental note to check the recent financial press.

§ § § § §

A few days later, Zoe arrived at Callaghan's home late on Friday night exhausted.

"Sit down, kick off your shoes, and I'll get you something cold and bubbly," he said.

Three minutes later, in only a T-shirt and shorts, she returned and flopped into a chair.

"Jesus, what a day!" she said. "Law would be really enjoyable if you didn't have clients."

"Ah, a typical day in the city," said Callaghan.

Two glasses later, she had started to relax. Callaghan brought in a plate of double cream brie, black olives, and sun dried tomatoes.

"Wow, you are becoming domesticated," she said.

"No, I felt hungry."

Zoe laughed. "So how was your day?"

"Very interesting," he said. He walked over to the desk and picked up the violin case.

"I had a call from the chap at the Violinery who I asked to fix it up. At least to make it look like a real instrument again. He said it was ready but that he would like to see me in person."

He opened the case and took out the violin. It had been restrung and sparkled. The deep luster of the varnish marked it as an instrument of true quality.

"Is that the same one?" asked Zoe in amazement.

"Not bad, is it? I thought it would polish up well. The owner of the shop asked me if I played and if I knew much about violins. I assured him that apart from singing in the shower, I was not musical. Then he asked me how I got the instrument. I thought, well, it's none of your business, but he seemed genuinely interested. I had nothing much to do this morning, so we sat down for coffee and I told him the story.

"When I had finished he was quiet for a minute and then said, 'I have been working with violins for over thirty years, and I have seen some fine instruments, but I think this is different. I am not really qualified to say but this may be an original Guarneri made in Cremona in the early 1700s. It is certainly a very old violin. At first, I thought it was only a copy, albeit a very good one. But looking at it more closely, I've come to the belief that it's not a copy. The maker's label is faded but you can clearly make out *Jofeph Guarnerius fecit IHS*. This suggests that it was made by the great Guarneri del Gesu, who some think of as being as good as Stradiveri. I am a little puzzled by some additional letters on the label that I can't find referred to in any of the literature.'

"'I'm no expert in old violins,' he said. 'I recommend you take it to Italy or London. There they have people far more experienced than I who can evaluate it.' I told him that I was shortly going to Ireland and it would be easy to detour to London.

"He was quite excited and gave me the names of several firms in London who may be able to help authenticate it, or, what is probably more likely, tell me it's a copy but a pretty one. I told him I would ring him from London once I had an answer. If it is a Guarneri, I assured him that I would give him full credit for finding it. This seemed to give him more pleasure than anything.

"As I was leaving, I asked him what a Guarneri would be worth; is it a collectible? 'Oh yes,' he said, 'they are very collectible; all of the great Cremona makers are. The important Viotti Stradiveri, which is said to be worth at least 3.5 million, was recently bought by public appeal for the Royal Academy of Music. Christie's sold another Strad, The Lady Tennant, for $2.3 million U.S. A rare Guarneri del Gesu could be worth millions.' Callaghan grinned. "Looks like I'm going to London," he said.

Zoe had not uttered a sound while he talked. Now, she said quietly, "Can I look at the violin?"

"Of course," he said, handing her the instrument.

She moved it closer to a side lamp so that she could look at the maker's label through the "f" hole. "That is an amazing story," she said, gently handing it back to him. "He said it was a Guarneri, did he?"

"Yes, and apparently they are rare." Callaghan grinned.

"How long had it been in your family?" she asked.

"Forever. My mother only spoke of it as if her family had always owned it."

Next morning, after a late and leisurely brunch, she said, "Will, I promised to go and visit my mother today; you don't mind do you?"

"Give her my best," he said. "I've got a bit of organizing to do anyway with London now on the itinerary."

§ § § § §

Mid-morning on Monday, Zoe called.

"Hi, Will. If that offer to go to London is still open, I'd like to come," she said.

"Great! Of course it is, but I leave at the end of the week; can you get the time off?" he asked.

"I think so. I'm due holidays anyway."

"You know what flights I'm on. Do you want me to book you?"

"No, thanks. I'll get my secretary to book it through the firm's agent. That way I might get a tax deduction for the fare." She laughed. "Anyway, we get very competitive prices because of the volume of bookings."

"By the way," he said "I haven't mentioned the violin to anyone. I wouldn't want to be embarrassed again if it turned out to be copy worth $5,000."

"I agree, Will, I won't mention it either."

§ § § § § §

Three days later Mix Kay watched a man, whom he now knew to be Will Callaghan, and Zoe Marranti, walk out of the townhouse with several suitcases each, get into a taxi and leave. They were obviously going away. He had to find out where.

When the idea first began to form, he didn't know who Callaghan was. He felt sure he had seen his photograph in the press recently. It took him the best part of a morning to go through the dailies for the last month, but eventually he found it. Nearly three weeks ago an article had appeared recapping the demise of the man with "the golden touch" along with a photo. He almost discarded the idea when he read that Callaghan had lost everything. Then, toward the end of the report the writer posed the question, "what is not known is, how much did this wheeler and dealer hide in offshore accounts?" *Cheeky,* Kay thought, *but bound to be right. Who doesn't have a secret cache overseas where the tax man can't touch it, and these high flying corporate types use every trick in the book.* The plan was back on track. In fact, it would be even better if Callaghan had secreted money offshore. He would not want any publicity about its existence or use. Kay smiled. Maybe the marina deal would work out after all. He might even make a profit.

Then he recalled where he had seen the two of them together the first time. At the opera house concert, when his foresight to buy another seat after losing the high-priced stalls ticket had paid dividends. He suspected the police who sat through the performance had not enjoyed it; *a bit highbrow,* he smirked.

After the taxi disappeared around the corner, he drove off.

By the end of the day, he knew where she was going and what hotel she was staying at. He also knew the name of the firm's travel agency. It had really proved quite easy. Ringing from a public phone, he posed as a very happy client wanting to send flowers for Zoe's arrival as a surprise. The receptionist had been touched and quickly determined that Ms. Marranti was staying at the Montcalm, Marble Arch, London. He then made a second call, also from a public phone, to the person in charge of administration.

"My name is Arthur Green," he said, "from the Australian Taxation Office. We are proposing to conduct a telephone audit of travel expenses among a range of professional firms such as yours. This is a preliminary call just to confirm that members of the firm do travel interstate and overseas and to get the name of the travel agency your firm uses. Once we've collated this data from a number of firms, the ATO will then decide on the nature and scope of the audit, and when it may go ahead."

Within minutes, he had the name of the travel agent, All Seasons Travel.

"Thank you for your cooperation," he said. "By the way, I wouldn't be too worried about this. These bright ideas of senior officers often don't go much further than the planning stage, unless someone reminds them about it."

He was confident the administration manager would not ring the tax office to ask about the audit. If the man never heard from them again, he would think himself lucky. It was a ruse he had used before.

He made his third call to All Seasons, where he passed himself off as the head of administration for the legal firm. He apologized that when she left, Ms. Marranti did not leave a full itinerary. The firm knew she was going to London and staying at the Montcalm but were unsure whether she would be in London the whole time, in case they needed to contact her. Within two minutes, he knew her itinerary. He declined an offer to fax the full details, just the main destinations and hotels would be fine, he said.

After booking himself on the next day's flight to London, he rang a number in the Cook Islands.

London

The Montcalm on Great Cumberland Street looks like a Georgian mansion from the outside and remained one of Callaghan's favorite hotels in London. It was discreet and only a few minutes' walk to Marble Arch. This time, however, he had booked a less expensive room at the rear with adequate space for two. In the past, he would have had one of the duplex suites with their own spiral staircases looking out through the original tall windows in the front of the hotel.

Callaghan suggested to Zoe she may prefer to go shopping instead of sitting talking to valuers, but she insisted on coming with him. They got out of the cab on King Street, St Jame's a few minutes before the ten o'clock appointment.

Philip Arbuthnot, the head of the Musical Instruments Department at Christie's, was a tall, aesthetic-looking man who you knew was the product of the better English public schools before he opened his mouth. Callaghan had been put through to a junior assistant when he first rang. Only on explaining exactly what instrument he had, had he spoken to Arbuthnot. After introducing himself, Arbuthnot introduced the woman with him.

"Ms. Wilkinson is a specialist in early Italian stringed instruments; she will do most of the work in establishing provenance. She has a detailed knowledge of the history of most of the great Cremona violins. She also has access, of course, to our own extensive database of information," he said. "May we see the instrument?"

Callaghan placed the case on the antique, leather-inlaid table and opened the lid. Fiona Wilkinson bent forward to look before carefully lifting it out and holding it up to the light. Holding the neck in her left hand she then tucked the chin rest against her shoulder. Adjusting the pegs with her right hand while plucking the strings with the fingers of her left hand, she tuned the violin. Satisfied, she picked up a bow she had brought with her and began to play. At first, it was a simple scales exercise. This quickly became the Romance from Shostakovich's *Gadfly*. The rich, romantic sound echoed around the room as she finished, placing the violin on the table.

"It has a beautiful sound, and the varnish is superb," she said, looking at Arbuthnot.

"Perhaps you could tell us how you came into possession of the violin," Arbuthnot asked Callaghan. He then told them the story of his mother's escape from China, and everything he could remember about how the violin had survived.

"Although she never said as much, I always had the impression that the violin had been with my mother's family for a long time," he concluded.

"Do you know why your great-grandmother would have impressed on her daughter the importance of retaining the violin?" Arbuthnot asked. "Do you think she knew its value?"

"I doubt she had any idea it was worth anything at all. It has been gathering dust in our attic for well over thirty years," said Callaghan.

"And you say she said it was important the violin be kept in the family?"

"Yes, although why I can't even begin to guess," replied Callaghan.

"May we see the letter you found in the lid?" asked Arbuthnot.

"Certainly," said Callaghan, handing it across the table.

Fiona Wilkinson had been studying the maker's label. "The label has the correct markings on it although just below the 'IHS' inscription, which is characteristic of Guarneri del Gesu, are letters and numbers I've not come across before: 'iv 76 na.' I can't be certain, Philip. I need to do further research before I can be more definite."

"Do you mind if we have some photographs taken?" she asked Callaghan. "We have a professional photographer in the office."

Sometime later, Callaghan had completed the paperwork to leave the violin with Christie's. He agreed to pay a valuation fee if he did not proceed with a sale through the firm. Before they left, he asked

Arbuthnot, "If this is a Guarneri del Gesu violin, what could it be worth?"

"That's difficult to be too precise about, but to give you an indication; about four years ago, we sold a Guiseppe Guarneri, Joseph Guarneri's (the del Gesu's) father, for 290,000 or nearly $500,000 U.S. Del Gesu's violins are of a much higher caliber than those made by other members of the Guarneri family. Some collectors say they are comparable to Stradiveri. Last year, we sold a Strad for over $2 million U.S., so I would suggest that a good example, such as this one, with good provenance could sell for well over $1 million U.S. I hope that, should you decide to sell, you will give Christie's the opportunity to handle the sale," Arbuthnot said as he said farewell to them.

Three days later, they were sitting in the same room with the violin laid on the table.

"We are reasonably satisfied that this is a Guarneri del Gesu violin," Fiona Wilkinson said, "however, its value would be considerably enhanced with better provenance. My research so far suggests that few Cremona violins can be reliably traced to Russia in the period up to the revolution. How a del Gesu came to be there is uncertain, assuming of course that it was acquired in Russia. Could it have been obtained in China? Perhaps from a fleeing aristocrat or maybe some another European. I understand that there were a large number of Czechs in Russia after World War I."

"I don't know," said Callaghan.

"What about if it was stolen and then on sold in Russia?" asked Zoe.

"That is, of course, possible," said Ms. Wilkinson, "but there is no record of such a thing happening in Russia at that time and without evidence that the violin may be linked to a crime we must assume that it is legitimately owned."

"One other thing," she added as they stood to leave, "the notation is still puzzling us, 'iv76na.' Do they mean this is type or style four, that this is the seventy-sixth violin Guarneri made? It cannot be a date as he was born in 1687 and died in 1745. And the 'na,' I'm not sure. My initial thought is that the whole notation refers to Nicola Amati, one of the greatest of the Cremona masters. He trained del Gesu's grandfather Andrea. Perhaps this is variation four of a design by

Amati created in 1676, eight years before his death. Andrea could have passed it on to his son, Guiseppe, (del Gesu's father) and del Gesu is rightly acknowledging the master's influence. We believe this is the best explanation as it ties in with the history of the Guarneri family. To try to confirm this, I've sent a request for details on all the known maker's labels issued by del Gesu to Italy, to the Juilliard Institute, the Royal Academy and the Smithsonian, as well as some private collectors who we know have considerable information on the Cremona violins."

"And who are also keen and wealthy collectors." Arbuthnot smiled, adding, "Should you decide to sell."

§ § § § §

When they entered their hotel room, the first thing they saw was a large vase filled with white lilies on the sitting room table. Alongside the lilies were several sheets of crumpled newspaper.

Zoe immediately rushed to the flowers and picked up the small envelope stuck in between the stalks and took out the card inside. "Zoe Marranti" was all it said. This time, the card had a black border.

"What's going on, Will?" she said handing the card to Callaghan.

Two days before, a similar sized bunch of lilies wrapped in an expensive white paper had been delivered to their room. It also had a card, plain white that time, with Zoe's name on it, nothing else to indicate who had sent them, or why.

"This is bizarre," she said, sitting on the couch.

Callaghan rang the concierge. After several minutes' conversation he put the phone down and shook his head.

"A different courier each time, two different firms, brought the flowers with explicit instructions as to the wrapping paper, he said, even included a tip to ensure that the instructions were carried out. The wrapping paper was to be left alongside the flowers. He assumed it was a joke from someone you knew. He was more concerned that he had done the right thing. I assured him he had."

"It's like some scene out of a 'B' grade movie," said Zoe. "Is it supposed to mean something? Should we call the police, Will?"

"And tell them what? That you received two deliveries of lilies from persons unknown. There's certainly been no crime committed, has there? You're the lawyer."

"No, you're right, but it's a bit unnerving," Zoe said.

"Well, we're going to Dublin tomorrow so that will put an end to it," Callaghan said.

"I was going to speak to you about that, Will. Would you mind if I didn't come with you, there are several people I would like to see while I'm here?"

"I'd much prefer you came with me, Zoe, darling. Dublin is such a charming city, and I like you by my side." He smiled.

"I know, Will, but there is something I need to do; it's family business," she said and kissed him lightly on the lips.

"Well, if you are sure you won't miss me too much," he said. "However, I'll only agree if you change hotels today."

"All right," she said.

§ § § § §

It was going according to plan. He expected they might move hotels after the second delivery of lilies and followed them. Once he was sure they had checked in, he returned to his own hotel and went over the next step. The flowers were the easy part; the next move had to be carefully planned and executed if it were to succeed. Timing was everything. He checked out of his hotel, and, within three hours, was in Paris, having caught the British Midlands flight out of Stanstead. This way there was a paper trail showing him leaving London as any tourist might.

He had just dropped off to sleep when the shrill tone of his mobile jerked him awake.

"Mix, where the hell are you? The police have been around asking questions."

"Shit, Joe, you don't have to yell," Kay said, instantly alert.

"The police have just left my office," said Garand, "They want to talk to all the members of the syndicate. They are trying to see if there is any link to the attempt on that banker's life. I told them not to be so ridiculous; it was only money, and we'll get it elsewhere. They said it's only routine. They're talking to a lot of people connected to the bank. They said that they have been unable to contact you, said you've left the country. Where are you?"

"I'm in Paris having a holiday. Tell them to relax. I'll be back in a couple of weeks and I'll give them a call then," Kay said.

After he had disconnected, Kay sat thinking for nearly an hour before going back to a sound sleep; he was confident he had nothing to worry about.

The next day, he bought a ticket on the early fast train to Brussels, paying in cash. From that city, he rang Callaghan's mobile number from a pay phone at the station. That way, if by some twist of fate the call was traced from Callaghan's phone it would be a dead-end.

§ § § § §

Callaghan delayed his flight to Dublin until he was sure Zoe was safe in her new hotel. He had agreed to Zoe's suggestion to leave the violin in London with her. It was one less thing to worry about. As a result, he decided when he landed in Ireland to stay in a bed and breakfast. On the recommendation of the taxi driver, he ended up in an excellent place just off St Stephen's Green, near the center of the city. He felt this would give him more flexibility and be less intimidating if he needed to leave an address with the people he was hoping to contact.

He was about to leave, after a generous and delicious Irish breakfast, when his phone rang.

When the call disconnected, he was visibly shaken. It had been a man's voice, distorted as if trying to disguise it. On the content of the call, he had no misunderstanding. The voice said he represented a dissatisfied investor who had lost a lot of money through Callaghan's failure. This investor was not the kind to accept such a loss meekly. What they required was the transfer of $1,000,000 to an account in the Cook Islands, $550,000 immediately, the balance within two weeks. He would be given the account number tomorrow. Callaghan laughed and said if he had a million dollars he would be well into his next deal and not holidaying in Ireland.

The voice replied. "We are confident you will find the funds, Mr. Callaghan." After a brief silence, it continued. "We trust Ms. Marranti enjoyed the lilies. Her ability to continue to enjoy lilies now depends on you. And when you hang up you will certainly consider going to the police. But what will you tell them? And even if they believe you and take this threat seriously (and it is a threat, Mr. Callaghan) what can they do? The British police are unlikely to provide twenty-four-hour protection for any length of time, nor are their Australian counterparts. Then, when the threat has been downgraded to crank status and withdrawn, she'll be vulnerable. Do you know there are hundreds of ways to kill a person, many of them very difficult to trace or almost certain to be deemed an accident? Her life will then be on your conscience, all for a small sum of money."

Callaghan sat going over the conversation in his mind. Notwithstanding that the voice was probably right about the police, he decided he must tell them. But he was in Ireland, they would not be interested here. He rang directories and got through to Scotland Yard, in London.

Then he rang Zoe. "Hi," he said as she answered the phone.

"Hi, Will. How is Dublin? Any success yet?"

"No I'm just about to go out. I've been delayed by a strange phone call. A man claiming to be an aggrieved investor called and demanded I pay him $550,000 immediately. God knows how he got my number, but then a lot of people used to have it. He seems to think I have millions hidden away overseas." He paused. "I think this may be connected to the lilies, and he's trying to get to me through you," Callaghan said. He had debated just what he should tell Zoe and decided not to be too dramatic in case Scotland Yard was right and it was all talk.

"What do you mean?" she asked.

"Well this crackpot says he wants money, money I don't have. I just want you to be careful. In fact, I am going to book a flight to come back to London today."

"No, don't do that," she said quickly. "I'm going to leave London to visit some family connections for a few days. I'll probably be away till the end of the week. And I may turn off my phone while I'm there so don't get worried."

"Well, when you come back, check into the Dorchester; let's have a bit of real luxury for the last few days," he said, feigning more jollity than he felt.

"Where is the violin?" he asked.

"I have it," she said.

"Before you leave, will you put it in the hotel safe. I'll collect it when I return," he said.

"I'll make sure it's secure," Zoe said.

If I have to pay a half million dollars that is all I've got, he thought.

"See you in a few days then and be careful. Don't tell the hotel where you are going in case 'Mr. Lilies' decides to follow you."

He still felt uneasy as he climbed into a cab and gave the driver the address.

Dublin

He stood outside the narrow-fronted, three-story terrace house in what was clearly a working class area in transition. It was close enough to the city to attract young professionals, and a number of the houses had been renovated. The one he stood in front of, number 32, had not. It was well maintained but had an air of authenticity about it. He pressed the bell. After a few minutes, a woman in her late fifties opened the door.

Seeing a stranger on her step, she said, "We're not buying or donating."

"I'm not doing either, ma'am," he said. "My name is Will Callaghan. I'm from Australia, and I am wondering if a Neave Ryan may have once lived here."

"There's no one of that name here," the woman said slowly. "Why do you ask?"

He explained about the violin and the letter and after several cups of strong tea established that this woman, Mary Flynn, was Neave Ryan's great-granddaughter.

"How sad," she said putting the letter down. "Katy was my great-grandmother's sister and to think that she thought to send her little granddaughter to Neave, it's very touching. My grandmother used to tell us Neave's stories about Katy. We always thought she sounded so romantic. Would you leave the letter with me for tonight; I'd like to show my husband—he's very interested in family history—and my brother. He lives close by."

Callaghan handed her the letter, and they agreed to meet the following day.

When he arrived late afternoon, he was greeted by a family council—Mary Flynn, Neave's great-granddaughter, Michael Flynn, her husband and Patrick O'Connor, Mary's brother.

On his way there, Callaghan bought a large bottle of what the publican assured him was the best Irish whisky in Dublin. He insisted it be opened immediately, and after the first round, the ice was well broken. He answered questions about Australia and Sydney, about kangaroos and koalas, about Kylie and rugby and the story of the violin and his mother.

Finally, Patrick O'Connor asked, "And what is it that you're expecting to find here, Will?"

"I came hoping to find out why my mother was to be sent to Dublin and to try to track her family. It's a part of me I know nothing about. And now I find I have relatives here in Dublin," he said, raising his glass. "I hope all of you will come and visit me in Sydney. My house is near the beach and has plenty of bedrooms."

An hour later with dinner being prepared and Patrick and his sister still telling stories about their great-grandmother's sister, Katherine, or Katya, as they said she was known in Russia, Callaghan had no desire to leave.

"How do you know so much about her?" Callaghan asked.

"We Irish are great story tellers," Patrick said, "and the stories about Katya Morozov are family favorites."

"Are they true?" smiled Callaghan.

"Oh, yes," said Mary Flynn. "Neave and Katya corresponded for years and our great-grandmother kept all Katya's letters. I think they're still in boxes in the attic, although no one has read them for many, many years."

After a pause, Callaghan said, "Would it be possible for me to read the letters? It may fill in a bit of the Russian end for me?"

Mary looked across at her brother, who shrugged slightly in agreement.

The next two days, Callaghan spent the daylight hours reading hundreds of neatly handwritten letters, all yellowed with age. In the evening, he insisted on taking the families to dinner. The first night they went to a restaurant they recommended; the second to a pub that had an irresistible warmth and life. Callaghan remembered playing darts, and losing. How many Guinness he drank, he could not remember. Late the next day, he returned to Mary Flynn's home and handed back the boxes of letters before taking his leave. Patrick O'Connor agreed to come on a visit to Australia in the next year, and Callaghan said he would certainly return to Dublin in the near future. Then, he was on the plane to London.

He looked through a notebook more than half full of jottings he had made as he read the letters. Much of it was out of chronological order, a task to be completed on the return flight to Sydney. Two items, however, stuck in his memory. The first was the name of a London legal firm, Freshman, Withers & Somerston. He wondered whether it still existed in these days of mergers and mega firms. *If not, he thought, the Law Society should have records to show what happened to it.* The Morozov family had clearly had a close relationship with the Somerstons of the firm, as that name appeared many times in the letters. What they could tell him, if they still existed, he had no idea. *Not much, he thought, but it's the only lead I have.*

The second thing came from one of Katya's later letters written from Harbin. She said that a large quantity of the tsar's gold had disappeared from the train the Czech Legion guarded. In a later letter, she said her daughter, Anna and her husband, Lt. Charles Macek of the Legion, had settled on a large farm outside Prague purchased soon after their arrival. The implication about the destination of at least part of the gold was there, whether intended or not. Callaghan wondered whether the Macek family had survived the repression of Communist rule. Maybe on a future trip to Europe, he would spend some time in Prague. However, the blood line was getting a bit remote in this Czech branch of what was becoming an ever-expanding family.

When he arrived at the Dorchester, he was surprised to find Zoe had not checked in. She had been due to arrive the day before. The hotel kept the room only because she had left her credit card details. She had also warned them that if she was a day late, a Mr. Callaghan would be arriving from Ireland to take the room. As he took the key, the desk clerk handed him a message in a plain white envelope. He opened the envelope in the lift.

"Please ring Mr. Paul Harding on arrival," it said and gave a telephone number.

London

After making the telephone call to Callaghan, Kay caught the train from Brussels back to Paris, then the afternoon high speed train back to London. There, he hired a car using a British passport in the name of Warren Cooper, his mother's maiden name. It showed an address in Kent, a dead-end if anyone took the trouble to check. Kay's mother had been born in England, and he had used this maternal link to get the passport with her name as his parent. The idea had come to him when by chance he had found out that his parents had never actually married. It had proved useful several times over the years.

He was waiting outside the hotel when Zoe Marranti came out and climbed into a hire car that had just been delivered. As she pulled out into traffic, Kay was right behind her.

§ § § § § §

Once Callaghan had left, Zoe spent most of the day on the telephone. Finally, she booked a rental car to drive to Bristol for three days. Callaghan's call from Dublin had stiffened her resolve to leave London as soon as possible; she had no desire to receive any more lilies. She paid the account and drove the Vauxhall Astra into the traffic. *The drive will help me clear my mind,* she thought, as she went over once again what she intended doing. Was she doing the right thing? Could she justify her actions? Emotionally, she felt it was right, but as a lawyer…hell! Several times she glanced in her rearview mirror to see if she was being followed before laughing out loud.

"How would I know?" she said to herself, "and, anyway, who knows I've left except Will? Maybe he's behind all this. Oh shit, that sort of paranoia is a step toward madness."

She drove on through the gathering dusk. Behind her, in another Vauxhall, one of thousands on the road, drove Mix Kay, concentrating on the number plate ahead.

§ § § § §

The traffic flowed steadily along the M4, and Zoe pulled off the road only once near Reading, to top off the fuel tank and get a cup of coffee. By the time she reached Bristol, she had decided she would continue with her plan and deal with the consequences later. Sometimes, she decided, you had to do what you felt deeply and strongly was right.

Kay watched her pull into the hotel car park and continued around the block. Ten minutes later, he parked twenty meters away in the same car park. Five minutes later, he started the engine and drove out, having determined she had booked in for three nights.

Kay arrived at the café across the street from the hotel the next morning, just in time to see Zoe picked up in a late model car and driven away. He was not really interested in where she was going, only that he knew where she was staying. He smiled and strolled away to explore Bristol. When he found a public phone, he called Callaghan's mobile. He tried three times without success. The phone was turned off. Annoyed, he walked away.

§ § § § §

Zoe kept busy all that day in meetings and discussions, returning to her hotel in late afternoon satisfied with the progress.

Next morning, the car picked her up immediately after breakfast, and she did not return until late in the evening after a celebratory dinner. The deal had been struck and the paperwork completed. She walked down the corridor toward her room feeling relaxed and happy.

She swiped the card key, opened the door, and turned on the light. At first, it was just a sensation that something was different. Then she saw them. A large vase of lilies sat on the side table. The shock was almost palpable. A cold shiver shot up her spine. As the horror of more lilies receded, a far more terrifying thought dawned on her.

Someone was stalking her. She saw the small white envelope. She knew what would be in it. But she could not resist the compulsion to open it. As she picked up the envelope, she screamed. There, in the middle of the lily stalks, were two dead fish. Flat lifeless eyes stared at her. She recoiled in horror. She had seen enough mafia films to know what this meant. To "swim with the fishes" meant the person was dead. If the lilies had not delivered the message, the fish certainly did.

Instinct took over. Without thinking, she threw her case on the bed and rapidly packed her possessions, jamming the lid shut. She grabbed the case and half ran out of the room, leaving the door ajar. By the time she reached the lobby, she had calmed down a little. She felt sure whoever was stalking her would be watching to see her reaction. She should probably wait until morning and tell the police or someone. However, she also knew she could not wait that long; she had to move, and fast. Hopefully, whomever it was would not expect such precipitate action

Across the street, Kay watched as the Vauxhall left the hotel. She had thrown her suitcase into the trunk. When he saw her leave, he was a little surprised. He thought she might but if he had been asked to bet on it he would have put the money on her staying until the next morning. He pulled out and followed.

At that time of night, the traffic was light and both cars were soon on the M4 heading back toward London. Kay carefully kept one car back from his quarry in case she got suspicious. He felt pleased with himself. His tactics had clearly worked. She was scared.

On his next call to Callaghan, he would give him the numbers for the new bank account in the Cook Islands. Immediately after the money hit that account it would be dispersed to half a dozen untraceable accounts in nominee names in tax havens around the world, finishing in a private bank in Lichtenstein. There, a lawyer who performed the same service for a wide variety of clients who valued their anonymity would deduct a 10 percent fee and convert the balance into U.S. bearer treasury bonds. On receipt of a coded phone call, these bonds would be posted to a one-time post office collection box in Brussels, where Kay would collect them. He smiled at the beautiful simplicity of the scheme. Bearer bonds were just that;— whoever held them owned them. There was no name on the bonds.

They were cashable anywhere in the world. It was the ultimate "Texan" asset. Possession was more than nine-tenths of the law.

A sudden change of speed interrupted his reverie. Zoe was accelerating away from him. There were now four cars between them. At first, he thought he had been spotted. Then he saw a red Range Rover alongside her in the fast lane. Instead of passing her, it matched her pace. After a mile, she slowed down and the Range Rover slotted in behind her. Three of the cars in front of him pulled out and overtook Zoe. He was relieved she slowed down to sixty miles an hour as the little Vauxhall felt less stable at higher speeds.

Now that he was closer to the powerful four-wheel drive vehicle, he could see two men in the front seats. They appeared to be laughing. As he watched, they pulled out and slotted in alongside her again.

Zoe had been watching the Range Rover for some miles in her rearview mirror, but not until they started to pass her did she begin to feel afraid. As they drew alongside, the passenger, a man in his late thirties with a shaved head, looked across at her. She knew she should ignore them but she could not resist. She glanced quickly to her right and locked eyes with the man. Immediately, a smirk appeared on the man's face, and as they began to accelerate past, he turned to the driver who quickly glanced over, smiled and nodded. He decelerated down to her speed. The passenger turned to her and grinned. When she increased her speed, they easily matched her. She slowed down and they dropped in behind her.

This could be a simple case of harassment, she thought, but she was in no position to take chances. She could not outrun them. If she pulled into one of the cafes along the route, they had such large car parks she could be assaulted or kidnapped before anyone knew. If she drove into London, then they would know where she was staying. A feeling of desperation began to grip her when she saw an exit sign, "Reading 2 m."Perhaps she could lose them but her timing would have to be precise.

Kay saw the Reading exit sign flash by. She had increased her speed again. He let her pull away with the Range Rover in pursuit.

They had almost passed the exit ramp when he saw the little Vauxhall swing violently to the left. He knew instinctively the turn was too sharp. The Range Rover braked hard. He followed suit. He watched, mesmerized, as the Vauxhaul swayed dangerously to the right. The left-side wheel lost traction as the driver tried desperately to regain control. For an instant, it looked as though she would make it. Then, the front mudguard hit the crash barrier on the ramp. The car flipped into the air, landing on its roof ten meters up the ramp. The heavy metal barrier crumpled the cabin as though it were paper.

The Range Rover slowed down before resuming its journey. Kay pulled over onto the verge and sat in his car, shaken. Several other vehicles had now stopped. He could see a number of mobile phones out, calling for the ambulance and rescue. Being so close to Reading, it took no time before flashing lights and sirens converged on the crash site. Kay got out and walked over to where a small crowd had gathered.

"Is the driver all right?" he asked one of the onlookers.

§ § § § § §

Mr. Harding turned out to be Senior Constable Paul Harding when Callaghan called the number given him at the Dorchester.

"Thank you for calling, sir," said Harding. "I'm afraid there's been an accident. I wonder if you could come down to the station?"

"Of course, I'll come immediately," said Callaghan.

Callaghan was shown straight into Harding's office.

"Do you know a woman called Zoe Marranti?" the policeman asked.

"Yes, she came with me to London. She was supposed to be at the Dorchester when I returned from Ireland," said Callaghan.

"I am sorry to have to tell you that yesterday evening she was involved in a motor vehicle accident on the M4 and was killed."

Callaghan sat there. He stared at Harding in disbelief. He asked the policeman to repeat what he had just told him. It couldn't be right.

"Would you like a cup of tea, sir?"

"Yes, please," said Callaghan, struggling to come to grips with what with what he had just heard.

Harding told Callaghan what had happened on the M4, how one of the motorists who stopped had told them about the red Range Rover. They turned out to be two fans returning from a football match. They probably didn't stop as they were over the limit.

"Do you know what Ms. Marranti was doing in Bristol?" asked Harding.

"No idea at all. She said she was going to attend to some personal business while I was away."

"What were you in Dublin for?" asked Harding.

"I'm trying to trace my roots," said Callaghan. Then, suddenly curious, he asked, "How did you know to leave a message at the Dorchester?"

"Ms. Marranti had a receipt in her bag. The hotel had your name. We also inquired of the hotel she stayed at in Bristol—the receipt was in her bag—to see if there was anyone that should be advised. She apparently had a number of meetings there outside the hotel. There was one curious thing though, sir. The manager said that when they went to clean her room the next day there was a large bunch of lilies with two dead mackerel in the stalks. Rather odd, we thought," said Harding looking at Callaghan.

Callaghan told him about the other deliveries of lilies. He also told him about the phone call demanding money.

"It doesn't appear as though the accident is related to the extortion attempt based on information from the crash investigation team," said Harding. "And from eye witness accounts it appears to be an unfortunate case of excess speed, for whatever reason. Please let me know if you have any more demands for money, or deliveries of lilies. We've asked the Australian police to advise her next of kin."

"Thank you," said Callaghan.

When he returned to the Dorchester, Callaghan paid the account and moved back to the Montcalm; he thought it seemed more appropriate.

§ § § § §

Kay could not believe his bad luck as he drove away from the accident. His beautifully elegant scheme lay in tatters. Trying to piece the events of the last fifteen minutes together, the only conclusion he could come to was that those two fools in the Range Rover had done something to cause Marranti to think that they were him, and she had panicked. He spent the rest of the journey into London trying to figure out a way to still get Callaghan to pay the $550,000. By the time he reached the end of the M4, he had decided it was no use. Marranti was dead. His leverage was gone. Threatening Callaghan directly would be unlikely to get a result. It involved a greater risk of exposure, particularly with the detective in Sydney wanting to interview him on his return. He toyed with the idea of one more call to the ex-investment banker but with the Marranti woman gone what threat could he use? With their roles reversed, if Callaghan threatened him, he would laugh, "and if you kill me who'll pay the money?" Clever and resourceful as he was, he could see no way out of the dilemma.

§ § § § §

Callaghan felt shattered. He now realized how much he loved Zoe and couldn't fully grasp that she was gone. Instead of the sound of her voice and the softness of her embrace, he had a black, gaping hole, a void. He had no idea how to deal with the numbness. He kept expecting the phone to ring and Zoe to be on the other end of the line, laughing at him. All this would turn out to be a horrible dream. But he knew deep down that would not happen. She was dead.

He sat alone in his room at the Montcalm trying to make sense of what had happened. The shrill stridency of the telephone snapped him back to reality.

"Mr. Callaghan? It's Philip Arbuthnot from Christie's," said the voice at the other end. "I hope you don't mind my calling but we always feel it better to check."

"Check what?" asked Callaghan.

"We were wondering if you had sold the Guarneri?"

"No, I haven't. Why?" said Callaghan.

"I see," Arbuthnot paused. "Well, we have been asked to place a valuation on what has to be the same violin. The coincidence of two Guarneris with the same unique markings on the maker's label are just too remote. Did you lend it to an orchestra?"

"No, as far as I know it is with Ms. Marranti," he said, before he stopped. Zoe was no more, so what had happened to the violin?

"Then could it have been stolen?" asked Arbuthnot. "We had a recent example of that occurring and happily we were able to recover the instrument for its rightful owner. It's just that in this case, the person who brought it in is reputable and well known in musical circles. I can give you his name and address and if we can be of any assistance please call me at any time."

Callaghan told the Christie's man about Zoe's accident and hung up. He sat there for some time considering the import of this information before the phone rang again.

"Mr. Callaghan? It's Paul Harding. We've received Ms. Marranti's belongings from the car, and I wondered if you would like to come by and collect them, or should we send them back to Sydney."

"No, I'll come and pick them up," said Callaghan. "Was there a violin among the items?"

"Not that I recall," said the policeman.

When Callaghan saw Zoe's personal things neatly stacked on a table in the police station, he knew finally it was not a dream from which he could awaken. She was gone forever.

"I rang the hotel where Ms. Marranti stayed in Bristol," Harding said. "They didn't have a violin in kept luggage. We made some further inquiries and the manager said the concierge remembers her carrying a violin case into the hotel. He says he thinks she left the next day with it but didn't return carrying anything. The manager said that the concierge remembers a Stanislaw Manowski coming to the hotel to meet Ms. Marranti. It stuck in his mind because he thought it unusual that a Manowski was meeting a Marranti. I don't know if that is of any assistance."

"Thank you. I am not sure either," said Callaghan, although that was also the name Christie's had given him. He decided not to tell the police about Arbuthnot's call until he had more information.

When he returned to the hotel, Callaghan rang the telephone number Arbuthnot had given him for Manowski. It turned out he was away touring with a visiting string quartet until the end of the week. After talking to the woman on the other end of the line about the musical activities of her boss, a possibility, way off in left field, began to take shape in his mind. In the meantime, he had no choice other than to await the return of Manowski. If his crazy idea turned out to be right, then it was likely he would need a good lawyer.

He sat in the hotel bar drinking a fresh brewed cup of coffee. He needed to keep busy to take his mind off Zoe, at least during the day. *I came here to trace my roots,* he thought, *I might as well finish the process.* My great-grandmother left Dublin over a hundred years ago and came to London. It was extraordinary that her mother and then her sister had kept all her letters. Where would he start? Immigration records? Marriage registry records? It would be too improbable to be able to trace the family she worked for. What was their name? Summers, Somersby—Somerston. That was it. Then he remembered, it seemed a bit odd reading the letters, but her employer Somerston seemed to be related to the legal firm mentioned in her later letters. What was it, a very traditional sounding English name? Three names?

Freshman, Withers & Somerston. If he were to need a lawyer maybe he could kill two birds with the one stone.

He finished the coffee, went back to his room and opened the telephone directory, the obvious place to start. Failing that, the Law Society. He turned to "F" and flicked through the pages. To his complete surprise, halfway down the first page he saw an entry for Freshman, Withers & Somerston in central London. It had to be the same firm. He dialed the number and made an appointment for the following morning.

Callaghan was shown into a meeting room with dark wood paneling halfway up the walls, just like the reception area. It looked old enough to have been in place for years before Queen Victoria died. Within minutes, a young solicitor, about thirty, came in and shook his hand.

"I'm Stephen St. John, Mr. Callaghan, how can we be of assistance?" he said in the crisp rounded vowels of the British public school, pronouncing his surname "Sin-jun."

"I understand you are from Australia."

"Will Callaghan," Callaghan responded. "Yes, I came over to the U.K. and Dublin to try to trace my ancestors."

Callaghan could see St. John was not really interested as the young man glanced at his watch. It was only when he mentioned the violin and the letter that St. John became more attentive. *Encouraging,* thought Callaghan. When he explained how he found the firm's name, St. John stopped him.

"Would you mind waiting a few minutes, I shan't be long," he said and without waiting for Callaghan's response left the room. Ten minutes later, he reentered with an older man.

"Mr. Callaghan, my father, John St. John, our senior partner."

"Good morning, Mr. Callaghan," said St. John Sr. "My son's told me your story very briefly. We acted for the Morozov family for many years, and I would be most interested to hear the story in more detail if you have the time."

For Callaghan, it was good to be doing something positive, and the two lawyers seemed to have a genuine interest, so he told them the whole story, beginning with the collapse of his takeover deal.

"You say you found a letter in the lid of a violin case," asked St. John.

"Yes."

"May I see it?"

"Of course," said Callaghan, handing over the yellowed pages.

St. John put the letter down on the table once he had read it and took off his spectacles. "Do you have the violin with you?"

Callaghan told them of Christie's and where he thought the violin now was, and of the death of Zoe.

"Christie's confirmed it was a genuine Guarneri, did they?"

"Yes, and that brings me to the other matter I would like your advice on. Would you be in a position to act for me in recovering the violin if it requires legal intervention?" Callaghan asked.

"Certainly, we would be pleased to, although it may be a police matter from what you've told us," said St. John. Callaghan nodded.

"Can you tell me about the Morozovs. It seems my great-grandfather was a very successful businessman in Russia. What happened to him?" Callaghan asked.

St. John turned to his son. "I think you might like to earn the firm some fees, Stephen, while I tell Mr. Callaghan some history." He smiled.

As the son left the room, a secretary brought in a tray with coffee and biscuits and set it down on the table.

"The Morozov history with our firm is well known to members of my family. I had the pleasure of spending quite some time with my great uncle, John Somerston, when I was completing my studies. From him, I know the broad detail.

"It was my great-grandfather, Bertie Somerston, who first met the Morozovs. My grandmother, Amanda, one of Bertie's children, married a rather dashing officer from the Boer War, Capt. Edward St. John, who was with Churchill in the Transvaal.

"Great Uncle John actually went to Russia and spent several years there working with the Morozovs before the revolution. He told the most marvelous tales of his adventures. He had great respect and affection for Mikhail, your great-grandfather, and his father.

"He lived his life heartily as a bachelor and died in 1967. He always said he owed a great debt to Mikhail Morozov, who saved his life on at least one occasion." St. John spent the next hour telling Callaghan what he knew of the Morozovs. Finally, he said, "Your own story is very interesting. It fits with what little we know about the fate of Katya and her family in China leading into the Second World War.

"There is, I should tell you, an estate left by Mikhail and Katya Morozov as the only descendents of Ivan. Our firm is the executor of that estate and if you can prove that you are the rightful heir then you would inherit the estate," said St. John, watching Callaghan's reaction closely. "The estate's instructions were set up by my great-grandfather. They are quite simple and quite irrevocable. The rightful heir will have the key to a code. Without it, the estate cannot pass. It's many years since I last looked at the estate's provisions. What I can remember is that the code contained words or letters. Beyond that I am not in a position to give you any information about the code or the estate."

Callaghan was intrigued. "I had no idea there was any estate," he said. "Is it estate of any value or simply some keepsakes and old books?" Callaghan smiled. "Having set me a puzzle, Mr. St. John, I'd hate to spend sleepless nights trying to crack a code only to inherit a few Victorian knickknacks."

"I suppose I'm permitted to tell you that it is not keepsakes and knickknacks," St. John said.

"Am I the first heir apparent to appear?" asked Callaghan.

"I am not in a position to answer that, Mr. Callaghan. However, you can draw your own conclusions," said St. John.

"Well, if the estate, whatever it is, is still here, I guess that either I am the first or no one else has been able to crack the code," said Callaghan.

"I don't think it is a matter of 'cracking' the code," said St. John. "The rightful heir will know it."

"I thought that after the elapse of a certain number of years unclaimed money was paid to the state."

"Yes, that's the case for unclaimed money," said St. John. "It's not necessarily the case in an estate matter. Of course, a claimant can always recover the funds from the state if proper title can be established."

"Well, thank you for your time, Mr. St. John. Each step along my ancestral road presents a new challenge." Callaghan rose to his feet.

"My great-uncle always mentioned the violin in the context of the estate, if that is of any help. Now that you tell me the value, I can understand why. In any event, you have possession of the violin, subject to locating it. If you need our assistance in recovering the instrument, please call me or Stephen," said St. John as he shook hands with Callaghan at the door.

Sydney

Mix Kay was in a foul temper as he walked out of Sydney International Airport. He had had little sleep on the twenty-two-hour flight from Heathrow. Try as he might, he could not think of any angle to help him recover his investment in the marina project. On top of that, he now had the prospect of an interview with Detective Sergeant Smith. In fact, he reminded himself as he climbed into a taxi, he had also just spent at least another $10,000 on the Marranti project with no prospect of a payoff.

The next morning, he rang his lawyer, Joe Garand, to tell him he was back. Three days later, he let DS Smith and another detective whose name he missed, into his apartment. He had decided to have the interview on his own territory rather than down at the police station. He had a strong aversion to the officious air that always seemed to hang heavily over any area where law officers congregated.

"Thank you for agreeing to see us so soon after your return, Mr. Kay," said DS Smith. "As I explained to you on the telephone, we are continuing the investigation into the attempted murder of Angus FitzWilliam. Part of this process entails interviewing a number of the bank's clients to see if they can shed any light on why this attack may have occurred."

Kay nodded.

"I understand that you are a member of a consortium that applied to the bank for a loan to build a marina project. Is that correct?"

"It is," replied Kay. One rule his father had always emphasized in dealing with police was never volunteer anything. Answer the question only, and then in as few words as possible. His father had quite some experience in such matters. In case he had forgotten, Garand had given him the same advice.

"The bank told us they rejected the application. Do you know why that was?" Smith asked.

"Actually, FitzWilliam told us that the bank would approve the loan. It was the bank board that rejected it, for reasons best known to them," Kay said.

"Did that cause you any problems?"

"Of course. We have to find another source of funding," said Kay.

"And has that been possible?"

"I don't know; I've been overseas," said Kay.

"Were your partners upset over the bank's decision?"

"Why wouldn't they be?" asked Kay levelly, "after having been told the loan would be approved."

"Do you know the other partners in the project well?"

"Not particularly," said Kay.

"How did you come to be involved then?" asked the detective whose name Kay didn't hear, the first time he spoke.

"Through Joe Garand, my solicitor," said Kay.

"Ah yes, Mr. Garand. He has an unusual list of clients, quite a number of whom are known to us," said DS Smith. "Have you always used his services?"

"He acted for my father for some years; that's how I got to know him," said Kay.

DS Smith nodded his head as though he already knew about Kay's father.

"How well do you know Eddie Ng?" Smith asked.

"I'd never met him until this deal," said Kay.

"Were you aware that there are allegations concerning drug trafficking against Ng?"

"I've since heard that," said Kay. "Have any charges been laid?"

"None that I am aware of," said Smith. "Not the best of company to be associated with. Then there were the bribery allegations concerning the local council and your marina project. Do you think that Ng could be behind the attack on FitzWilliam?"

"I have no idea," said Kay.

"Well, thank you for your cooperation, Mr. Kay," said Smith as he stood up. "I noticed that you've kept a clean record since the baseball bat allegations," Smith added as he stood at the door to the apartment.

Kay was momentarily taken aback. "What do you mean? I've never been charged with anything."

"Quite so," said Smith. "However, there were allegations, which were never proven, I concede, by several university students years ago that you attacked them with a baseball bat. One of them was quite badly injured, as I recall from the file. I think their story was that it was a revenge attack. Seemed a bit extreme to me, but then you come across some strange things in this job…Well, thanks again. We may need to talk to you again so please let us know if you're planning any more trips."

When they were back in their car, DS Smith turned to the detective and said, "What d'ya think? Is he a possible suspect?"

"He's certainly very cool, and if that baseball bat story is true he'd be violent enough."

They drove in silence for some minutes before Smith said, "I had a call from the bank this morning. The bank's lawyer on the marina project, Zoe Marranti, died in a car crash in the U.K. a few days ago. Apparently, the British police said it was a simple traffic accident. Didn't Mr. Warren Kay say he had just returned from England? It may simply be a coincidence, but I believe all coincidences are suspect until proven otherwise. When we get back, let's do a little more digging on Kay, and let's also look up his father; you never know what might turn up."

London

As he waited for the end of the week, Callaghan idly began to draw a diagram showing his immediate antecedents before he realized he had enough information here and in Dublin to construct a family tree from the bottom up. He would be the starting point. Within a day, he realized he needed to return to Dublin. This time he would look at the letters with new eyes.

Having decided that he would not contact Manowski by telephone, he arrived outside the house on the outskirts of Bristol at six o'clock that evening. He rang the bell twice. The door opened no more than a few inches and a woman's face appeared in the gap.

"Hello," Callaghan said, "Is this the home of Stanislaw Manowski? Christie's of London suggested I call."

"One moment please," she said in a heavy, Eastern European accent. "Stanislaw, a man from Christie's is here," she called out.

"Please come in," said Manowski, a tall, thin man with high Slavic cheekbones.

"I've come about the violin," said Callaghan as he was ushered into a sitting room.

"Yes, of course," said Manowski. "But first, would you like a vodka? I have some of the best Polish vodka. Not available in this country."

"Thank you," said Callaghan.

When the vodka had been served and glasses clinked, Callaghan said, "My name is Will Callaghan and the Guarneri violin that you are currently holding is my property. How you came to have it I do not know. I have informed the police that it has been stolen and that Christie's has advised me you are in possession of it. However, Philip Arbuthnot assures me that you are well known in musical circles and highly regarded as a man of integrity. So, I thought I would come here in person to speak with you."

Manowski looked at him steadily.

"You English—"

"Australian," corrected Callaghan.

"—are very direct and lack, if I may say so, a little subtlety. So, I know who you are and what you want. Let me be direct in return. The Guarneri was given by deed of gift to the Polish nation to be used by our national orchestra. As far as I know, it is now in Warsaw."

"When you took the violin to Christie's for an insurance valuation, they rang me as soon as you had left the building. At my request, they notified British Customs that it is a prohibited export. They have also notified the Art Section of Interpol. Unless you smuggled it out, and I do not believe you would do that, the violin is still here," said Callaghan evenly.

"On what basis do you claim ownership?" Manowski asked, looking at Callaghan appraisingly.

"The violin was brought by my mother from China sixty years ago. It was owned by her family for at least forty years prior to that. In all we have owned it for one hundred years. I was coming to London on other business and brought it to be evaluated by Christie's. I also can produce original letters dated in the early 1900s referring to the violin."

"Then how do you account for the deed of gift that I have?" asked Manowski.

"I can't, other than to say that it is fraudulent. It's not possible to perfect title to an asset by creating a false document claiming title, my solicitors advise. May I see the deed? I suspect that may clear part of the mystery," Callaghan said. He watched Manowski evaluate what he had just been told. The man was clearly no fool and was rapidly coming to the conclusion that perhaps he had a problem.

"Please wait here," he said

When he returned, he handed Callaghan a single printed sheet headed "Deed of Gift." Callaghan did not bother to read it; he went straight to the signature.

Sadness clouded his eyes as he looked up.

"It's as I suspected; this is Zoe Marranti's signature. This is a fraudulent deed."

He then proceeded to tell Manowski the full story of the violin, the letter in the lid, Zoe's mother's obsession over a lost family violin and Zoe's tragic death.

"I think Zoe was coming back to London to try to persuade me to the transfer of the violin to the Polish National Orchestra when she was killed."

"You make a very convincing case, Mr. Callaghan," said Manowski, although it was clear he was not yet wholly convinced. "However, I have a problem. The acquisition of the violin by the Polish government has already been announced in Warsaw. It will cause extreme embarrassment to have to admit that this is not so and, worse, that it was the result of an attempted theft. If what you say is true, there seems little alternative," he said, shaking his head in dismay.

"Can I see the violin?" asked Callaghan.

"Certainly," said Manowski, opening a cupboard beneath a bookcase and pulling the case out.

"Not a very secure hiding place," observed Callaghan.

"What thief would look twice at a battered old violin case left in such an obvious place by an old music teacher?" smiled Manowski. "Valuables are often best hidden out in the open."

Callaghan opened the case, took out the violin, and looked at the maker's label, then at the tear in the lining of the case lid. Satisfied, he replaced it on the table.

"I have Philip Arbuthnot's private number here if you would like to ring him to confirm what I have just told you," Callaghan said.

Manowski returned five minutes later.

"As you said, he confirmed what you have told me. He also said that you may have a proposal to put to me."

"If you will return the violin to me now, I propose the following: I will give the violin on loan to Poland to be used only by the national orchestra as you proposed. The loan will be for an initial period of five years and after that by mutual agreement. Poland will acknowledge my ownership of the violin and the whole deal will be drawn up in a loan agreement by my solicitors and signed by the

Polish ambassador in London on behalf of his government. The announcement about a gift can be blamed on faulty translation." Callaghan stopped. "Oh, one final thing. Poland is to insure it at Christie's valuation."

A smile broke out over Manowski's face.

"Please, give me your telephone number and I will call the ambassador tomorrow," he said.

As he sat on the late train back to London, the Guarneri on his lap, he tried to make sense of Zoe's deception. She was a lawyer, so how did she think she could have got away with it? Why not suggest the plan to him? Perhaps she was going to claim her family's ownership prior to the Morozovs.' She couldn't have proven it, but the legal case could have dragged on for years, with a national government having physical possession in the meantime. Maybe she thought he would look at the likely costs and capitulate. He felt hurt and betrayed. In truth, he had to admit he was unlikely to sell the Guarneri in any case; it had too strong a family connection for him. He may well have ended up doing a deal like the one he had just struck with Manowski. After all, he was not musical and could barely sing in the shower without protest. The difference being, he would liked to have made the gesture.

He opened the case, picked up the violin, and looked idly at the maker's label. If only the other passengers in the carriage knew that he had well over a million dollars in his hands.

He left the violin and his instructions with Freshman, Withers & Somerston on Monday and caught the mid-morning flight to Dublin. When he explained to Mary Flynn why he wanted the letters again, she willingly handed them over. This time he had the advantage of St. John's history of the Morozovs. He also knew who John was—great-uncle John Somerston. This time, the letters made more sense. As he went, he sketched out the family tree on a large sheet of paper.

As the tree grew, he made sure he added in the patronymic to each of the Russian names; he felt it gave the family a certain gravitas.

As he read the detail in Katya's letters over a period of nearly forty years, he began to build a mental picture of each of his relatives, although, after 1918, there were few letters and most had little real information in them. It was as if Katya had been afraid they might be intercepted.

The overall impression he formed was one of a happy, loving family, with the patriarch, Ivan, setting the example. Katya, or Katy, and Mikhail were clearly very much in love. Mikhail Ivanovich, he corrected himself.

Katya mentioned the date of birth of each of her children when she wrote to her sister so Callaghan started to write in all the important dates as he went. He was able to work out both Katya's and Mikhail's year of birth from the letters Katya wrote in high excitement about her engagement and wedding. She speculated on whether she was too young at nineteen, although she went on to reassure herself that he was "quite mature at twenty-one years." The letter was dated 1898.

In another letter at about the same time, Katya, struck a slightly melancholic note when she confided to Neave how sad it must have been for Mikhail not to have had the benefit of a mother. "His mother Nataliya died bringing him into the world," she wrote. From another letter, he deduced that Ivan and Nataliya had only been married for a year. Yet, he had never remarried. *He must have missed her,* thought Callaghan, Zoe's loss still fresh in his mind.

After two days, he had most of the blanks filled and could glean no more from the letters. He made a copy of the family tree for Mary, returned the letters, and took his leave. On his way back to his hotel, he stopped at a bookshop and purchased a short history of Russia. He felt he should at least know the rudiments of the environment in which his ancestors lived.

§ § § § §

In Sydney, D-S Mike Smith's investigations went nowhere. He had no new leads and no hard evidence, just suspicions.

His digging on Warren Kay had not turned up anything new, although the father had been a different matter. He was surprised to see the thickness of the file, with only one conviction, for loitering in a suspicious manner outside a girls' school. The rest of the file contained allegations of a variety of sexual offenses and violence, none of which had been pursued. It looked as though Kay senior had preferred to settle his problems out of court. *Could such traits be inherited?* he wondered, not for the first time. Had Mix Kay inherited a liking for violence from his forbears? If not from his father, then maybe from *his* father? It would be interesting to know more about

Mr. Kay's family history. However, since his father was a migrant he didn't fancy his chances. The only other item of interest, though D-S Smith felt it really had no relevance to the present, was that Kay's father had changed his name as a young man. His original name had been Volodya Koslinski. He changed that to become Vince Kay. *I think I would have changed my name if I had one like that,* Smith thought.

He would keep on digging. Police work was largely a process of persistence, patience, and never giving up.

§ § § § § §

After an early breakfast the next morning, Callaghan left the Montcalm, crossed Oxford Street via the underpass at Marble Arch, and began walking around Hyde Park. He needed the repetitive monotony of steady walking to get his mind back in order. He walked for nearly two hours, down the avenue of trees, through the squirrel-infested gardens, past Kensington Palace, around The Serpentine and on and on. When he finally stopped, he had no idea where he was. It took him several minutes before he could orient himself. He hailed a taxi and headed back to the hotel.

The walk had cleared his head. He decided there was little to keep him in London now. Within a few days, he would return to Sydney. First, he needed to place the Guarneri violin safely into the hands of the Polish government. Secondly, he decided he owed it to his mother, even though she had never known about her real family, to pursue the estate whatever it may turn out to be.

To achieve his second objective, however, meant he had to find the key to a code. No, it was worse than that. He had to find the code itself. How he could achieve this he had absolutely no idea. He decided to rely on his experience in business. Many times, he had found solutions to seemingly unsolvable problems often presented themselves if he let his mind wander freely. Thinking outside the square was the jargon.

He called St. John, who confirmed the documentation for the loan of the violin would be completed on schedule. Satisfied, he picked up the short history of Russia he had bought in Dublin. From the formation of the city state of Kiev by the Rus, to the establishment of the Romanov dynasty unifying a scattered group of principalities centered on

Moscow, the history of Russia seemed one of missed opportunities. Two overwhelming factors dominated Russian history, the author said. The first was the harshness and extremes of the weather. The second was the relative isolation of the country from the rest of the world. These weapons Tsar Alexander I used to defeat Napoleon.

Not all the tsars were bad, Callaghan thought, reading about the genuine efforts of Alexander II to improve the lot of the serfs in 1861 with far-reaching reforms. This was about the time Ivan Victorovich was growing up. He put the book aside. He unfolded the family tree. He did not have a firm birth date for Ivan or Nataliya so Callaghan had estimated it as being early to mid 1850s and arbitrarily decided on 1853.

The only other missing piece was Nataliya's patronymic. For completeness, he decided he should add a most likely name. He referred back to the history of Russia. The most likely names were the names of the tsars or other important historical figures. He flicked through the book, Mikhailovna, Victorovna, Petrovna, Vladimirovna—none of them seemed to fit. He realized it was foolish. How could he possibly know Nataliya's full name, and why did it matter? Yet, he felt sure that when he had the right name he would know.

The tsar at the probable time of her father's birth would have been Nicholas I. Would he have been named after that tsar? *The other possibility was more than likely the conqueror of Napoleon, Alexander I,* he thought. A national hero. Very likely the choice for many newborn sons. So, her father could have been Alexander. Idly, he wrote down, Alexandrovna. He looked at it, Nataliya Alexandrovna. It looked right; it also sounded right. Without any further thought, he wrote the patronymic into the family tree. He sat there for some time looking at the finished result. Satisfied he now had it as complete as he could make it, he folded the papers to a manageable size and put them on top of his suitcase.

Next morning, he began to pack his cases. After the disaster of the failed takeover in Sydney, he no longer had the funds for a long stay in a city as expensive as London. Over breakfast, he felt irritated. He was missing something.

Today he would go and see St. John to finalize the documents for the Guarneri loan. Back in his room, he rang Freshman, Withers &

Somerston to arrange a time. As he told St. John how he had completed his family tree, it hit him.

"I know the key to the code," he said. Like the last clue to a cryptic crossword it fell into place. "I'll tell you when I arrive."

§ § § § §

Callaghan signed the last of the agreements for the Guarneri. The violin would be handed over to the Polish ambassador in a ceremony Manowski had arranged for later that morning.

John St. John pushed the pile of documents to one side and sat, quiet and expectant.

Callaghan reached into his attaché case and pulled out several sheets of folded paper that he opened and smoothed out on the boardroom table. He then pulled out a copy of a photograph he had obtained from Christie's, the only other paper in his case, and laid it beside the other sheet.

"Have you had an opportunity to check the code set out in the estate documents?" he asked.

"I have," replied St. John.

Suddenly, Callaghan did not feel as confident as he had earlier that morning. It had seemed so clear and obvious, perhaps too obvious.

He cleared his throat.

"The code is iv76na," he said and held his breath as St. John opened a leather-bound document case and glanced at a page marked for easy access.

"That is incomplete," he said after a long pause as he considered the folder in front of him. "Unless the code is expressed in full the requirements of the estate are not fulfilled."

Callaghan stared at the lawyer and then looked at the papers in front of him. He had not been prepared for this. He had expected the recitation of the code would suffice.

He looked at the large sheet; it was his family tree.

"Ivan Victorovich married Nataliya Alexandrovna in 1876—iv76na," he mused out loud.

"Correct, that completes the code, Mr. Callaghan. I am pleased to welcome you as the only known heir to the Morozov estate." St. John smiled, extending his hand across the table.

"Is that it?" asked Callaghan now surprised that it seemed so insubstantial.

"The fact that you have possession of the violin and your mother was charged with it by Katya Morozov on its own presented a very persuasive argument. The letter you found in the violin case lid really put the matter beyond doubt. If you had come into my office with only the code, even if correct, we would have felt obliged to undertake more detailed investigations.

"However, even with all your credentials, we could not have admitted you as heir without the full code. As it is written in Ivan Morozov's will, the expression of the code is slightly different, no doubt a function of its translation from Russian. Notwithstanding that small translation difference, what you have provided satisfies me you are the heir in terms of the will. As I understood from my great-uncle and more recently from my father, Ivan Morozov held the view that only a direct family member would have the information to open the code. The fact that his wife died in 1877 giving birth to Mikhail made it all the more unlikely that any non-family member could know the code. How did you find the solution?" St. John asked.

Callaghan handed the photograph across the table. It was a detail of the Guarneri taken through the "f" hole with a macro lens and showed the maker's label with the added notation "iv76na."

"When Christie's experts insisted they had never come across such a notation on a Guarneri label, it started to raise questions. But their explanation sounded so plausible I began to accept it. It was only coming back from the meeting with Manowski that I began to wonder if maybe it had been added later. The story my mother told me about her escape from China always included the exhortation "do not ever part with the violin." My sister and I used to think it must have been magical," said Callaghan.

"It was the family tree which gave me the key. If I'd not embarked on a project to trace my family's roots I couldn't have come up with the answer." He slid the large sheets of paper across. St. John could see right at the top beneath the heading Morozov Family Tree, "Ivan Victorovich 1876 m Nataliya Alexandrovna."

"Great-uncle John Somerston said that after the 1905 revolution, Ivan became increasingly worried about what might happen in Russia," said St. John. "Apparently, the violin was damaged after an assassination attempt at a recital. Perhaps the code was added when it was being repaired. Perhaps that is why your mother was exhorted not to part with it. We'll never really know.

"After the 1917 revolution, we eventually received word that Ivan had been murdered in Moscow and that the family had fled. It was some years before we heard from them again. This time it was from Katya in Harbin to advise that Mikhail had been killed and that she and her children were intending to remain in Harbin.

"We often wondered why Katya did not leave Harbin. We know they had some business interests there although we have no details. Perhaps she chose to remain close to her children; we don't know. What we did know is that she had three surviving children, two sons and a daughter. We continued to hope that one of them at least had survived and would make contact. To date, you're the only descendent to do so. After all these years and with you having possession of the violin, I think it most unlikely any other claimant will emerge."

St. John sat back in his chair. The two men regarded each other. Callaghan liked the lawyer. He had heard that English lawyers could be rather obtuse. St. John was not, and he felt he could trust the man.

"What have I inherited then?" Callaghan asked. He felt sure he knew what it was going to be, Imperial Russian bonds (worthless except for framing and decorating a wall), one or more rare musical instruments and some family heirlooms.

"Firstly, I strongly suggest that you plan on remaining in London for some time. If you will speak with Stephen, he will arrange a more appropriate and less expensive place than The Montcalm for you to stay. Secondly, as we are intimately familiar with the estate, having administered it for the last hundred years, we would be pleased to offer our services into the future."

St. John paused, as if uncertain how to proceed.

"The Nataliya Trust, which is the peak entity in the Morozov estate, had a collective worth when last valued about ten years ago of over 500 million pounds—that would be well over a billion dollars, I should think," he said.

§ § § § §

Callaghan lay back in bed thinking on the extraordinary events of the last few weeks, particularly the last two days. Stephen St. John had driven him to a superb four-story Victorian townhouse overlooking a large garden square in one of the more exclusive areas of London. A retired former prime minister, now a life peer, lives on that corner, he confided as they arrived. The house was beautifully maintained and had a full-time staff of two who would be at his disposal. This house is now yours, Stephen said.

Not quite, Callaghan thought, *not yet.* He was pleased to see St. John was thorough; he had not simply accepted Callaghan's story. The lawyer proceeded to verify it. After dropping him at his new home, Stephen intended flying to Ireland to read Katya's letters himself. As Callaghan climbed out of the car, Stephen said, "Of course you also own several houses in Dublin. The Morozovs bought them after visiting Dublin so that Katya's family would have secure lodgings."

St. John requested certified copies of Callaghan's birth certificate and his mother's marriage certificate from Sydney. These had arrived by secure PDF e-mail late yesterday. Today he was to meet with St. John to take formal title to the estate and to find out just what it included.

At two minutes after ten o'clock that morning, a secretary showed Callaghan into the Somerston boardroom. After confirming he had satisfied himself Callaghan was who he claimed to be, St. John passed a two-page list of assets across the table.

"This summarizes the assets of the estate," he said.

Callaghan began to read. Most of the assets were properties whose addresses meant little to him. When he reached halfway down the second page, he stopped, astonished.

"Is that the right number of shares?" he asked.

"Yes," smiled St. John. "Apparently, the Morozovs had singular success investing in oil in Kazakhstan and grabbed the opportunity to invest in oil in the London market. The shares in Royal Dutch Shell plc were bought in the first decade of the twentieth century and have expanded over the years. As you can see, there are only two holdings of company shares, both in oil companies. The other holding, in British Petroleum plc, has an interesting history.

"They joined a consortium to search for oil in Persia, or Iran as it is today. Burmah Oil also joined the search at this time. Even so, after nearly three years, more capital and no oil, the money dried up. They sent a cable to the field manager in Persia ordering him to cease activity and to sell the residual assets. After receiving the cable, the manager decided two things. Firstly, he needed the instruction in writing. This, he reasoned, would give him about a month. Secondly, as he was halfway through drilling a well, albeit the final well, he would complete it.

"Two weeks later at four in the morning, the rig struck oil. It was a massive strike and the field, Masjid-i-Sulaiman, the "Mosque of Solomon," is still in production today. Burmah Oil subsequently issued shares to acquire the syndicate's interest and it in turn ultimately became BP. All dividends paid by both companies have been reinvested in their shares in the absence of any instructions to the contrary."

Callaghan turned to the last item on the summary, then looked inquiringly at St. John.

The lawyer nodded his head. "Even British Treasury bonds can be a satisfactory investment over time if left to compound," he said. "I am told that a capital sum invested at 5 percent per annum interest when the interest is reinvested will double over approximately fifteen years. And these funds have been compounding for nearly a century," he reminded Callaghan.

Callaghan nodded slowly and checked the figure again, just over 60 million in bonds.

"All the properties are rented, with the exception of your new home, which has only recently become vacant. The rents have accumulated and additional properties purchased when appropriate. For instance, several badly damaged sites were bought at the end of WWII and later redeveloped by third parties who pay rent to the estate. At the end of the ground lease, the property, including the development, reverts to the estate," said St. John.

"What is required now for me to assume control of the estate?" he asked.

"When the trust was set up, Bertie Somerston formed it in the Channel Islands, which are not subject to British taxes. As the beneficiaries were foreign nationals, there was no British jurisdiction at all. The trustees are long established companies in Jersey specializing in this area. All assets are registered in the name of the trustee on behalf of the estate. However, no investment decisions can be made by the trustees; they must come from this firm. Any use of funds must be authorized by this firm and the trustee. Twice a year, the trustees report on the composition of the trusts. Thus, there is a two-way check on the disposition of the funds and assets," explained St. John.

"There is a simple and failsafe second level of verification that a claimant must pass to satisfy the trustees before finally taking control of the assets. First, we must be satisfied that the claimant has the correct code, amongst other things. This you have done. Secondly, the trustees must be satisfied that the claimant is a direct descendent of Ivan Victorovich Morozov. I have discussed this with the trustees and they have advised that the only truly satisfactory evidence will be official documentation. So we have requested certified copies. Katya's birth certificate arrived this morning from Dublin. Certified copies of your own birth certificate and your mother's marriage certificate are expected by the end of the week. By early next week, I also expect to have copies of Mikhail Ivanovich's birth record, the marriage of Katherine Mary O'Connor to Mikhail and the birth of Yuri Mikhailovich. We have also sought documentation of Yuri's marriage to Larissa Andreovna from Harbin, and the birth of your mother. Of those two, I am not as confident and think we will need to rely on Katya's letters to Neave, more crucially, the letter you found in the lid of the violin. Your possession of the violin will also carry significant weight in the trustees' minds."

Two weeks later, Callaghan and St. John sat side by side on the flight from Jersey to London. The trustees had been satisfied Callaghan was a direct descendent of Ivan Morozov and on the advice of St. John had consented to hand control of the Morozov estate to William Callaghan.

"Due to Bertie Somerston's clever use of blind trusts and nominee companies, I doubt even the trustees know the full extent of the estate's assets. It would be impossible for any outsiders to unravel the total value," said St. John.

"Good, lets keep it that way," said Callaghan. "Anonymity can be very useful."

"And provide excellent security for such a large fortune," added St. John.

"John," said Callaghan, "I hope Freshman, Withers & Somerston will continue to act for me."

"We would be delighted to do so," said St. John.

As the plane circled London airport, Callaghan said, almost to himself, "It's strange how random acts can set events in motion. If some cold-blooded killer hadn't sliced Angus FitzWilliam's throat in Sydney, I wouldn't be sitting here the owner of a billion dollar fortune."

St. John continued looking out the aircraft window.

Sydney

Warren Kay could not be described as a great reader, with the exception of the business press. This he read avidly. He prided himself in being up to date with the latest trends in the financial world. Nevertheless, when he read the small paragraph reporting that Australian Development Bank, the largest investment bank and fund manager in the country, proposed establishing a leisure trust for investors, he did not initially pay it much attention.

Several days later, reading a supplement on the leisure industry, a feature article on the boating industry caught his eye. *Sometimes, the obvious just doesn't stand out,* he thought. Of course, boating was part of the larger leisure industry.

"And where do owners park their boats?" he asked rhetorically out loud. "In a marina."

Over the next week, he found out that the ADB was indeed interested in marinas; they had put offers in on two already. That was in addition to theme parks, sporting complexes, entertainment venues, golf courses, etc., they said.

"At the moment we are in an acquisition phase until the first tranche of investment funds is committed," the spokesman said. "Then we will take a breather for about a year before the next round."

Kay explained the bank interest to Garand on the phone and met with the lawyer to discuss their next step a week later.

"They're looking to buy now, but one of their conditions is that they own 100 percent. We'll all have to sell out," Kay said.

"That may be a problem," said Garand. "Ng reckons they'll pay a lot more if it's completed. He thinks he can get the funding with ADB buying when it's finished."

"And what if the ADB have bought all they need for round one, or decided they don't need any more marinas," Kay said. "Fucking Asians. I told you they were problems. If they're that certain they can buy me out now. Tell them, Joe, it's one or the other; sell to ADB or buy me out. There's no other choice."

Two days later, Garand rang Kay.

"Sorry, Mix, they insist that the deal will make more money if it's completed," he said.

"Persuade them, Joe," was all Kay said before he hung up. He had no intention of missing the opportunity to cash out of a bad deal. Twenty-four hours later, he took action. The strategy had a slightly better than 50 percent chance of success, but it had much less risk for Warren Kay. He called Ng's office from a suburban public phone. He spoke to the accountant, a recently graduated Asian girl.

"Good morning. My name is Richard Hescott from the Australian Taxation Office." If she rang to check, she would be told that a Mr. Hescott did indeed work for the tax office, but he was not in today. Kay had confirmed Hescott would be on leave for the next two weeks.

"I'm from the Asian Task Force," he went on, "and we're investigating businesses and individuals who seem to have asset holdings not supported by their declared income levels. It may be that there's a simple explanation. In such cases, the file is marked 'clean' and no further activity is undertaken. If, on the other hand, we're unable to satisfy ourselves as to the disparity between assets and income declared, a full, detailed investigation will be initiated. In this case, all the parties' assets and bank accounts would be frozen pending determination as to the amount of tax and penalties due. This process can take several years."

"Is there an investigation under way?" the accountant asked, unable to hide her anxiety.

"Not yet," Kay said. "We're ringing to advise that a forensic accounting team may call you in approximately two weeks to arrange a time to visit your offices. Please ensure that all the key management personnel will be available for interview at that time."

Kay continued in this vein for some minutes until he was sure the accountant believed her employer and his companies were under investigation for tax evasion. He further implied they had a case to answer. *That will get to bloody Ng,* he thought. *Unless I'm very wrong the bloody drug dealer will then start to panic.*

Two days later, he handed an envelope to a person he had done business with before. After going through several hands, including cut-outs that were dead-ends, the envelope was given to Ng's ten-year-old daughter on her way home from school.

She handed the envelope to her father when she arrived home. It had his name on it. He pulled out two pieces of paper. The first was a photo of his daughter leaving school. The second said, "DIRTY ASIAN DRUG DEALERS GET OUT OF AUSTRALIA OR DIE."

Toward the end of that week, Ng received a second envelope, this time through the mail. It had one sheet of paper in it. He unfolded the paper. It was a digital photo of his other child, a son at university, in full color lying in a pool of blood on the ground. His throat had been so savagely cut the head was nearly severed from the body.

Ng's face went white. It could not be right. His son had left for lectures only this morning. It took him several minutes before he regained a semblance of equilibrium. Then he grabbed his mobile phone. Within an hour, his son arrived home, safely. A digital photo had been "enhanced." Neither child left the house the next day.

When Ng arrived at his office the next morning, the third letter awaited him. It was pinned to the body of a dog. Ng's wife had complained for the last three days that "little Paw Paw has disappeared." The dog's throat had been cut. Spurting blood had soaked the curly fur and the pure white poodle now looked a bedraggled dirty red. Ng gagged as the sickly stench of blood mixed with decomposition reached his nostrils.

When he cleared the vomit off his face, he pulled two sheets of paper from the blood-stained envelope. One showed a recent photo of his home. The second was a digitally manipulated view of the same house. This time it looked as though a bomb had exploded in the house; flames shot high over the roof. The rapid escalation in events convinced Ng—a family member would be next.

"What happened to Ng?" asked Kay as he and the remaining partners in the marina sat around the board table in Garand's office.

"He and his family have left Australia for somewhere in Asia," Garand said. "I don't know all the details, but I gather he received a number of threats which he took very seriously. So they upped stakes and left in a hurry."

"Triads?" asked Kay.

"Could be," Garand said looking speculatively at Kay. "I don't know. And I didn't ask."

"Where does this leave us with the marina and the ADB then," said Kay.

"ADB have confirmed their offer. They want Nic to manage the completion of the project. They refuse to budge on paying any more than cost, however," said Garand. "Fortunately, before he left, Ng gave me power of attorney to deal with his interest. So we can deliver full ownership."

Kay smiled. He would get his money back. Very soon.

He had one final hand to play before this game ended.

London

It was nearly a year to the day since Callaghan first knocked on Mary Flynn's door in Dublin. His lifestyle had not changed markedly. He had a new but modest motor vehicle in Sydney. He dressed well and traveled business class when he flew. Those who knew him assumed he was back doing small deals. He nodded with a smile when they put this to him. When asked about his backing, he replied vaguely that he dealt with a small legal firm in London and in fact his address in London was care of St. John. He maintained the beachside house in Sydney because he liked it, liked being able to go for a surf. And it represented a last link to his parents. In London, he operated out of his new house and drove a supercharged Jaguar S-Type, which in that part of London did not even rate a second glance.

One of the first decisions he made on assuming control of his inheritance was to transfer the two Dublin properties into the name of his great-grandmother's descendents. He was certain that would have made her happy. By pure chance, the transfer deeds were registered on a day the oil price spiked so the value of his holdings did not change.

About six months ago, he had employed an assistant, Sarah Longhurst, a Cambridge graduate with a doctorate in life sciences and an honors degree in mathematics. She was attractive, played competitive tennis, and held a black belt in judo. The latter, she told Callaghan in her first interview, so that there could be no misunderstanding as to her position. Callaghan liked her. That and St. John's recommendation—he had known the family since before she had been born—had been enough. Her business card now introduced her as "Chief Analyst."

Early on, Callaghan came to the conclusion that with strongly rising oil prices, selling his oil shares would not be sensible. So far, all of the property holdings seemed worth keeping. That left Callaghan with nearly 100 million to invest in the first year, including the Treasury bonds, interest, property rents, and dividends from Shell and BP.

Sarah Longhurst's analytical skills soon made her indispensable in the slow process of assessing investments and strategies. Investment ideas first had to pass her intellectual rigor.

"I've been looking at that proposal you brought back from Australia," she said one day as she spread the sheets of her analysis on the board table for their daily meeting. "Who is Warren Kay?"

"No idea," said Callaghan. "I've never heard of him. The papers came to my beach address in Sydney. Maybe he thought I was back in business. Is it worth looking at?"

"It's an intriguing concept. A bit riskier than I would usually consider, but worth a closer look," she said.

Author's Note

In writing this story, I saw an unpublished diary of a Russian whose parents went to Harbin to build the Trans-Siberian Railway. Here he grew up and met his wife. He was not a wealthy industrialist, but there were many wealthy Russians who escaped to Harbin. Most of these Russians later fled the Japanese. Some came to live in Australia; some of their descendents are my friends.

There was a real Morozov family in pre-revolutionary Moscow— they are not my Morozovs. Most of the events described in the story actually happened; most of the background characters were real people, such as Sir Algernon Law (head of the FO Commercial Division), Eugene Ysaye, the Belgian violinist who was popular in London of the period, and General Dubasov, who commanded the forces that used artillery against the strikers in 1905. There were many bombings and assassinations of leading figures in Russia during those tumultuous years.

The streets of tsarist Moscow in this story are much as they would have been in those days. The Purlov tea shop really existed. Each year, one of the major social events in Moscow was the Rose Ball. A number of horrific murders occurred in the Moscow of those years, many of them unsolved.

It is often forgotten that by the time of the 1917 revolution, Russia had one of the great empires of the era. It ranked as the fourth largest industrial power in the world with many large and successful businesses. The textile businesses described would have been typical of the period. Kornovalov's huge complex actually existed. Russian agriculture of that time, notwithstanding the extremes of poverty in so many villages, was far from unsuccessful. The huge harvest of 1913 was not again equaled until the early 1960s, after more than forty years of Bolshevik control.

In the years leading up to the revolution, over 70 percent of the industrial workforce took part in strike action as the tsar and his ministers dithered over badly needed reforms.

In the period immediately after the Bolsheviks seized power, the well-organized and disciplined ex-prisoners of war, the Czech Legion, did in fact make their way to the east via the Trans-Siberian Railway and from there back to Europe by ship. During their fighting retreat, the Czechs came to guard the tsarist government's gold reserves as described in the story. When the Legion finally handed over the gold at Irkutsk in exchange for safe passage, in excess of $200 million U.S. in gold (at 2008 prices) remained unaccounted for. The Czechs assured the Soviets they had handed over all the gold, but mystery still surrounds its fate. Over 300,000 ounces weight of gold is not some trivial amount that could be lost. There has been speculation over the years that this gold was spirited away for use by the tsar and his family when they escaped from Russia. That did not happen. Recent DNA tests using DNA samples from the Duke of Edinburgh, a direct descendant, proved that the last of the Romanovs died in a fusillade of bullets in a cellar in Ekaterinburg. The most likely explanation for the missing gold is that the Czechs used some of it to pay for provisions along the way but that the bulk went with them when they left for home.

Over 1,600 Russian women married members of the Legion and followed their husbands to what became Czechoslovakia.

The Japanese invasion of northern China and Manchuria and the atrocities they committed there are well documented. They are still largely unacknowledged by subsequent Japanese governments. The excesses and atrocities of the Kempeitai mentioned in the story (and many others) actually occurred, as did the kidnapping and murder of Simon Kaspé in Harbin.

The attempt by Imperial Japan to annex the area as Manchukuo nearly succeeded. Japan sucked the area dry as the country struggled to pay for its own invasion and occupation.

Rare musical instruments such as violins are occasionally discovered in unlikely places. When they are, they cause a minor sensation in circles that follow such matters. These instruments are keenly sought as an asset class that is certain to increase in value, and for the beauty of their sound. Recent sales of Cremona violins through the international auctions houses, generally handled by Christie's, are listed later.

Did any pre-revolution Russian millionaires secret part of their fortune in the West? Almost certainly. Did any of them set up trusts in the Channel Islands? It is most unlikely that without specific and accurate information anyone would be able to find such funds if in fact they did. They guard their secrecy jealously. Those seeking the Nataliya Trust will be disappointed; that is not its real name.

Geoff Lambert

Sydney

2010

VIOLIN SALES

Christie's

(published figures)

1990 Stradiveri—"The Mendelssohn" £902,000

1998 Stradiveri—"The Kreutzer" U.S. $1,582,000

1998 Stradiveri—1714 Cremona U.S. $932,000[1]

1998 Stradiveri—1698 Cremona U.S. $710,000[*]

2000 Stradiveri—Taft Ex-Heermann U.S.$1,326,000

2002 Giuseppe Guarneri (del Gesu's father) U.S. $459,833

2004 Stradiveri—1679 £255,250

2005 Stradiveri—"The Lady Tennant" U.S. $2,032,000

2007 Guarneri del Gesu—"The Carrodus" A $10,000,000[2]

---

[1] These prices exclude buyer's premium.
[2] Sold by J & A Beare Ltd, London.

www.ingramcontent.com/pod-product-compliance
Lightning Source LLC
Chambersburg PA
CBHW030239030726
47493CB00023B/190